"EVERY TIME I TURN AROUND THERE YOU ARE."

Ryan's voice was rough with longing as he added, "Beautiful, desirable and totally out of reach."

Karen started nervously. "Ryan, I'm still not—"

"Hush!" With his lips he silenced her, with his arms he drew her close. The first touch of his tongue was an intimacy she had never dreamed of. Nor could she have imagined her response—a shaft of pure pleasure that shot through her being.

The kiss went on and on, a honey-sweet exploration, and when he finally released her, Karen could only cling to him, her eyes dark pools of wonder. "I don't understand what's happening...."

"You're coming alive, Karen." Ryan's smile was a triumphant promise. "You're coming alive!"

JOCELYN HALEY

CRY OF THE FALCON

A SUPERROMANCE FROM

WORLDWIDE

TORONTO · NEW YORK · LONDON · PARIS
AMSTERDAM · STOCKHOLM · HAMBURG
ATHENS · MILAN · TOKYO · SYDNEY

Published November 1983

First printing September 1983

ISBN 0-373-70088-1

Printed in Canada

CHAPTER ONE

As the train clattered between stations, and passengers came and went, the woman sitting by the window near the back of the coach attracted more than one interested glance. It could have been because of her appearance—the contrast between her fragile long-lashed beauty and her very ordinary clothes—or it could have been because she looked much too happy for a wet July day. Her gray eyes were warm with some inner satisfaction, and her gentle, vulnerable mouth curved in a smile quite without provocation or self-consciousness. Certainly she was oblivious to any attention she was getting as she stared out of the rain-streaked window.

Had she been asked why she looked happy, Karen Smythe would have answered simply, "Because I know where I'm going." And she would not have been referring to the train journey. Far from it.

For more than a year Karen had been employed at a drop-in center in downtown Montreal, an enterprise financed by the city in an attempt to cope with the increasing number of homeless teenagers who thronged the streets—and who so frequently became involved in prostitution, drug dealing and crimes of violence. The year had not been an easy one, for

Karen had found it impossible to remain anonymous. And as the daughter of a very rich woman she had been forced to prove herself over and over again.

While the rain spread in horizontal ribbons across the dirty windowpane, blurring the houses, stores and streets into a gray montage, Karen found herself remembering as vividly as if it had happened yesterday one particular episode dating back to her sixth week at the center. The ugly words were as clear in her ears as when she had overheard them.

Sue had said them. Nothing surprising about that, of course. Although only eighteen, Sue was as hard as nails and as amoral as an alley cat, notorious for her foul language yet clever enough to use the system for all it was worth. She came to the drop-in center when she needed a place to stay or a free meal, then sneered at its efforts. "Karen Smythe's nothing but a rich bitch," Sue had said to Margie—gentle, lost Margie who at nineteen already had two children out of wedlock. "Her mother's loaded. They live on the Lakeshore with a swimming pool and tennis courts. And then her ladyship waltzes in here spreading sweetness and light and expecting us to feel grateful. She makes me sick." She had added an epithet that had made Karen blink. "It's all right for her. It's easy to be a do-gooder when you can go home to a mansion full of servants."

Sue's right, Karen had thought sickly. *I am just another do-gooder. Guilty because of all that money, trying to help those less fortunate, yet never able to really do anything because they know and I know that I don't belong in their world.*

After Sue had left, slamming the door behind her, Karen had gone straight to her little desk, squeezed in the hall under the stairs, and had written out her resignation. Dropping it into the director's box, she had picked up her handbag and walked down the hallway toward the front door.

She was never sure what had stopped her. The memory of Margie's desperate need for affection and security? The knowledge that she, Karen, had no other visible alternatives short of a return to dependency on her mother—a move that would be in itself an admission of defeat? A streak of stubbornness in her, inherited from her father, that refused to allow her to quit? Whatever the reason, Karen had turned around, torn up the letter and gone back to her desk.

As the weeks passed by she had gradually gained acceptance. Quietly persistent, she had an innate dignity that the teenagers couldn't help but respect. In time she became less and less afraid of showing the very real warmth and empathy that lay behind her reserved exterior.

The work horrified her, frightened her and exhilarated her. Often it made her weep; more rarely it made her laugh as she never laughed at home. She was levelheaded enough to realize that the center wasn't perfect. At times it was only a bandaid treatment for a wound that screamed out for radical surgery, its programs and resources placebos in a neighborhood that needed basic reforms. But the center was all there was. And though imperfect, though its staff had all the normal human frailties, it was at least an attempt to give meaning and purpose to young lives bogged down in a morass of poverty, violence and ignorance.

She would never change the world; the most she could hope for was to influence for the better the lives of a very few people. But Karen soon knew her decision to stay on at the center had been the right one. She belonged in this kind of place and began to plan a career with that in mind.

Today had been Karen's last day at work. The staff had treated her to a rather protracted and very enjoyable lunch, and now she was on her way home. In the fall she was going back to university, not to continue the general arts degree she had started three years ago, but to study social work. She had trained her replacement and was looking forward to several weeks of freedom to do some preliminary reading and to rejoice in her newfound sense of direction. She felt like a hurdler who has won a very important race: she had overcome her mother's opposition and her own self-doubts to accomplish something she knew was worthwhile. No wonder she was smiling as the train repeatedly stopped and started.

The train jolted to a halt, and Karen realized this was her station. After hurrying along the aisle, she jumped down the steps onto the pavement. The rain was falling steadily, and ruefully she realized something else: she had forgotten to clean out her locker at the drop-in center, and in it were her raincoat and umbrella. She hesitated momentarily, wondering if she should call Mandy to come and get her, or take a taxi. But she was in no hurry to get home, and she loved walking in the rain. She set off at a brisk pace down the sidewalk.

It was July, and warm enough that the droplets of water trickling down Karen's face felt pleasantly refreshing. The tires of passing cars swished on the wet pavement. Rain dripped from the graceful maple trees that lined the streets and dewed the petals of the roses that grew in the flawlessly tended gardens. The air was scented with wet grass.

With a lift of her spirits Karen realized that at this precise moment no one knew where she was; by no one, of course, she meant her mother. For the space of five or ten minutes, until she reached the big house on Lakeview Crescent, she was free.

Flinging her bag over her shoulder, she began to run, her sandals slapping on the wet sidewalk. The rain was coming harder, bouncing on the surface of the road, gathering in puddles in the ditches. She was getting soaked to the skin but she couldn't care less. Suddenly exhilarated, she ran faster, her slender legs carrying her as effortlessly as wings.

The houses were more imposing now, the grounds more spacious. On her left through the trees she caught the pewter sheen of Lac St. Louis. Approaching the intersection of Roselawn Avenue with Huntingdon Terrace, she slowed down to check for traffic. Not until then did she notice that a car had pulled to the side of the road and had slowed to match her pace. A nondescript car, a dark green compact. Nothing about its appearance to account for the panic that exploded within her. Karen stopped dead, her eyes riveted on the vehicle.

The car stopped, too. Then the window on her side was rolled down and a man's face appeared in the opening. Quickly she took a step backward.

A deep pleasant voice, cultured and very sure of itself, said, "Can I give you a lift? It's rather wet for an afternoon run."

Some of the tension ebbed from her body. As usual she was overreacting. "No, thank you," she said clearly.

"Come on, you're soaked."

She should have kept walking. Instead she glanced down at herself. Her red shirt was molded to her body, her denim skirt clinging damply to her bare legs. She always wore inexpensive clothes at the drop-in center. "It doesn't matter, I'm nearly home anyway. Thank you," she added as an afterthought.

There was open amusement in the deep voice. "I'm not a rapist, you know."

Her chin snapped up. "I never said you were. I simply prefer not to accept rides from strangers." She glanced both ways and resolutely began to walk across the road.

"A well-brought-up girl, I see. I thought they were obsolete."

Lifting her chin a little higher, Karen ignored him and walked briskly past the geometrically clipped hedges of the Rawlinsons' estate. They were friends of her mother, and their son Duke, a cheerful young man with not a subtle bone in his brawny athletic body, was one of Karen's male friends. He would be at her mother's party tonight, she was sure, because Nancy Smythe cherished hopes he would become more than a friend to her elder daughter. Karen's heart sank abruptly; she had forgotten the party.

Glancing to her left, she saw that the car was still following her. Damn the man! He'd not only disrupted her well-earned sense of self-satisfaction, he'd also destroyed that ephemeral sensation of freedom, the joy of being, only too briefly, at one with her body. From past experience she knew it might be weeks before she felt it again.

"Sure you won't change your mind?" he called.

"Positive," she said crisply, not even looking at him, yet knowing from the low purr of the car engine that he was still there.

"A pity—I'm really a very respectable citizen."

She whirled around, glaring at him. "Look, would you please leave me alone? I hate being. . . being importuned. Just go away!" He had the bluest eyes she had ever seen, she thought irrelevantly, like patches of summer sky gleaming through the clouds.

"All right, I can take a hint. It's too bad, though."

To her relief she saw the car pull away from the curb and accelerate, and watched it until it was out of sight around the corner. Only then did she let out her breath in a long sigh. Walking more slowly, for she was so wet now that a bit more rain wouldn't matter, she found herself wishing the incident hadn't happened. Not even to herself could she admit why it had so frightened her. She only knew it had, knew in her bones that she would have had to be dragged screaming into that car. The old black fears swirled around her, beating at her with their batlike wings, and to get away from them, to lock them in the past where they belonged, she began to run again. But this time her limbs felt heavy as lead, the fears dragging on them, pulling her back. And when she crossed the street and rounded the curve of Lakeview Crescent, her heart was thudding in her chest.

She did not see the car at first, for the driveway of her mother's house was flanked with tall privet hedges. Her mother's house.... The words were indicative of a great deal, Karen thought wryly, regarding the handsome Tudor-style mansion with neither affection nor appreciation. Mellow brick, aged timbers, leaded glass; manicured lawns that stretched to the water's edge, formal gardens, immense trees. None of it touched her heart or offered her a welcome. She had hated it from the first day they had moved there so many years ago, and she would hate it, she was sure, until the day she finally managed to escape from it.

She jogged across the crescent and turned into the driveway. And there she stopped, her breath rasping in her throat. Parked near the house was the same nondescript green car that had followed her a few minutes ago. The man was standing beside it, apparently checking the house number on the huge, dark-stained oak door, then comparing it with whatever was written on the small piece of paper in his hand.

She saw him before he saw her, and in those few seconds she absorbed an indelible impression of him. He was wearing a trench coat over what looked like a business suit. Although he carried his clothes well, his blond hair was thick and unruly, somehow belying the civilized garb. He was a very big man, tall and broad shouldered, and something in his build caused the fear to erupt in her brain again. Ever since she was fourteen she had been afraid of big men.... As if he had sensed her scrutiny, he turned his head and saw her.

Attack was the best mode of defense. "What are you doing here?" Karen said sharply.

He put the piece of paper in his pocket and walked toward her, stopping only a couple of feet away. Mockingly he let his eyes run over her from head to foot, missing not one detail, from the strands of wet hair plastered to her face to the cheap sandals on her feet. "I could ask you the same question."

"I live here." She was obscurely pleased to see that her words had disconcerted him.

"Do you now. You surprise me."

"Oh?" Her tone was not encouraging.

He glanced over his shoulder at the imposing facade of the house, then back at her. "For one thing, you don't exactly fit the image. For another, it's rather a strange coincidence...."

"What do you mean?"

"I wanted to meet you—and now I have." His expression was very serious. "When I saw you running down the street a few minutes ago, I realized I hadn't seen anything more beautiful in a long time. You were like a little girl running through a field full of daisies, running for the sheer joy of it. As graceful as a bird on the wing and as free as the wind. That was why I stopped the car—because I wanted to meet you. It had nothing to do with the rain. I could tell you were oblivious to it."

In a few words he had caught her mood exactly, and this frightened her more than anything else. "I did feel that way until you came along," she said with deliberate rudeness. "You ruined it."

"Then I'm sorry. That wasn't my intention."

Karen couldn't doubt his sincerity. Biting her lip, she said, "I asked you what you were doing here."

"I'm looking for the daughters of Dr. Laurence Smith. Karen and Amanda. I believe I have the right house, don't I? Are you one of them?"

"I'm Karen Smythe, yes."

He said dryly, "Spelled with a *y* and an *e*."

She flushed. "My mother changed our name several years ago. I had no choice."

"I see." And she had the feeling that he saw rather more than she had intended.

"Why are you looking for us?"

He ran his fingers through his hair, which was rapidly becoming as wet as hers. "Look, do you think we could continue this conversation indoors?"

Much as she disliked the house, it still at times represented a sanctuary to her, and she knew she did not want this self-confident, good-looking stranger invading it. "I suppose so," she said grudgingly. "I don't know if my mother's home or not."

"I came to see you and your sister, not your mother." He gestured for her to precede him.

Reluctantly she walked up the driveway and over the flagstone path to the front steps. Taking her key from her purse, she unlocked the door and stepped inside. She heard him close the door behind them and she bent to remove her sandals, not looking at him.

As if by a signal, her mother's housekeeper appeared through the stone Gothic archway that led into the dining room. "Hello, Mrs. Houndsel," Karen said with the careful politeness she had cultivated over the years—she thoroughly disliked Emily Houndsel. "Is mother home?"

"No, miss. She's at a meeting for the symphony auxiliary." *Which, as a dutiful daughter, you should have known,* was the implication.

"And Amanda?"

The primly pursed mouth softened slightly. If Emily Houndsel liked anyone, it was Amanda. "She's out driving with young Mr. Manley."

Karen was not at all surprised that her sister was out driving with young Mr. Somebody-or-other. Manley was a new name to her, but then Mandy changed boyfriends as easily as she changed clothes. The trouble was that today it left only Karen to entertain the stranger. "Please, would you bring some tea to the library, Mrs. Houndsel? This gentleman wishes to see me and Amanda."

The rigid, iron-gray head nodded. "Certainly, miss. May I take your coat, sir?"

Karen said briefly, "Mrs. Houndsel will show you to the library. I'm just going up to change. I won't be a minute." Feeling shamefully as though she was beating a retreat, she hurried across the oak flooring to the wide staircase with its stained-glass windows and beautifully carved railing. After taking the white-carpeted stairs two at a time, she crossed the hall to her bedroom.

The room was perfectly tidy. The books stood

straight as soldiers in the bookshelves, all the clothes were hung up, the bed neatly made. There was none of the clutter that might have been expected in a young woman's room, no football pennants or dance invitations or dried-up corsages, no photos on the walls. A close observer would have noticed that the books represented a wide range of interests, however, and that they had nearly all been read. Would have noticed the two exquisite oil paintings in the alcove by the bed, their jewellike colors a denouncement of the stark severity of the rest of the room.

Quickly Karen went into the adjoining bathroom, stripping to her skin and drying herself on one of the luxuriously thick towels. From her closet she selected a plain linen skirt and a white shirt, while she slipped her feet into high-heeled sandals. Lastly she dried her hair, brushing it back from her face. For a moment she regarded herself gravely in the mirror, wishing she did not have to go downstairs and drink tea and make polite conversation with a man whose presence she already resented. If she had only stayed at the drop-in center until five, as she would normally have done, she need never have met him.... But he was here, so she'd better go down and deal with him. Hopefully it would be easy enough to get rid of him.

She went back downstairs and crossed the hallway to the library. Of all the rooms in the house, this seemed the one that most epitomized her mother's dependence on the taste of others and her compulsive need to do the right thing. The room was lined with bookshelves replete with sets of leather-bound volumes tooled in gold: Shakespeare, Dickens,

Thackeray, the Greek classics—the list was endless. There were hunting prints on the walls, brass fire tongs on the hearth, leather-covered armchairs tastefully arranged on the antique Persian rug. The library of the perfect English gentleman, Karen had often thought, knowing all too well that Nancy had never opened any of the books, let alone read them.

But the stranger was reading one now. He was standing near the tall windows, his back to the door, absorbed in the book he was holding. His dark gray business suit with its narrow pin-stripe design fitted him to perfection, sitting easily on his wide shoulders and long lean body. He wore it with a grace and distinction Duke could never have achieved in a hundred years. Yet for some reason she was sure the stranger could match, if not surpass, Duke's considerable physical strength and coordination. The thought touched her nerves with fear.

She cleared her throat pointedly. "You haven't yet told me your name."

He looked up, almost as if he had forgotten where he was. His eyes seemed the focus of all the light in the room, so brilliantly blue were they. "Oh. . .Ryan Koetsier."

"Coot-seer?" she repeated uncertainly.

"Koetsier." Impatiently he spelled it for her. "My father is Dutch. Now listen to this. It's called 'A Prisoner's Song.'

> "But though my wing is closely bound,
> My heart's at liberty;
> My prison walls cannot control
> The flight, the freedom of my soul.

"Written in the seventeenth century by Jeanne-Marie Guyon. It gives not a bad impression of the way you were running... 'the flight, the freedom of my soul.' "

But Karen's brain had stopped at the mention of prison walls. How much did he know, this stranger with the disconcertingly blue eyes. "I'm sure you didn't come here to discuss seventeenth-century poets," she said tightly. "Oh—Mrs. Houndsel. Thank you." What a genius the woman had for appearing at the wrong moment! "Yes, by the fire will be fine. Please sit down, Mr. Koetsier, and let me pour you a cup of tea."

As he obediently walked across the room toward the fireplace, her earlier impression was confirmed, for he had an athlete's economy of movement. A man who spent much time outdoors, she decided, noticing his deep tan and the fan of tiny wrinkles at the corners of his eyes. He was not a classically handsome man—there was too much strength and character in his features for that. But he was certainly arresting, with his broad cheekbones, straight nose and very determined jawline. His chin had a slight cleft in it, while the line of his mouth carried a contradictory message of humor and sensuality. Mandy would undoubtedly call him sexy.

The tea service was antique Georgian silver, the cups Spode. Having something to do steadied Karen's nerves. She added a slice of lemon to his cup and passed him one of Mrs. Houndsel's admittedly excellent scones, saying levelly, "Why *are* you here?"

"So there's to be no small talk on the subject of poetry or freedom. You're a very direct young woman, Miss Smythe."

Karen stirred her tea, her head downbent so that a sheaf of dark, silky hair fell forward to lie on her cheek. When she spoke, her words were as much a surprise to herself as to him. "I want to know why you mentioned my father's name."

"Your father is a very good friend of mine."

Her spoon clattered on the saucer, but when she looked up her gray eyes were steady, giving away no secrets. "Did he send you here?"

"He asked me to come, yes."

Anger licked along her veins. "Could he not have come himself?"

"Not easily, no. Certainly not as easily as I."

She had the feeling they were fencing with each other, neither one giving anything away. "Perhaps you could explain that to me."

He put his teacup down on the table, his hands surprisingly deft for so large a man. "Look, let's get to the point," he said with a touch of the impatience she had noticed earlier. "I'm here because your father asked me to come. I'm also here to ask something of you and your sister. Particularly of you, because you're the one he speaks of more often."

"I don't even know where he is."

"You must know he's in the Arctic."

"The Arctic's a very big place, Mr. Koetsier."

He leaned forward. "You know, it's a long time since I've met a woman who riles me the way you do. First of all, enough of this Mr. Koetsier stuff—my name is Ryan and yours is Karen. Secondly, your father needs you, I'm convinced of that. I want you to go and see him.''

"So after all these years my father suddenly evinces a desire to see me—how nice!'' she snapped, twin patches of color in her cheeks. "Unfortunately I won't be able to go.''

Before she could guess his intention, he reached across the table and seized her by the wrist, his fingers like steel. "What's with you, anyway? I don't—''

"Let go of me!'' There was an edge of sheer terror in her voice as she jerked her wrist back. He must have heard it; he released her instantly, his eyes intent on her face.

"What are you so scared of?'' he asked slowly. "You made me angry but I didn't mean to frighten you.''

Karen rubbed her wrist as if she wanted to erase the feel of his hand. "I don't like being touched, that's all.''

Once again his eyes traveled over her from head to foot. This time there was assessment in them rather than mockery as he took in the severity of her clothes, unadorned by jewelry or a scarf. She wore no makeup. Her features were exquisitely modeled, her lashes dark and very thick, her brows like wings. There was intelligence in the wide, beautiful forehead. But the curve of her mouth was far too sensitive, and her gray eyes were guarded, accustomed to keeping their own counsel.

She shifted uneasily under his scrutiny. "You still haven't told me where my father's living.''

Ryan Koetsier seemed to come to some kind of a decision. "He's based at Pond Inlet. That's a tiny village in northern Baffin Island, a thousand miles above the tree line, four hundred miles north of the Arctic Circle. I worked with him up there last summer and then this summer again."

"So you're an archaeologist, too."

He smiled. In a clinical, detached way Karen had already realized he was a most attractive man, his features strongly carved to a very definite statement of masculinity and determination. But his smile brought his face to life, injecting it with a personable warmth that was hard to resist. "Beside your father I'm a rank amateur," he said cheerfully. "It would take me a lifetime to learn what he's forgotten. He's worked from Siberia to Greenland, and he's made some amazing discoveries and deductions over the years. I consider myself most fortunate to be associated with him...quite apart from which I value his friendship."

"There's never been any doubt of his competence," she said coolly. "But of course he's had no family ties for the past several years. It's easy to be competent when you're responsible only for yourself."

"It's never easy to achieve his level of excellence." Ryan had not raised his voice any more than she had, but there was no question of the animosity that smoldered between them.

"I would have thought you were too old for hero worship, Mr. Koetsier."

"At your age you should know the difference be-

tween hero worship and friendship, Miss Smythe,''
he countered.

The tea and scones were forgotten. ''He may be a
great archaeologist, but he's been a lousy father. You
can tell him that for me, if you like.''

''Why don't you do your own dirty work and tell
him yourself?''

''Because I don't care if I ever see him again, that's
why.''

His eyes narrowed. ''Do you blame him for the
divorce?''

''I'm not quite that naive.'' She had had enough of
this conversation. ''Look, I don't care what you tell
him. Tell him I'm busy or I'm on my way to Timbuc-
too. Or tell him to come and visit me himself. Because I'm not going to Pond Inlet or anywhere else to
see *him*.'' She sat back in her chair, wishing she
hadn't been quite so vehement. She should have
played it cool, saying with just the right degree of
detachment that she was working and would be unable to get away. Up until this afternoon that would
have been the truth. Instead she had let her feelings
show to a man who was far too intelligent to miss
what such a display might mean. His next words
proved her right.

''Why do you hate him so?''

''I don't see that that's any of your business.''

''At the risk of sounding repetitious, your father
happens to be a very good friend of mine. He's not a
man to talk about personal matters, but the fact that
he asked me to come and see you is of significance,
I'm sure of it.''

"And what messages do you bring from him?" she interrupted. "A letter, maybe? Or even a note?"

"Nothing specific. He wanted me to see how you both were, what you were doing with yourselves."

It was a weak reply, and they both knew it. Mercilessly Karen pressed her advantage. "So the suggestion that I should visit him emanates totally from you."

"That's right." His blue eyes held her gaze, refusing to allow her to look away. "I can't give you a rational explanation, Karen, but I feel it's very important that you should see him. For his sake."

"No."

His face hardened. "And maybe for yours, too. Or do you want to go around for the rest of your days carrying such a burden of hatred and resentment toward him?"

Her hot reply died on her lips and briefly she closed her eyes, hiding the pain and bewilderment in them. "I won't go," she whispered stubbornly. "You don't understand...."

"Try me," he said, oddly gentle.

"I can't go, I just can't! It's too late, you see. Much too late." Her earlier hostility had vanished, to be replaced by a kind of desperate sincerity. "I can't ask you to understand, but please accept that I'm telling you the truth."

"I can see you are," he answered. "Whatever's wrong, Karen?"

She stared at him dumbly, recognizing with one tiny part of her brain that she liked the sound of her name on his tongue. What a man of contradictions!

Tough and unyielding as the land he lived in, yet not afraid of offering gentleness and understanding.

Then, to her infinite relief, she heard the front door open and close and her mother's voice call, "Hello! Anyone home?"

She was rescued. Her face mirroring her emotions, Karen called back, "In the library, mother!"

Nancy Smythe came to the doorway. "Why, it's you, Karen. What are you doing home so early?"

Karen smoothly evaded the question. "Mother, I'd like you to meet Ryan Koetsier. Ryan, my mother, Nancy Smythe. Mr. Koetsier is a business associate of father's, in the Arctic." And that, she thought with faint satisfaction, should divert her mother from any further queries about Karen's unexpected afternoon home.

Ryan Koetsier had stood up when Nancy entered the room. He towered over her, for Karen had inherited her height from her father rather than her mother. "Good afternoon, Mrs. Smythe," he said in his deep, lazy voice, his smile calculated to charm the birds from the trees, Karen thought maliciously. "I hope I'm not intruding. Laurence asked me to visit your two daughters while I was in Montreal."

"Not at all," Nancy fluttered, no more immune to the intensity of those blue eyes than Karen had been. "A pleasure, I'm sure. Has Karen offered you a drink? Oh, I see you've had tea. I expect you'd like something a little stronger, wouldn't you, Mr. Koetsier?" It was one of Nancy's firm beliefs that men should always be plied with hard liquor, preferably whisky, regardless of the hour of the day. This conviction had done her reputation as a hostess no harm.

As if he had read her mind, Ryan Koetsier made exactly the right reply. "A Glenfiddich on the rocks, perhaps?"

"Fine!" Nancy rang the bell, walking over to the fireplace and rubbing her hands. "A dreadful day, isn't it? Oh, there you are, Houndsel. A Glenfiddich on the rocks and my usual, please. Karen?"

"No, thanks." Karen smiled quickly at the butler. He was frail, white haired and sweet tempered, and his improbable marriage to the stout, dour Emily was always a source of wonder to Karen.

"A little sherry wouldn't hurt you, dear," Nancy reproved. "You need to relax more. Why are you home so early, anyway? Surely they didn't shut down that place because of the rain?"

The drop-in center had always been "that place" to Nancy. Karen said evenly, "No. I told you today was my last day there."

Anyone at all sensitive would have picked up the repressive note in her voice. Not Nancy. "So you did—they found a replacement for you, didn't they? A very good thing, too. I never did like the way you were wedded to that place. I couldn't see the attraction at all." She glanced over at the man standing on the other side of the hearth. "A drop-in center downtown. Quite unnecessary, if you ask me." Which nobody had. "Just encouraging people to use drugs and have babies and walk out on their husbands."

"Mother, it's *not* like that—"

"That's what you say, but then you're prejudiced, aren't you, dear? *I* think it's a blatant misuse of the taxpayer's money. One should take responsibility for one's actions, and if those girls get in trouble, they shouldn't expect other people to bail them out of it.''

Karen said tautly, ''Some of those girls, as you call them, live in a poverty you can't begin to imagine.''

She should have known better than to argue. Nancy opened her light blue eyes very wide and said guilelessly, ''Then why aren't you down there helping them? Normally you're not home until five-thirty.''

''We all had lunch together because it was my last day, and then Peter sent me home. But I'll be going back and forth to borrow books from him. I want to do some preparatory reading before classes start in the fall.''

''It's a ridiculous idea, your taking up social work.'' It might just as well have been prostitution Karen was about to take up from the tone of Nancy's voice. ''I'm by no means sure I'll allow it.''

Humiliated that Ryan Koetsier should be exposed to a family quarrel, Karen muttered, ''Mother, please. . . .''

Ryan Koetsier said smoothly, ''Ah, here come our drinks.'' Just as smoothly he usurped the tray from Houndsel, passed Nancy her glass of bourbon and began a lengthy exposition on the virtues of various malt whiskies.

It was impossible for Karen not to feel grateful. Her mother had, at least temporarily, been diverted from the topic of Karen's job and was listening to their visitor, her head tilted at an angle an admirer had once called utterly charming. She was a pretty woman in her early forties, and she spent a considerable amount of time and money preserving that prettiness. Her soft brown hair showed not a trace of gray in its artfully casual curls, while her makeup was subtle and her silk dress discreetly flattering. Every morning she worked out in front of the television screen with a childlike faith that this would somehow make her figure comparable to that of the svelte Swedish beauty who lead the exercises. She tried every fad that came on the market, from sunlamps to mudpacks, and twice a year she spent a great deal of money visiting a health spa in California. But mudpacks and health spas could not erase the lines of discontent around Nancy's mouth. She was a woman with too little to occupy her time and too much money—money that had not, moreover, purchased her the social position she craved. She had never remarried, although she must have had opportunities; instead she clung obsessively and ruthlessly to her two daughters as a guard against a loneliness she could never acknowledge even to herself.

Karen poured herself another cup of tea, wondering without much hope if she could escape from the library without anyone noticing. The tea was cold. She put the cup back on the tray, tensing herself for escape, unaware that the deep blue eyes were watching her. Then from the doorway another voice spoke, a light voice with the same conscious charm in it as Nancy's. "Hello, darling! What an awful day! Mmm, are those some of Emily's scones?"

The only one who called Mrs. Houndsel Emily was Mandy, Karen's sister, younger than she by four years. Nancy looked up, evincing a warmth she had not shown for Karen. "Did you have a nice time, darling? Amanda, this is Ryan Koetsier. Ryan, my younger daughter, Mandy." She might as well have said favorite daughter, for it was written all over her.

Amanda crossed the room holding out her hand. She was as graceful and immaculately groomed as a model, from her burnished chestnut hair to her slender feet in their handsome Italian shoes. She was as lovely as a model, too, and as accustomed to male adulation. Like a decorative butterfly, she flitted from pleasure to pleasure and man to man, losing her heart to none of them. Fickle she might be, but she was also essentially harmless, as good-natured as she was flirtatious. Two things she took seriously: her mother's money and her own appearance.

Looking up between thick, curled lashes she said sweetly, "Good afternoon, Mr. Koetsier. Do you live in the city?"

Briefly Ryan Koetsier explained the purpose behind his visit, ending as he had with Karen with the suggestion that Amanda visit her father. Mandy smiled prettily. "Oh, I couldn't right now, my calendar's booked up solid for the next two or three weeks. I'm very busy, you know."

"I'm sure you are." His reply was grave, not a trace of a smile showing on his face. Why then did Karen have an absurd urge to giggle? "Perhaps in three weeks you could manage a trip north then?"

Mandy sank down on the arm of one of the chairs, exposing her silk-clad legs to best advantage. "Maybe. Although the Merritts have their annual garden party around that time, and I wouldn't miss that for the world. But you can give him my love.''

"I'll certainly pass on your message." There was an unmistakable hint of dryness in his voice this time.

Amanda said anxiously, "You do understand, don't you, Mr. Koetsier? I couldn't possibly just drop everything and leave all my friends in the middle of summer. Besides—" she wrinkled her delightful little nose "—I'm a city person. The wide open spaces aren't my thing." She suddenly brightened. "Just to show there are no hard feelings, why don't you come to our party tonight? Do come! We'd love to have you, wouldn't we, Karen?"

Again Karen felt that irrational clutch of dread. She did not want him to come to the party. She wanted him to leave, and to take the shadowy figure of her father with him. "Of course," she said with patent insincerity, not looking at him.

Nancy shot her elder daughter a reproving glance. "Do sound a little more enthusiastic, Karen! After all, I would think you had something to celebrate tonight—you don't have to get up tomorrow and go to that place. Mr. Koetsier, we'd all be delighted if you could join us. It's a dinner-dance around nine, formal, if you can manage it."

"That's very kind of you, Mrs. Smythe. I'd be delighted to attend." He stood up, putting his empty glass down on the table. "I must be going. I'm sure you have a lot to do before this evening."

Houndsel appeared in the door. "Excuse me, madam, the telephone. Mrs. Rawlinson."

"Thank you, Houndsel, I'll be right there," Nancy

said briskly. "Goodbye, Mr. Koetsier, we'll see you this evening."

"I'll get my keys," Amanda intervened. "I'm parked behind you."

So, briefly, Karen was left alone with the visitor. In a low voice he said, "You don't want me here this evening, do you?"

She didn't bother to prevaricate. "No, I don't."

"Are you against men in general, or is there something particularly repugnant about me?"

She flushed angrily, the color in her face highlighting the elegant curves of her cheekbones. "You'd better hurry. Amanda will be waiting to put her car in the driveway once you're gone."

She might just as well not have spoken. "What are you going to wear tonight? Something as sexless as you're wearing now?"

Karen gasped in outrage. "I like tailored clothes."

"That make you look like a nun?"

Amanda's voice drifted from the hallway. "Are you ready, Mr. Koetsier?"

Karen smiled maliciously. "You'd better go. Mandy's not used to being kept waiting."

"I'm sure she's not," he said lazily. "The experience will be good for her."

It was difficult for Karen not to smile, for she was used to seeing men fall all over themselves to get Mandy's attention. Ryan Koetsier's attitude made a pleasant if unexpected change. Keeping her thoughts to herself, she said with distant politeness, "Goodbye."

"Goodbye." He raised one eyebrow, his expression quizzical. "And don't forget what I said. Try looking like a woman tonight, even if you don't want to act like one."

A dozen hot-tempered retorts trembled on Karen's tongue, but before she could select the most scathing of them, he was gone. She heard his voice mingling with Mandy's, and then the front door closed behind them both.

Quickly she left the library and hurried upstairs before her mother could get off the phone and continue the argument about her social-work degree. In her room she pulled open the closet and surveyed the row of clothes hanging there, her lips set mutinously. There was a full-length shirtwaist of unrelieved black, with a black leather belt and long sleeves; it would serve him right if she wore that. Or—her eyes brightened as she reached into the back of the closet and pulled out a plastic-covered garment—she could wear this. Mandy had talked her into buying the dress a year or two ago, but she had never had the courage to wear it. It, too, was full-length, but that was the only thing it had in common with the black dress. This gown was made of silver lamé. Sleeveless and backless, it had a slit up the side and was cut low in the front. The price had made her blanch, Karen remembered, but Mandy had only laughed, saying that the principle was the same with bikinis: the less material, the higher the cost.

She had slim-heeled satin pumps with silver bows on them, and she could put her hair up and wear those diamond drop earrings her mother had given her for her twenty-first birthday. The overall effect, she knew, would be not at all nunlike. It would be worth the effort just to see the expression on Ryan Koetsier's face.

There was a light tap at her door, a signal the two sisters had shared for years. "Come in," Karen called.

"What a dream of a man that is—oh, Karen, are you really going to wear that? Do! You'll knock his eyes out."

"Don't you want him for yourself?" Karen asked dryly.

"Well, he *is* gorgeous, isn't he?" Mandy replied with the frankness that was one of her most likable attributes. "Those eyes...mmm, real bedroom eyes."

"Mandy!"

"Well, they are," her sister said unrepentantly. "And he's so tall and well built—imagine being kissed by him."

Karen bent to search for the satin shoes, her cheeks flushed from more than the activity. She didn't want to imagine any such thing. Yet this was the man whose attention she was proposing to get by wearing an outrageously seductive dress. "I expect I'll wear my usual, the blue chiffon," she said with attempted nonchalance from the depths of the closet.

"No, you won't! You'll wear that silver dress and you'll let me make your face up—please, Karen. After all, if he's been stuck in the frozen north for the past six months, he deserves a treat. And he said he's going back in a couple of days, so it can't do any harm. Promise me you will?"

It was hard to resist Mandy in a coaxing mood. "All right, I will," Karen said rashly, regretting her decision almost as soon as she'd spoken.

Mandy knew her sister well enough to say firmly, "A promise is a promise." She stretched to her full height, the collection of gold bangles on her wrist jingling together. "It's going to be a great party. I invited Craig Manley. He really is a doll. . . not to mention all the money he has."

Karen couldn't help laughing. "You're horribly mercenary, Mandy! If Craig didn't have a sports car—a Jaguar, in all likelihood—you wouldn't have gone driving with him, right? Admit it!"

Mandy grinned, pivoting in front of the mirror and smoothing her culottes over her hips. "I like money, I might as well be honest about it. Now you—you wouldn't care if we went bankrupt tomorrow, would you?"

"I don't suppose I would, no."

"It seems a pity you can't enjoy it more."

Karen's fingernails were digging into the satin-covered shoes. "I hate it," she said fiercely. "I hate how it's changed our lives. I'd like to go back to being thirteen again, living in the country with both our parents. We were happy then. . . ."

"I'm happy now, and so is mother. It's only you who's not. Oh, Karen, I know it must have been terrible, what happened to you after we got the money, but can't you forget about it? Put it all behind you?"

It was the forbidden subject. Karen's face closed. "Will you let me use that new frosted lipstick you bought last week?"

Mandy sighed. "I know, I should learn to keep my big mouth shut.... Of course you can." She recovered some of her insouciance, for none of Amanda's serious moods lasted for long. "And don't forget, you promised to wear the silver dress."

She must have been a fool to do so. "I'll wear it," Karen agreed.

"I wonder if Ryan will be able to come up with a tuxedo at such short notice."

"So it's first names already?"

"While we were changing the cars around he told me to call him Ryan. After all, it's hard to be formal when the rain's dripping down your neck."

"He strikes me as the resourceful type, so I'm sure he'll come up with something appropriate."

"He'd look dreamy in a tux. What a waste, that lovely man living in the Arctic miles from anywhere."

"Well, you've got an invitation to go and visit him up there."

Amanda made a moue. "He doesn't look like the kind of man who'd drop everything to squire a woman around. But I'm kind of surprised you don't want to go. That sort of thing's much more up your alley."

"Why would I want to visit father?" Karen demanded with suppressed violence. "After these years he's never bothered writing or coming to visit us, just as though we don't exist anymore."

"He wasn't home that much beforehand," Amanda said reasonably. "He was always going off to some godforsaken spot to dig up bits of pottery or bones or whatever it is that archaeologists do." Still eyeing herself in the mirror, she sucked in her stomach. "Do you know, I think I've put on a bit of weight."

"You'll have to start exercising like mother," Karen said, relieved by the change of subject.

"Heaven forbid! I hate the woman who does that show—she's so gorgeous and she looks so smug. Besides, I think she's a sadist underneath it all, making you do all those dreadful contortions." Mandy tilted her head to one side, taking out one of her tiny gold earrings. "By the way, what did mother mean when she said you didn't have to go to work tomorrow?"

"I'm finished for the summer."

Mandy gave a surprised gurgle of laughter. "Already? Good for you! I never did think they were paying you enough."

"They couldn't really afford to pay more," Karen said loyally. "The thing is, they found a permanent replacement for me earlier than they'd expected and they couldn't pay both of us."

"So you *would* be free to go north for a visit.... I wish you'd go, Karen. It seems like fate, somehow, that you ended your job on the very day Ryan came here."

"I'm not going!" Karen said irritably. "Stop going on about it, Mandy."

"Okay, okay, don't bite my head off," Mandy responded good-naturedly. "I'll come and do your face about eight-thirty, and I expect to see you in the silver dress. A promise is—"

"A promise," Karen finished neatly. "Out—I'm going to wash my hair."

But once Amanda had gone Karen didn't head toward the bathroom. Instead she locked the door and sat down on her bed, looking out of the window that overlooked the back of the house. The rain trickled down the pane, while the leaves of the old elm tree hung sodden and dripping from their branches. She felt very tired, for too much had happened in too short a time: her last morning at work; the car following her down the street just as a car had followed her so many years ago; Ryan Koetsier's plea that she visit her father, and Ryan Koetsier himself, with his deep voice and those piercingly blue eyes that missed very little of what went on around him.

She lay down on the bed, pulling the coverlet over her. A trick she had learned long ago was to deliberately empty her mind of all its fears and concerns, letting it fill instead with an image of beauty. An empty beach on a bright spring day with the waves curling on the sand, or a field full of wild flowers, sunshine and the drowsy humming of bees. . . . Her breathing slowed until it was deep and regular.

CHAPTER TWO

THERE WAS A FEELING of suppressed excitement in the house when Karen came downstairs a little after nine. A florist had brought attractive arrangements of roses, carnations and freesias for every room. The maids had set the long mahogany table in the dining room, and the caterers were running back and forth between there and the kitchen. Under the benign direction of Houndsel a crew of uniformed young men was organizing the bar. A rock band with amplifiers and strobe lights was ensconced in the big ballroom at the back of the house, while a chamber group was tuning up in the lounge at the front. Nancy, meanwhile, was bustling around getting in everyone's way, her cheeks pink with anticipation.

"Karen!" she exclaimed with an unflattering degree of surprise. "Don't you look lovely...I've never seen that dress before, have I?" Without waiting for a reply, she added, "Find Houndsel and tell him we need six more chairs in the lounge, would you? I must remind the caterers about the champagne." She rushed off, completely happy, for she loved a party.

Karen did as she was bid, to be reassured by Houndsel that the chairs had already been looked after. Going back through the hall, she caught sight of herself in the gilt-edged mirror there and felt a pang of mingled surprise and unease. Was that seductive-looking creature really her? The dress hugged the curves of her figure, exposing a considerable amount of lightly tanned skin and more than a comfortable amount of silk-clad leg. With her hair in a loose knot on the back of her head, her neck looked very long. When she moved, the glittering dress moved with her, and the diamonds flashed at her ears.

In sudden panic, knowing the image in the mirror was nothing like the real Karen, she contemplated running upstairs and changing into her old blue chiffon with its high draped bodice and full skirt. Safe and ordinary and very proper.... But as she was standing transfixed, one of the uniformed young men approached her with a tray of punch. "A drink, madam?" he asked politely. In his eyes she saw the same flash of admiration she had so often seen when men looked at Amanda.

From long experience Karen knew that her mother's punch was dangerous stuff, its very pleasant fruit flavor concealing a lethal combination of rum and vodka. She hesitated for only a second. Smiling at him so that her face lost its strained look, she said, "Thank you, I will." Raising the glass to her lips, she took a long drink. Then the doorbell rang and the first of their guests arrived.

By ten o'clock the party was in full swing. In the lounge Nancy's friends sipped champagne, ate lobster canapés and waltzed sedately on the inlaid oak floor. The ballroom was in direct contrast. There the flowers shook in the alcoves and the lights flashed white, red and blue on the gyrating dancers. The music was too loud for thought or conversation, the rhythm throbbing primitively like a heartbeat.

Karen by now had had three glasses of punch and had stopped looking for every new arrival. Something must have happened to prevent Ryan Koetsier from coming, and she could not have said whether she was glad or sorry. She had been dancing steadily for nearly an hour. The alcohol had removed her usual inhibitions, and this kind of dancing was no threat to her; although one had a partner, one was never required to touch him. So she gave herself up to the music, feeling it pulse through her veins, her body a swaying silver flame.

She was dancing with Duke when a tall, blond-haired man appeared in the archway. He stood still, only his eyes moving as they searched the crowd of dancers under the flashing lights. It did not take him long to find the one he sought, for the silver dress caught the light and held it, splintering it into a thousand shiny bits. Karen did not see him. She was totally absorbed in the music and in her own almost pagan movements, hips swinging from side to side. Her eyes were half-closed, her expression almost trancelike.

He watched her intently. She was no longer the girl-child running through the rain, nor the prim young lady pouring tea. She was a woman, a mature and beautiful woman whose voluptuous dancing was an invitation in itself.

Even as he stood there the music ended. Karen slowly straightened, blinking a little. As her partner, a florid, black-haired young man, started to take her by the arm she casually stepped back out of his reach, and her lips moved as she said something. The two of them edged their way through the crowd to the long, linen-covered table set up along one side of the room, and helped themselves to food and drink.

When the lead singer announced the next number, the girl quickly downed her glass of punch, and the couple moved back onto the dance floor. Again Ryan saw how she evaded the arm her partner would have put around her waist, and how quickly she gave herself up to the loud, insistent beat of the music.

"Ryan, you came after all! I'd just about given up on you."

It was Amanda, looking gorgeous in a flame-colored dress of raw silk and quantities of chunky gold jewelry. She had a red-haired man in tow and swiftly made the introductions. "Craig," she added, "be a darling and let me have this one with Ryan."

Craig grinned amiably at them both. "Only one, mind you," he said and purposefully headed for the bar.

"Only one," Ryan repeated firmly, "and only it we end up in the vicinity of your sister."

Mandy opened her eyes very wide. "So that's the way the wind's blowing...."

"Never you mind which way the wind's blowing," Ryan replied equably. "But I want the next dance with her."

"Maybe Duke won't like that."

"She's not engaged to him, is she?"

"Karen? Engaged?" Mandy gave a short laugh. "Not a chance."

His eyes narrowed, but he did not take the opening she had given him. "Then Duke will just have to make the best of it," he said easily. Almost in spite of himself he added, "She looks very beautiful."

"I hope you realize that I'm the one who made her promise to wear that dress. She's never worn it before."

"Then you're to be congratulated."

With a salvo of chords on the guitar and a roll of drums the next piece began, and conversation, of necessity, came to a halt. Ryan and Amanda moved in among the dancers, and obligingly Mandy edged them nearer and nearer to the slender figure in silver. Karen didn't even notice them. It took the sudden deafening silence at the end of the song and Mandy's clear voice to bring her back to reality. "There you are, Karen. Ryan did come, after all. Isn't that great? I think he wants to dance with you. Duke, why don't you take me over to the bar. I'm dying for a drink." She tucked her arm in Duke's and led him away before he had the chance to say a word.

Ryan began to laugh. "That sister of yours is something else—a fellow hasn't got a hope around her. You're looking very beautiful, Karen."

His sudden appearance had thrown Karen off balance. Her breast still heaving from the exertions of the dance, her cheeks flushed, she murmured, "Oh...thank you." She had forgotten how tall he was. Even in her high heels, and she was a tall woman, she had to look up at him. It was not the moment to recall Mandy saying, "Imagine being kissed by him," yet those were the words that flashed through her mind. Blushing even more deeply, she stammered, "Would you like a drink?"

"No. I'd like to dance with you. Your partner's been commandeered, or hadn't you noticed?"

"Yes." She made a frantic effort to pull herself together, to show at least a semblance of intelligence or wit, but before she could say anything he was talking again.

"This Duke—is he a friend of yours?"

"Yes, he is."

"I've been watching you. You never let him touch you, not once."

"I already told you that I hate being touched."

"Why, Karen?"

"Why don't you ask Mandy, if you get along so well with her?" she said shrewishly.

"I don't want to ask Mandy. I want you to tell me."

The next song was announced, and Karen said in a brittle voice, "Do you want to dance with me or don't you?"

"Yes, Karen, I want to dance with you." The words were simple, yet weighted with a significance beyond their normal meaning. She shivered as though someone had walked over her grave.

The music had started up again. She waited a second or two to catch the rhythm and began to dance. But this time was different. Ryan was not Duke; she could not shut him out as though he didn't exist. Instead she found herself admiring the grace of his big, loose-knit frame, the perfect coordination that must come from a body at the peak of fitness. Dressed as he was in tuxedo and starched shirt—very civilized clothes—she was in danger of forgetting that he was a man of the outdoors used to roaming the Arctic tundra, surely one of the world's most demanding environments. A tough, resourceful man, very different from Duke.

Her body would not obey her. Her movements were jerky, not always in time with the beat; she couldn't recapture that sensation of complete unity with the music, of a fluidity of movement that freed her from her own physical being. And already she knew Ryan well enough to know he must be all too aware of the difference and would be drawing his own conclusions as to the reason.

She tried. She closed her eyes in an effort to blank him out. She focused on the loud, repetitive rhythm, trying to let it flow through her limbs, played the old game of thinking of the empty beach and the long white curls of waves. But nothing worked. She felt like a teenager: awkward, uncoordinated and painfully self-conscious.

It seemed to take forever for the music to end, but when it did the silence was sheer relief after what had been rapidly becoming unendurable. Then the announcer's voice boomed across the room. "We've had a request for a slow number, ladies and gentlemen, so we'll play you a waltz."

Karen said lightly, "I need a drink, Ryan." It was the first time she had used his name; she didn't even notice.

"Let's dance this one first."

She saw the calculation in his eyes and knew he was playing with her, pushing her to the limit. She raised her chin. "I don't want to."

They might have been alone in the crowd of other guests. Soft and seductive, the music floated across the room. Ryan started to reach out for her, and she shrank back. He said evenly, "It's only a dance, Karen. Nothing's going to happen to you in the middle of the dance floor."

"I don't want to," she reiterated. "Please, Ryan, don't do this to me."

There was genuine pleading in her voice, and abruptly he relented. "Find me that drink and let's go someplace where we can talk," he said levelly. "Lead the way."

She threaded through the swaying couples, murmuring her excuses. Fortunately there was no sign of either Duke or Mandy at the bar, only another of the smartly uniformed young men. Because she was thirsty after dancing so much, she drank a glass of punch right away then asked for a refill. Her voice seemed to come from a long way away as she said, "Where do you want to go?"

"Somewhere quiet."

"The sunroom's the best place." It was her favorite room in the whole house, a glass-walled solarium with a southern exposure. From the ceiling hung flowering begonias and vivid red fuchsias, while the cedar benches were crowded with bushy green ferns and stately, waxen-petaled lilies. It was deserted and serene, the conflicting strains of Styx and Strauss reaching them faintly. The only light came from Chinese lanterns strung in the trees outside, and the room seemed very peaceful after the crowded, noisy ballroom. Karen sank down on one of the soft cushions on a bench, her face as pale as the petals of the lily beside her. "That's better," she said softly, leaning her head back and closing her eyes.

"Isn't it just? I never was much of a one for crowds."

She smiled. "You must enjoy the Arctic, then."

He was still standing, leaning on the railing in the corner across from her, his drink in his hand. For a moment he looked at her in silence, as if debating what course to follow. "Do you like crowds, Karen?"

It seemed a safe enough topic. "At times I do, yes. You're anonymous in a crowd, just one person among many with no one caring what you're like or where you're going. In a small group everyone knows about you. You have no freedom, no room to breathe."

"You find that true in your family situation?"

"Heavens, yes! You heard my mother talking about my job—she hated every moment I was there. And she's going to hate it even more when I go back to university in the fall."

"So it's important enough to you that you'll fight for it?"

The alcohol had loosened her tongue. "I don't know if I can explain it to you," she said, absently brushing the white petals of the lily with the tip of one finger, her profile against the shadowed wall as clean-cut as a cameo. "The job made me feel needed and useful. There can be so many rules and regulations in the welfare system, so much red tape—it's all too easy to hide behind the system, so that you're just a machine processing other human beings. I wanted as much as possible to humanize it all, to invest the handout of money with dignity, even with caring...."

"I understand exactly what you mean." He paused. "Judging by what I've seen of your home environment, you don't need to work, Karen."

"Not for money, no. There's always lots of that." There was no mistaking the bitterness in her voice.

"There are people who would give a great deal to be in your shoes."

"I know that, of course I do!" She bit her lip, glad of the concealing gloom in the sunroom, aware that she had drunk too much.

"A desire for independence, is that it?"

In only two meetings he seemed to know as much about her as she knew herself. "I love earning my own money—money that has nothing to do with my mother. But it's more than that. It's the whole question of what one does with one's time. Mandy can get along fine going from day to day and party to party, but I can't. Lots of times I wish I could—it would certainly make life simpler."

His relaxed posture hid from her how intently he was listening. "Your mother inherited the money, didn't she? I think your father once mentioned that."

"Yes. A great-aunt died in Vancouver, and mother

was her only living relative.'' Her voice was so low he had to strain to hear it. ''That changed everything.''

''Tell me about it.''

Whether it was the alcohol and the darkness, or some strange intuition of his solidity and strength, Karen didn't know; all she knew was that she did want to tell him. ''I was only thirteen at the time and I didn't understand a lot of what happened. Looking back on it, I think the money went to mother's head. She's my mother and I love her, but she's not a particularly wise or sensible woman. We had been living in southern New Brunswick because my father taught in a university there. Our house overlooked the Tantramar Marshes, great tidal flats that stretch for miles.'' She smiled reminiscently, almost forgetting her listener. ''I had a German shepherd, and the two of us would roam the marshes for hours. I loved it there. . . .

''But when my mother inherited the money, she decided we should move. It so happened that a position opened up for my father in Montreal at the same time. That's why we came here. She bought this house and devoted herself to becoming a leading light in the local society circles. I think she's found out subsequently that money can't always buy social position, but that's neither here nor there. My father never liked his job here, so he started cutting himself loose from the academic community and spending more and more time at actual digs. I don't know if he has any university affiliations now.''

''He winters in Vancouver and does some lecturing at the University of British Columbia.''

"I see. That's about as far away from us as he can get and still be in Canada, isn't it?" She paused, for she had lost the thread of her story. The fruit punch she had drunk was causing her brain to whirl, and for a moment all she could remember was a skinny, long-legged thirteen-year-old running through the grass on the marsh with a big dog lolloping at her side.

"Mandy and I started school in Montreal," she said vaguely. "Mandy was nine and never seemed to have any problem adjusting, but right from the start I hated it. Too many houses, too many people, nowhere to get away from it all.... I suppose like most teenagers I didn't have much sense of proportion. Black was black and white was white and there was nothing in between. Then when I was fourteen I—" She suddenly broke off, her brain braking with frantic speed as the black abyss yawned in front of her. Oh, God, she had nearly told him. The dark wings rose around her, surrounding her, smothering her with their soft, deadly weight. She put a shaking hand to her forehead. "I...."

"Karen, what's wrong?" In two swift strides Ryan had reached her, unceremoniously pushing her head between her knees and holding it there.

As the blackness retreated, Karen became aware of her forehead pressing into the fabric of her dress and of the coldness of one of the diamond earrings against her cheek. "I'm all right," she mumbled, and felt his hands release her. Slowly she raised her head to find him kneeling beside her, his face on a level with hers. He was so close that she could see the tiny lines around his eyes and the vivid blue of his irises.

"I'm sorry," she said more clearly. "I've had too much to drink."

From his expression she could tell Ryan knew she was avoiding the truth. But all he said was, "I thought you were going to faint."

"So did I. Mother's punch has done that to me before. It tastes so innocuous you don't realize how much you're drinking." She sat up straighter. It seemed important to end her narrative as quickly as possible, so she said lightly, "Well, to make a long story short, I was sent off to boarding school, where I indulged in all the adolescent pains of introversion and rebellion. I even ran away at one point, and I managed to fail two years in a row. Not exactly what you'd call a well-adjusted teenager. However, I eventually finished my schooling, went to university for a few years and got the job at the drop-in center." She smiled determinedly. "The story of my life. Not very exciting, is it? And now don't you think we'd better go back to the party?"

He refused to smile back. "It's what you haven't told me that interests me," he said heavily. "However, I don't think this is the time to push you."

Ryan stood up, took her hand and pulled her to her feet. He must have felt how her fingers quivered in his hold like a frantic, trapped bird and must have seen how she instinctively recoiled, her gray eyes very wide. For a moment he held her prisoner, his eyes traveling over her parted lips, the tense set of her shoulders and the shadowed valley between her breasts, his expression inscrutable. Then, without haste, he released her and stepped back a pace.

"Let's go back and find you something to eat. Your friend will no doubt be looking for you, anyway."

Karen gazed up at him, unable to think of anything to say. For some reason she found herself wondering how old he was. Mid-thirties, perhaps? Certainly no younger, for his was a rugged-looking face. Somehow she always distrusted people in their thirties or forties whose faces showed none of the marks of day-to-day living. Such people were detached from life, she had decided, without involvement, or care or concern for others. Ryan Koetsier was not like that. His interest in her, whatever his motives, was genuine.

Stumbling a little, she preceded him from the sun-room, the strands of a strawberry begonia brushing against her hair. The music grew louder. The seething crowd in the ballroom could have been from another planet.

Karen felt almost a relief to see Duke standing by the bar—safe, ordinary Duke who, like Mandy, had no desire to look beneath the surface of things. She gave Ryan a brilliant, empty smile. "There's Duke—I'd better go. Goodbye, Ryan." She couldn't have prevented that note of finality in her voice if she had tried.

"Let's rather say au revoir." No smile, no hand-shake, nothing. He simply turned on his heel and walked away from her. He had nearly reached the archway when Mandy darted out of the crowd, followed by two or three of her friends. He was encircled and drawn into the dance.

Feeling oddly deflated, Karen walked up to Duke,

"I'm hungry," she said without ceremony. "Are you?"

It was an unnecessary question, for Duke was always hungry. He was the classic picture of a college football player: burly, not overly endowed with brains, yet relieved from ordinariness by a good-tempered nature and an often surprisingly apt sense of humor. When he said with a grin, "The best food's in the dining room," she was not surprised; he *would* know that. Neither was she surprised that he did not question her about her disappearance with Ryan Koetsier. Live and let live was very much Duke's motto; he seemed to expend all his aggression on the football field.

The evening wore on. Karen ate, drank sparingly, danced and talked, going through all the motions like a marionette on a string. And finally people started leaving. It was not until then that she realized Ryan Koetsier must have already left. He was not with Mandy and her group, nor was he with her mother's friends. She felt an unaccountable pang of disappointment that he had gone without saying something, yet knew at the same time that she was being illogical. Hadn't she said goodbye to him earlier?

She couldn't imagine that she would be seeing him again. He would go back north, carrying her father the message that neither of his daughters wanted to see him. Tears pricked at her eyes. The situation was all so wrong, yet it was beyond her to mend it.

By the time the last of the guests left, the caterers were starting to clear everything away. Mandy yawned widely. "Great party," she said. "But my feet are killing me. I'm going to bed. Night all." Carrying her shoes in her hand, she trailed up the staircase.

"It was a good party, mother," Karen said. "You must be pleased."

"The Westons didn't come," Nancy answered peevishly. "I'd hoped they would."

Karen knew the Westons were considered the elite of the neighborhood, an invitation to their gray stone mansion akin to a royal command. "Never mind. The Martocks came, and the Lees." Two of the lesser lights, but nevertheless good catches in Nancy's eyes.

Nancy frowned. She was tired and, consequently, in the mood to find fault. "I wonder why Mr. Koetsier left so early."

"Oh—did he?"

"I'm rather surprised he came at all."

"He wants me to go to Baffin Island and visit father." Karen had had no idea she was going to say that until the words were out.

Something flickered in Nancy's eyes and was gone. Fear? Yet why would it have been fear, Karen wondered. Her mother said sharply, "That's quite out of the question. A ridiculous idea."

"Why, mother?"

"If your father had wanted to see you, why didn't he come to Montreal himself?"

It was the argument Karen had used with Ryan "I don't know...maybe I'll go and ask him."

"You'll do no such thing! Karen, I'm very tired and I don't want to hear any more about it, now or in the future. You should be more considerate—you know how tricky my blood pressure's been lately.''

The same old strategy. Karen said quietly, "Sorry, mother. I guess I'll go to bed, too. Good night.''

But as she climbed the stairs, she had forgotten her earlier tiredness. She was aware of only one thing: her mother's opposition had aroused in her a strong desire to go to Pond Inlet, to confront her father and demand of him why he had so callously cut off all contact with her. She had sworn to Ryan that she would not go. Now she was beginning to wonder. . . .

CHAPTER THREE

KAREN SLEPT LATE THE NEXT MORNING, a restful, dreamless sleep that left her refreshed. Through the chink in the curtains a narrow beam of golden sunlight spilled onto the carpet; birds were chirruping in the elm trees. Her first waking thought was not of the job she had finished or even of Ryan Koetsier, but of Pond Inlet where her father was based. She felt excitement stir within her. She had the time, because she had no job. She had the money, for she had saved most of her salary. Did she really want to go?

It would mean a major battle with her mother, she knew that already, and over the years the winner of those battles had rarely been Karen. It would also entail coming face to face with her father, a figure who had become less and less distinct to her as the years of silence had passed.

Rolling over in bed, she pulled open the drawer of her bedside table, rummaging among the contents until she found what she was looking for—an enlarged black-and-white photograph mounted on cardboard. Her father was wearing an old lumberman's jacket and a turtleneck sweater, his eyes looking beyond the photograph to a horizon Karen could only imagine. Somehow it seemed characteristic of him that he not meet the photographer's eyes. His was a handsome face, but not an approachable one, for there was impatience, perhaps even intolerance in the rather thin line of his mouth, and a forbidding intelligence in his far seeing gray eyes. Although she had searched that face many times for clues to the person behind it, she had never found much of herself in it.

What would he look like now, she wondered, gazing at the stubbornly unrevealing piece of cardboard. This picture had been taken nearly ten years ago, so he must have changed in the interim. Certainly he must have aged. Would the mouth soften to a smile were he to see her? Would the gray eyes drag themselves from the illimitable horizons to focus on his own daughter and see her need for his love and approval?

She suddenly shoved the photograph facedown into the drawer and slammed it shut. She must be crazy even to think of going to Pond Inlet, for doing so would only cause her more grief. She was letting Ryan Koetsier's words outweigh her judgment. Her eyes narrowed as she recalled that conversation with Ryan over tea and scones in the library. Her father had asked Ryan to come and see her and Mandy. But he had not asked them to visit—that was Ryan's addition. At the time she had been too angry and upset to make much of the distinction, important though it was. She wished now that she could have the opportunity to question Ryan further. Why did he think her father needed to see her? How could Laurence Smith possibly need anything from her?

But it was too late to ask Ryan anything. She certainly wouldn't be seeing him again. He might even be flying back to Baffin Island today.

The other thing that a visit to Pond Inlet would mean, of course, was that she would see more of him. Ryan was her father's close friend and associate, so where Laurence Smith was, presumably he would be, too. In her mind's eye she saw his big, powerful body, his well-groomed hands, his all-too-astute blue eyes and knew in her bones that he spelled danger. Duke and his football cronies she could handle; Ryan was a far different proposition, someone with whom she could easily be out of her depth and whom she would therefore be wise to avoid. In the privacy of her bedroom she could admit to herself that he both fascinated and frightened her.

Restlessly Karen got out of bed, pulled back the curtains so that the sun flooded the room and outlined the long, lissome curves of her figure in the thin cotton nightdress. She was oblivious to her own beauty, for her body as a sexual object was something she chose to ignore. She could not be oblivious to the beauty of the morning, however. She'd go jogging for a half hour before it got too hot, she decided, and maybe that would help clear her head and drive from her mind the recurring image of Laurence Smith's remote features—and Ryan Koetsier's handsome ones. She pulled open the closet door to get her running shoes.

A light knock came on her door and Houndsel called apologetically, "Excuse me, miss, are you up?"

She wrapped a housecoat around herself and opened the door, smiled at the old man. "Only just."

"Telephone for you, a Mr. Koetsier."

"Oh," she said blankly. It was as if her thoughts had conjured him up. "I—I'll take it downstairs."

She ran down the stairs, belting her housecoat as she went, and picked up the receiver. "Hello?"

"Karen? Ryan here."

"Hello," she repeated foolishly.

"Would you be free to have dinner with me this evening?" He sounded very sure of himself over the phone.

She didn't stop to think. "No. No, I don't think so."

"Do you mean you're not free, or do you mean you don't want to have dinner with me?"

Her hand gripped the receiver. "There's no need for us to see each other again."

"So you *are* free. Good. I'll pick you up at seven." The connection was cut and the dial tone buzzed in her ear.

Crossly she banged the receiver back on the hook. He could think again. There was no way she was going out with him this evening. She dialed Duke's number and when he came to the phone said without preamble, "Duke, would you take me to the movies this evening?"

"I'd love to, Karen, but I can't. Didn't I mention that a bunch of us are going to Dave's summer place for an overnight?" He hesitated. "You can come if you like, although I'm not sure it's your kind of party."

"I'm sure it's not," she said ironically. "Never mind, another time." She ran upstairs to her sister's room, but Mandy was going sailing with Craig Manley. "Just the two of us," Mandy explained airily. "Goodness, Karen, if Ryan asked me to dinner, I'd go like a shot. And for heaven's sake wear something pretty."

So Mandy was no use, either, and by an offhand question to her mother, Karen discovered Nancy was going to a bridge party. No help there.

She went jogging. She took some of the flowers from the party to the hospital. After lunch she went for a swim in the pool and read for a while. Then, without being aware that she had made a decision, she went indoors and showered the chlorine from her skin and hair. After experimenting with different hairstyles she finally settled on a tight knot at the nape of her neck, hair pulled back from her face. Karen had the forehead and profile for such a ruthless style, which stressed the beauty of her dark brows and wide-spaced eyes. She applied more makeup than usual, using it as a disguise to hide behind more than anything else. And finally she slipped on a very plain white dress, gathered at the waist with a wide black belt. With a black-and-white scarf at the neckline and delicate black sandals on her feet she presented an elegant, aloof figure in the mirror. Black and white, she thought mischievously, the colors of a nun.

She kept Ryan waiting for five minutes while she painted her fingernails, and then sauntered down the staircase. He was wearing a pale gray suit, with a light blue shirt and a darker tie that emphasized the blue of his eyes. He was watching her intently, and again she received the impression of an outdoorsman only temporarily tamed. He could function more than adequately in the city, but he would prefer the challenges of the wilderness to those of urban living, she knew.

Karen paused for a moment, wishing it were Duke who was waiting for her, easygoing Duke whom she could wrap around her finger. Makeup, hair and dress suddenly seemed a most inadequate facade; she was sure Ryan Koetsier knew she was afraid of him. "Good evening," she said coolly.

"You never cease to surprise me," he said. "I've seen you running in the rain, pouring tea like a maiden aunt, dancing like a call girl. And now this. You could have stepped out of the pages of *Vogue*."

She flushed. "I did not look like a call girl!"

"I'm glad to see you're real under all that makeup. Shall we go?"

"Are we going to spend the evening fighting with each other?"

He quirked an eyebrow. "Only if you want to."

He looked so damned sure of himself. She hesitated on the bottom step of the staircase. "I told Houndsel I'd be back by eleven."

"Back to the cloister, eh? In that case we'd better not stand here any longer."

She heard herself say, quite out of the blue, "Are *you* real, Ryan?"

The mockery left his eyes. He said quietly, "Yes, I'm real, Karen. I asked you out tonight because I like you and I want to know more about you. You're beginning to fascinate me—so free and graceful one minute, so closed and defensive the next. I want to discover what makes you tick.'' He must have seen the very defensiveness he had just mentioned shutter her eyes. More lightly he added, ''It's not all part of a plot to coerce you to visit your father. I've said all I'm going to say on that subject.''

''Oh. You mean it's my decision now.''

''That's right.'' He smiled. ''The evening's ahead of us, I'm going to relish walking into the restaurant with a startlingly beautiful young woman on my arm, and I'd like us both to enjoy ourselves. I'm leaving for Quebec City tomorrow and I fly back to Pond Inlet the day after, so I'm no threat to you.''

Her gray eyes troubled, she said, ''How do you know. . .?''

''That I'm a threat to you? It's written all over you, Karen. Even though I don't understand why I should be. But I promise I'll do nothing that you don't want me to do, nor will I badger you to tell me anything you don't want to share. We're going to enjoy good food, good wine and each other's company—is that a deal?''

Disarmed, unable to believe he was anything but sincere, she favored him with a rare, generous smile that did indeed make her look startlingly beautiful. ''It's a deal,'' she said with a little laugh of mingled delight and relief, for she had been worrying that he was going to pressure her about her father; his words about herself dropped to the bottom of her mind. ''Let's go!''

On the way downtown they talked about books they had read; they moved to plays, movies, and music over their meal in one of the fine restaurants in Old Montreal, discovering a number of similar tastes and some intriguing differences. Earlier Karen had thought the word outdoorsman described him, capturing the impression he gave of leashed physical power. Now she realized that that was far too simplistic, for he was demonstrating other traits—a breadth of knowledge, and a tolerant and balanced judgment that she could only admire. When the talk moved on to the field of art, she discovered him to be equally knowledgeable. She had recently seen a collection of Robert Bateman's wildlife prints, and she said reflectively, "There was one of a white gyrfalcon that I particularly liked. That's an Arctic bird, isn't it?"

"Indeed it is," he said easily. "It's very rare, though. Last summer I saw a pair nesting on Bylot Island, but they're the only ones I've ever seen in all my trips to the Arctic."

"Is Bylot Island near Pond Inlet?"

"Right across the way. It's a federal bird sanctuary. Your father and I were there because some Dorset remains have been found on the island." Briefly he described how the Dorset culture was a part of the Canadian Eskimo's prehistory, and how the Dorset people had died out about a thousand years earlier, leaving a legacy of artwork closely connected to witchcraft and magic.

She listened, fascinated. "Has my father been associated with the site on Bylot Island?"

"Not that particular one, no. He described others farther west. At the moment he's involved with a dig of a Thule settlement. They're a more recent culture, hunters of whales, and the ancestors of the present-day Eskimos—who, as you probably know, prefer to be called Inuit."

She said curiously, "What's Pond Inlet like, Ryan?"

He paused. "It's mountains with ice caps that never melt, and glaciers with names like Aktineq and Narsarsuk. It's the wide open stretch of the tundra, where willows grow only a foot tall and Arctic flowers bloom in places you wouldn't think a plant could exist. It's the croaking of the raven and the wail of the loon—"

"You love it."

He grinned shamefacedly. "I do, yes. You spoke of the sense of freedom you felt on the Tantramar Marshes when you were a young girl, Karen. . . I feel the same way about the Arctic tundra. Space and light and a vast expanse of sky. At this time of year the sun never sets."

She was playing with her fork, her expression wistful. "It sounds lovely."

He added abruptly, "I've given you a romanticized picture, I'm afraid. It's also oil drums and broken-down snowmobiles littering the landscape, temperatures that rarely climb above 12°C and three months of total darkness in the winter. A land that doesn't forgive mistakes. They call it Toonoonik-Sahoonik, the land of many bones."

It was almost as if he was trying to discourage her

from going there. "Where do you live when you're there?" Karen asked.

"There's a hotel."

"Do they get many tourists?"

"Very few. Construction workers, people associated with the oil companies, government workers. A few tours, maybe. That's all." The waiter had brought their bill and Ryan said, "We'd better get going if I'm to have you home by eleven."

"Is it that late already?" Karen asked, conscious of a faint feeling of dismay. The time seemed to have flown.

Once they were back in the car Ryan changed the subject to the French-English situation, and obediently Karen followed his lead, though her mind was still preoccupied with visions of dazzling white glaciers under a sun that never set. But somehow there did not seem to be an opening where she could ask any further questions. Before she knew it, they were turning into the driveway. Ryan put out the lights and took the key from the ignition, moving to open his door.

Without premeditation the words burst from Karen's lips. "My mother would totally oppose my going."

The lamp over the front door was on; through the tall hedge it cast a mottled pattern of light and shadow on Ryan's face as he turned to look at her. "Going where?" he said obtusely.

"Pond Inlet, of course."

"I thought you said you weren't going."

"I'm not! I just want you to understand why."

With heavy patience he said, "I understood the reason to be your antipathy toward your father—now you're saying it's because of your mother. Make up your mind, Karen. Besides which, I fail to see how your mother could stop you. You're free and surely over twenty-one."

"Her health is very poor. She gets upset when either Mandy or I go away."

"You mean she holds her health over you like a weapon. That's one of the oldest tricks in the book."

Karen sighed. "I know. The trouble is that sometimes she really is ill. And I never know which it is." She hesitated, looking down at her hands, which were locked together in her lap. "Once, when I was sixteen, I ran away from school. I think I already mentioned that to you. I went to Toronto, got a job, rented a little bed-sitting-room. Everything was going fine. But I had to let mother know where I was so she wouldn't worry. A couple of weeks later I got a telegram saying she'd had a severe gallbladder attack and was in the hospital recuperating from an operation. So I had to go home—what else could I do? I couldn't leave Mandy alone to cope with it all. My mother was very loving, very forgiving, and clever enough to make me promise not to run away again. And ever since then whenever I try to assert myself or do something she doesn't want me to do, she gets ill. She *does* have high blood pressure, that's genuine enough. But I never know whether she's faking her illnesses or whether they're real."

"So what are you planning to do, dance to her tune for the rest of your life?"

She glared at him. "*I* don't know! You think I'm being a typical hysterical female, don't you?"

"No, I don't think that, Karen," he replied soberly. "But I think you are allowing your mother to manipulate your life. If you do decide to go to Pond Inlet, or anywhere else for that matter, I think you should make your plans and tell her afterward. Otherwise ten years down the road you'll find yourself still living at home and catering to your mother's whims—because she'll probably live to be a hundred."

Karen had a horrible feeling he was right. Stirring restlessly in her seat, she said, "I'm still not going to Pond Inlet. But it's good advice for the future."

"Is there somewhere we can walk?" he said abruptly. "Does the backyard go down to the water?"

"Yes, but—"

"Come on then. I hate being cooped up in a car." He got out, then strode around to open her door.

"But I don't really want—"

"Stop arguing." Not waiting to see if she was coming, he went to the end of the driveway and unlatched the gate that led into the garden.

For Karen the moment suddenly became charged with significance. She could leave him and go into the house; he would go back to Pond Inlet and that would be that. Or she could follow him. He frightened her, because he had a way of seeing through all the chinks in her armor and mercilessly attacking her at her weakest points. Yet she was honest enough to admit she had enjoyed the evening with him. There had been a meeting of minds, she thought, deliberately ignoring that there could be anything more to it than that. She and Duke had very little in common apart from a love of the outdoors and of physical exercise; she and Ryan had already discovered many other mutual interests, so that she had felt alive and stimulated in his presence....

It had taken only a split second for all these thoughts to rush through Karen's brain. Then she was slipping through the gate as well, her dress and face a ghostly white in the gloom. Ryan had apparently assumed that she would follow him, she realized resentfully, for he was weaving purposefully through the trees on his way down to the water, his path lit by the spotlight on the corner of the boathouse. Nor did he stop until he had reached the shore, where little waves lapped and splashed on the rocks. He turned to watch her slower progress down the hill, keeping his hands in his pockets and not offering to help her even though her shoes made walking difficult on the uneven terrain. When she was within fifteen feet of him, he said roughly, "I know damn well I promised I wouldn't pester you about going to Pond Inlet. But, Karen, I wish you would go."

She stopped dead. "Why is it so important to you, Ryan?"

"Your father needs you. Don't ask me how I know that, I just do."

There was a silence. "And is that the only reason?"

"Of course it's not. You don't even have to ask that question."

Her temper flared. "Perhaps I'm a little slow. . . why don't you spell out the other reasons for me?"

"There's only one other reason. You," he said heavily. "I want to keep on seeing you."

"What's so special about me?"

As he walked up the slope toward her, Karen instinctively retreated a few steps until her back touched a tree trunk. Holding on tightly to her anger as her sole means of defense, she waited for his answer. When it came, she knew she would never have guessed it in a hundred years.

"You're the most beautiful woman I've ever seen."

She stared up at him in blank astonishment, forgetting to be afraid. "Don't be silly! Mandy's much prettier than I am."

"Mandy's a very pretty girl. But I didn't say you were pretty, I said you were beautiful. They're two very different things."

"Oh." She digested this in silence, wondering why his words had startled her so much. If she was not a vain woman, she was at least a realistic one, and it needed only a passing glance in the mirror to tell her she *was* beautiful. Perhaps it had surprised her because she had never tried to see herself through a man's eyes.

"Has no one ever told you how beautiful you are?"

There was a thread of laughter in her voice. "Duke thinks I'm cute."

"Cute—for heaven's sake! Duke's blind."

"You really mean it, don't you?" she said curiously. "That I'm beautiful."

"Oh, yes, I mean it."

"You're not just stringing me a line?"

"There wouldn't be much point in that, would there, Karen?"

A smile pulled at the corners of her mouth. "Thank you," she said, feeling oddly breathless.

Leaning forward, Ryan kissed her, a brief, gentle touch of his lips that he must have thought wouldn't frighten her. For an instant she was absolutely still, caught in the wonderment and pride he had instilled in her. Then she tensed, jerking her head away. "Don't!"

"It was only a kiss."

Her lashes flickered. "I hate that kind of thing. So don't do it again."

He said slowly, "There's a reason you feel that way, isn't there? Something happened to you as a child or as a young woman. Something traumatic." She could see him searching his memory, his brow furrowed. "When you were a teenager, fourteen or fifteen... that was when it happened, wasn't it? You nearly told me in the sunroom, and that was why you almost fainted."

"Don't be ridiculous! Nothing happened to me. I just don't like being mauled, that's all."

"You don't want a man within ten feet of you."

"So what?" she said raggedly.

"It's not exactly what you'd call normal."

"So maybe I'm different and I don't like sex. Why should you care? I'm sure you never have any problem finding somebody willing."

"You're quite right. I don't. Maybe that's the trouble, that it's always been too easy."

"Well, don't get interested in me as some kind of a challenge," she said shortly. "I'm not available."

"I can ask Mandy what happened to you, or your mother."

"Go ahead."

He laughed, a sound without humor. "You know damn well I won't, don't you?"

Karen shrugged with pretended indifference. "I really don't care one way or the other. Be honest with yourself, Ryan—the only attraction I hold for you is that I'm saying no."

"That is by no means the only attraction." With an urgency and a lack of finesse she was beginning to recognize as characteristic of him he added, "Come to Pond Inlet, Karen. For your father's sake and for your sake. There's room there for you to breathe and be yourself. To be free."

Shaken by a surge of longing for the kind of simplicity his words had evoked, yet knowing it to be a false hope, she said flatly, "No. It's not that easy."

"So you'll stay in your golden cage, hedged in by your money and your mother from any kind of relationship that has reality or personal responsibility," he said savagely.

She flinched. "You persist in oversimplifying."

"I'm telling the truth and you know it. You're so scared of your own shadow you won't face up to it, that's all."

Perilously near tears, she stamped her foot. "You've always had your own way over everything, haven't you?" It was only a shrewd guess, but she saw immediately that it had hit home. "And now that you're not getting it, you're throwing the blame on me. For once and for all, I don't want to see my father. And I don't want to see any more of you. So you can go to hell, Ryan Koetsier!'' She whirled and ran up the hill, her feet soundless in the grass as she dodged between the tall straight tree trunks.

She had almost reached the driveway when Ryan caught up with her, grabbing her by the shoulder. Automatically she ducked, slicing out with the flat of her hand and jabbing with the heel of her shoe, her movements smooth and fluid from long practice. But he was quicker and she met only empty air. Off balance as he released her, she spat, ''How many times do I have to tell you not to touch me?''

He did not bother acknowledging this. ''You've taken lessons in self-defense, haven't you? Another bar on the cage.''

''So, obviously, have you.''

He was breathing hard, but it was nothing to do with his dash up the hill or his lightning-swift deflection of her defense tactics. In the shadowed light his eyes were dark and fathomless, his mouth hard with purpose. ''Come to Pond Inlet, Karen. I won't promise to leave you alone. In fact, I'll challenge you and harass you every chance I get. But you won't be bored. The place will fascinate you, and at least you'll know you're alive.''

''Miserable maybe, but alive,'' she replied sarcastically.

''Are you happy now?'' His voice was very quiet.

She shivered. Without much conviction she said, ''I was until you came along.''

''If you really believe that, then there's no hope for

you.'' He searched in his pocket for his keys. ''Good night, Karen. I'm not going to say goodbye.''

''Goodbye, Ryan.'' There was cold finality in the words.

He got into the car and turned on the engine, twisting his head around as he reversed out of the driveway. The sound of the vehicle faded as he drove away, and Karen was alone. She pressed her trembling hands to her face, wishing with all her heart that she had never met Ryan Koetsier.

CHAPTER FOUR

A WEEK PASSED. Karen went sailing, golfing and swimming with friends of Mandy. She obligingly made up a fourth at her mother's bridge party, went to the theater and the movies and dined out. Then early one morning as she was out jogging it hit her what she had been doing all week.

She was pacing along the grass verge of the sidewalk in her shorts and T-shirt, her steps light and easy, her breathing only slightly accelerated. There was a hint of coolness in the dawn air, to be savored after the series of hot, humid days. No one was around, for she had risen earlier than the rest of the world. Yet despite the different circumstances it was impossible not to remember her first meeting with Ryan. Then, too, she had been jogging along a sidewalk. Her steps slowed.

She had been running from the thought of him all week, she realized, trying to forget him and the conflict he had aroused in her by submerging herself in a deluge of physical activity. But the tennis balls she had slammed at her opponents had really been directed at Ryan's disturbing blue eyes—and at the shadowy, indistinct features of her father. She saw that now. She had literally been running away from both of them.

She slowed to a jog, her gray eyes introspective.

What had it accomplished, all that running? The days had passed. She had killed time—a dreadful phrase, she decided with a shudder—and that was all. She had done nothing of significance; she hadn't even been able to concentrate on the books she had brought home from the center. The week had been a parade of busy, useless days, totally meaningless. Was that what she wanted for the rest of her life?

When I go to university in the fall, everything will be all right, she told herself. But would it? Ryan had said she was living in a golden cage, sheltered from any real relationships. Was he right? Were there other matters she needed to settle before she went to university? Other ghosts to put to rest?

The tempo of her steps picked up again, and her face was thoughtful. Life didn't have to remain that way; if she wanted to make changes she could. Ryan had said that, as well. And the logical place to start was to go and see her father. Confront him with the cruelty of his silence over the years, ask for an explanation for his disappearance at the time when she had needed him most.

In an instant the decision was made, so rapidly that she knew it was the right one. She was going. Automatically she turned right at the next corner and headed back to the house, already planning all the things she had to do to get ready and filled with a heady sense of exhilaration. By seeking out her father she might find answers to questions that had plagued her for years. More than that, it would be a step toward freeing herself from her mother's domination. The possibilities were endless.

Once home, it proved to be astonishingly easy to make her reservations, necessitating only two phone calls. In four days' time she could fly from Montreal to Pond Inlet, changing planes at Frobisher Bay. She gave her credit-card number to the Nordair and First Air ticket agents and that was that.

The next thing was the hotel. She knew neither its name nor its telephone number. Furthermore, she had the idea that Pond Inlet was so small that were she to register there, Ryan and her father would find out she was coming. She didn't want that to happen, she realized. She simply wanted to arrive and surprise them both. Surely there would be no problem getting a room, for Ryan had said the town had very few visitors.

The next question was luggage and what clothes to take with her. Feeling absurdly excited, she opened her closet. Nine-tenths of what she had would be useless, she was sure. Rather than dresses and skirts and high-heeled shoes she'd need jeans, sweaters, a heavy jacket and rainwear. And a backpack would be far more suitable than her expensive leather suitcases. She pulled out her hiking boots from the back of the closet and began to rub a coat of silicone into them. She'd have to buy a couple more pairs of socks and some film for her camera and she'd go to the university library to see what she could find to read about Baffin Island.

The one thing Karen didn't do was tell her mother. That she left until the day she was due to leave, waiting until Nancy had had her first coffee and cigarette of the day and was curled up in an armchair in the living room reading the paper, the glasses that she wore only in the presence of her daughters and her servants perched precariously on her nose. Karen had been out jogging, rehearsing what she wanted to say. As she flopped down in the chair facing Nancy and bent forward to take off her sneakers, she remembered the last occasion when she had changed the pattern of her life, a year or more ago. That was the day she had told her mother she was taking the job at the drop-in center instead of going back to university. The discussion had ended in hot and angry words, with Nancy taking what she termed a weak spell and neither of them speaking to each other for more than two weeks. Karen didn't want that scenario repeated.

Carefully she lined up her sneakers on the carpet and wriggled her toes. "Mother, I'm going away for a few days," she said pleasantly.

Her mother rattled the newspaper. "With Duke?"

It was not the answer she had anticipated. "Goodness, no."

"He'd be a very good match, Karen."

Refusing to allow herself to be sidetracked into a discussion of Duke's virtues, Karen said firmly, "By myself. I'm going to Baffin Island to see father."

Nancy lowered the newspaper with a snap, the glasses sliding down her nose. "You're joking."

"No, I'm not. I think it's time I go and see him, because there are things we need to resolve." Karen could have understood anger in Nancy's expression. But consternation and alarm? Why should she be afraid?

"Quite out of the question, darling. The Rawlinsons' big dance is next week. Surely you hadn't forgotten that?" Nancy turned to the society page; the matter was closed.

"Mother, I don't think you quite understand. My reservations are all made. I'm leaving later this morning."

"This morning? Nonsense! That's enough, Karen—I don't want to hear any more."

It was a strange time for Karen to think of Ryan. But she suddenly felt as if he were beside her, encouraging her to keep calm and remember her objectives. She said gently, "You can't make the situation go away by not listening. I'm leaving with or without your blessing. I would much prefer to have it."

Nancy gave up any pretense of reading. "You'll certainly never get it for such a harebrained scheme. I suppose this is all Ryan Koetsier's fault, coming here and stirring up trouble."

"I only want to visit father, I'm not proposing taking up residence with him. I'll be back in a week or two."

"I forbid you to go."

"Why?" Karen asked bluntly.

Flustered, Nancy said overloudly, "Your place is here with me, not gallivanting all over the north by yourself."

"I'm twenty-three years old and well able to look after myself." She sought for the right words. "And I love you, you know that. It *was* Ryan's idea that I go north, and maybe father won't think any more of the idea than you do. But even if he and I have a really good visit and are able to get close to each other, that won't make any difference to the way I feel about you. Surely any daughter can love both parents?''

There was a hunted expression on Nancy's face and patches of color in her cheeks. "I don't want you to go, Karen. Your father's neglected you for years, and now at the slightest overture you're running to him like a. . .like a puppy with its tail wagging.''

The simile was rather too apt. Karen said grimly, "Nevertheless I'm going.''

Nancy folded her hands in her lap. "Then I'm afraid I shall have to tell you that I have an appointment at the end of the week with a heart specialist. Dr. Waring thinks I need a thorough checkup. I didn't mention it because I didn't want you to worry.'' The hunted look was gone, replaced by muted triumph, for this was a strategy that had never once let Nancy down.

Ryan had warned her about this.... "Which day is it? I'll be sure to phone you and see how your examination went," Karen said brightly, her fingernails digging into the arm of the chair.

"You mean you'd go anyway?''

At any other time Nancy's affronted look would have been amusing. "Yes. Ever since I was sixteen you've used your health as a way of keeping me in line, mother—now admit it. First thing you know I'll be an old maid of forty still dancing to your tune.'' Decisively Karen got to her feet and dropped a kiss on her mother's forehead. "I've got to shower and change. I'll be down to say goodbye in a few minutes.''

"When did you make your reservations?"

"Three or four days ago."

"So you've been willfully deceiving me."

"I was afraid you might stage a scene if I didn't."

"Really, Karen, that's a horrible thing to say. Does Mandy know?"

"Not yet. I didn't think it would be fair to tell her and not you."

"I'm glad to see you have that much decency left." The pale blue eyes abandoned artifice; for a moment there was naked pleading in them. "Please, Karen, give up this foolish scheme. Perhaps it's time the three of us took a trip. We could go to Europe together, London, Paris and Zurich."

Slowly Karen shook her head. "No, mother, not right now. Pond Inlet is more important."

"Then I wash my hands of you," Nancy snapped, picking up the paper and burying her nose in it. But the pages fluttered very slightly, for her hands were trembling.

Torn by pity, guilt and love, Karen paused irresolutely; Nancy, had she but known it, was within a hair's breadth of winning. Then she turned on her heel and left the room, trying to block out of her mind that last glimpse of her mother's frightened, ravaged face. She looked so much older, the wrinkles showing all too clearly. That had been no act. Why it should matter so deeply that Karen wanted to see her father she had no idea. But matter it did, there was no question of it.

If ever Karen had been going to weaken it was then. But something drove her up the stairs and into her room, where her backpack, already full, lay on the bed. Hurriedly she turned on the shower.

Mandy must have heard her moving around. She came in, yawned, as Karen was getting dressed. "Where are you off to?" she said in amazement.

"Baffin Island. To see father."

"Good heavens! What does mother think of that?"

"Not much. She almost seems frightened."

"Probably afraid you won't come back." Mandy grinned. "Maybe you won't. Maybe you and Ryan will fall in love and drive off on your dog sled into the midnight sun."

"People don't use dog sleds anymore," Karen said pragmatically. "They use snowmobiles."

"Oh, dear, that's not nearly so romantic. Well, if you decide you don't want him, let me know and perhaps I'll come up, as well."

"Mandy, I'm going up there to see father!"

"Sure." Mandy leaned over and kissed Karen on the cheek, a rare gesture of affection for her. "Have a good time, don't behave yourself and give father my love."

Smiling reluctantly, Karen responded to only the past part of her sister's statement. "I will." She began lacing up her boots. "I'm scared of seeing him again, Mandy."

"It'll be fine, you'll see. You worry too much."

"I guess I do. Anyway, I'll see you in a week or so."

"Make it longer. You never know, you might get snowed in. Imagine that, you and Ryan sharing an igloo."

"It sounds very uncomfortable," Karen said firmly, checking that she had her tickets and traveler's checks in the pocket of her haversack. "Besides, they don't have igloos anymore, either."

"You're destroying all my illusions. I've got to go, love, I'm meeting Craig in half an hour." A blown kiss, and Mandy had drifted out of the room in a wave of delicious scent, leaving Karen feeling considerably more cheerful. Even her mother's frigid goodbye a few minutes later could not entirely dampen her spirits.

Taking a taxi to the airport, she checked in at the counter and went to the Nordair lounge to wait for her flight. It seemed as though the journey had already begun, because the group of people waiting for the plane was a very different group than the one at the Air Canada counter—men in boots and work clothes, and a sprinkling of black-haired Inuit. No business-suited executives, no stylishly dressed women. Karen was glad she was wearing jeans and a rain jacket, her hair pulled back in a ponytail, for it gave her the anonymity she was looking for.

The plane left on time, and as it climbed into the sky Karen had a last glimpse of the massed houses and straight streets of the city. She was leaving all that behind, she thought with an irrepressible lift of excitement, and for all the reading she'd done, she had very little idea of what she was going to. She leaned back in her seat as banked clouds hid the ground and let her mind leap ahead to the two men she would be seeing later in the day—Laurence, her father, and Ryan, who was responsible for her being here. Would Ryan be surprised, she wondered with a faint smile. Or would he have known that sooner or later she would arrive? Somehow the latter seemed more likely....

En route to Frobisher Bay they stopped at Fort Chimo in northern Quebec. The clouds had been sculpted by the wind into a long range of rolling hills whose seeming solidity vanished only as the plane descended into them. The aircraft broke free of the vapor into a cold, gray light that revealed a drab, lake-spotted landscape, where the rocks had been scraped raw by the retreat of mighty glaciers 10,000 years earlier. In the valleys there were tiny pockets of green marsh grass and the spikes of stunted spruce trees. They were the most northerly trees in Eastern Canada, Karen knew, for this was the limit of the tree line. The cluster of houses and sheds around the runway looked so totally out of place in these bleak surroundings that she could not begin to imagine what it would be like living in such isolation.

The stop was only brief. They crossed Ungava Bay and Hudson Strait and came in to land at Frobisher Bay. After Fort Chimo, it seemed almost cosmopolitan, with tiny flat-roofed bungalows in neat rows, an apartment block crowning the hill and a white, windowless school—shaped like an igloo—standing beside a church. No trees, only grass and stretches of bare brown sand.

At the terminal Karen checked her luggage for the First Air flight, admired the carvings in the co-op upstairs, and then filed with the rest of the passengers onto the plane, which was propeller-driven yet reassuringly large. She had already traveled 1,300 miles, and for another four hours she would be carried still further north.

Their first stop was Pangnirtung, the entrance to the Auyuittuq National Park, where the flat-roofed bungalows that she had already come to expect were clustered against the hillside. Rain was pouring down, and to Karen it all looked incredibly bleak and forbidding. Hundred-mile-an-hour winds were common here, the man sitting next to her informed her; they came tunneling through the pass and had recently blown the roof off the Hudson's Bay warehouse.

Feeling very far from home, Karen was cheered by a game of peekaboo, surely a universal game, with a moon-faced Inuit boy in the seat ahead. He was plump and cuddly, with lustrous dark eyes. When they took off again the rain and fog cleared, and she saw below her the jagged peaks of the mountains thrusting up through the clouds, fresh snow dusting their steep flanks. She saw drift ice that from the air was a vivid turquoise color; her first iceberg; fiords cut into the mountains; gaunt cliffs topped with fields of dazzlingly white snow untouched by human or animal. It was incredibly beautiful, alien from anything she had ever seen before. That it was also totally inimical to habitation went without saying. For the first time she understood why their flight attendant wore overalls, hiking boots and a down vest as her uniform.

They made two more stops, at Broughton and Clyde River. By now Karen was growing used to the gravel-surfaced runways edged with orange and yellow oil drums, and to the deceptively casual air with which the flight was conducted. When she got off at Clyde to take a photograph, the pilot, also in overalls, was helping to load freight into the nose of the plane, and the flight attendant nonchalantly called her back when they were ready to leave.

Last leg of the journey. Massed white clouds were again hiding the landscape, so Karen sat quietly in her seat, her eyes on the far horizon where the pale blue sky merged with the clouds. She was growing increasingly nervous now that she was nearing her destination. For the first time it occurred to her that Ryan and her father might be off at the dig, virtually unreachable. Her idea of surprising them both began to seem more and more foolish the nearer she got; she should have phoned from Frobisher Bay.

The pitch of the engines changed as they began their descent. Mist shrouded the windows, then she saw a line of mountains clear-cut against the sky, and below her the dun-colored tundra. They approached the end of the runway, then once again the tires were bouncing on the gravel. The flaps screamed in the wind, the plane slowed to a stop and the engines died. She had arrived.

Karen got to her feet, feeling stiff and cramped after so many hours of sitting. She smiled a goodbye to the flight attendant before trailing after the other passengers to the small corrugated green hut where they would wait for their luggage—a far cry from the massive terminal building at Dorval. Inuit children in parkas and baseball caps wandered in and out of the overheated office, where a voice blared over the radio, apparently unnoticed by anyone. On the far wall three brightly colored posters warned of the dangers of polar bears. Stay Alert, Stay Alive, she read. The Hand That Feeds Could Get Eaten. She shivered, blaming it on the blast of cold air that whipped around her ankles every time someone opened the door. Then the pilot came in, announcing their luggage was unloaded, and she went outside again.

Her backpack and canvas haversack were leaning against the side of the building. She picked them up and looked around uncertainly, wishing she had arranged for Ryan to meet her. Three men were talking together beside her, the syllables of a strange language falling gutturally on her ears. She knew it must be *inuktitut*, the language Inuit people used from Alaska to Greenland. One of the men, short and stocky with a lined, genial face, said in English, "Do you want to go to the hotel? I'm driving there in a few minutes."

Karen smiled gratefully. "Thank you. I'd appreciate that."

"Just wait by the van."

She shouldered her luggage and walked over to the van, feeling the cold air sting her cheeks; 7°C, the pilot had said. Ahead of her, orange, green and yellow, were the houses and sheds of Pond Inlet, set like a child's building blocks on the bare sandy soil just as the buildings had been at Frobisher Bay. It was a utilitarian arrangement, without trees or gardens to soften it, and she might have found it depressing had it not been for the surroundings. On all sides of her were mountains, the closest directly ahead of her on the far side of a stretch of blue water that must be the inlet. The mountains of Bylot Island! They were capped with snow, some of the peaks vanishing into the clouds, while a vast white glacier snaked to the sea down one of the valleys. The air was clear, cold and fresh, the very essence of the north. She drew a deep breath, thinking, *I'm in the Arctic, two thousand miles from home. I'm really here.*

"First trip north?"

It was the pilot speaking. He was a dark, bearded young man with an uncomplicated smile that revealed two teeth missing. She smiled back. "Yes. It's very beautiful."

"Yeah." He shifted his wad of chewing gum to the other side of his mouth. "God-awful place in the winter."

"You surely don't fly up here then?"

"Sure we do. All year round. The winds keep the runway clear, but it's nothing for the temperature to be thirty below." He spat reflectively. "I'll tell you, the bright lights of Toronto look pretty good from here sometimes. Particularly when it's been pitch-dark for two months at a stretch."

"Why do you do it, then?"

He grinned at her. "Can't help it, lady. The Arctic's in my blood. I last about a week in Toronto and then I gotta come north again. You'd better watch out because it gets all kinds of people that way. This your luggage?" He threw it in the back of the van and sat down beside her on one of the vinyl-covered seats.

"Have you ever crashed?" she asked curiously.

"No, ma'am! You think I'd be sitting here if I

had? Had a few close calls though...icing up, engine trouble, one thing or another.'' He shrugged philosophically. ''If my time's up, my time's up. Until then I'm gonna enjoy life. You just up here for a visit?''

''I'm here to see my father,'' she said reluctantly.

''Yeah? What's he do?''

''He's an archaeologist. Laurence Smith.''

''Sure—he's staying at the hotel. He's an okay guy. Got a one-track mind like most of those scientific types, mind you.'' He stuck out his hand. ''Mike Riley.''

''Karen Smythe.'' She tried not to wince at his crushing grip.

''Got reservations?''

''No. I hope it won't be a problem.''

''Not likely. I'll put in a word for you with Lucas. He drives the van and runs the hotel. Nice fella.''

The van jolted off down the dirt road, first heading toward the inlet, then crossing a creek, the bridge built not of stone or brick but of two closely packed rows of oil drums filled with sand. Along the banks of the creek Karen saw a team of huskies chained to metal posts; an Inuit woman drove past them on a three-wheeled Honda. ''She had her baby in the hood of her parka,'' Karen murmured to Mike.

''Sure. It's called an *amautik*. Practical kind of getup. Here we are.''

They had drawn up in front of a one-story building prefabricated in a bright yellow metal with white trim, a rough wooden porch built around the front door. There was no sign to indicate that it was the hotel. In fact, the sole indication of occupation was a red dirt bike parked by the door. "This is it?" Karen asked.

"Yeah. Don't look like much but the beds are comfortable and the food's great. I'll get your stuff."

Glad that Mike had taken her under his wing, she followed him up the wooden steps and into the porch, where a neatly written sign requested that they remove their boots. Mike unlaced his Kodiaks, putting them with the half dozen or so other pairs of boots, all men's, all well worn. Karen's hiking boots looked small beside them. Leaving her gear there, Mike led her through a lounge with deep armchairs and a television set and into the dining room, on the far side of which was a counter with a telephone resting self-importantly on it. Somehow it was the last thing Karen had expected to see.

Following her gaze, Mike said, "You can call from here to Ottawa free—government subsidy."

"But how does it work?"

He grinned tolerantly. "Didn't you notice that saucer-shaped thing on the edge of the runway? Satellite. Here's Lucas now." The man who had driven the van had let himself in behind the counter. "Got a room for this lady?" Mike asked.

"The hotel's full. I could put you in a Parcoll, miss."

Puzzled, Karen looked from one man to the other, and Mike explained, "It's a glorified tent. Insulated, with a wooden floor and a stove and windows. A great rig."

"That would be fine," she said to Lucas, feeling very much out of her element.

"You staying, Mike?"

"Nope. Flying back to Frobisher this evening."

Lucas took out a register and wrote down Karen's name. The price he mentioned, even though it included meals, made her blink, and as she took out her bundle of checks, Mike intervened again. "You gotta remember all the supplies come by air and that the water's trucked in. Expensive business running a hotel up here. Which one's she in, Lucas?"

"Number three."

"C'mon, I'll take you there and show you how the stove works."

"Just a moment," Karen murmured. "Is there a Laurence Smith staying here, Lucas?"

"He's in number four, along with Ryan who's in number five. They should be around. If not, they'll be in for dinner, for sure. Meal hours are posted by the door." Lucas smiled at her, revealing terrible teeth. But his dark eyes were friendly and Karen smiled back warmly.

Back on the porch she discovered dinner was from six to seven. She pulled her boots on again and went outside, with Mike carrying her luggage. When they went around the back of the hotel, Karen saw five Quonset-type silver tents, all with aluminum doors and windows, all connected by a plank boardwalk. Mike led her to the third one, opened the door—which had no lock, she noticed—and ushered her in.

It was Spartan in its simplicity: four single beds pushed into the corners, a metal oil stove, two chairs, one bedside table and a lamp. However, the floor was carpeted, and the bedding looked very clean.

Mike knelt by the stove, showing her how to turn it on and off. "I'll light it now," he said. "That'll take the chill off the air. There we go." He stood up. "You'll be okay now?"

"I'll be fine. I'm going to unpack, then I'll see if my father's around."

He went to the door. "I'll see you at dinner, then."

She held it open for him. "Thanks so much for all your help, Mike." His friendliness had sprung from a seemingly boundless store of good nature; she sensed that already. There had been no ulterior motives. He had not, for instance, as much as laid a finger on her.

"My pleasure—" He broke off. "Oh, hi there, Ryan. How's it going?"

Ryan had been striding along the boardwalk toward them. He stopped dead as his eyes fastened on the woman in the doorway of the Parcoll. "Karen!"

He looked very different from the man she had met in Montreal, for he was wearing wool pants tucked into steel-toed Kodiaks and a heavy wool sweater over a checked shirt. But his thick blond hair was the same, disordered now by the wind, and his eyes were just as blue. Karen felt a rush of pleasure, ascribing it to the fact that he was a familiar figure in an alien place. "Hello, Ryan, it's nice to see you again," she said inadequately. But her gray eyes were warm, her smile obviously unfeigned.

"You know each other?" Mike said resignedly.

Karen answered, since Ryan still seemed to be struck dumb. "We met in Montreal."

"Always my luck. Meet a woman and find out she's already taken. See you later, Karen."

"Thanks again, Mike," she called after his retreating form. Then she turned her attention back to Ryan, noticing with a touch of unease the rigid set of his mouth and chin, his hooded eyes. She had forgotten how big he was and how formidable he could look. She said weakly, "How are you?"

"Are you staying here?" he demanded.

"Yes."

"What the hell was he doing in your room?"

She flushed. "Showing me how to light the stove. What do you think he was doing?"

"Knowing you, nothing else, I'm sure. What made you decide to come?"

Karen's cheeks were still pink with indignation, for whatever reception she had anticipated, it had not been this. "Ryan, aren't you pleased to see me? I thought you wanted me to come here."

"Yeah. . . . I'd forgotten the plane comes in today. It was a shock seeing you standing there."

But he was still not smiling. She crossed her arms over her chest. "Where's my father?"

"He's in the Parcoll." He indicated the neighboring tent.

"Then I'd better go and say hello to him, hadn't I?" she said steadily.

Ryan made an effort to pull himself together, running his fingers through his hair. "Sorry, Karen, I'm not handling this very well, am I? Listen, let me go and tell Laurence you're here first. I think that would be better.''

"Warn him, you mean?'' she said with a touch of bitterness.

He disregarded her words. "I'll be back in a minute. You should shut the door, by the way. You're going to lose all the heat.''

Karen watched him go along the boardwalk, open the door to the next tent and disappear inside. She hesitated only fractionally before following him, walking on the ground rather than on the creaking planks, and going behind the Parcoll to stand near one of the windows, which was open an inch or two. From there she could hear as clearly as if she were inside. The voice speaking was not Ryan's; it was higher pitched, very clipped, as if verbal communication was a waste of valuable time. "Did you forget something?''

"No.'' A pause. "Laurence, we've got a visitor.''

"That's the last thing we need with all this new data to correlate. Who is he?''

"It's not a he. It's a she. Your daughter Karen.''

There was a silence that seemed to the waiting woman to last forever; passionately she wished she could see her father's face. "*Karen?* You mean she's here now?''

"Yes,'' Ryan replied dryly. "In the next Parcoll.''

"What the devil's she doing here?''

"She's come to see you.''

"For God's sake, why?'' Laurence Smith's voice altered. "What's going on, Ryan? What did you tell her?''

"I didn't tell her anything. I did suggest she come and see you, as much for her sake as for yours."

Karen held her breath, knowing Ryan was picking his words with great care. Had he anticipated this kind of a reaction? Was that why he had not allowed her to walk in unannounced?

Laurence was speaking again, with a flatness that to the listener at the window carried absolute conviction. "I don't want her here."

"Don't you bloody well tell *her* that." Ryan must have made an effort to control his anger, for he went on in a more conciliatory way, "Come on, Laurence, she's your daughter, for heaven's sake. She's a beautiful young woman you should be proud to call your own."

Laurence sounded very tired. "I see. This is the worst possible time, Ryan."

"When would have been a good time?"

"You're really on her side, aren't you?" It was the first, wintry touch of humor. "Is she that beautiful?"

"You can judge for yourself. I don't know her very well, but I do know this—she's got a hell of a lot of things to sort out."

"And are you suggesting I'm responsible for that state of affairs?"

"I'm not suggesting anything!" Ryan burst out. "All I want you to do is spend a little time with her. Be nice to her."

"Talking of time, it's nearly time for dinner. No doubt I'll see her in the dining room."

"Laurence, you can't leave a meeting with your

daughter whom you haven't seen for how long—seven or eight years—to a public place full of construction workers and government officials. Have a heart.''

"Then what do you suggest?" Laurence retorted silkily. "As you seem to be the instigator of this little show."

"I'd suggest you go to her room right now. You might even try sounding pleased to see her."

Karen had heard enough. She fled across the space between the two tents and almost fell into her own, pulling the door shut behind her. The stove had already warmed the air. She flung her jacket across one of the beds and bent to undo the cord on her backpack, her fingers shaking. Ryan had been wrong, horribly, catastrophically wrong. Her father was not the slightest bit interested in seeing her, would have preferred her to be anywhere else in the world but here. Oh, God, why had she come?

She heard the sound of footsteps on the plank walk, slow, heavy steps, like the approach of an executioner. Then knuckles rapped on the door. She stood up, rubbing her wet palms down the sides of her jeans, more frightened than she had been for years. "Come in."

The door opened and a man stepped over the threshold. A tall, lean man with thinning gray hair brushed neatly across a lined forehead, where two vertical frown marks were permanently engraved. His mouth was tightly held, inevitably reminding Karen of the photograph in her drawer at home. But for the rest, he had aged far more than she could have anticipated. He looked at her in silence, his gray eyes giving nothing away, until she could stand it no longer.

"Hello, father," she said, hearing her voice quaver with nervousness.

His movements seemed to take place in slow motion as he closed the door behind him and then stood with his back to it, examining every detail of her appearance. A convulsion of feeling swept across his face, but as quickly as a summer squall it was gone, and the inscrutability Karen was soon to recognize as characteristic of him clamped over his features. He cleared his throat, the sound very loud in their confined quarters; it took two attempts for his voice to make itself heard. He said inadequately, "Well, Karen...it's been a long time." He smiled, a difficult smile behind which for all her searching she could detect no real warmth. "I'd hardly have recognized you."

"No, I suppose I have changed.... You've changed, too."

A spasm of some indefinable emotion twisted his mouth, and she knew that somehow she had said the wrong thing. "May I sit down?" he asked with an old-fashioned politeness that seemed to increase the distance between them.

"Oh, please...." She pulled one of the chairs forward and perched on the edge of a bed, only half noticing how carefully he sat down, gripping both edges of the chair.

"How is your sister?" he asked.

At least it was a question she could answer. Sheer

relief made her prattle, "Mandy's fine. She has a new boyfriend so she's in love again, a state that will no doubt last at least another two weeks. She's going to start an arts program at McGill in the fall."

"And you?"

"I've been working at a downtown drop-in center for more than a year. In the fall I'm going to study social work."

He raised his eyebrows. "You surprise me."

She tilted her chin defiantly. "Why?"

"Oh, I don't know. I'd have thought skiing and going south in the winter would have kept you busy enough without trying to cure all the ills of the world."

She flushed, touched on the raw. "I have no ambitions to cure all the ills of the world, as you put it. If I can be of use to even one or two people, I'll be doing well."

He nodded slowly, as if he had got the response he wanted. "A good answer, Karen. So you have a social conscience, eh?"

"Maybe. The skiing and going south routine has never been enough for me."

Laurence did not inquire why. Instead, glancing over at her bags, he asked, "Will you stay here long?"

"Perhaps that's up to you," she said boldly.

"You've caught us at our busiest time."

She bit her lip; he was hardly being encouraging. "In that case, probably not long, no. Mother didn't want me to come at all."

"I'm sure she didn't. Has she conquered the citadels of Montreal society yet?"

Karen was not blind to Nancy's snobbery, or to her considerable skill at manipulating those around her to fall in with her wishes. But she loved her mother and disliked this cold-eyed stranger's question. She said sharply, "Mother enjoys life. Although her health is not all it could be."

"You jump very quickly to her defense."

"She *is* my mother, after all. But I don't want to take sides. Surely that's no longer necessary."

He did not allow himself to become involved. "I suppose not. That was all a long time ago, wasn't it?" Getting to his feet, he said with a distant smile that did not reach his eyes, "No doubt we'll see a fair bit of each other over the next few days, since all the meals are eaten communally in the dining room. It's unfortunate I'm so busy, but it can't be helped. I'm hoping to publish a definitive paper this winter so there are a lot of loose ends to tie up. The season is extremely short, as I'm sure you realize. Permanent snow can fall in September and the sea ice forms in October."

It was his longest speech, and Karen did not think it coincidental that it should deal with his work and the weather rather than with his family; he had always been so inclined even when he was living with them. "Maybe I could come and see your dig," she ventured.

"Perhaps. It's very isolated."

Another snub. Trying to keep her composure, she stood up and followed him to the door. "I'll see you at dinner, then."

"Yes." As he half turned to face her, she caught

her breath, for there was the same fleeting pain in the gray eyes that she had caught when he first entered the room. He said awkwardly, none of the assurance in his voice that had been there when he had spoken of his work, "I've got so used to my own company the past few years that I've lost whatever social graces I used to have—not that I ever was much of a one for words. But I want you to know I'm glad to see you again... you've become a very lovely young woman."

"Thank you." Deeply grateful for even these words, she briefly rested her hand on his sleeve. He moved to open the door, but not before she had felt the faint tremor in his arm. Nervousness? Surely not. "It's good to see you, too," she said, unable to prevent a certain wistfulness from creeping into her voice. Laurence nodded in acknowledgment, not looking at her again, and started walking back to his tent.

Karen closed the door, leaning her back against it, and felt tears crowd her eyes and spill down her cheeks. Despite that last speech, which had almost been dragged from him, he had not kissed her or touched her, had not in any real way reached out to discover what kind of a person she had become. She should not have come here. At least at home she had grown used to his absence; it was another thing to come face to face with him and be rejected.

"Karen? Want to go for dinner?" Ryan's voice, speaking outside her door.

"Just a minute," she replied, hurriedly grabbing a Kleenex from her bag and blowing her nose, scrubbing the tears from her cheeks. Then she opened the door. "I just want to find my lipstick—can you wait a moment?'' Bending over her haversack, taking her time, she carefully outlined her lips and brushed her hair loose of its ponytail so it would at least partially hide her face. But when she turned to face him her eyes were still suspiciously bright and her lashes wet and spiky.

He had stepped into the tent. "It didn't go too well," he said, more a statement than a question.

She stared down at the carpet. "I shouldn't have come."

"Don't say that yet, Karen...give him time. He's a difficult man to get close to, I know. Besides, I'm sure there's something worrying him, although I can't figure out what it is."

"It certainly isn't his daughter," she answered flippantly. "I'm hungry. Let's go and eat."

Ryan reached out a hand as if to touch her, but then let it drop to his side. He said roughly, "You've been crying, and I'd like to put my arms around you and give you a hug. But that won't do, will it, Karen? You wouldn't want me to do that."

Torn, she gazed at him, seeing the slight cleft in his chin, his deep-set eyes, his generous mouth and realizing how familiar his features had already become to her. Knowing also that it would take very little to make her start crying again. One part of her longed to run to him for comfort, for her father's visit had upset her more than she wanted to admit. But the thought of physical closeness had terrified her for so long that she could feel herself automatically drawing back from him. "No...I wouldn't," she faltered.

"Sooner or later you're going to have to resolve

your phobia about sex," he said flatly. "Unless you want to be an emotional cripple for the rest of your life."

"Don't call me that!" she retorted, stung.

"Why not? It's true, isn't it?"

"No!" she said vehemently, rather spoiling the effect by adding illogically, "Anyway, even if I am, it's none of your business."

"That's where you're wrong. You see, I'm beginning to want you very much, Karen Smythe. I thought when I came back up here that I'd forget about you. But I didn't. And now that you're here, I'm realizing just how strong the attraction is."

If anyone had asked her, she would have said she valued honesty. But Ryan's bluntness terrified her. "You're crazy," she whispered.

"Why? Because I show the instincts of a normal male around a very beautiful woman?"

Frustrated and frightened in equal measure, she snapped, "You only want me because you can't have me."

"The attraction of the forbidden? There's probably an element of that in it. But it's a hell of a lot more than just that."

"You *can't* want me," she said stubbornly. "I've never been appealing or attractive to men."

"Oh, for heaven's sake! Haven't you ever looked in a mirror? Didn't you notice the way the men in the restaurant were eyeing you the night I took you out? I sure as hell did. Where have you been all these years, Karen?"

"Men go for Mandy, but not for me."

"Perhaps that's because Mandy puts out a bit—lets it be known she likes men's company. Whereas you act as if any man's a cross between Jack the Ripper and King Kong."

"If the shoe fits...."

"Don't be bitchy.... At first I thought you had a classic inferiority complex—Mandy's prettier, Mandy's more popular. But those are just words you're hiding behind so you won't have to look the problem in the face. You could have any man you wanted, Karen, and you damn well know it."

"You certainly don't pull any punches, do you?" Her eyes were bright with anger now, not tears, and part of it was anger that he could be so infuriatingly accurate. She loved Mandy dearly, not envying her her string of conquests and her ease with men one whit.

"I think it's time there was a bit of plain speaking as far as you're concerned. I meant what I said, Karen—you'll be an emotional cripple for life unless you can resolve whatever's making you frigid."

Karen flinched. "That's a horrible word."

"It's an apt one. You told me yourself that you hated being touched."

"Maybe that's just by you," she said waspishly. "Did that ever occur to you? Or do you think you're irresistible?"

Incredibly, he laughed. "That's a cheap shot, Karen, and you know it. Look, we're obviously not going to resolve it all right now. Let's go and eat, I'm starving."

She drew a deep breath, not knowing whether to

stamp her foot or laugh back, and consequently did neither. "You really are the limit," she said warmly. "Dr. Ryan Koetsier, resident psychiatrist. And then the next minute all you've got on your mind is dinner."

He grinned at her. "A man has to keep body and soul together," he intoned piously.

"The trouble is, I can't help liking you." She hadn't known she was going to say that, but as soon as the words were out she knew them for the truth. With Duke and his friends she was often bored, inwardly impatient with their immaturity; with Ryan she was far from bored. Angry, amused, frightened—but not bored.

"Good. That's a beginning, anyway."

"It's not the beginning to anything," she said. "Surely it can be an end in itself?"

"It could be, I suppose. But it's not going to be. Come on—food."

Aggravating man, she fumed, as she tramped over the boardwalk. Other adjectives clicked through her brain: infuriating and unpredictable, arrogant and ruthless. She took off her boots in the front porch and followed Ryan into the dining room.

A battery of male heads swung around to face her. The conversation died and in the sudden hush the wolf whistle that came from the youngest of them sounded very loud. The flush in Karen's cheeks heightened. She was the only woman in the room.

Standing slim and straight in her jeans and sweater, her dark silky hair falling around her face, she heard Ryan begin a round of introductions. Joe,

Jean-Pierre, Guillaume, Claude, Archie. It was Jean-Pierre who had whistled. "This is Karen Smythe," Ryan finished. "Laurence's elder daughter."

Gathering every scrap of her poise, she smiled in acknowledgment and sat down at a table with Ryan, thankful when everyone started to eat again. "You could have warned me," she hissed.

"And spoil the fun?" he replied lazily. "They don't see many women up here, let alone one as gorgeous as you. All of which goes to prove the point I made earlier."

"You never let up, do you?"

"As far as you're concerned, I don't plan to."

She spread her hands helplessly. "But *why?*"

"I don't want to answer that right now." He looked over her shoulder. "Good. Here comes our food."

The waitress, an Inuit who smiled a lot to compensate for her lack of English, brought them salads and then heaped plates of beef stew, piping hot and very tasty. "Most of the men here are working outdoors, surveyors or construction workers. If you're digging down to the permafrost and pouring cement all day, you need a good meal at the end of it," Ryan explained. "Hello, Laurence, come and join us."

Karen had not heard her father approach. She smiled at him tentatively as he sat down across from her. His frown lines were very much in evidence, and as the meal progressed she could not help but be grateful for Ryan's presence. He drew Laurence out to tell Karen about their work, interposing the occasional question, always making sure Karen was included in the conversation. Skillfully and discreetly done, it allowed her to ask questions directly of her father and to warm to the genuine enthusiasm in his voice as he described some of their latest finds. It established a rapport of a kind, fragile and tenuous though it might be.

Ryan walked her back to the Parcoll afterward. Outside her door she said, "I'm very tired, so I think I'll go to bed. The day's catching up on me."

"There's some dark plastic stuff above the windows. Pull it down if you want the illusion of darkness."

"Oh, of course—it's not going to get dark, is it?" She hesitated. "Thank you for keeping the conversation going in the dining room, Ryan. That made it a lot easier."

"No problem. See you tomorrow." A casual salute of his hand and he was walking away from her.

More or less unconsciously she had been braced to discourage him from kissing her good-night. It was now obvious he had had not the slightest intention of doing so. Served her right for trying to anticipate him, she thought with a touch of wry humor as she went inside. If there was one thing she could count on with Ryan Koetsier, it was his lack of predictability....

CHAPTER FIVE

KAREN AWOKE to the sounds of children playing close by, to shouting and the rattle of rocks, and a puppy barking. It surely wasn't morning already? Squinting, she peered at her watch. Twelve-thirty. Children playing at midnight? Rubbing her eyes, she looked out the window. A crowd of boys and girls in boots and parkas was playing tag around a deserted shed just down the hill, while the puppy, tied up by a frayed piece of rope, was yelping frenziedly, obviously wanting to join in the fun. She grimaced, for it did not look as though the game was about to end.

To see children running around in daylight at midnight gave her a strange sensation; ''land of the midnight sun'' began to seem a very appropriate description for the north. Wide awake now, she let the plastic curtain fall, then got up and walked restlessly around the room. She didn't feel like going back to bed. The outdoors, so bright, so different from home, beckoned to her. Without consciously making a decision, she began to get dressed.

When she went outside, the children were still chasing one another over the rough, rocky ground. Someone had taken pity on the puppy and untied it so it could leap and run with them, its pink tongue

What made Marge burn the toast and miss her favorite soap opera?

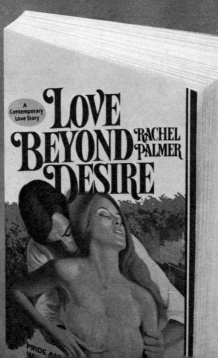

A Contemporary Love Story

LOVE BEYOND DESIRE

RACHEL PALMER

...At his touch, her body felt a familiar wild stirring, but she struggled to resist it. This is not love, she thought bitterly.

PRIDE AN

A compelling love story of mystery and intrigue... conflicts and jealousies... and a forbidden love that threatens to shatter the lives of all involved with the aristocratic Lopez family.

⌐—Mail this card today for your FREE gifts.

TAKE THIS BOOK
AND TOTE BAG FREE!

Mail to: SUPERROMANCE
2504 W. Southern Avenue, Tempe, Arizona 85282

YES, please send me FREE and without any obligation, my SUPERROMANCE novel, *Love Beyond Desire*. If you do not hear from me after I have examined my FREE book, please send me the 4 new SUPERROMANCE books every month as soon as they come off the press. I understand that I will be billed only $2.50 per book (total $10.00). There are no shipping and handling or any other hidden charges. There is no minimum number of books that I have to purchase. In fact, I may cancel this arrangement at any time. *Love Beyond Desire* and the tote bag are mine to keep as FREE gifts even if I do not buy any additional books.

134-CIS-KAGV

Name	(Please Print)

Address	Apt. No.

City

State	Zip

Signature   (If under 18, parent or guardian must sign.)

SUPERROMANCE ™

EXTRA BONUS
MAIL YOUR ORDER
TODAY AND GET A
FREE TOTE BAG
FROM SUPERROMANCE.

☞ Mail this card today for your FREE gifts.

lolling from its mouth. Pulling on her gloves and zipping up her jacket, Karen began to walk along the street, her eyes taking in detail after detail of her surroundings: the wolflike profile of a husky chained to a post between two houses; the row of Arctic char nailed to the eaves of a blue bungalow; a clothesline with sheets hanging at one end and a sealskin draped over the other, and a pair of caribou antlers on the roof of a shed that had a motorbike parked beside it. She could not help seeing it all as an uneasy amalgam of two cultures, a mingling of the ancient and the modern.

She walked on. She had reached the road that ran parallel with the beach, where a trawler was pulled high off the sand, flanked by smaller motorboats. There was a long blue-and-white trailer, labeled RCMP, with a Canadian flag hanging on its flagpole, and behind it were the waters of the inlet and the mountain range of Bylot Island. Even as she watched, the door of the adjoining bungalow opened and a man came out, calling a goodbye to someone inside. He waved at her, then ran across the grass toward her. It was Ryan. To her consternation she felt a quickening of her heartbeat at the sight of him. The mountains, the sea and the drift ice were a fitting backdrop for his big, rangy body. He belonged in this dark northern setting, she thought, for he was self-reliant enough that it posed no threat to him.

He smiled at her, his teeth very white in his tanned face. "Saw you through the window—I was ready to leave anyway. Couldn't sleep?"

Briefly she explained how she'd woken up, finishing lamely, "I just didn't want to waste any of this."

"Want to go farther along the beach?"

"I'd love to."

In companionable silence, or so Karen thought at the time, they crossed the grass, which was littered with bleached white whalebones. When they reached the pale sand of the beach and began to walk briskly along it, her eyes were never still. Now that they were leaving the houses behind, the hills rose barren and rocky along the shoreline. At their base another team of huskies was chained, the dogs thin flanked and mangy, their deep-throated howling sending shivers up Karen's spine. On the beach ahead of her a dead seal had been washed up by the tide, and a cloud of glaucous gulls rose complaining in the air as they approached. Across the water drifted the low put-put of a boat engine.

It was the light that fascinated Karen. Far to her right she could see the golden glow of the sun behind the massed purple clouds that overhung the mountains. It cast a soft, luminous light over everything, so that the mountains looked mauve and the sea was splashed with pink and orange. There was a gentleness to the sun, like a benediction.

"It makes me wish I could paint," she said. "Although I think it would take a genius to capture the quality of the light.... I hate darkness!" She had spoken the last three words with unexpected harshness.

Ryan looked at her reflectively. "Are you frightened of it?"

Somehow knowing it was not going to get dark, that nothing she could do could make the sun sink below the mountains, gave Karen the courage to speak. "Terrified of it," she said, trying to sound flippant. "Ridiculous, isn't it? Twenty-three years old and scared of the dark. Oh, look, Ryan, what kind of a bird is that? It's flying right at us."

"A jaeger." They both watched the slim, sooty-gray silhouette sweep past them. "If you get too close to their nest, they'll dive-bomb you with an earsplitting screech. Scares you out of a year's growth if you don't see them coming. Why are you scared of the dark, Karen?"

She should have known he would not let the subject drop. Regretting her frankness, she said vaguely, "Oh, I don't know that there's any specific reason."

"I'd prefer you to be honest with me and say you don't want to tell me, rather than lie."

She stopped dead in her tracks. "All right, then. I don't want to talk about it, Ryan."

"So let's keep it all hidden and tucked under the carpet and pretend it doesn't exist. Is that the way you'd prefer to deal with it? You reacted the same way when I said you were frigid."

"I don't want to talk about that, either! Nor about being an emotional cripple, as you so succinctly phrased it."

"You didn't like that, did you?"

She started walking again, shoving her hands deep in her pockets. "I certainly did not."

"The truth hurts."

"Oh, do be quiet," she snapped.

"How deep does it go, Karen? Did your first boyfriend get a bit rough with you, is that what it is? Or did you get jilted, so you've decided to hate all men as a result?''

"I said I don't want to talk about it."

There was something merciless in the blue eyes. "I intend to find out."

She glared at him. "If you really want an answer, I could tell you any number of reasons, couldn't I? Maybe I was raped, attacked on the subway, roughed up by a boyfriend. Which version would you prefer?''

"How about the true one?"

"Oh, the truth," she said bitterly. "I don't even know what that means anymore. If you're going to keep on at me, I'm going back to the hotel."

She did not see the hard line of his mouth, the growing resolve in his face; if she had, she might well have turned around. He said flatly, "Let's go as far as Salmon Creek. There are some remains of old whalers' shelters there, and you'll see why they call the area the land of many bones."

Intrigued, as perhaps he had known she would be, she began to walk faster. A small flock of sandpipers streaked past them, peeping back and forth to one another, and farther out on the surface of the water oldsquaw ducks bobbed on the waves, diving for food. There were no other signs of life. Wanting to keep the conversation on safe ground, Karen said, "Would we be likely to see foxes or caribou? Or polar bears?"

"You don't want to see a polar bear," Ryan answered grimly. "You're not likely to see too much in the way of ground mammals at all, Karen. The caribou are farther inland, and all the hare and ptarmigan have been killed off around the hamlet.''

"No gyrfalcons?" She scanned the sky, almost as if expecting to see a great white bird hovering high above her.

"You'd be very lucky. If we were to climb the hill, we'd see Utuk Canyon about twelve miles away. There might be a pair nesting there." Because she looked a bit crestfallen, he added, "You'll see seals and whales, I'm sure. And there are lemming runs up at the creek."

The ground had leveled out when they got to Salmon Creek. The grass was a luxuriant green around a series of raised mounds, hollowed out in the center and littered with rocks and bones.

"People used to live here?" Karen asked curiously.

"Several families at a time. Each mound was a shelter. They'd use whale ribs to hold up a roof made of skins," Ryan replied, watching as she knelt in the grass and picked up a piece of bone encrusted with lichen, pitted and worn. "That's probably well over a hundred years old, because things decay very slowly here. It looks like a piece of rib."

She picked up a huge vertebra, finding that doing so required nearly all her strength. "Bowhead whale," Ryan said briefly. "They're very rare now, hardly ever sighted. Why don't we walk up to the cache?" The cache turned out to be a coffin-shaped arrangement of weathered rocks, low to the ground, the roof partly collapsed. There were more bones littering its floor. "When the hunting was good, they'd store meat here for the hungry days ahead."

Karen knelt beside it, spellbound. It seemed an integral part of the landscape, tangible evidence of an ancient way of life that the coming of the white man had disrupted. A hard, dangerous way of life, certainly, but one to which the Inuit had been superbly adapted. She shivered, visited by a flashing insight into the transitory nature of life, of its essential fragility in the face of forces far beyond its control. Standing up, she said in a brittle voice, "Where are the lemming runs?"

They were actually quite near the mounds, a whole network of narrow tunnels, some on the surface, some underground. Karen was the first to see one of the little creatures, sighting a white-furred snout poking up from one of the holes. When she moved, it disappeared in a flash. But then, less than a minute later, it reappeared, nostrils testing the air before it made a mad dash for the next tunnel. For almost ten minutes she followed it around its various burrows, laughing out loud at some of its antics, convinced it was putting on a show for her.

Ryan was sitting on the grass, his arms resting on his knees, his face unexpectedly somber when she'd finally had enough. Karen sat down beside him, content to be silent as she let her eyes wander over the distant mountains and the purple-shadowed glaciers, drinking in the silence and the peace. Afterward she was to wonder how she could have been so insensitive to Ryan's mood; at the time she was only grateful for his undemanding presence in the face of the vast panorama of sea, mountains and sky.

When he moved closer to her, she scarcely noticed.

It was not until his arm curved around her waist that she glanced at him in quick inquiry. His face was very close to hers; there was something in his expression that suddenly made her uneasy, and she said lightly, "What's the trouble? Have I got a smudge on my nose?"

"Karen, I . . . ."

"What's wrong?" She tried to move away from him, but his hands clasped her shoulders so strongly that even through her jacket she could feel the imprint of his fingers. Then he was pulling her toward him, and she read the intent in his face. The isolation that only moments ago had seemed such a blessing, so peaceful, changed instantly into threat. They were alone, cut off by the hills from sight of the village, out of earshot of any other people. Her breath caught in her throat, but she fought back her almost instinctive panic, certain she could still appeal to his reason. "Don't, Ryan," she said evenly. "Please, you know I don't like it."

There was no altering of his resolve; she might just as well not have spoken. He lowered his head, one hand moving to clasp the back of her neck so rigidly she couldn't move. At the first touch of his lips fear raced through her veins, conquering reason, and she abandoned herself to it. Striking out with her knees, she twisted in his grasp.

But he must have anticipated what she would do. He moved so fast that everything blurred in front of her eyes until she found herself flat on her back in the grass, wrists pinned to the ground, hips crushed by his weight. She couldn't kick or bite or scratch. She was caught, helpless. She allowed herself to go limp, hoping he would relax his hold, then she put all her strength into one frantic twist of her body, kicking out at him with her boots.

He was not deceived by her trick. His thighs pushed her legs to the ground and he flung his whole weight on her, driving the breath from her body. She wrenched her head to one side, hearing her voice, as if it belonged to someone else, shamefully pleading over and over again, "No, no...please, no."

Then he brought his face down to hers, his body covering her, smothering her, and her frantic, fear-crazed eyes were lost to the light. She was scarcely aware that he was kissing her, his mouth moving against hers with a gentleness at variance with his brutal hold, as if he was searching for a response that he knew must be there and that he desperately need-ed. Mad with terror, she felt the darkness gather, the black wings swooping down to cover her eyes and her ears, blinding her, deafening her. The scream that filled her throat died to a whimper. The walls of the room rushed in, walls without windows, crushing her, suffocating her, and the body was not his but another man's.... The horror that was too great to be borne was lost in the blackness that swallowed her. Her body went limp, her lips slack.

Ryan must have known this was not a trick, must have known he had caused her to faint. He levered himself up on his elbows, seeing her crumpled body and paper-white face, her hair tangled in the grass. In sudden self-revulsion he wiped his mouth with the back of his hand, his eyes like chips of ice. Slowly he raised himself, sitting beside her on the ground, knowing he could not pick her up and hold her as every instinct screamed out to him to do. He pulled off his jacket, covered her with it then leaned his head on his knees, waiting.

KAREN LAY VERY STILL, wondering if she was dead but not really caring one way or the other. Then she became aware of a rock digging into her hip, of another under her shoulder, and she knew she must be alive. Furthermore, there was grass under her cheek. Grass and rock.... So she was not in the room. The floor there had been rough planks, and by the time she was released she had memorized every crack and knothole in it. She felt a great flood of relief knowing that she was no longer in the room. But then where was she?

Carefully keeping her eyes shut, she realized next that the ground was very cold, and that something was covering her. She huddled her face into its folds, and elusively to her nostrils came a clean masculine scent compounded of soap and after-shave and body warmth.

Memory rushed back. Ryan...Ryan had been kissing her, and she must have fainted. Oh, God, why had he done it?

Her lashes flickered open. Above her were gold-tipped clouds, remote and majestic. To her ears came the thin cry of a seabird. Slowly she turned her head. Ryan was sitting on the grass beside her, not touching her, his head resting on his knees. He could not have known that she had recovered consciousness. Bewildered and frightened though she was, there was something in his attitude that kept her silent as she fumbled in her brain for a way to best describe it. Exhausted? Defeated? Ashamed? Why *had* he done it?

"Ryan?" she whispered shakily.

His head jerked in her direction, his hand reaching out to her, stopping in midair, slowly withdrawing. "Karen," he said heavily.

She could see him struggling for words. But she could see more than that. His face was haggard, white about the mouth, his eyes sickened. He had not enjoyed what he had done, she thought dazedly. "Why did you do that?" she burst out.

"I had to," he said hoarsely, not looking at her. "I had to know how deeply it went with you, this business of not being touched or kissed or held. I thought, God help me, that it might have just become a kind of habit, a useful trick to keep men at a distance. Genuine enough in your mind, but not deep-rooted." He ran his fingers through his hair, still staring down at the ground. "I found out differently, didn't I? It's useless to say I'm sorry, Karen, but I am. More sorry than I can say. I terrified you, didn't I? So much so that you fainted."

So it had been deliberate, a cold-blooded attempt to break through her defenses. Yet she could not find it in herself to be angry with him, for it was all too obvious that he was bitterly ashamed of what he had done. She sat up, hugging the jacket around her and fighting back a last wave of dizziness. "Ryan, look at me," she whispered.

Slowly he brought his head around, his eyes full of

self-contempt. Before she could open her mouth, he said, "It won't happen again, Karen. I promise you that."

The windowless room and the rough plank floor receded even further from her consciousness as her own fears were superseded by concern for her companion. "I believe you."

"I've never done anything like that in my life before." The words were wrenched from him.

"I'm sure you haven't." She spoke the simple truth, for she knew in her heart that no one could fake such remorse and self-castigation. Shaken by a wave of compassion for him, she tentatively stretched out her hand, and for a moment, as lightly and warily as a wild bird, rested it on his sleeve. "It's all right, Ryan, really it is."

He looked down at her hand. Her fingers were long and slim, unadorned by rings or nail polish, the blue veins evident under her tanned skin. Her wrist was very fragile. Even as he watched, she snatched her hand away, as if frightened by her own action. He said dazedly, "Do you know what you just did? That's the first time you've ever voluntarily touched me, Karen."

"It was only because you looked so awful," she said defensively, shoving her hands in the pockets of her own jacket. "Here, you'd better have your jacket back, it's cold."

He gave his head a little shake as though he was not quite sure where he was. "I guess you're right." Then the blue eyes were looking straight at her, filled with a strange pleading. "You can't tell me what it was that frightened you so? When you were a teen-ager, I mean. Were you raped? If you were, that's nothing to be ashamed of, Karen. You don't have to be embarrassed or afraid to tell me, I'll understand."

Her face was anguished. "I—I can't tell you! I've never told anyone. Maybe you would understand, but I still can't say. It's all locked up inside me and it's been that way for years."

"It would be far healthier if you could bring it out into the open."

"Oh, I know! Do you think I wasn't told that, over and over again until I was sick of hearing it?" she said violently. "My mother insisted that—that afterward I go to a psychiatrist, one she chose herself. Dr. William Huntley-Davis, with a string of letters after his name as long as my arm. I can see his face as clearly as if he was here right now. He was very good-looking in a cold sort of way, perfect features, an expensive haircut, Gucci shoes, Brooks Brothers shirts. He was a successful man, and didn't he know it. And he was the one I was supposed to talk to!" She gave a short laugh. "Under the best of circumstances he wasn't the kind of person I could have confided in. At that time...well, it was hopeless. I sat there in his office for minutes on end, not saying a word. I could tell you every detail in that room if you asked me. One hundred fifty dollars an hour he charged. My mother's wasted some money in her time, but that was the worst. It was after that that I was packed off to boarding school."

"And ran away, and failed for two years in a row."

"You have a good memory," she said ruefully. "It seems rather a childish way to have acted now, but at the time it was real enough." She hugged her knees, her face pinched and pale.

"I'm sure it was.... Karen, you look worn out. We'd better head back."

"I suppose so." She grinned weakly. "We'd better not wait until it gets dark, had we?"

"Rather a long wait." He got up, pulling his jacket on over his sweater, and she got to her feet as well. She felt very tired, yet the tiredness was overlaid with a kind of peace, as though the last hour had been a catharsis. She glanced over at her companion, noting not for the first time his determined chin, the intelligence and character in his strongly boned face. He was a man to be reckoned with, a man who would not be put off by easy or evasive answers. It occurred to Karen that she had never told anyone else about her reaction to Dr. Huntley-Davis, yet she had told Ryan. Maybe, she thought painfully, if there had been a Ryan around nine years ago, things would have turned out differently.

"Are you okay?"

"Mmm." She managed to smile at him. "Are we going back by the beach?"

"If you can take a bit of a climb, we could go along the hills. That'll end us up at the runway."

Side by side, yet a careful two feet apart, they began walking across the tundra, past the mounds and the cache and along the bed of a stream. Wanting to end the silence, Karen said impulsively, "Tell me about yourself, Ryan. Are your parents living? Do you have any brothers and sisters? Have you ever been married?"

"Yes, yes, and no. Although I came damn close once. She was a nice girl, pretty, wanted to have a family; and all our friends were getting married, so it seemed the thing to do. But something stopped me. I'm not sure what. Maybe I sensed even then that something was missing." His steps slowed, his shoulders hunched against the wind that was blowing across the face of the hill. "I never felt with her the way I feel with you," he said with a calculated deliberation that made Karen blush. "It's rather ironic, when you think about it."

She did not want to think about it. "Your parents, where do they live?"

"On the Gaspé coast. You'd like them, I'm sure. Dad's a big, easygoing Dutchman. Mum's Irish, half his size, red haired with a temper to match."

"You're very fond of them."

"Sure I am. They brought up six children with just the right mixture of discipline and love. I hope someday I can do the same."

So he wanted children. Hurriedly Karen changed the subject. "What does your father do?"

"He's more or less retired, so he passed the farm along to me, although he keeps an eye on things in the summers when I'm away."

"You mean you're a farmer as well?"

"Dairy and market gardening."

Intrigued, she asked, "How many acres do you own?"

"About five thousand. A fair bit of that's woodland, mind you, but it's still a big operation."

"How lucky you are to own a place in the country! But you must be wealthy," she added suspiciously.

" 'Fraid so. So I'm not after your money, Karen."

He had a trick of always bringing the conversation back to her; she found it disconcerting. They had reached the top of the hill so she paused for breath, seeing the sprawl of the hamlet ahead of them. To her ears came the chugging of motorboats, a half dozen of which were circling in the inlet to the east of them. Then a shot rang out, echoing against the hillside, and another, sharp as a whipcrack. "What are they doing?"

"Hunting narwhal. I heard the tags were issued today."

"Narwhal?"

"A type of whale. The male grows a spiral ivory tusk, which can be up to nine feet long and which fetches quite a price. They're slaughtered for the tusks."

"Who buys them?"

"People with more money than brains. The kind of people who don't care if a species becomes extinct as long as they own something their neighbors don't."

"The acquiring of the very rare by the very rich," she murmured.

"Exactly. It's an attitude I deplore. You mentioned gyrfalcons earlier. They're poached on a regular basis and shipped to countries in the Middle East. A single bird will fetch thousands of dollars, with the result, of course, that they're becoming more and more rare."

Another volley of shots resounded against the hillside. Karen began walking again, her boots crunching the lichen and dwarf blueberry, dry from lack of rain. "What do they do with the falcons?"

"Oh, some sheik or other keeps them in his aviary, and maybe trains them for falconry. A white-phase bird is considered a real prize, and has been for generations. The Emperor Frederick II hunted cranes with gyrfalcons, and one was presented annually to Louis XVI. They were reserved for kings and nobility, not for ordinary people, who had to make do with goshawks and kestrels."

"And that practice is still carried on today?"

"Yes. There are very strict laws against poaching, but in a country as big as Canada it's almost impossible to prevent."

They had reached a small graveyard with handcarved wooden crosses and heaps of rocks marking the graves, many of which were so short they must belong to children. Karen didn't want to linger there. The killing of the narwhals, the confinement of proud white birds and now the reminders of human mortality had made her realize all too clearly that she could not romanticize this northern land, could not see only the stark beauty of its mountains and fiords. As anywhere else, there was greed and ugliness and death.

Depression settled on her with an almost physical weight. She began to walk faster, wanting only to be alone in the temporary sanctuary of her tent. Her father didn't want her at Pond Inlet. Ryan wanted from her something she couldn't give. She herself didn't even know what she wanted. To be left alone, she thought grimly. That would do for a start.

In silence the two of them tramped along the runway, then cut down toward the hotel. Outside her tent Karen said expressionlessly, "I'll see you tomorrow."

"Breakfast is at eight. Do you want me to turn the stove off for you?"

"No, thanks." She didn't want him anywhere near her, she just wanted to be by herself. "I'll probably sleep in tomorrow. Good night."

"Good night, Karen."

She closed the door, checked that the windows were all covered, then pulled off her clothes and got into bed. She fell asleep almost immediately, for she was emotionally and physically exhausted.

CHAPTER SIX

KAREN SLEPT until late in the morning. She got up in a leisurely fashion, went to the hotel and showered and washed her hair, then purposely arrived quite late for lunch, thereby avoiding meeting either her father or Ryan. She didn't feel ready for that until well into the afternoon, for she still was uncertain of her welcome. Perhaps subconsciously she had hoped Laurence would seek her out, rather than the reverse, but he didn't do so. At two-thirty, therefore, with the trumped-up excuse that she wanted to borrow a book to read, she walked along the planks to the next Parcoll and tapped on the door.

"Come in." Her father's voice, curt and impatient, responded.

Wishing she didn't feel afraid of him, she slowly opened the door. "Hello," she said pleasantly. "I'm wondering if I can borrow something to read."

He was alone, seated at a makeshift desk shoved against the vertical end wall of the Parcoll. Two of the beds had been removed, and the others were covered with a litter of papers and artifacts. A temporary set of bookshelves had been built into the near wall. Laurence frowned at her. "I'm not sure I have anything you'd want to read."

She suppressed a quick flicker of irritation, wondering if he was patronizing her. "I'd enjoy reading some background material on the work you're doing."

He made no attempt to get up. "Check on the third shelf down for a blue-covered book by McGhee. That'll give you a general overview, at least."

Karen ran her eye over the closely packed titles. "I don't think it's here."

He clicked his tongue irritably. "What about the bottom shelf? I'm sure it's there somewhere."

She knelt, flipping through the shelf with her finger to make sure she didn't miss the one she was looking for. "No."

She heard the chair scrape back and out of the corner of her eye, saw her father lever himself upright, standing for a moment with both fists resting on the desk before crossing the room toward her. She said, "It's not down here, I'm sure. But if it's too much trouble, I'll come back another time."

As she stood up he said testily, "Here it is. I don't know how you could have missed it."

She bit back the retort on the tip of her tongue; she didn't remember that her father had been an irritable man. He reached up for the book, which was on the top shelf tucked between two much larger volumes, then everything seemed to happen in slow motion. Halfway to the book his hand began to shake uncontrollably. Puzzled, Karen stared at him, wondering for a wild moment if he was drunk. He muttered something under his breath, lowering his arm and bringing it up again. The shaking was less violent this time, enough so that he managed to extract the book. But as he started to pass it to Karen, it slipped from between his fingers and fell to the floor.

The book was suddenly the least of her concerns. "Is something wrong?" she said. "Your arm—"

"It's nothing. I've been sitting at the desk too long, that's all." He stooped to pick up the book, but somehow he lost his balance, his shoulder crashing into the bookshelves. If Karen had not instinctively grabbed him, he would have fallen. Using all her strength, she was able to help him to his feet, for he was thinner than he appeared. She could feel the tremors running through his body.

"You're ill," she began. "You'd better lie down—"

He struck her hands away with vicious strength, his face ugly with fury. "There's nothing the matter!"

"There has to be. I—"

"Nothing's the matter. Do you hear me?"

She fell back before the naked rage in his voice. "Please, father—"

"Get out!" he snarled.

The color drained from her face. "You hate me, don't you?" she whispered. "You don't want me anywhere near you."

"Just get out!"

"Oh, I will...don't worry." Her voice rose, his image blurring as tears crowded her eyes. "And I'll never come back!"

She whirled and ran for the door, slamming it shut behind her, then stumbling down the steps and across the planks to her own tent. She didn't even see Ryan until she ran full into him, the force of the collision driving the breath from her lungs. In a reflex action his arm went around her. She beat against his chest with her fists. "Let go," she choked. "Let me go!"

Instead he picked her up bodily, opened the door of her tent and carried her inside, then closed the door before depositing her on her feet again. She was still flailing at his chest, sobs racking her body. He grabbed her hands in his, holding them captive. "Stop crying, Karen," he said sharply. "What the devil happened?"

His lack of sympathy was like a dash of cold water. A sob rattled in her throat and died. She opened her eyes, looking up at him, and said the first thing that came into her head. "I didn't even see you there."

"I know you didn't. Now answer my question— what happened?"

"I need a Kleenex." Only when Ryan released her did she realize he had been holding her hands; she hadn't even noticed, and that in itself was enough to throw her off balance. Taking a couple of tissues from the box by her bed, she blew her nose vigorously and wiped her cheeks. Then she said flatly, "I should never have come here."

"Why not?"

"You were wrong—my God, so wrong! My father needs me, you said. He doesn't need me." In a spurt of defiance she added, "And I don't need him."

"Will you kindly tell me what happened?"

Again there was no sympathy in his voice, only exaggerated patience. Glaring at him, Karen briefly described the scene in her father's tent. "Twice he told me to get out," she finished, a last sob catching her breath. "I told him I'd never come back. And I won't. I'm going to find out when the next plane leaves, and I'll bc leaving on it."

"Running away again, eh?"

"Just cutting my losses, Ryan. I'm not a masochist."

"Look, what you've told me just confirms that he needs you here—"

"Sure," she jeered. "How in hell do you arrive at that conclusion? He doesn't need me or anyone else. He's like one of those icebergs out in the inlet, just as cold and hard."

"A good analogy, but for a different reason," Ryan said dryly. "Nine-tenths of an iceberg is under water, or didn't you know that? Laurence is in trouble, I'm convinced of it, Karen. I've noticed his shaking and his loss of balance, and wondered what the cause could be. I wish to heaven there was a doctor up here."

"Do you really think he'd go, even if there was?"

"He'd go," Ryan said grimly. "If I had to tie him to a *komatik* and drag him there myself."

Momentarily she was diverted. "A what?"

"A *komatik*. It's a long wooden sled."

Karen sat down on the bed, pulling off her boots. "Maybe he is ill, Ryan. But the fact is, healthy or ill, he doesn't want me here. You don't hit someone and tell her to get out if you love her."

"So you're going to tuck your tail between your legs and run home to mother."

She said coldly, "You're mixing your metaphors. I'm going to be sensible and not let myself get hurt any more than I already have been."

"Do you expect everything in life to go easily? And do you always run away when it doesn't?"

Her chin snapped up. "You're a fine one to talk! It sounds to me as though your life has been pretty easy. Parents who love each other and their children, lots of money, two careers, land of your own—and, of course," she finished nastily, "women falling all over themselves to go to bed with you."

He strode over to her and pulled her roughly to her feet. "So that's what you think, is it? That life's always been a bed of roses for me? You're not the only one who's had problems, Karen, and maybe it's time you stopped thinking about yourself for once."

Hurt, as perhaps he had intended her to be, she snapped, "I don't always think of myself!"

"Oh, yes, you do. I don't know what happened to you, but whatever it was, you've been hiding behind it ever since."

He was getting too close to the truth. Eyes glittering with rage, she retorted, "So what were your problems, Ryan? Don't tell me I'm not the first woman to say no to you?"

His breath hissed between his teeth. "You can be a real bitch when you want to be, can't you?" His blue eyes were implacable, and unconsciously Karen braced herself for what was to come, knowing that it was going to be unpleasant. But she was not prepared for his next action. He pulled his shirt free of his waistband and began unbuttoning it.

"What are you doing that for?" she said nervously.

His answer was to take it off and turn his back to her. The scars leaped out at her, a mess of ridged and whitened tissue that followed the line of his spine, distorting the powerful muscles, shockingly obvious against his tanned skin. Her anger died. She faltered, "Ryan. . .Ryan what happened?"

Slowly he turned around. "It was a car accident. I was driving. The only other passenger was my youngest sister—my favorite sister, if you want the truth. She was killed."

His voice, his face, were raw with pain. Utterly appalled, Karen said, "How did it happen?"

"It was dark and rainy. There was an oil slick on the other side of the road. The truck that was coming toward us didn't see it and collided with us head-on."

"Then it wasn't your fault."

"We'd been talking, Sally and I. I took my eyes off the road just long enough to say something to her, and that's when it happened. She had time to scream and that was all. I'll never forget that scream as long as I live."

"So you blame yourself." She was stating the obvious, she knew.

"Of course I do. If I'd been watching the road, I might have been able to avoid a collision. Or at least taken the worst of it on my side."

"No one drives with their eyes on the road all the time," she said helplessly. She was standing so close to him that his pain seemed to become hers; something must have shown in her face, for with a muffled groan he dropped his head onto her shoulder, resting his face against the silky dark hair.

She could no more have pushed him away than she could have stopped breathing. Clumsily, like one unused to making such gestures, she put her arms around his naked torso, holding him, hearing him mutter, "She was nineteen. . . her whole life in front of her."

Karen could think of no answer to this. Perhaps there were no answers. So she simply held him, standing very still. It was an awkward pose, for Ryan was so much taller than she, but she would not have moved for the world. Under her palms she felt the curves of his ribs, the smooth texture of his scars. His skin was warm. He was heavy, yet she didn't want the embrace to end. From the depths of her being, where it had lain stifled for years, welled up a generosity that made her want to give something to a man, a generosity that was stronger than all the inhibitions that normally hedged her in.

It was he who moved first. When he raised his head he must have caught the soft, unguarded warmth on her face. Unconsciously he gripped her shoulders as if he would draw her closer. But then, by an effort of will she could only guess at, he let his hands drop to his sides and he moved away from her.

Of necessity she had to let go of him, too. To her nostrils drifted the elusive scent of after-shave and clean, male skin, reminding her inevitably of another embrace, the one by the creek that had ended in an agony of fear. Yet only moments ago she had touched him voluntarily and had been happy to do so. How could that be? With her face reflecting her conflicting emotions, she gazed up at him in silence.

His shirt had dropped to the floor. He bent to pick it up, saying gruffly, "I shouldn't have told you about Sally—I'm sorry."

"Please don't apologize," she said quietly. "I think I should do that. Because you're right, I *have* been blind to other people's problems. Maybe we all have burdens from the past, things we can't escape from."

"Some are heavier than others, Karen." He was buttoning up his shirt as he spoke. "At the risk of sounding as though I'm sermonizing, sharing the burden can lighten the load."

In sudden distress she cried, "But I *can't*! I told you it's all locked up inside me—I just can't."

"I think you can. And I'll help you in any way possible."

She swallowed hard. "Why, Ryan? Why do you care what happens to me?"

He must have sensed her genuine confusion. He said soberly, "I keep getting glimpses of the real you. For more than a year you worked in a tough, alien neighborhood in the city—that must have taken a great deal of courage and persistence, particularly with your mother opposing you every inch of the way."

"I—I guess so. Lots of times I nearly quit."

"And do you remember the first time I saw you? You were running along a rainy street with wings on your feet . . . you looked so graceful and unfettered.

Then that same day I saw you dancing in a crowded ballroom, and you were at one with the music. I want you to be like that all the time, Karen. To be free as a woman to express all the warmth and passion that's in you. Instead you're ruled by fears whose source I don't understand but whose effects are crippling. You're only half a person as you are, you must know that.''

A week ago she would have fiercely denied what he was saying. But yesterday she had fainted in his arms from sheer terror, an only too vivid proof of his words. And today...today she had been able to offer him, however briefly, the comfort of a woman's embrace. The swing of the pendulum from one extreme to the other, she thought numbly. And where was she on that trajectory? She made a tiny, helpless gesture, more telling than words. ''I—I don't understand what's happening.''

''You're coming alive.'' He smiled crookedly. ''It can be a painful process, Karen. Something in me died after that accident, so I know what I'm talking about.''

She felt a pang of the same terror she had felt the night before. If what he said was true, and she had the feeling that it was, then she would be robbed of the safe, placid attitude toward the opposite sex that she had so carefully fashioned for herself. Something would have to replace it. Yet what that would be, she had no idea. ''I was all right as I was,'' she said, not sounding particularly convincing even to herself.

''I'm not going to bother answering that. But I am

going to ask you one more thing. What are you going to do next, Karen—go back to Montreal?''

Her father... she had forgotten him. Her shoulders slumped. ''He hasn't made the slightest overture to me.''

''He's a proud and independent man, too much so for his own good. If there *is* something wrong with him, he'd find it horribly difficult to tell anyone, I'm sure. A bit like someone else I could mention.''

She pulled a face at him. ''Thanks.''

''Give him another chance, Karen,'' he said forcefully. ''I can't guarantee what will happen, but I think you'll regret it if you don't.''

But giving her father a second chance also meant that she would have to remain in Pond Inlet, exposed to the continual demands that Ryan seemed to make on her, to the tensions he created simply by being around her. To go was to flee to the known, the familiar.

She did not see the telltale whiteness of Ryan's knuckles as he waited for her response. She saw instead a young girl running across the marshes and a young woman running through the rain, and it was they who spoke for her. ''I guess I'll stay,'' she said at last.

She heard him release his breath in a sigh of relief and only then realized he had not been certain of her response. ''I'm glad, Karen.''

''I hope I will be, too,'' she answered wryly. With a deliberate lightening of her tone, she added, ''Well, now that that's settled, I might as well tell you that the original reason I went to see my father was to borrow something to read. I did bring a sociology text with me, but I'm not in the mood for anything that heavy. Do you have anything besides massive archaeological tomes?''

"A whole shelf of mysteries," he replied promptly. "Too lowbrow?"

"By no means!"

"Let's go, then."

She had not been in Ryan's Parcoll before. Compared to Laurence's, it was scrupulously neat, the papers, books and clothes arranged in tidy piles. But there was a homelike atmosphere to it that Laurence's lacked, created by the photographs crowded together on the wooden dresser, the Cape Dorset prints taped to the end walls, the brightly patterned quilt on the bed. "May I look?" she asked, walking over to the photographs.

She picked out his father immediately, for he was an older version of Ryan, a big, blond-haired man with his arm around a petite, vivacious redhead who had vibrant green eyes. There was a group picture of the two of them with their six children, a studio portrait of a sweet-faced blond that was signed in one corner, "Love, Sally," and various photos of the brothers and sisters with their respective spouses and children. She said wistfully, "You're lucky to have such a big family. It must be fun when they all get together."

"Christmas and Thanksgiving are traditional family reunions. I have a hard time keeping all my various nephews and nieces straight."

Envy was not a very admirable emotion. Karen said abruptly, "Where are the books?"

She was down on her knees thumbing through a new P.D. James she hadn't read when a sharp knock came at the door. "Ryan, are you there?"

Her father—the last person she wanted to see. Wishing she could disappear through the floor, Karen stayed where she was, her gray eyes clouded.

He did not see her at first. "Have you got the charts for the winter house? I can't lay my hands on them."

"I'm not surprised," Ryan said equably. "Karen, they're in that white folder on the shelf above you. Pass them to me, would you?"

Her father had no choice but to notice her presence. "Karen," he said stiffly. He hesitated. "I owe you an apology for the way I spoke to you."

She waited a moment, but apparently that was all he was going to say. No reasons, no excuses. "Yes, I think you do," she said steadily.

But Laurence's nose was buried in the folder Ryan had passed him. "These are the right ones, thanks. You've got the diagrams finished, have you?" He did not look at Karen again, but the implication was obvious.

"No," Ryan said, meeting the older man's gaze squarely. "Karen was upset, and I thought it was more important to talk to her than to rush back and get at the diagrams."

Laurence's eyes fell. "I see. Well, don't forget we need them as soon as possible."

"I won't."

Laurence left without another word and Karen scrambled to her feet. "I've got to go, too. I'll borrow these three if I may, and let you get back to work."

"Karen—"

"Bye." Quickly she closed the door behind her. It was a retreat and she knew it, but she had had enough emotional conflict for one day. Her father's grudging apology could only confirm her conviction that he had cut her out of his life many years ago and did not want her back. Yet she had told Ryan she would stay, so stay she must. *Freedom,* she thought caustically. *There's no such thing. You're either caught by your own nature, or by the demands of other people.*

She went to dinner early, sitting with some of the construction workers and gradually sorting them out. Claude, the foreman, a soft-spoken, wiry little man was from Chicoutimi. Jean-Pierre was the youngest of the men, with romantic dark eyes and a fledgling beard. Guillaume and Joe, equally overweight and equally taciturn, were electricians working at the generating plant—Tweedledum and Tweedledee, she thought mischievously. She had the chance to use her French with Claude and Jean-Pierre, and then a chance question got Guillaume talking about the mysterious and daunting internal problems of the generator, which he called "she" with the kind of possessive affection a man usually used toward his wife. The explanations he gave would have been complicated enough in English; in French they were mind-boggling, the more so when Claude and Jean-Pierre added their own solutions—with which Guillaume manifestly disagreed. Joe said not a word. He ate his way through the menu, drank three cups of coffee and then lit an evil-smelling pipe, staring soberly at the far wall through clouds of blue smoke.

Karen thoroughly enjoyed herself, promising to inspect Jean-Pierre's surveying and Claude's construction work the next day. When she pushed back her chair, Ryan and Laurence were still eating at one of the other tables; she gave them a cool nod and left the hotel, deciding to go for a walk by herself. She went east instead of west, and soon found herself on the open cliffs beyond the hamlet. Unfortunately she also came to the dump, littered with broken snowmobiles and rusting oil drums. Its only redeeming feature was a brilliant carpet of wild flowers cascading down the cliff where once the sewage must have seeped. She knelt to examine the flowers more closely, wondering what they were called. Now that she was alerted to their presence she began to see many more, although none as luxuriant as the first. There were tiny white, yellow, and pink flowers cowering in the cracks between the rocks or hugging the bare ground. She saw birds as well—brown sparrowlike birds, and ones of a similar size with white wings, as well as gulls and ducks offshore. And she couldn't name a single one of them, she thought humbly. She must ask Ryan if he had any field guides.

It was peaceful out on the cliffs by herself. She sat for a while, watching the play of light on the water and the slowly moving drift ice, not thinking of anything in particular. Once she was disturbed when a small plane came in to land, and later she heard a boat leave its mooring. Otherwise there was only the vast, primeval silence of the Arctic overlying the thin chirping of the birds.

Even when she began to get cold she didn't move immediately, conscious of a strong reluctance to go back to the hotel where she might meet either Ryan or her father. Away from the mesmerizing blue of Ryan's eyes, she recognized that she was afraid of his forceful personality and his aptitude for interfering in her life—all for her own good, of course. Somehow when she was with him his often brutal honesty and his sheer strength of will had a way of making her behave quite atypically. She could not help remembering the way she had put her arms around him, hands on his naked flesh, and she felt a frisson pass along her spine as she did so. Right now she found it almost impossible to believe she had touched him. But she had, and willingly.

It mustn't happen again. There had been nothing sexual about it, of course, or so she told herself. It had been simply for comfort, and she would have done the same for anyone. But even so, it mustn't happen again. Ryan must get no closer to her than he already was, for any other way spelled danger.

Rather pleased with herself for this decision, and blithely ignoring the fact that she was also making a decision for another person, she got to her feet, stretched and wandered back toward the hamlet. She was just passing between the first row of bungalows when a voice hailed her. "Hello! Are you a visitor here?"

Karen looked around. The woman who had called was standing on the steps of a mud-colored house, a wide smile on her face. Karen walked over to her, smiling back. "Yes, I am. My name's Karen Smythe."

"And I'm Mary Ann Delaney. I'll be honest and say I saw you walking out to the cliffs, and so I watched for you to come back. We get so few visitors here." She had been joined by a vital-looking, dark-haired young man who had slipped a proprietary arm around her waist. "My fiancé, Don Kavanaugh," she beamed, introducing Karen. "Please, won't you come in and have a coffee with us?" With her tangled dark curls and her generous full-lipped smile she was hard to refuse, and Karen's policy of staying uninvolved went by the boards.

"I'd love to."

The bungalow was cheaply furnished, although with a few well-chosen prints and some attractive plants Mary Ann had done her best to give it touches of hominess. A large gold-framed photograph of Don had a place of honor on the end table. Following Karen's gaze Mary Ann said, "We've only been engaged for ten days, so it's all very new."

"Is it only ten days? Seems like forever," Don teased.

Mary Ann consulted her watch. "Ten days in one hour and thirty-five minutes."

"I didn't realize you had it timed," he laughed, hugging her. For a moment she leaned against him, the two of them encased in a little world of love and happiness that needed no outsiders. But it was more than that, Karen thought with a lump in her throat. For all her own inhibitions, she was not blind to the interactions of others, and briefly, like a hot blue flame, sexual awareness had flared between Don and Mary Ann, a memory of passion shared and hunger renewed. They had made love earlier, Karen was sure, and probably, once she was gone, they would make love again. It made her feel like an outcast, abnormal, shut off from an activity that others seemed to find both necessary and enjoyable.

Mary Ann disengaged herself, her cheeks pink. "Do tell us what brings you here," she said, and somehow it was impossible to be offended by her bright-eyed curiosity.

"I'm visiting my father," Karen replied, hoping she sounded suitably filial. "Laurence Smith."

"He's your father? I never would have guessed. You don't look a bit alike... you're *very* beautiful," Mary Ann added without a trace of envy.

"Thank you." That Ryan's words should be repeated with such artless enthusiasm was disconcerting; Mary Ann, certainly, could have no ulterior motive.

"And such a gorgeous figure." Mary Ann sighed, looking down at her own rather plump curves. "I'm always planning to diet but somehow I never seem to get around to it."

"I like you exactly as you are," Don said calmly. "Want me to put the kettle on?" Very much at home in Mary Ann's bungalow, he disappeared into the kitchen.

"I'm sorry if we seem a bit smug," Mary Ann said. "It's all so new to us, and I don't think I, for one, can quite believe how happy I am. We both lived here all last year—I'm the nurse and Don's the junior-high teacher—and we were friends and that's all. We went to our respective homes for a month this summer, came back here and everything had changed. Suddenly we realized we were in love. Very strange. But nice," she added with naive pleasure.

"When will you be married?"

"Next month. But I've talked enough about us. What do you do, Karen?"

Karen explained briefly about her job at the drop-in center and her plans for university in the fall. "It had been a while since I'd seen my father," she finished with purposeful vagueness, "so I thought I'd come up here and see a bit of the north as well."

"You must have met Ryan, then. What do you think of him?"

About to make another politely vague reply, Karen said instead, "I think he's a very overbearing man far too used to getting his own way."

Mary Ann blinked. "Well, that's interesting. *I* think he's the best-looking man I've ever seen."

"Talking about me again, eh?" Don said, coming back with a tray of coffee and some date squares.

"Not this time," Mary Ann chuckled. "Ryan." It was obviously a long-standing joke between them. "Karen thinks he's overbearing."

Wishing she'd kept her mouth shut, Karen heard Don say thoughtfully, "Confident and competent, certainly. But I wouldn't have said overbearing. He's always struck me as being particularly sensitive to the needs of others."

"Perhaps there's something about me that rubs

him the wrong way," Karen said hurriedly. "Mmm, this is good coffee, Don."

"Sorry we can't offer you anything stronger, but we never bring alcohol up here. We could get a permit, I suppose, but it seems better not to."

"Come to think of it, there isn't a bar at the hotel," Karen remarked. "Why is that?"

"The Inuit themselves run the hamlet, so they have a committee that keeps a very watchful eye on the alcohol situation. It's done such a lot of damage to Inuit and Indian peoples over the years that I think they're very wise to keep this virtually a dry community. As we're so isolated, it's manageable. Frobisher Bay is another story."

"So they do it themselves," Karen murmured. "Much more effective than having white people impose some kind of restraint on them."

"Exactly."

They talked for well over an hour, Karen learning a fair amount about the village and its surroundings, and accepting with pleasure Mary Ann's loan of wild flower and bird books. Finally she stood up. "I must go—I'm monopolizing your evening. Thank you both very much, and thanks for the books, Mary Ann."

"A pleasure. You must come again."

Warmed by the knowledge that she had made two new friends, Karen walked back up the hill toward the hotel. Although it was ten o'clock, it seemed too early to go to bed. On impulse she went into the hotel lounge, where Guillaume, Joe, Claude and Jean-Pierre were watching the television news. A newcomer was seated in one of the deep armchairs, a man Karen had not seen before. He got to his feet when she came in, saying with a roguish twinkle in his eye, "Well now, things are looking up. Rusty McNeill at your service, ma'am."

He was tall and lean, with a shock of red hair and a red beard. He also had that mysterious attribute called charm, Karen thought ironically. Oodles of it. Women must fall like ninepins for Rusty McNeill. She held out her hand, saying coolly, "Karen Smythe."

"And what brings you to these benighted parts, Karen?"

For some reason she had no compunction about using Laurence's name. "My father is an archaeologist here. Dr. Laurence Smith."

"A very famous man."

"And what about you?" she countered.

"An ornithologist. Doing surveys for a group of oil companies. I just got in tonight."

She remembered hearing the sound of a small plane coming in to land while she was on the hillside. Smiling, she indicated the book she was holding. "You're a godsend. I was out on the tundra earlier this evening and a lot of birds were flying around, not one of which I could name."

Something in him that had tensed when he'd seen the book in her hand relaxed infinitesimally. "Sure, I'll be glad to help. In fact, why don't you come with me tomorrow? I've made arrangements to rent a boat and go across to Bylot Island. Providing the weather cooperates, that is."

"I'd love to. When are you going?"

"After breakfast. I'll get them to pack us a lunch. Wear warm clothes, won't you?"

It wasn't until Karen was back in her tent that she wondered about the wisdom of her decision. She had agreed to spend a day in very isolated surroundings with a man about whom she knew virtually nothing. Except that he had charm, not always the most reliable of traits. Yet she understood her instant acceptance of his offer all too well: she had been lured by the promise of getting closer to the gaunt cliffs and the stark, snowcapped mountains that had been beckoning to her across the blue waters of the inlet ever since she had arrived.

I'll tell my father where I'm going, she decided as she started to get undressed. *And I'll make sure Rusty knows I've told him. I hope it will be a sunny day....*

CHAPTER SEVEN

THE GODS MUST HAVE BEEN LISTENING. When Karen awoke the next morning, bright sunlight was streaming into her room at the edges of the plastic coverings on the windows. Sitting up in bed, she pushed the plastic aside and looked out. The waters of the inlet were mirror smooth, reflecting the clear blue of the sky, while the glacial snow was so white it hurt the eyes. *A perfect day,* she thought excitedly, jumping out of bed and dressing in her warmest clothes.

In the porch of the hotel Rusty was just taking off his boots. She greeted him with a lilt in her voice. "Good morning!"

"Hi, there." He looked with approval at her flushed cheeks and the shiny hair under her scarlet toque. "All set?"

"Really looking forward to it."

They went into the dining room together, Rusty leading her to the table nearest the window, which happened to be the table farthest from her father and Ryan. Karen waved at them casually across the room, pleased that she was not dependent on either one of them for her entertainment today. She missed the sudden tightening of Ryan's features as he saw how at ease she was with her companion. For Rusty was good company, there was no doubt about that. He had never married, she soon discovered, preferring to remain footloose and fancy-free; he had worked on oil tankers and chartered cruises in the Caribbean, and traveled widely in Asia and the Middle East, never really settling long in any one place. And for every country he had been, he had a host of amusing and entertaining stories. Her own life seemed very circumscribed in contrast.

They had nearly finished eating when Ryan stopped by their table. With no great warmth he introduced himself to Rusty, then said to Karen, "I've got a pile of work to get through this morning. But by lunchtime I'll need a break—do you want to go for a walk for an hour or so?"

Her father had not bothered to stop, she noticed. She gave Ryan a brilliant, empty smile. "I can't, I'm afraid. Rusty's taking me over to Bylot Island."

Ryan's eyes hardened. Turning to Rusty, he said without even the pretense of politeness, "Whose boat are you taking?"

"Lucas's," Rusty responded lazily. "And yes, I know how to handle it."

"You take good care of her, McNeill." Naked antagonism had flared between the two men; the words were more of a threat than an admonition.

"I'll do that."

Ryan nodded curtly at Karen. "I'll see you later."

"Do say good morning to my father for me," she replied silkily. "As usual, he hasn't bothered acknowledging that I exist."

"He knows you exist, Karen."

"Then he has a strange way of showing it. Good-bye, Ryan." She turned back to Rusty, finishing the last of her tea despite the fact that it was almost cold.

"Well, well," Rusty said softly. "And who is that very large and irate gentleman?"

Suddenly ashamed of the way she had spoken to Ryan, she found she didn't want to discuss him. "He works with my father," she said lightly. "Where do we pick up the lunches, Rusty?"

"He seems to have more than a passing interest in you."

She should have known someone with Rusty's knockabout life would not be so easily put off. With just the right touch of casualness she added, "He probably feels responsible for me, since it was his idea I come up here in the first place. I'd better bring mittens, hadn't I?"

"Yes." For a moment his eyes, which were an un-usually pale blue, were very cold as he looked over at Karen. "I don't like being told what to do."

It was a side to Rusty she had not seen before: the opposite side of the coin to charm. "Do you still want me to come with you?" she asked directly.

The pale eyes widened and warmed. "Of course I do! And don't worry—I'm extremely competent around a boat."

Knowing it for the truth, Karen replied, "I think you'd be extremely competent at whatever you chose to do."

Pushing back his chair, Rusty gave her a mock bow. "Meet you outside in ten minutes."

She went back to the Parcoll, where she automatically gathered up the things she thought she'd need: the bird book, one extra sweater, mittens, her dark glasses. But her thoughts were elsewhere. The little scene between Ryan and Rusty had shaken her more than she liked to admit. In his own way, each was a tough and able man; if it came to a contest between them, she wasn't sure who would win.

She shivered, chiding herself for being over-imaginative. There was no contest. Ryan had simply been annoyed because she was not available that afternoon. As she had taken such pains to point out to Mary Ann, he was used to getting his own way. She shouldered her haversack and zipped up her jacket, putting Ryan out of her mind. Today was hers to enjoy, and no one was going to spoil it.

Nor did anyone. Lucas's boat was a sixteen-foot aluminum powerboat, more than roomy enough for the two of them. It didn't take long for Karen to realize that Rusty's assertions were true, for he was completely at home on the water. She sat near the bow, catching a glimpse of some seals bobbing and diving near a chunk of drift ice, and by perusing her book and using Rusty's binoculars, she discovered the difference between a Thayer's gull and a glaucous gull, a kittiwake and a fulmar. They passed the pyramidal peak of Mount Herodier, the smaller peaks of Beloeil Island, and finally the graceful, frozen sweep of Narsarsuk glacier where the cliffs dropped sheer to the sea, with snow in the shadowed crevices. The primitively carved landscape was virtually untouched by man, as beautiful as it was unaccommodating.

When they rounded Button Point, the open waters

of Baffin Bay stretched eastward, the nearest land and the vast frozen bulk of Greenland four hundred miles away. Dead ahead were the gaunt cliffs of Cape Graham Moore. Rusty slowed the motor to an idle.

The first thing Karen noticed was the noise, an incredible din set up by thousands of seabirds. They were like a totally undisciplined choir, she thought fancifully, all bass voices, all determined to be heard at once, all very suave in their slick black-and-white plumage. "What are they?" she yelled.

"Thick-billed murres. More than twenty thousand of them. This kind of colony is called a bazaar— rather appropriate, wouldn't you say?"

He passed her the binoculars. The cliff face was streaked white with droppings. There were no nests at all, only fluffy gray chicks perched horribly close to the edge of the ledges. As well, there was a constant coming and going of adult birds, narrow wings beating the air so rapidly they were almost a blur, bodies splashing into the sea as they dived for fish. They never collided, nor did a single chick tumble from its precarious perch.

There were kittiwakes, too, Karen realized, their wing tips looking as though they had been dipped in ink, their flight very much more graceful than that of the murres. But it was the latter that dominated the scene, raucous, argumentative, never still.

Reluctantly she handed the binoculars back to Rusty. "Sorry, you're the one who's supposed to be doing the survey. What exactly do you do?"

"Oh, I'll have to set up a pattern of grids and do counts," he said easily. "I'll come back another time. In fact, I may camp here." He was looking through the binoculars as he spoke, focusing not so much on the murres as on the surrounding cliffs.

Karen had no idea what brought the great white falcons to mind. Curiously she asked, "Rusty, have you ever seen a gyrfalcon?"

His head snapped up, the binoculars forgotten. "Why?" he asked sharply.

Taken aback by his strange reaction, she said uncertainly, "Ryan told me about them—said they were very rare. I just wondered if you'd seen one."

Belatedly Rusty smiled, although it did not quite reach his eyes. "No, I've never been fortunate enough." He shrugged. "I've heard they nest around here, though. You should keep your eyes peeled."

"I'd love to see one," she said longingly.

"Let me know if you do. I'll write it up in the ornithological journals."

They ate their sandwiches, then shortly afterward left for home. Karen was not sorry to go, for she did not think anything could equal the spectacle of the bazaar of murres. More practically, also, the wind had freshened and it was growing cold on the water. By the time they got back to the hamlet, her hands were numb inside her mittens and her knees were stiff from sitting so long. Rusty walked back to the hotel with her to find Lucas, and as she left him at the door she said simply, "Thanks, Rusty. I wouldn't have missed that for anything."

His charm was very much in evidence. "My pleasure, Karen. Maybe we can do it again sometime."

She walked behind the hotel to the row of Parcolls,

somehow not at all surprised to see Ryan coming toward her. "Hello," she said politely, as if he were Claude or Jean-Pierre. "Cold, isn't it?"

Her hair was tangled by the wind, which had whipped color into her cheeks; her eyes were very bright. Ryan said flatly, "You're back."

"Oh, yes—did you expect otherwise?" she replied provocatively.

"I heard the boat so I came out to meet you. That guy's an adventurer if I've ever seen one—not your type at all, Karen. So take it easy, okay?"

Her cheeks were pink from more than the cold. "Are you presuming to tell me how I should spend my time?"

"I'm just giving you a word of warning, that's all."

"I assure you, it's quite superfluous," she said angrily. "I'm perfectly capable of looking after myself, thank you."

His jaw tightened. "I wouldn't trust McNeill an inch. That's all I'm trying to say."

That she had had a few doubts herself was beside the point. "At least he didn't try to kiss me," she said nastily. "Not like some people I could mention."

"Oh?" He took a step closer. "You tempt me to try again."

The wind ruffled his thick blond hair. His eyes were brilliant with an anger that matched her own. "Perhaps you'd better not," she said sweetly. "My father's just come out of his tent and he's watching us. You wouldn't want to give him the wrong impression, would you, Ryan?"

He muttered an expletive under his breath. "He won't be there next time."

She widened her eyes innocently, knowing she was behaving atrociously but unable to help herself. "Then I'll have to make sure there isn't a next time, won't I?"

Ryan smiled, running a finger lightly down her cheek, judging her withdrawal so accurately that his finger left her face a fraction of a second before she moved back. "Oh, there'll be one, Karen."

She forced herself to hold his gaze, although her hands were clenched into fists at her sides. "Father's waiting for you. Don't you think you'd better go?"

"Don't expect to win the next round." Swiftly he kissed her full on the mouth, then turned and strode along the planks to where her father was still standing. The two of them disappeared into the tent.

Karen stood still, her mouth open. It had been so brief a kiss that it had left only sweetness, not fear. A memory of warmth and a fleeting pressure, the tantalizing scent of his skin. She had liked it, she thought dazedly. She had actually liked it.

Coming back to the present with a jolt and knowing she must look like an idiot gaping after Ryan, she hurried into her own tent and closed the door. It was deliciously warm inside, so she huddled by the stove, turning it up a notch and rubbing her hands together to bring the circulation back. Although she sat there for some time, the only conclusion she came to was that she had to avoid Ryan. So she had enjoyed a kiss that had been over almost before it had begun—so what? If it had been prolonged, the familiar panic would have usurped any pleasure she might have felt; she knew that in her bones. So it must not happen again.

That evening she joined Jean-Pierre and Claude for dinner again, noticing that Rusty was sitting with a stranger. The dour, black-haired man was badly in need of a shave, and he shoveled in his food as if he hadn't eaten for a week. Following her gaze Claude said sardonically, "A nice-looking guy, eh?"

"Who is he?"

Claude shrugged. "*Je ne sais pas.* I think he arrived with the other one, what is his name? McNeill? But what he does in the meantime, I don't know. Gets drunk, by the look of him."

He did look as though he had a hangover, Karen had to agree, and she found herself wishing that Rusty didn't have such a sinister-looking companion. Not that it was really any concern of hers, she thought hurriedly.

She spent the evening playing cards with the French Canadians, even managing to win a few hands of a particularly bloodthirsty variation of poker, much to the stolid Guillaume's amusement. The game did not break up until after midnight. She slept late the next morning, almost missing breakfast and certainly missing Ryan and her father, who were always among the first to be up. It was another gloriously sunny day, warmer than the day before, the sky a cloudless blue from horizon to horizon. Checking with Lucas, she discovered that she could follow the creek that ran through the village up into the tundra, and that she'd eventually come to the lake that sup-

plied the hamlet with its water. Packing the bird and
flower books into her haversack, and taking a lunch
with her, she set off.

She wanted to get clear of the village and of the
scraps of garbage that fluttered across the tundra
from the direction of the dump, so she walked steadily for a while, discarding first her toque and mittens,
then her jacket. By diligently perusing the bird book,
she discovered that the striking black-breasted birds
whose thin, piping calls echoed back and forth across
the stream were golden plovers. Then, by muddling
her way through the key in the botany book she identified the white-petaled mountain avens, the pea-like
purple *Astragalus* and the deep pink willow-herb.
The Arctic poppy she had read about; their pale yellow petals cupped the sun, swaying on slender, hairy
stems that seemed far too fragile for so harsh an environment.

Because her progress had slowed considerably,
Karen had been aware for some time of a chorus of
voices ahead of her and had found herself rather resenting this intrusion into her privacy. However,
when she rounded the next bend in the creek, she saw
a crowd of young boys playing in a dammed-up part
of the stream, some of them skinny-dipping, others
content to float boats from the edge. She had already
tested the water and knew it to be ice-cold. How
could they bear to swim in it?

As she came into sight, the boys scattered for their
clothes. Then there was a chorus of hellos. "What's
your name?" the boldest one demanded. He was
wearing jeans, oblivious to the wind on his wet skin.

"Karen." They giggled, apparently finding this very funny. "What's yours?"

"Tuglik. You staying at the hotel?"

"Yes."

"Lucas is my father."

"I see." On inspiration she took a chocolate bar out of her pocket and divided it among them. It was gone in a flash and she was left with a circle of round expectant faces. "Sorry—no more." She stayed and talked for a little longer, then went on her way again, the shouts and laughter gradually diminishing until they sounded like a distant chorus of birds fighting over scraps on the beach.

The ground had leveled to a marshy area surrounding a lake. Cotton grass was growing so thickly that the marsh looked like a field of drifting snow. Karen picked a piece, finding that the white tuft at the top of the stem was deliciously soft to the touch, like a tiny powder puff; from her reading she knew the Inuit used to use cotton grass as wicks for their soapstone lamps.

Climbing the hill behind the lake, she walked on. By now she was on high enough ground that she could see how the distant mountains encircled her. There were no other humans, for the little boys had retreated out of sight long ago, and for a moment Karen closed her eyes, enjoying the sun's warmth on her lids. She felt suffused with a sense of unity with her surroundings, so wild, so spacious, so free. All too briefly that elusive emotion called happiness filled her with wonder. Even as she wished she could capture such a perfect instant and prolong it forever, it faded, and she was simply a woman standing alone on a hillside on the tundra.

Nevertheless, she was still smiling when she wandered on. She picked a few flowers she was unable to identify, having first ascertained that they were common species, and carefully pressed them between the botany book's enigmatic pages. She ate her lunch perched on a rock that faced the mountains of Bylot Island, shimmering in the sunlight; she identified the brown sparrowlike bird as a Lapland longspur. And then civilization intervened, in the form of a dirt road that presumably led to the water supply. Following it, she eventually came to a lake that had a wooden ramp for the water truck, and as if on signal she heard the faraway roar of an engine. So her solitude was to be invaded. Philosophically she went back up the hill to watch the truck's approach.

It had a passenger—Rusty. He jumped out, giving her his mercurial smile. "Fancy meeting you here!"

Pleased to see him, she began telling him of her various discoveries, and she was rather disappointed when he barely glanced at the pressed flowers. He had his binoculars with him and began methodically sweeping the horizon, not offering them to her until he had done a complete circle. "See any interesting birds?" he asked casually.

"Plovers and longspurs. Maybe a jaeger, I wasn't sure."

"Nothing else, eh?"

"No. What are you looking for?"

"Oh, nothing in particular." Again he scanned the horizon.

Something did not quite ring true in the whole conversation, but Karen couldn't have put her finger on what it was. When the water truck was full and the driver hailed them, she said on impulse, "I think I'll go back with you."

She squeezed in between Rusty and the driver, a cousin of Lucas's named Noah, and they rattled off down the road. Rusty was drinking a can of pop. He offered her one but she declined, too busy watching every detail of the scenery. They were in sight of the runway when she exclaimed, "Look over there—is *that* a jaeger?"

"I guess it is." He didn't sound very interested.

"Then I was right. But which kind is it? Aren't there three different species?"

"I'd have to be closer to tell." He rolled down the window and flung the empty pop can out onto the ground.

Karen sat very still, all her doubts coalescing. Surely no qualified ornithologist who cared about the environment would discard his litter like that? And surely a qualified ornithologist would know a long-tailed jaeger from a parasitic jaeger with or without binoculars? Hoping her thoughts weren't showing, she said brightly, "Is that your plane parked by the shed?"

"The Twin Otter. Yeah."

"Do you do any aerial surveys?"

"Probably we will."

"I'd love to come with you. It's all so interesting." She was babbling on like an idiot, she thought disgustedly—although Rusty didn't seem to notice.

"We'll see."

Which means no, she decided shrewdly.

He glanced over at her, perhaps reading her mind. Flashing her his quick grin, he said, "Sorry, Karen, guess I'm preoccupied. I'm sure we can arrange a flight sometime."

"Thanks, I'd love that, I really would," she gushed. "Goodness, here we are, home already. Thank you for the ride, Noah." Noah nodded his head, laughter lines crinkling around his dark eyes. She clambered to the ground, avoiding Rusty's helping hand. "Thanks for the lift. I'd walked farther than I realized."

"Distances are deceptive up here. See you later."

That flashing, unreliable smile and he was gone. She stared after him, frowning.

"You look as though you've just lost your best friend," Ryan said disagreeably.

She hadn't seen him there. She began, "It's not—"

"Karen, I wish you wouldn't go off with him so much."

She said icily, "I beg your pardon?"

"You heard. That's two days in a row."

"First of all, where were you this morning when I wanted to go for a walk? In your tent with your nose buried in a book, no doubt," she snapped.

"I am being paid to work, you know."

Ignoring him, she swept on, "And secondly I did not go off with him. He and Noah gave me a lift home from the lake. Not that it's any of your business." She was standing on the ground, Ryan on the wooden walkway, so he towered over her more than usual. She had to force herself not to retreat.

Obviously making an effort to sound impartial, Ryan said, "For some reason I don't trust him, I don't know why."

It suddenly struck Karen how ridiculous this all was, and she began to laugh, her eyes sparkling. "Don't laugh. . ." he began.

"I can't help it. Because *I* don't trust him either." Briefly she described the episode of the jaeger and the pop can. "So why are we standing here arguing?"

He grinned reluctantly, his eyes trained on her up-turned face. "I don't know. You have a beautiful smile."

"Ryan, we're not discussing my smile—"

"I am."

"I don't know what happens to me when you're around," she blurted, fumbling for the right words. "You make me feel. . .different. I don't know how to describe it."

"Like a woman?"

"Maybe. . . ." Her cheeks warmed. That *was* it. Standing there so close to him she was very conscious of his size, of the breadth of his shoulders under the Levi's shirt and of the muscles of his forearms bared because his sleeves were rolled up. His strength and humor, the sheer maleness of his features were immensely attractive. And something about him made her aware of her own femininity, of how differently she was built, of softness and curves that could only complement the planes and angles of his own body. For so many years she had totally refused to think of herself as a woman, let alone as a desirable or beautiful one. Yet Ryan found her both desirable and beautiful, she knew that. Standing there in the sunshine she felt the first stirrings of pride that he should find her so, and at the same time an intimidation of the vulnerability this could bring her.

He was speaking, "And it's very new to you, isn't it?"

She nodded. "Yes."

"You don't have to be frightened of me, Karen. What happened that evening by the creek will never happen again. Anything I do will be because you want it."

"But I don't want...." She stopped, utterly confused.

"You don't know what you want. But I hope someday soon you will."

She managed to break the spell long enough to step backward. Her boot slipped on a rock so that she stumbled, almost dropping her book, and a couple of the pressed flowers fell to the ground. She bent to pick them up. "I couldn't figure out what these are."

Ryan said knowledgeably, "*Pyrola*, that one with the white flower. The common name's wintergreen. And the tiny yellow one is *Draba alpina*."

Delighted that he should know them, she said, "Do you mind if we go to my tent for a minute so I can write the names down? I'll never remember them otherwise."

In the Parcoll she spread the specimens on the bed, getting a notebook and a pencil as Ryan began locating the plants on the key. As she sat down beside him, waiting for him to finish, her attention was distracted from the descriptions of leathery, netted-veined leaves and drooping petals to more immediate concerns. He was very close to her. Blond hair covered his arms. His hands were well kept, the nails short and very clean.

For a moment she saw superimposed on them another pair of hands, coarse and dirty, the nails chewed to the quick, and her world rocked. By a sheer effort of will Karen forced herself back to the present, and a small voice in her brain said, *Ryan's not like that. Ryan's different.*

"Are you all right?"

She was looking at him as if she had never seen him before, and she pushed a strand of hair back from her face with fingers that were not quite steady. "Yes, I'm all right." More convincingly, "Really I am."

He rested his hands on her shoulders, then bent to kiss her with infinite gentleness, releasing her while her body was still pliant and unafraid. Struck dumb, she knew she had felt it again, that fleeting wonder, the pleasure of his kiss. But before she could say anything he had picked up another of the flowers. "This looks like a saxifrage. There are too many species for me to remember which one. Do you want to look it up in the index?"

She did as she was asked, obediently writing down the name, her emotions in a turmoil. Ryan dealt with the rest of the flowers in a very businesslike way, then said calmly, "Karen, I've told your father I'm taking tomorrow off. Told him, not asked him. He and I have worked every weekend since the end of June and I need a break. So why don't we hike over to Janes Creek? You haven't been that way yet.''

A whole day with him, alone on the sweep of the tundra. But this time the old familiar fears had mingled with them a touch of anticipation, even of recklessness. "I'd like that,'' she said breathlessly.

"Okay. We'll leave after breakfast. I'll have to work this evening to make up for it, so I probably won't see you until then.''

"How is my father?'' she asked in a small voice.

"In a foul mood. I wish I knew what was eating him.''

"So do I. I'll see you tomorrow, then.''

"I'll look forward to it.''

Ordinary words, but Karen knew he meant them. He didn't try to kiss her again, and as the door closed behind him, she was conscious of an emotion that could only be disappointment. She would have liked him to kiss her, she thought dazedly, putting her hands to her cheeks. What was happening to her?

CHAPTER EIGHT

EVERYTHING CONSPIRED TO GO WELL the following day. The sun was shining, and because there was not even a breath of wind, it was warmer than the day before. Karen and Ryan set off after breakfast, each with a haversack and a pair of binoculars, for Ryan had borrowed Laurence's for Karen. Walking at a steady pace past the dump and the green-painted oil tanks, they reached the crest of the hills that over-looked the beach. Although the ground was rocky, it was fairly easy walking, so they had covered a fair distance by the time they stopped for lunch near the canyon. Beyond it Janes Creek meandered toward the sea, and beyond that again was the distinctive peak of Mount Herodier.

Their lunch, simple though it was, tasted delicious. Afterward Ryan carefully folded the pieces of waxed paper and put them back in his haversack, an action that inevitably reminded Karen of Rusty. "Do *you* think Rusty's an ornithologist?" she asked.

"I don't know, Karen. For some reason I have the feeling he's up to no good. Maybe I'm just being bloody-minded because I don't like seeing him with you."

"You don't? Why not?" She had not meant to ask

that; it was as though some force greater than herself had caused her to speak.

"Because I want you for myself."

"Ryan, you mustn't...."

"Mustn't I?"

"Oh, *I* don't know. Let's go." Not looking at him, she got to her feet, bundling her jacket into her haversack and adjusting it on her back, an action that strained the thin cotton of her shirt across her breasts. She looked over to find him watching her and blushed fiercely, knowing instantly what he had seen. "Let's go," she repeated sharply.

His face grim, he led her to the edge of the canyon. It looked very steep, its near side a tumble of rocks, the far side a sheer cliff smeared with bird droppings. "Ravens' nests," Ryan said briefly. "We'll go down side by side. That way if one of us starts a rock slide, the other's not below. Test your footing as you go. Ready?"

Karen nodded, not wanting him to see she was nervous. The first part was not too difficult, for there was grass growing on the slope and it was easy to find footholds. Snow buntings were chirping back and forth on the cliffs and it was very warm, so warm that Karen was glad to stop for a minute when Ryan called her over to see a fern growing in the hollow between two rocks. It was the tiniest fern she had ever seen, the fronds no more than an inch in length, the fiddleheads a quarter the size of the buttons on her shirt. Delighted, she said, "It's like a perfect miniature, isn't it?"

"Another adaptation to the Arctic climate. In effect, it's a northern desert up here. You must already have noticed how small and low to the ground all the plants are, and how many there are that have hairy stems and leathery leaves.''

She brushed her fingertip along the tiny frond. "It's almost a textbook illustration, isn't it?''

"I thought you'd be interested." Deliberately he backed away from her. "If I were you, I'd go around that big rock."

They began the descent again, Karen unashamedly clinging to every handhold she could get as the slope grew steeper. Once she started a rock slide, the jagged chunks of granite bouncing down the hill until they hit the canyon floor, the noise echoing like gunshots from the opposite cliff. And once she nearly slipped and fell, clutching the cliff face to save herself, her heart racing in her breast. But finally she made it, dropping to the boggy ground beside the little stream that gurgled along the canyon floor. "We don't have to go up the other side, do we?" she asked, gaping up at the rugged cliffs.

"We could try if you like."

"No, thanks!"

Laughingly he relented. "We'll walk along the canyon floor."

He started off in front of her, and at first the going was easy, for they followed the course of the stream. But gradually the walls of the canyon narrowed in above them. The stream disappeared beneath a jumble of rocks that were tossed in all directions as if by a giant hand, rocks that were encrusted with lichen and clumps of dry, dead moss. From beneath them the water gurgled menacingly. Karen soon found that no two steps were on the same plane; it was necessary to climb over the rocks, edge between them, skirt around them, until she was breathless.

But she was honest enough with herself to admit that more than the exertion was bothering her. It was dark at the foot of the canyon, the cliffs and rocks casting deep, sharp-edged shadows. The air was cold and damp. The boulders, some of them twice her height, seemed to be closing in on her, so that she found herself glancing over her shoulder, half expecting them to be moving behind her back, creeping up on her to crush her. She scolded herself for letting her imagination run away with her. But the black shadows and the hulking monoliths cast too powerful a spell to be so simply exorcised, and when she rounded a ledge and came face to face with a gaunt slab of rock angled sharply toward her, she gasped in panic. She had to get out of there, she thought blindly. Scrambling back the way she had come, she squeezed between two vertical chunks of granite to bypass the angled rock. For a fatal moment she paused, the hush of the waiting rocks drumming in her ears. "Ryan?" she called, panic edging her voice. No answer. "Ryan!"

Through the darkness pressing against her eyes Karen heard the scrape of boots on the rocks. For a wild moment she was convinced it was not going to be Ryan—that another man would lower himself from the ledge, a big man whose name was Paul. A man who bit his nails to the quick.... She jammed her fist into her mouth to stop the scream that rose in her throat.

Ryan jumped the last three feet from the ledge. He must have seen how her fingers clutched the rock, her body cowering against it, and how her eyes were as dark shadowed as the crevice. Yet when he reached out to her she flinched, turning her face away as though she couldn't bear to look at him. She was trembling, and he could hear whimpering in her throat.

Ryan hesitated only briefly. His mouth a tight line, he slapped her across one cheek and then the other, the impact of his fingers sounding shockingly loud.

Karen sagged against the rock, her eyes clearing. "Oh, Ryan, it's you," she gasped, one hand groping to close on his arm, so warm and so very real. "I thought—" She broke off, passing her other hand over her face. "I'm sorry. I get claustrophobia in places like this. Especially when it's dark."

"You should have told me."

"I didn't realize it would be like this.... Is it much farther?"

"A quarter of a mile." He was looking at the red marks on her cheeks, his face bleak. "I'm sorry I hit you—I didn't know what else to do. I only want what's best for you, Karen, and yet I always seem to end up hurting you."

"I'm glad you did." Her fingers tightened on his arm. "You got me out of that other place and back here."

He must have known it was a direct reference to whatever had so terrified her in the past. "What was the other place like?" he asked very casually.

"Like this, only pitch-dark. I was always afraid

the walls were closing in on me.'' She shuddered, then suddenly dropped his arm and recoiled from him as she realized what she had done. Her face shut against him. ''I never talk about it,'' she said raggedly.

''Then it's time you did.''

She shook her head in helpless denial. ''No!''

His shoulders slumped and for a moment he looked tired and defeated, older than his years. ''Come on, then, let's get out of here,'' he said gruffly.

Trying not to think about anything, past or present, Karen followed him step by step, ignoring the aching of her muscles and the stitch in her side. She was grimly determined not to give way to panic again. Twenty minutes later the canyon widened with dramatic suddenness, and there was grass underfoot, the gleam of a lake to her right and the open spaces of the tundra in front of her, leading all the way down to the sea. She let out her breath in a long sigh. ''That's better.''

Ryan shot her a quick, inscrutable glance. ''Do you want to rest here? Or we could go straight down to the creek and stop there for a while.''

She wanted to put the canyon behind her as quickly as possible. ''Let's go to the creek,'' she said promptly.

It was downhill most of the way, to the accompaniment of the plovers' whistling calls and the sun's dazzling brightness. But the walking was hard for all that, and Ryan explained how the bitter winter temperatures froze the ground unevenly, leaving tussocks of grass islanded by wet, peaty soil so that one had the choice of balancing from tussock to tussock or letting one's boots sink into the wet mud.

"Hobson's choice," Karen said, pink-cheeked from the exercise. "Listen—what's that, Ryan?" From the nearest range of hills came a deep croaking call. "A raven?"

He already had his binoculars trained on the slopes. "Look to the left of that outcrop of rock—it's a sandhill crane." Following his instructions she found in the field of her binoculars a large brown heronlike bird stalking along the ground on long, spindly legs. "That's quite a rarity," Ryan said. "It's a young one, for the adults are slate gray. It lives on insects."

"Insects? Up here?"

"Oh, yes. Spiders and so on."

It seemed amazing to Karen that such a large bird could survive on the limited insect life of the tundra. Wondering if Rusty would have known as much about the crane, she walked on, the guttural, far-reaching calls following her. The ground had evened out now, for they were near the streambed, and Ryan said cheerfully, "This is the nearest thing you'll find to a forest in Pond Inlet."

She already knew that the willow was the only woody plant to grow this far north, but any specimens she had seen so far had been vinelike, creeping along the ground. These were all of eighteen inches tall, the stems gnarled and twisted, the seed pods a fluffy white. Forest was a misnomer. Yet that they should grow at all seemed something of a miracle.

The willows thinned as she and Ryan approached the creek, where Ryan pointed out a couple of late-flowering clumps of vivid purple saxifrage on its banks. The water rushed over the stones, but it wasn't crystal clear as she might have expected. Instead it was opaque, the color of watered-down milk. Ryan smiled at her, anticipating her question. "It's glacial runoff, so it's full of silt. Why don't you dip your feet in it? You'll find it refreshing after all that walking."

He was unlacing his own boots, pulling off his socks and rolling up his trouser legs, and she followed suit. The water was, not surprisingly, as cold as ice. Numbingly cold. But she did get used to it. "Or else," she said jokingly to Ryan, "all the feeling's gone because my feet are frozen."

He splashed her, and she shrieked as the icy droplets hit her skin, retaliating instantly by scooping up a handful of water and flinging it at his chest, then retreating for the shore as fast as she could. He caught her at the edge, rubbing his cold wet fingers up her bare arms as she laughed up at him, struggling to free herself.

The laughter died from his face. His hands moved to her shoulders and he bent his head, his eyes closing as he found her mouth. His lips were very warm, very sure of themselves. Her own were still. Then, very tentatively, there was the first quiver of response, the softening of her mouth under his, the first unmistakable yielding of her body.

Perhaps it went to his head. His grip tightened, his mouth demanding more of her. She tensed, pulling back, and the fleeting moment of rapport was gone. But as Ryan looked up, his eyes gazing straight into hers, they both knew it had happened.

Her eyes fell. "My feet are cold."

"I've got a towel in my haversack. I'll get it for you."

Karen perched on a rock as he pulled a towel out of his pack, passing her an apple as he did so. Then he knelt at her feet, picking up one foot and beginning to rub it. "I can do that," she said shyly.

He glanced up at her. "Let me."

She bit into the apple, knowing she was blushing. His downbent head was very close to her, so close she could see how the sun had streaked his hair. It was thick hair with a slight tendency to wave, and she was suddenly visited by the urge to run her fingers through it to see if it was as soft as it looked. Quickly she took another bite of the apple.

He was being very gentle as he kneaded her flesh back to life, although through the towel she could sense the latent strength of his hands. Beside his tanned skin hers looked very pale, the veins a delicate blue tracery over her fine-boned ankles and slim feet. In her innocence she had made no real protest when he had offered to do this for her, for what harm could come of him drying her feet? Yet as she watched his soothing, rhythmic movements, saw how his fingers lingered on the fragile lines of her ankle, she knew she had been wrong. What he was doing was more intimate than anything he had done to her before, more intimate even than that brief, shattering kiss. Then she felt him lift her foot, bending his head to kiss her instep, his mouth sliding over her cool, soft skin.

Deep within her something stirred to life, a sweet

wild ache that she had never experienced before. Lightly as a butterfly wing her hands rested on his hair, holding him there, prolonging the birth of something she could not have named. He laid his cheek against her ankle and murmured her name.

She came back to reality, the shock running through her body as she pushed him away. "Don't!"

Slowly he straightened, passing her her socks and boots, then he began to dry his own feet, the brilliance fading from his eyes until he looked very thoughtful. Lacing up his Kodiaks, he said quietly, "Karen, you're as capable of passion and desire as any other woman."

"Don't be silly," she said shortly.

"I'm not. Look, we've always tried to be honest with each other, haven't we? We both know what happened just now, and earlier, when I kissed you. You liked what I did, didn't you?"

As though she was confessing to something shameful, her head drooped and her voice was so low he could hardly hear it. "Maybe I did. But—"

"I know you did." He couldn't disguise the exultant note in his voice. "I was afraid that all your feelings were buried so deeply that I'd never be able to reach them. But I was wrong, and thank God for it."

Her hair had fallen forward to hide her face; her fingers were twisting in her lap. More gently Ryan added, "It's nothing to be ashamed of, Karen. It's normal and natural and right."

"You don't understand!" she burst out incoherently. "It's only because I feel safe with you that I—that I can respond. You promised you'd never be rough with me again, not after I fainted.'' Her gray eyes were troubled as she sought to make him understand. "I don't know why I believe in that promise but I do, Ryan. I trust you. So you see, I know I'm safe. I know nothing's going to happen."

He would not allow her eyes to drop. "By nothing you mean I won't actually make love to you, don't you? But, Karen, what happened here this afternoon was something far more significant than if I had made love to you. *You* responded. However briefly, and however much you might wonder right now how it happened, you did respond. Because you can't fake that."

"But only because I knew I was safe," she repeated helplessly.

"And I promise you'll always be safe with me. But safe can mean many things, and the day will come when we will make love, and you'll be safer in my arms than you have ever been anywhere else or with anyone else in your life. I swear that."

She shook her head. "No—that can never happen! You don't understand."

She might just as well not have spoken. "I'll never do anything you don't want, I promise that, too. But I'm going to bring you back to life, Karen. Make you a whole and passionate woman."

Almost hypnotized by the intensity of his eyes, she said faintly, "But why, Ryan? Why are you bothering to do this?"

For the first time he looked away from her, across the creek to the eastern range of mountains and the blindingly bright snowfields trapped in their heights.

"Because I care what happens to you," he said finally. "I think I'm falling in love with you. Or maybe I already have. I know the thought of you haunts me day and night."

Shaken to the core of her being, Karen whispered, "Oh, Ryan, you mustn't do that—I'll be no good to you. I'm *not* like normal women, no matter what you say."

"Maybe you're not now, but you can be," he said stubbornly.

It was perhaps not irrelevant that once again she noticed the determination in his chin. "I'll never marry," she said flatly.

He quirked an eyebrow at her. "I haven't asked you yet."

It disconcerted her, as he must have known it would. She stammered, "Well, I didn't mean . . . ."

He was laughing. "Sorry—but I couldn't resist it."

She couldn't resist his laughter, and the tension between them dissolved. Ryan stood up, stretching to his full height, his shirt taut over his flat stomach and the breadth of his chest. "We'd better get going if we're going to be back for supper. We've got to follow the creek to the sea and then go along the beach."

She tightened the laces on her boots and stood up too, putting the much-lightened haversack on her back. "How far is that?" she asked resignedly.

"Four or five miles. No distance at all."

She winced theatrically. "A pleasant afternoon stroll. Lead on."

He picked up his haversack, the sun limning his figure. Then he hesitated for a moment. Moving closer, he smiled down at her. "You're a lovely woman, Karen Smythe, and don't you forget it."

She half closed her eyes, knowing he was going to kiss her, waiting for that warm, firm pressure. She should have known better than to try and anticipate him. Instead of a kiss his lips brushed hers back and forth tantalizingly. Then his teeth caught her lower lip, nibbling at it with exquisite gentleness. Swiftly he drew her to him so that her breasts touched the hardness of his chest. Then just as swiftly he put her away from him, his hands falling to his sides. The pulse at his throat throbbed against his skin.

Her breasts were tingling, the tips pushing against her shirt. Her lips felt soft and swollen. And he had done this to her, this big, handsome man with his devil-may-care smile and his contradictory mixture of toughness and sensitivity.

He said softly, "Shall we go?" Not waiting for her to answer, he began cutting across the rock-strewn bed of the creek in a direct line to the sea.

They were late for supper, for the four or five miles that Ryan had mentioned entailed crossing a bog, clambering over boulders on the beach and climbing two ranges of hills. They ate together, Ryan firmly keeping the conversation in impersonal channels, then he disappeared to his tent to do some work. "To placate your father." He grinned. "That was a nice day, Karen—thanks."

"I enjoyed it, too," she said, knowing it for the truth and sorry to see him go. However, she was very tired, so she soaked in a hot bath, changing into clean clothes. After chatting briefly with Lucas and Tuglik she went to bed, there to sleep the clock round.

She was to regret missing breakfast, for when she wandered over to the hotel at ten-thirty to get a cup of coffee, Lucas handed her a note, her name in a forceful, angular script on the envelope. "Ryan left this for you," he said.

"Left it? Where's he gone?"

"Him and your father went to their dig near Cape Hatt. Said they'd be gone four days."

"Oh." Karen digested the news in silence, rather horrified by the intensity of her disappointment. She had been looking forward to seeing Ryan again. "Thanks, Lucas."

"There's boxes of cereal under the counter and milk in the kitchen if you're hungry," he added, giving her his gap-toothed smile.

"Sounds like a great idea." She went into the empty dining room, sat down and tore open the envelope.

The note was very brief and seemed to have been written in considerable haste, its gist being that her father had decided first thing that morning that it was necessary for him and Ryan to spend more time at the dig. "So we're leaving right away," Ryan had written. "He's not in the best of tempers, Karen, so I haven't suggested you come along. I'll see you as soon as we get back. Take care of yourself. Love, Ryan."

Love, Ryan. The words seemed to leap off the page at her. Did he put that on every letter he wrote, casually, without thought? Or did he mean what he had said yesterday about falling in love with her? She bit her lip, wishing that he was here or that she had been able to go with him. But her father would never have countenanced that, she thought bitterly.

How Laurence had changed! All through her childhood he had been away a lot—that had been part of the pattern of their family life. But when he was home he had been a loving and attentive father, and she had many happy memories of picnics, trips to museums and holidays at the beach. If only he would show the slightest interest in her now, she would find the courage to ask for an explanation for the drastic change in his relationship to her. It had happened, of course, after his separation from Nancy. But it was Nancy he had divorced, not her and Mandy. Why, then, those years of obdurate silence?

She ate her breakfast and went outside. The sky was overcast and the wind had a bite to it; after so much exercise the day before she didn't feel like going for a walk. Particularly alone, she was honest enough to admit to herself. She'd go to her tent and read the sociology text she'd brought, and maybe she'd try classifying some of the flowers she'd pressed. And this evening she could visit Mary Ann and Don....

As it happened, Mary Ann was alone, because Don was working on the greenhouse he was building behind his own bungalow. "I think he's crazy," his fiancée said frankly. "But he's convinced he can grow stuff like cabbages and peas and lettuce up here. And if he could it certainly would be marvelous to have the fresh vegetables. I'm so glad you came for a visit."

There could be no doubting her sincerity, and Karen relaxed. They sat in the tiny living room with coffee and homemade doughnuts and indulged in what Mary Ann called "girl talk," although they soon moved from superficial chatter to some of the very real problems that the Inuit were facing in places like Pond Inlet; to the scope of Mary Ann's job as a nurse in a village without a resident doctor; to Karen's job at the drop-in center as well as some of her difficulties with her mother. Karen soon discovered that Mary Ann was both honest and kind, tougher-minded than Karen but by no means insensitive. The talk had passed on to marriage, Mary Ann's future and careers versus babies. Somehow Karen was emboldened to say, "Mary Ann, can I ask you something very personal?"

"Sure."

"You and Don—" She gulped, embarrassed. "This is none of my business, I know, but—do you *like* making love, Mary Ann?"

The other woman offered no false protestations that she and Don had not slept together. "With Don I love it. But then I love Don."

"So it's a question of loving the person?"

For a moment the nurse hesitated. "Not always, I'm sure. But as Don's the only man I've ever slept with, my experience isn't exactly vast." She paused, her curly head on one side. "Are you saying that you don't? Like it, I mean."

"I've never done it." Karen stared down at her lap. "You see, something happened when I was a teenager, and it completely put me off the idea of ever making love with anyone. I've always just assumed I'd never marry or have any kind of a normal relationship. But then, when I see you and Don together...."

"Look," Mary Ann said bluntly, "I'm only a nurse, not even a psychiatric nurse. If you've got some kind of deep-rooted aversion to the thought of having sexual relations with anyone, then I think you should get professional help. But having said that, let me say something else."

She paused, sorting out her thoughts, giving Karen the chance to say in a small voice, "I think you must be a very good nurse. Even if you're not a psychiatric one."

Mary Ann laughed. "Thanks! I hope I can say what I want to say. You see, sex to me isn't just the act itself. It's a way of communicating, of sharing, of being intimate in far more than the physical sense. It means taking a risk, too, because you're making yourself vulnerable to another person and trusting he won't take advantage of it. But if everything goes right, then you can be closer to another person than I, at any rate, ever thought possible. Do you see what I mean?"

"Yes. Yes, I think I do."

"Maybe part of your problem is that you've never met the person you want to take that kind of risk with—which has nothing to do with whatever happened to you. Don't confuse the two things. I'll bet they're quite different."

Oddly enough it was Ryan's face that was in the forefront of Karen's mind. She could almost feel the weight of his hands on her shoulders, the gentle, questing warmth of his mouth on hers. He had talked of trust, too.... "Thank you, Mary Ann," she said simply.

Recognizing that the subject was closed, the other woman said lightly, "Anytime. I'll send you a bill at the end of the month!" She cocked her head. "That sounds like Don. I'd better put on some fresh coffee."

When the two of them came into the living room, Don had his arm around Mary Ann, whose rosy cheeks and yielding body told their own story. Karen stayed long enough for appearance' sake, then left to go back to the Parcoll, her gray eyes very thoughtful as she mulled over everything Mary Ann had said.

THE FOLLOWING DAY Karen went out on the tundra to photograph some wild flowers, and then took her father's binoculars to the beach, where the sandpipers and shore birds totally confused her. They all looked alike, she thought in exasperation. It was very well for the book to say that whether the middle tail feathers were more obtuse or the bill broadened near the tip would readily distinguish one species from another. The birds didn't stand still long enough for her to even focus on the tail feathers or the bill.

Back at the hotel Rusty was just leaving the dining room as she arrived. "I really needed you an hour ago," she said jokingly. "How do you tell all those wretched little sandpipers apart?".

He smiled, although his pale eyes shifted to the door. "They're a bit of a nightmare, aren't they? I'm in a hurry, Karen—"

She detained him a minute longer. "I know what else I wanted to tell you—Ryan and I saw a sandhill crane the other day out by Janes Creek."

"Did you? Good for you."

No real interest appeared in his face. On sudden inspiration she added, "It was a young one, so it was slate gray all over."

"You're turning into quite the bird-watcher, aren't you?" An indefinable note in his voice sent a shiver down her spine. "I've got to go. See you later."

Wherever he was going, he plainly did not want company. And a young sandhill crane was a rusty brown color, not gray; the adults were gray. Surely as an ornithologist Rusty should have known that? Ryan was not an ornithologist, and he had known. Frowning, she stared after him.

The evening passed quickly, for the First Air flight had come in that afternoon while she was down on the beach and the crew was staying overnight. Mike Riley, the pilot, was flatteringly pleased to see her again, particularly in the absence of "that big blond fella," as he called Ryan. The air crew joined with the construction workers in a lengthy game of cards, as a result of which Karen lost three dollars and thirty-five cents and Mike won nearly seven dollars. "You must have cheated," she said amiably.

"How can you say such a thing, and me as honest as the day is long?"

The sunlight was still streaming in the window even

though it was past midnight. "Say that again in December," Karen remarked primly.

Amid general laughter she said her good-nights and went to bed. But she did not sleep well that night. She found herself thinking about Ryan, wondering what he was doing, wondering if he had thought of her at all since he had left the inlet. She knew she would have enjoyed the evening more if he had been there. Mike might not have won the seven dollars quite so easily, either, she thought with a smile. She wished Ryan was coming back tomorrow. But he had said four days, which meant the day after tomorrow. . . .

She did sleep eventually, but the next day she felt restless and out of sorts, particularly after Mike and his crew left. With the feeling that she was trespassing, but using the fact that she had finished the mystery books as an excuse, she went to Ryan's Parcoll and pushed open the door; none of the tents had locks. Quickly she picked out another book, then studied the array of family photographs with a certain wistfulness, for they all looked so happy to be in each other's company.

There were other traces of Ryan in the tent as well: a pile of notes on the desk in the angular handwriting she now knew; a book open on his bed; a shirt flung across the back of the chair. She found herself picking it up as if to fold it, then holding it to her face, catching from it the elusive scent of his skin. It made him seem very close, almost as if he was in the room with her. So acutely that she was frightened, she wished that he was there. Yet why, she wondered, staring at the shirt in her hands as if she had never seen one before. What did she want of him?

It was a question she either could not or would not answer. Putting the shirt back on the chair, she looked around her once more, knowing that she had been there long enough, that she must go back to her own tent and decide what she was going to do with the day. Then her eyes fell on a couple of rolled-up bundles on the floor at the foot of the bed, and with a quickening of her pulse she knew it was a tent and sleeping bag.

She had done some camping with Duke and his friends, enough to know that she enjoyed it. She could carry the gear in her backpack, get some food from the kitchen and camp out on the hills tonight. It wouldn't get dark, so she wouldn't mind being alone, particularly on the wide open stretches of the tundra. She could go beyond Salmon Creek to the river, and maybe follow it part of the way up to Utuk Lake. She might even see a gyrfalcon.

She unrolled the sleeping bag, discovering it to be of top-quality down, then checked the tent. A one-man pup tent, bright orange, it had all the necessary poles and pegs. No problems there. Forgetting her earlier sensation of trespassing, she rummaged through the gear stashed in the far corner, finding a small stove complete with fuel that she could use to heat her food. The last real find was an ensolite pad that would make sleeping a great deal more comfortable.

Finding pencil and paper on the desk, she wrote Ryan a note, explaining what she had taken and where she was going. Hesitating for a long moment, she merely signed the note *Karen*. Then she gathered everything and went to her own tent to pack, first scrounging some food from the kitchen.

She packed extra socks, waterproof matches, toque and mittens, a book to read. Regretfully she had to leave the bird book behind, for it was much too heavy to carry that far. A last-minute check to see that she hadn't forgotten anything and she was ready. Putting the pack on the bed, she turned and eased the wide padded straps over her shoulders, fastening the hip band and adjusting the weight a trifle so it rested more comfortably on her back. Then she left the Parcoll, carefully closing the door behind her.

She cut up behind the hotel and tramped along the runway, partly because she didn't want to see the team of mangy-looking huskies on the beach again. She took her time, resting often, studying the flowers and the lichens, and for well over an hour perching herself on the crest of the hill to watch a group of seals in the water. There were three lemmings dashing around the network of tunnels by the creek; they took up more of her time.

She ate her lunch midafternoon, and it was well into the evening before she selected a campsite. She had gone beyond the creek to the river, following its curving course for some distance before branching off toward a lake to the west. The lake was crystal clear and very still, the mountains of Bylot Island reflected on its surface, its bottom smooth yellow sand. A built-in water supply, Karen thought in some satisfaction, feeling rather pleased with herself as she flattened out an area for the tent and began to erect it. Then she prepared her bed and cooked her evening meal, a can of spaghetti with some of the hotel's homemade bread, followed by an apple with some cookies and a mug of tea, milkless but nevertheless very good.

Her watch read ten-thirty. She turned out the little stove and carefully stacked her garbage by the tent, ready to be carried home with her tomorrow. *She* wasn't going to leave any cans lying around the tundra, not like Rusty, she thought decidedly. She cleaned her teeth at the edge of the lake, then slid into the tent, taking off her boots and her heavy sweater, but leaving on her trousers and her thin T-shirt. Zipping up the bag, she soon felt her body heat warm it up and almost immediately fell asleep.

Outside the sun continued its lingering circle over the mountaintops, while the deep, slow currents carried the drift ice toward the frigid waters of Baffin Bay....

CHAPTER NINE

KAREN AWOKE WITH A START, her first sensation that of having been asleep for quite a while. Her second sensation was of sheer terror. Something or someone was moving around outside her tent. There was a rattle of stones, then the clatter of a tin can against the rocks and a heavy, snuffling breathing. Not a person then, she thought with fleeting relief. An animal. But what?

From the noises she could tell that the can was being very thoroughly investigated. At another time she might have been amused by the snorts of apparent exasperation only a few feet away from her. But an unpleasant musky odor was seeping into the tent, and she knew with a chilling of her blood that so much noise could only be produced by a large animal. A polar bear.

Across her brain flashed the memory of the posters at the air terminal. The Hand That Feeds Could Get Eaten. Stay Alert, Stay Alive. She should never have left the empty can outside the tent, she knew that now. She should have buried it. She should never have come out here alone to start with.

Rigid with fear, she lay absolutely still. The bear seemed to have abandoned the can and was nosing at her boots, which she had left outside the flap. She could see its huge shadow thrown against the end wall of the tent. It flipped one of the boots into the air and let it drop, grunting almost as though the solitary game amused it.

Please go away, she prayed. *Oh, God, why did I come out here alone? Please let the bear go away.*

It was still playing with her boots, the growls growing louder. Then its paw must have swiped the tent, catching one of the guy ropes, for the whole corner of the tent sagged inward. The animal began snuffling along the edge of the tent, which was swaying unsteadily.

Karen could feel the scream gathering in her throat. She fought it back, knowing instinctively that her best—indeed, her only—defense lay in staying absolutely still. Her nails were biting into her palms. Her eyes were wide open, her mouth a tight line. She would not scream. She would not.

But then the bear reared up on its hind legs. She knew it had for she could hear it snorting over her head. A paw descended, ripping the tent open down one side.

She closed her eyes, unable to move, knowing with a strange sense of detachment that this was the end. She was going to die, alone on the tundra, and she would never see Ryan again.

The new noise scarcely registered in her brain. A sharp crack, like a gunshot, she thought confusedly. And then a man's voice yelling at the top of his lungs.

She was so close to the bear that its confusion became her own. Through the gaping holes in the nylon fabric she could see yellow white paws and sensed that it had dropped to all fours, the better to assess this new threat. The voice yelled again, and with a wave of relief that almost made her ill, she knew it was Ryan.

She heard the paws scuffle on the ground, heard the low grumble of the bear's breath. It seemed to move away a bit and she bunched her muscles, wondering if she should try to make a dash for safety. As if he had read her mind, Ryan shouted, "Karen! Stay flat—don't move!"

The shadow had fallen across the tent again, and suddenly the bear roared. A primitive and ferocious sound, it echoed in her brain. Ryan had come too late, she thought numbly. He would not be able to save her.

The second gunshot was closer, and to the end of her days she would remember the horrible sound of the bullet striking flesh. She heard the great body thud to the ground. The tent quivered and was still.

Then footsteps sounded across the stones. A man's voice, in an agony of fear, demanded, "Karen! Are you all right?"

She sat up, fumbling ineffectively with the zipper on the sleeping bag. Then Ryan was hauling her bodily through the gaping hole in the side of the tent, his hands running over her to ascertain that she was indeed unhurt. "It didn't touch you?"

"N-no." Scarcely able to stand up, she sagged against him, burying her face in his sweater. "Oh, Ryan, I was so sc-scared...." She was shaking all over, and it took her several moments to realize that the heavy pounding under her cheek was the pounding of his heart, not hers.

"*You* were scared," he said grimly. "What the hell do you think I was? I could see the bear around your tent when I was much too far away to do anything. I certainly couldn't shoot from that distance in case I hit you as well. I've never felt so bloody helpless in my whole life."

"I—I really thought I was going to die." She was still shuddering, the memory of those terror-filled minutes horribly real. But if she had expected sympathy, she was soon disappointed.

"It would have served you right if you had." His hands tightened around her upper arms, and he gave her a shake. "What possessed you to do such a damfool thing in the first place?"

"Wh-what do you mean?" She gaped at him, shrinking from the fury in the blazing blue eyes.

"Coming out camping like this by yourself. Don't you know that one of the cardinal rules of the wilderness is never to travel alone? That's common sense, damn it!"

He was shaking her again, although with one part of her brain she was sure he didn't know he was doing it. "I—I knew I couldn't get lost," she stammered. "And I knew it wasn't going to get dark. I didn't think there'd be any danger." But his anger didn't abate. His nails were digging into her skin through her thin cotton shirt and she added rebelliously, "Stop it! You're hurting me."

"I feel like hurting you," Ryan grated. "Not only did you scare me out of ten years' growth because I thought you were going to be mauled to death in front of my eyes—''

"Would it have done that?"

"Polar bears can kill seals by crushing their skulls. They've been known to do the same to humans. Surely you've seen the posters at the airport? They're not just there for fun, you know."

She had been foolish, incredibly foolish. A stranger in a cruel land, she had ventured out alone with all the bravado of the ignorant. "I'm sorry," she said, trying to meet his eyes without flinching from them. "I do see I shouldn't have come."

Her apology didn't placate him in the least: if anything, it seemed to make him angrier. "Saying you're sorry is useless," he snarled. "Because do you know what else you've done? You made me shoot a wild animal, a species that's called this land home for thousands of years and that's marvelously well adapted to it. Or was, until the white man came with his guns and his lust to kill." He broke off, taking a deep breath. His voice was flat when he spoke again. "I like to think of myself as a conservationist. I want to preserve the wildlife here, not kill it off indiscriminately. But because of you, I had to kill that animal."

Karen pressed trembling hands to her cheeks. He might forgive her the scare she had given him, but he would never forgive her for the killing, she thought numbly. For she had made him act against his own nature. He was a strong and resourceful man, but he was far too knowledgeable of the consequences to be a killer. Not for him the polar bear rug in front of the fireplace, the narwhal tusk polished and hung on the wall.

As if drawn by a magnet her eyes left him and looked over her shoulder toward the tent. The rifle was lying on the ground. Ryan had felled the bear with one shot; it had been a quick, clean death. The bear was lying crumpled on its side, and in one glance its image was imprinted on her brain—the black pads on its paws and the great claws, useless now, that had ripped through the tent. The black snout and the small, rounded ears set close to its massive and beautiful head. The thick, luxuriant fur, more yellowish white than pure white.... The trickle of blood on its chest was startlingly red, and he was the one responsible for the shedding of that blood.

Ryan said coldly, ''We'll have to leave everything as it is because I'll have to come back here with the police constable. Get your jacket and your boots and we'll go.''

To fetch her jacket from the tent she would have to go very close to the bear. Feeling as though it was a form of penance, she knelt at the tent flap and pulled out her jacket and sweater, the odor of the bear rank in her nostrils. Forgetting for a moment about Ryan, she rested her palm on its flank, feeling the fur under her fingers and wishing with all her heart she could undo the wrong she had done. Then she got up and retrieved her boots from the hollow in the ground where the bear had tossed them. When she saw the tooth marks in the thick leather, she began trembling again in spite of herself, and it seemed to take a long time to lace and tie her boots.

Ryan didn't offer to help her. When she got to her feet, doing up her jacket and fumbling in the pockets for her mittens, he had already started walking toward the river. There was something in the set of his shoulders that discouraged any urge she might have had to say anything. Pulling up the hood of her jacket against the cold, she trudged after him.

The sun had disappeared behind the clouds. To the south more clouds hung low over the mountains, blurring the slopes with a whiteness that she realized was new snow. The nearer hills looked almost black against the gray sky, black and lonely. The plovers were silent.

Ryan was setting a killing pace, his long legs striding across the rocky ground. Too proud to ask him to slow down, Karen hurried after him, the exercise at least having the effect of taking the chill from her bones and stopping the trembling of her limbs. She tried very hard not to think, to concentrate solely on putting one foot in front of the other, but it was an impossible task. Bleakly she was forced to face one inescapable conclusion: she had forfeited Ryan's good opinion of her, certainly any love he might have felt for her. She had acted foolishly and thoughtlessly, and while she had been lucky to get away with her life, the net result was that she'd forced Ryan into an act he would find hard to forgive himself for, let alone her. Now that she had lost his esteem, it occurred to her with utter clarity how much she had come to value it. She had regarded him as a friend, as someone she could trust. The loss of his friendship just when she was beginning to appreciate it came as a bitter blow. She found herself watching the loose-limbed grace of his movements, the way the breeze stirred his hair, while inwardly she wept for the ending of something that had scarcely begun. At an even deeper level she was frightened by the intensity of her grief. How had he gained such a hold on her in so short a time? Her thoughts circled around and around, going nowhere, numbing her with depression.

He kept up his merciless pace until they were within sight of the hamlet. Then, so abruptly that she almost cannoned into him, he stopped. They were standing above the little cemetery with its stark rows of wooden crosses and its mounds of rocks. Staring downward, he said flatly, "Karen, I've finally started to use my brain. That bear was a young one, a male. He must have got marooned on land when the ice broke up, because normally they stay on the floes all summer hunting seals. But he wasn't in particularly good condition, so he'd probably been subsisting on lichens and berries and whatever carrion he could find. Sooner or later he would have been attracted to the village, especially to the dump, and he would have had to have been shot anyway...it would have been inevitable. But it's taken me this long to figure that out. I guess I was so angry at first I couldn't see straight. It wasn't fair of me to throw all the blame on you—I'm sorry."

She looked at him warily. "Oh. You're not just telling me that to make me feel better?"

He produced the semblance of a smile. "You should know me better than that."

Somehow his honesty loosened her own tongue. "But I did a very foolish thing, Ryan, I see that now."

"Thank God you left me a note, or I'd never have found you."

"You came back early?" An unnecessary question, but it helped to bridge the gap between them.

"We finished sooner than we thought. I was anxious to get back to see you."

No particular emotion in his voice, simply the stating of a fact. She tucked it in the back of her mind to examine later, knowing there was another fact that needed to be stated. "You saved my life," she said simply. "I haven't even thanked you for that."

"I can hardly blame you. I wasn't exactly in an approachable mood, was I?"

"No, you weren't," she said honestly. "But perhaps I'd have been just as angry in your shoes."

His hands were shoved in his pockets, his shoulders hunched against the wind. "Maybe so," he said hoarsely. "You see, I was afraid it was going to be Sally all over again, another death for which I'd be responsible. If it hadn't been for my urging, you wouldn't have come up here in the first place. And if Laurence and I hadn't left for three days, you wouldn't have gone camping on your own." He swung around to look at her, his eyes anguished. "I don't think I could have borne to have had your death on my hands."

She didn't stop to think. Swiftly she closed the gap between them, putting her arms around his unyielding body and tilting her head up to his. "I'm safe,

Ryan," she said fiercely. "Don't you see—*you* saved me. You saved my life. Surely in some small way that negates any part you had in Sally's death."

He put an arm around her, stroking her cheek with his free hand. "I'm not sure it's that simple, Karen. But thank you, anyway."

Longing to comfort him, yet not knowing how, she took his hand in hers and held it to her cheek. "Your fingers are cold."

"Oh, Karen," he said helplessly. Cupping her face in his palms, he kissed her, a kiss so full of tenderness that for a heart-stopping moment she thought the very bones would melt in her body. His mouth still against hers, he murmured, "Do you realize what you're doing? You're touching me of your own free will. You're kissing me as though you enjoy it." He slid his lips up her cheek and across her closed eyelids, exploring all the delicate contours of her face, before seeking her mouth again. "Sweetheart...."

Only one word, but it was enough to break the spell. She jerked her head away. "Ryan, don't—" For a moment she thought he was going to resist her and she pushed hard against his chest. "Let go!"

Without hurrying he let his arms drop. There was a reckless light in his blue eyes. "The day—or night—will come when you won't ask me to let go."

She shook her head in passionate denial. "You're wrong. I'll never be able to...." She faltered to a stop. "I'm not like other women, Ryan. I will never be."

"Three weeks ago when we first met did you think

you'd ever reach out with your hand and touch me, or take pleasure in being kissed?"

"No. But—"

"Of course you didn't. You're changing, Karen. It won't happen overnight, but it will happen. I know it will. And, believe me, I'm patient enough to wait. I'll wait for months if I have to."

Her lashes flickered. "I'm cold—let's go back."

She was not surprised when he followed her lead; it wasn't his policy to force her, she knew. "Yes, we'd better. Laurence will be worried."

"Sure," she said with more than a touch of sarcasm.

"Don't underestimate him, Karen."

"Oh, we've been through all this before," she answered edgily. Too much had happened in the past few hours and all she wanted now was some time alone. "Let's go."

They covered the rest of the distance in a determined silence, which Ryan broke when they reached the hotel. "Before you go to bed, I want you to see your father."

"You can tell him I'm all right."

"You're going to do it, Karen," he said inflexibly.

She was quite sure there was no point in arguing with that tone of voice, for he'd pick her up bodily if she refused to do as he asked. "Damn you, Ryan Koetsier," she seethed. "The last thing I need right now is another rebuff from my father."

He put a hand under her elbow, herding her along the plank walkway. "Come on."

Laurence must have heard the sound of their footsteps. Before they reached his Parcoll, he had flung open the door and was walking toward them, both hands outstretched. "Karen! I was so worried about you. Are you all right?"

Somehow his arms were around her and she was being pressed against his shirtfront. He was painfully thin, she thought, stupefied. "I'm fine," she managed to say.

"You're cold. Come inside."

The three of them went inside, Laurence still holding on to her. The warmth felt exquisite, while the clutter of books and papers looked miraculously ordinary. Karen was trembling again, as much from exhaustion as from delayed shock. "What's wrong?" her father said sharply.

Humiliatingly she knew she was going to cry. She tried to pull away, her eyes blurring with tears. But Laurence pulled her close again, patting her back awkwardly, like a man not used to such contacts, and for some reason that was the final straw. Karen began to cry, deep sobs bursting from her, her hands clutching at her father's shirt as if it was all that kept her upright.

The storm of weeping had to end. She felt a handkerchief pressed into her hand and blew her nose, then heard Ryan explaining what had happened. "I left the rifle and all the gear there," he finished. "I'll have to go back with the constable later on."

"You could have been killed," Laurence said shakily to his daughter.

"She very nearly was."

"Then I'd have lost you for the second time. Ryan, I'll never be able to thank you enough."

Karen was calmer now, for the tears had eased her tension. "What do you mean, you'd have lost me for the second time?" she demanded.

Laurence looked faintly surprised by her question. "The first time was when your mother and I separated. We lost contact then, didn't we? Although I never intended that to happen."

She straightened, unable to keep the resentment from her voice. "It was your fault that it happened. You never wrote."

There was a frown on the lean, tired-looking face, but he said mildly enough, "Come now, you know that's not true. Although I can hardly blame you if you thought the separation was my fault. I should never have married Nancy. Young as I was at the time, I knew right away that we weren't suited."

She hardly heard him. "You didn't write! I waited and waited for letters from you, particularly after I was sent to boarding school. You never answered any of mine."

The frown was more pronounced. Laurence said slowly, "Do you mind if we sit down while we sort this out? I'm rather tired." As he lowered himself carefully into the room's only chair, Karen perched on the bed, unlacing her boots and tucking her feet under her, dimly conscious of Ryan standing quietly in the corner. She, too, was tired, but not for anything would she have gone to bed right now. It was time for some plain speaking; time for the truth.

She said, trying to keep her voice expressionless,

"I wrote you at least half a dozen letters. The last one I wrote, from the boarding school, came back address unknown, and when I asked mother what your new address was she said she didn't know, you hadn't told her. She said that I should accept the facts: that you didn't want to keep in touch, that your work was more important than your family and that you wanted to be left alone. So after that I didn't write any more."

Laurence said deliberately, "I gave your mother a forwarding address. I was doing a lot of traveling at that time, most of it in inaccessible places, but I had a box number in Yellowknife and she knew that."

Karen stared at him in consternation. He had not welcomed her visit to Pond Inlet, and he had been distant and cold to her, but it never occurred to her now that he was telling her anything but the truth. He was a man of probity, she knew. If he said her mother had known his address, then she had. Finally she found her voice. "But didn't you get any of the other letters? The earlier ones?"

"No, I didn't." Very gently he added, "Who mailed them, Karen? Did you?"

She had seen it coming. "No. Mother did. For a while after . . . ."

"After the kidnapping," he supplied gravely.

She gulped. "Yes. Afterward for quite a while I wouldn't even go outdoors. So she took the letters for me. She never mailed them, did she?"

"I don't think she did, no. I could understand one going astray, or maybe even two. But five or six?"

"Why would she have done such a thing?" Karen was leaning forward, her face anguished.

"I don't know, Karen," Laurence answered soberly. "I don't think your mother copes very well with the idea of being alone. Perhaps deep down she was afraid you and Mandy would leave her and go and live with me—maybe not then, but at some time in the future. So she saw to it that you both lost contact with me. That way she'd be safe."

It fitted the facts. Karen knew all too well Nancy's abnormal possessiveness, the illnesses, genuine or imagined, that kept her two daughters close at hand. "Did you write to us back then?"

"I certainly did. But when I didn't hear from you, I wrote less often. Looking back, I think I should have persisted. But so much of the time I was in out-of-the-way places, hundreds of miles from a telephone or a post office, and, in all honesty, enjoying both the work and the newfound freedom. As I said earlier, I don't think I should ever have married."

"Mother is exceptionally possessive," Karen said quietly.

He shot her a quick glance. "You realize that now, do you?"

"Oh, yes. I think she did hold back all my letters, and intercept yours to me and Mandy. It was very wrong of her." She paused. "It explains something else, too. When I told her I was coming up here, I sensed she was afraid of something, although I couldn't understand what. I know now. She was afraid I'd find out that she'd intercepted your letters."

Laurence stirred restlessly. "Try not to be too hard on her, Karen. The whole setup was wrong. Ironically, it was the kidnapping that really revealed how fragile our marriage was. We fought tooth and nail over everything. She wanted to go to the police right away, I wanted to pay the money and get you home and then go to the police. In the end we did it my way—"

"You mean you're the one who insisted on paying the ransom?" she interrupted, stunned.

"Yes. Why do you ask?"

"Mother always told me the exact opposite. That you were more interested in catching the kidnappers than in getting me home safely."

"That's simply not true, Karen. We paid the money, we got you home and only after that did we put the police on their trail. As you know, none of them was ever caught."

Karen's head was bent, her shining dark hair parting at her nape. In the shadows Ryan stood motionless. "I fought her about the psychiatrist, too," Laurence continued. "Couldn't stand the man, a pompous fool with enough letters behind his name to paper a room and not the slightest understanding of what made people tick. The whole idea of boarding school was hers as well. I thought you'd be better off at home, in an environment you knew, with your family around you. But your mother didn't know how to handle you after the kidnapping, you'd changed so much, you were so quiet and withdrawn. So she got rid of the problem by enrolling you in a very expensive private school, convincing herself it was all for your own good."

There could be no mistaking the resentment in

Laurence's voice. Karen said gently, "It was some-where around then that you left."

He nodded. "She controlled the purse strings after the inheritance, of course, although I could have coped, I think, if that had been all. But she wanted to control everything and everyone. You, me, Mandy, the house, my job...so I left. In exculpation, may I say that I genuinely believed you and your sister would be better off with your mother in your own home. I knew I'd be living a pretty rootless existence, not the best kind of life-style for two young girls."

"But you meant to keep in touch with us." It seemed important to Karen to have that absolutely clear.

"Certainly I did." He hesitated. "When I knew Ryan was going to Montreal a couple of weeks ago, I acted on impulse when I asked him to go and see you."

Again she was careful to iron the emotion from her voice. "You weren't very pleased to see me when I arrived up here."

"No." The hesitation was longer this time. "I can only ask you to believe that there was nothing personal in that, Karen. That I was genuinely torn. Part of me was delighted to see you again, my own daughter, my firstborn child." He cleared his throat. "But part of me didn't want you here. I was...afraid. However, that's another matter altogether." His tone was dismissive.

"Won't you tell me about it?" she pleaded.

She had forgotten about the listener in the corner, although possibly Laurence had not. "I can't right now," he said heavily. "Maybe later on."

She was disappointed; nevertheless, she knew they had made immense strides towards a new, more adult relationship. "Do you mind if I stay longer in Pond Inlet?" she asked. "I'm really enjoying it up here."

"I'd like you to stay."

She gave him her generous smile. "I'm glad," she said simply.

"Just promise you won't go camping again," he added wryly.

"You don't have to worry about that—I learned my lesson!" A huge yawn caught her unawares. "I'd better get to bed. You must be tired, too."

He stood up, holding on to the back of the chair. "Tired enough. But I'm glad we had this talk, Karen."

Her answer was to walk over to him and kiss his cheek. He hugged her, adding gruffly, "You're a good girl."

They were heartwarming words. She turned to leave, shoved her feet into her boots and bent to lace them loosely. Ryan walked across the room, opened the door. "I'll walk over with you."

She jumped. "You don't need to do that."

"Come along."

There was no point in arguing with him. Over her shoulder she said quickly, "Good night, dad," the words seeming very natural even after the gap of so many years.

She was rewarded by Laurence's rare smile. "Good night, Karen."

Outside Ryan took her elbow in a no-nonsense grip, steering her relentlessly toward her own Parcoll, where he opened the door and pushed her inside. Following hard on her heels, he closed the door behind them, and without preamble he said, "The kidnapping is behind it all, isn't it? That's why you're so terrified of men."

He had been listening, of course. She tried to remember exactly what had been said. Nothing very much, surely. "Perhaps," she said noncommittally. "Ryan, it's late—"

"There's no perhaps about it. You never told me about it because you can't stand talking about it. Look at you now—you're as tense as a bowstring."

She said tightly, "Look, it's been a long night, and you're absolutely right, I don't like talking about it."

"How long did they hold you, Karen?"

"Eleven days, that's all."

"That would be enough. More than enough. How old were you?"

"Fourteen," she snapped, resenting his inquisition.

"Did they rape you?"

"No."

"But they did something to you, didn't they? Something that still haunts you, that's between us whenever I get near you." His face relaxed, his hands kneading the rigid line of her shoulders. "Karen, can't you trust me enough to tell me? Because you've never told anyone, have you, and that's part of the problem."

"I do trust you, Ryan," she said in a small voice. "More than I've ever trusted anyone, even Mandy or my father. But I can't tell you, I just can't. It's. . .it's as though there's a huge steel door bolted over all the memories. I cannot open that door. I don't *want* to!''

Her lips were quivering, her eyes dark with panic. She didn't see his blue eyes, bleak with purpose. She only heard his voice say with deliberate brutality, ''You've got away with that line for years, Karen. With your father and mother, with the psychiatrist, with Mandy and Duke and all your other friends. But you won't get away with it with me. I'm going to find out what happened in those eleven days, because you're going to tell me.''

Deep within her something snapped, and fear was banished in a glorious uprush of pure rage. ''Oh, am I?'' she retorted, adding with a childish but very satisfying stamp of her foot, ''That's what *you* think!''

''That's what I know. You're twenty-three years old, Karen Smythe—too old to be hiding behind a clutter of repressed fears that have no existence outside your imagination.''

''What the *hell* do you know about it?'' she stormed. ''It wasn't you who was kept all alone in a pitch-black room where you didn't even know if it was day or night. Tied up a lot of the time. Never knowing whether they were going to kill you or—'' She broke off, pressing her hands to her face. ''You tricked me, didn't you?'' she whispered. ''Made me lose my temper so I'd start telling you what you want to know.''

''Maybe I did. But I've proved something, haven't I? It's not locked up, Karen. It's all there.''

"Damn you!" she shrieked. "Go away and leave me alone. I don't want you poking and prying around, thinking you know what's best for me. Who do you think you are—God?"

He shook her, not a trace of gentleness left in his face. "I think you're a coward, that's what I think. You're afraid of loving, of being a whole woman— you're afraid of life!"

Her anger dissipated as quickly as it had come, leaving her feeling tired and frightened and very lonely, miles away from this hard-eyed stranger whom she had thought she could trust. "Go away," she said with the brevity of exhaustion.

"Yes, I will. And maybe next time you'll have to come to me. I'm tired of chasing after a woman who hasn't got the guts to be honest or the desire to be human."

He had spoken with contempt; without ceremony he turned and left her alone, the click of the door catch sounding very final.

CHAPTER TEN

KAREN ALMOST CALLED HIM BACK, his name rushing up from some deep elemental need in her. But she fought it down, her lips a thin, tight line, until she could no longer hear the sound of his footsteps. For the first time since she had come to Pond Inlet she shoved the only chair in the room under the door handle before she began to undress. It seemed to take twice as long as usual to do everything, her fingers reverting to the clumsiness and lack of skill of childhood. Undoing the belt and the zipper on her slacks seemed terribly complicated. She couldn't remember where she had left her nightdress, and when she eventually located it in the most logical place, under her pillow, she discovered she was crying, tears of utter weariness that trickled slowly down her cheeks and dripped onto the bed. Too tired to care, she huddled under the blankets, trying in vain to erase from her mind a pair of ruthless blue eyes and an angry voice hurling accusations at her....

She must have fallen asleep, because when next she looked at her watch it was eleven in the morning. Too late for breakfast, too early for lunch. She burrowed her head into the pillow but, after fifteen minutes of tossing and turning, knew she was not going to get to sleep again. As she sat up in bed, she realized she was dreading going over to the hotel, for in all likelihood the first person she would meet there would be Ryan. She had nothing to say to him, she thought drearily. Nothing.

But your father will be there, too, a little voice whispered encouragingly in her ear. *You have plenty to tell him, now. There's an eight-year gap to fill in.*

In front of Ryan? Who are you kidding, she argued back.

Ryan had to go back to the scene of the shooting this morning. Remember?

So he had. She got out of bed, putting on a pair of tight-fitting jeans and a sweater that did considerably more than hint at the curves of her breasts. If it was a gesture of defiance directed at Ryan, then it was wasted, so she discovered when she went for lunch at noon, for her father was sitting alone at one of the tables. She waved at Guillaume and Claude and sat down with Laurence. In the bathroom she had done her best to repair the ravages of her tears; apparently she had succeeded, for her father said, "You look very nice, dear. But did your jeans shrink in the wash?"

Karen had caught the glint of mischief in his eyes and was disarmed by it. "Mmm. Unfortunately I washed the sweater at the same time."

"I have a feeling they must be for Ryan's benefit, not mine."

She tossed her head. "Nonsense. Where is he, anyway?"

"He went back to Salmon River with Josh Crooks, the local police officer. He'll probably stay and have

lunch with him afterward. They're good friends."
He buttered a piece of bread. "Tell me about the job
you had—a drop-in center, did you say? And what
stage is your university career right now?"

To Karen's delight they talked nonstop throughout
the entire meal. At the end of it Laurence fished in
his pocket, producing a small bundle wrapped in
white tissue. "On our way home from the dig I
bought this for you from an old Inuit friend of mine
who lives with his family on Paquet Bay. He carved it
nearly thirty years ago."

She took the package from him, carefully unwrap-
ping the paper. Inside was a ptarmigan carved in
ivory, perhaps three inches long. The details were
simple, the lines flowing into one another, and the
ivory had been polished to an exquisite sheen.

"It's made from a walrus tusk," her father interposed, and from something in his voice she knew he
was nervous.

She said softly, "It's beautiful." Cupping it in her
palm, she rubbed its satin smoothness, unashamed
tears in her eyes. "Thank you...I'll treasure it. It's
the first present I've had from you for years, isn't it?
Do you remember the teddy bear you gave me when I
was five? I still have it in my room, although he's lost
one eye and I keep having to patch him to keep the
stuffing in."

"Yes, I do remember.... I'm glad you like the
ptarmigan. I thought you would." He cleared his
throat. "Well, I have to get back to work. What are
you going to do this afternoon?"

"I might go and look for some more wild flowers.

I've started photographing all the species I can identify. I'll see you at supper, won't I?''

With a touch of the formality that seemed to be
Laurence's retreat from too much emotion, he said,
"That will be delightful." Squeezing her shoulder
briefly, he left the room.

Karen carefully rewrapped the ivory bird, enjoying
the feel and the weight of it in her hand, and then
pushed her chair back. She had been so absorbed in
her conversation with her father that she hadn't
noticed Rusty was also in the room; she hadn't seen
him for a couple of days. He was ready to leave at the
same time as she so she smiled at him brightly.
"How's it going?"

He looked disgruntled and irritable, although he
said automatically, "Fine."

She persevered. "Have you been back to Bylot
Island?"

"Yeah, a couple of times."

They had crossed the lounge to the porch where the
boots were lined up. "Did you see anything interesting?"

"Nothing out of the ordinary," he answered
repressively.

The door swung open and a big black-haired man
came in. Karen recognized him as Rusty's partner.
Although she had not met him, she had seen them together in the dining room. He would be hard to forget, she thought wryly. He must weigh well over two
hundred pounds, his belly ballooning out over his
belt, his prognathous jaw and low forehead devoid of
intelligence, humor, or friendliness. He looked like a

bouncer in a sleazy club, she decided, hearing him say—or rather growl—to Rusty, "All set?"

"Are you going somewhere?" she said, knowing she must seem insatiably curious, but not really caring.

Rusty looked at her coldly. "Yes."

"May I come?" The words were out before she had thought.

"Look, Karen, we're only going on a short reconnaissance flight. You wouldn't be interested. Some other—"

"Oh, but I would," she said, widening her eyes ingenuously. "You mean you're going up in the plane? I haven't met your friend, by the way, Rusty."

Short of outright rudeness, Rusty had no choice but to introduce his black-haired cohort. "Steve Mettinger," he said grudgingly. "Karen Smythe."

"How do you do, Mr. Mettinger?" She glanced at him through her lashes, hoping she was managing to combine shyness with admiration. "Are you a pilot, too?"

He grunted, an indeterminate sound that could have meant anything. A man of few words, obviously, she thought, giving Rusty the full benefit of her smile. "Do let me come, Rusty," she coaxed. "I promise I won't get in the way, or bother you."

He didn't smile back. In fact, his pale eyes were so inimical that for a moment her smile wavered, and she wondered if her insistence was the height of foolishness. She was not sure why it seemed so important that she go. Certainly there was no rational reason for it. Yet it was important enough that she was standing there making a fool of herself, the picture of a brainless female trying to get her own way. "Please?" she added, head to one side.

"Okay," Rusty said impatiently. "I'm sure you'll be bored to tears, Karen. All we're looking for is snow geese."

"Are you really?" she prattled. "I haven't seen any yet. Do they nest around here?"

They were going down the steps to a ramshackle old van that Rusty apparently had the use of when Karen saw Lucas over by his family's trailer, which abutted on to the hotel. "I'm just going for a plane trip with Rusty," she called. "Would you mind telling my father?"

Lucas raised a hand in salute and she climbed into the back seat of the van, rather glad that at least two more people would know where she was going. Determined not to show any qualms, she chattered away artlessly to Rusty about her botanical collection as they drove the short distance to the airport, trying to ignore that he was barely bothering to be polite to her.

The clouds were high in the sky and the striped wind sock was tugging at its pole as they walked across the gravel surface of the runway to the Twin Otter. Its tail and wing tips were painted bright orange—in case they crashed, Karen thought uneasily. For a moment she contemplated abandoning the whole trip, for she had no idea what she hoped to prove by it. Moreover, the propellers looked distressingly frail. She had never flown in such a small plane before.

Perhaps her thoughts showed in her face. Steve had already climbed up the steps into the cabin;

Rusty took her by the arm and forcibly lifted her up, his fingers too tight for comfort. "In you go—too late to change your mind now," he said mockingly. "As you're our only passenger, you can sit anywhere you like. Fasten your seat belt for takeoff, won't you—it can get quite rough in a small plane." With an unpleasant smile he went up into the cockpit.

Hoping Lucas wouldn't forget to pass on her message, she did as she was told. The engines started, the propellers blurred into a tight circle, and they began taxiing down the runway. The takeoff, contrary to Rusty's threats, was very smooth, and in no time they were flying over the hills that led to Salmon Creek and the river beyond. Knowing she was risking another snub, but knowing also she wouldn't learn anything by sitting back in the cabin by herself, Karen unbuckled her belt and edged her way up into the cockpit, seeing with no great delight that Steve was at the controls, Rusty consulting a map in his lap. "Where are we going?" she asked over the roar of the engines, in one quick glance orienting herself on the map. They were heading up Salmon River toward Utuk Lake, she saw with a stirring of excitement. Hadn't Ryan said gyrfalcons were supposed to nest near Utuk Lake? It was her first overt linking of Rusty with the gyrfalcons; she knew it was the reason she had so blatantly invited herself along today.

"We'll fly up the lake," Rusty said, "because they often nest along the shores," and it took Karen a moment to realize he meant snow geese, not gyrfalcons. "There'll be turbulence over the lake. You should sit back in one of the seats."

"Oh, I can see so much better up here. I'll just hang on," she said blithely, ignoring the dirty look Rusty gave her. "That's Salmon River below us, isn't it? How white the water looks."

"Glacial runoff," Steve said. Karen jumped. It was the first time he had spoken and she was somehow surprised to hear coherent words issuing from him. His voice suited his appearance, a low-pitched, bearlike growl.

"I see," she said, neglecting to tell them that Ryan had already given her the same explanation. "Look how tall the cliffs are. Are we really going between them? And that's new snow on top of the mountains, isn't it?" She was glad Ryan couldn't hear her performance as a wide-eyed ingenue; acting did not seem to be the ideal career for her.

Rusty didn't answer. He had the binoculars out and was scanning the fast-approaching cliff faces. Karen didn't know much about birds, but she was fairly sure snow geese would nest in marshes and flat places, not halfway up the side of a cliff. Her own eyes darted from side to side, searching for she knew not what. Utuk Lake lay ahead, just visible through a gap in the cliffs. It was long and narrow, its murky green waters lying in a deep gorge surrounded by snow-dusted mountains.

She sensed rather than saw Rusty stiffen to attention. Following the line of his binoculars, she felt her heart leap in her breast. Soaring halfway up the cliff was a large bird, its plumage startlingly white against the dark rock. Its pointed wings cleaved the air with effortless grace. . .*kingavik*, the white gyrfalcon.

She said, her voice squeaky with excitement, "What's that? That big white bird?"

Rusty lowered the binoculars. When he spoke his voice sounded almost bored, and Karen might have been deceived had she not seen how tightly his hands were clenched around the binoculars. His nails needed cleaning, she noticed abstractedly. "What bird?" he said. "Oh, look—down along the shore there. Those are snow geese, Karen."

The gyrfalcon was out of sight. Two large white patches at the edge of the lake did indeed signify the presence of snow geese. She murmured, "I must have seen one flying, I guess. Aren't they beautiful?"

They, too, passed beneath the plane. Steve was flying the length of the lake now, the cliffs towering above them on either side, the plane bucking and jerking in the air currents. Karen held on tightly, her brain in a turmoil. She would swear on a stack of Bibles that she had seen a gyrfalcon, and she would also swear that Rusty had seen it. But he had said nothing about his discovery, and that could surely mean only one thing. He was one of the poachers Ryan had described to her. He was hoping to trap the gyrfalcon and sell it into captivity.

She remembered the dead polar bear, its great white body sprawled on the ground by her tent. This was her chance to redeem herself, she thought fiercely. If it was anything to do with her, Rusty was not going to succeed. She had had only one brief glimpse of the falcon, but that had been enough for her to sense its regal bearing, its freedom to fly where it chose among the cliffs and rivers of the tundra. It did not belong in an aviary, no matter how luxurious; it should not be a plaything, no matter how rich and powerful the owner.

They were at the far end of the lake by now, where she pointed out two more flocks of geese. Under cover of the engine noise Steve muttered something to Rusty that sounded like "go back." Rusty said flatly, "No. Keep going."

If she had not been there, they would have circled in an attempt to get another sighting of the gyrfalcon, she was sure. She took a vicious pleasure in thwarting their plans even in such a small way, although she knew Rusty well enough to be certain he had pinpointed the exact location. The plane was racing low to the ground over the plateau at the end of the lake, the terrain a jumble of snow-covered rocks—terrible country to cross on foot. Then they had soared over the edge of the cliff, and far below were the steel-gray waters of Oliver Sound. For the next few minutes Karen almost forgot about falcons and snow geese, for they were crossing a landscape of such desolate beauty that her breath was taken away. Deep fiords, smooth as glass, between gaunt, snow-ridged crags. Scattered islands rearing up out of the water like the backs of giant whales. And as they crossed the narrowest part of the inlet to Bylot Island, two gigantic icebergs, their meltwater brilliant turquoise against the white.

The western end of the island was a sweep of low-lying tundra, dotted with hundreds of tiny ponds and lakes. What Karen had thought at first glance were patches of snow turned out to be several large flocks of snow geese, one flock taking to the air in a concerted beat of white wings as they passed overhead. The scenery had so awed her that she was beyond the stage of making flip remarks; in silence she watched the birds circle and sink out of sight behind the wing tip.

The tundra stretched on for miles. Then she saw ahead of them a vast, interlocking network of streams and rivers, the water the same milk-white color she had come to expect, and into sight came the tongue of a glacier, a sheer cliff of dirty, melting ice.

"Aktineq," Rusty said conversationally. "Give her the scenic tour, eh, Steve?"

Afterward, she was to wonder if Steve had been trying to frighten her, for he flew very low over the glacier, and stationed as she was in the cockpit, the sensation of speed was alarming. Yet it was also exhilarating. Between the sharp-peaked mountains they followed the winding course of the glacier, which was traversed by rivulets of turquoise water and edged by the heaped rocks of the lateral moraine. Then they flew between two vertical cliff faces, the jagged rock so close Karen felt she could have reached out and touched it, and over a blindingly white field of snow that the mountain winds whipped into phantasmagoric shapes as they passed. Another glacier, another range of mountains. . . .

She became very conscious of the fact that all three of them were depending upon a fragile, man-made piece of machinery to keep them aloft. Had they crashed in such a hostile landscape, they would never have survived, for there was no life in sight at all. No trees, no plants, no animals or birds. Only rock and snow and ice, on and on for miles.

It had to end. They flew down the last of the glaciers, Kaparoqtalik, and then they were over the inlet again where the water was dramatically discolored by the melting ice, a sharp-edged cloud of white in a blue sea.

The landing on the runway was pure anticlimax. Karen had gone back to her seat and buckled her belt, wanting to be alone with all the visions that were whirling in her head. The plane taxied to a stop near the little terminal building, and she got to her feet. Rusty preceded her down the length of the cabin, opening the door and lowering the metal steps. Jumping to the ground himself, he reached up a hand to her.

Still bemused, she took it and awkwardly climbed down the steps, stiff as she was from sitting for so long. Looking up at him and forgetting how she had virtually forced her company on him, she said sincerely, "Thank you, Rusty. That was an unforgettable experience."

He, however, had not forgotten. His pale eyes scanned her rapt, upturned face. "It was, was it?" he said silkily. "Let's make it even more unforgettable."

It took her a couple of seconds too long to realize what he intended. By the time she had tensed in resistance, one arm had pulled her close, throwing her off balance, and with the other hand he had grasped her chin. He used the kiss as a means of expressing his anger with her, for there was no tenderness in it, not even any genuine desire. It was a violation, a brutal grinding of his lips against hers, a forcing of his tongue into her mouth.

She whimpered in protest, desperately trying to wrench her head free. It was like another kiss, one that had violated her when she had been fourteen. As if they had never been, the years fell away from her and she was that same young girl, trapped, understanding very little of what was going on, terrified out of her wits every moment she was awake and racked by nightmares when she was asleep.

She fought to free her hand to scratch his face, but he was far too strong. Kicking out at him, she felt sickness rise in her throat, as well as a helpless anger that he should be stronger than she and able to force his will on her.

Then two things happened at once. A man's voice spoke, a voice so raw with anger as to be almost unrecognizable. "Let go of her!" And the kiss ended as Rusty looked up.

Karen gulped in air, her chest as tight as if she had been running, and looked over her shoulder. It was Ryan; she had known it would be. He was not even looking at her; his attention was wholly on the man whose arm was still around her. The words edged with menace, he repeated, "Let go of her."

Behind her she heard Steve clamber down the ladder, but neither Ryan nor Rusty even looked at him. Rusty's fingers were digging into her back. She could hear his quickened breathing. He said with a lightness that did not deceive her, "Well, now, she was brash enough to invite herself when she wasn't wanted, and now she takes the consequences." He glanced down at Karen, still in his arms. "It was only a kiss, after all. Not even a particularly good one. She's a cold-blooded little bi—"

Karen did not even see Ryan's fist. She felt a wind pass her cheek and felt Rusty stagger, his arm falling away from her waist as she flung herself free. The force of the blow knocked him to the ground, his head narrowly missing the fuselage, his boots scrabbling in the gravel. Very slowly he raised himself up on one elbow, wiping at the trickle of blood that ran from the corner of his mouth.

Beside her she felt Steve move, heard Rusty's barked, "No!" Steve fell back, his huge ham fists clenched at his sides. Rusty said softly, "You'll pay for that, Koetsier."

His eyes had the cold, amoral flatness of a killer's. Terrified, Karen looked over at Ryan. There was primitive violence in his stance and in his blazing blue eyes; he was spoiling for a fight, she thought sickly. He didn't at all look like the civilized, intelligent man she knew; he was like an animal, ready to fight tooth and nail for his. . . . She fumbled to a stop. For his mate? Was that it?

When he spoke to Rusty, it could only bear out her thoughts. "Keep away from her from now on—do you hear me?"

Rusty levered himself upright, leaning against the wing for support. "Tell her to keep away from me then," he said vindictively. "She didn't get anything she didn't deserve."

In a horrible twisted way, it was true. Ryan took a

step forward. "You wouldn't have let go of her if I hadn't been here. But you knew she was terrified—"

"She asked for it." Rusty straightened to his full height, deliberately adding an obscenity so crude that Karen flinched.

In a split second she saw Ryan move in, his fists already raised, saw Rusty's hand fly to his pocket. A knife? A gun? She was never to know what he was reaching for. She threw herself between them, screaming at them to stop. Impelled by its own momentum, Ryan's big body knocked her sideways. As he grabbed at her to keep her from falling, she cried out incoherently, "Don't you see? He *wants* you to fight! He's got a knife or a gun, I know he has!"

There was naked fury in Ryan's blue eyes. "Do you think I don't know that? Get out of the way."

She clung to his arm with the strength of desperation. "No—you mustn't!"

"How touching," Rusty sneered. "Maybe you should pay attention to her, Koetsier. I fight dirty and I fight to kill. And if she got hurt in the process, that would be just too bad."

Under her fingers she could feel the rigidity leave Ryan's arm and she knew she had won, at least for now; he would not risk putting her in physical jeopardy. "Okay," he grated. "But next time she won't be around—remember that."

"I will. Because I owe you one. You might do well to keep that in mind."

It was a hollow victory that she had won, for the antagonism between the two men was as sharp and as deadly—and as real—as the weapon she knew to be in Rusty's pocket. She let go of Ryan's arm, feeling the sickness rise in her throat again, knowing this time she could not force it back. Covering her mouth with her hand, she whirled around and ran for the ditch. She made it in time, but barely.

Crouched over the ground, involuntary tears pouring down her cheeks, she was dimly aware that someone had come up to her. A jacket was put around her, then her shoulders were grasped in a no-nonsense way. "Go away," she gasped.

"It's the worst feeling in the world, isn't it?" Ryan said calmly. "I had food poisoning once, and when I wasn't feeling as though I was going to die, I was wishing I would. There's a restroom in the terminal building. I'll take you there and you can wash your face...that always helps."

As the spasms ceased, Karen drew a deep, shuddering breath and passively allowed herself to be led to the restroom. Once there, she closed the door behind her and doused her face in cold water, patting it dry on some paper towels. Not even bothering to comb her hair, feeling every bit as miserable as she looked, she walked outside. The Twin Otter was still parked on the runway, although there was no sign of Rusty or Steve; Ryan was waiting for her at the foot of the steps. She said flatly "I'll go back to the hotel by myself."

If he saw the mutinous set of her lips, he paid no attention. "Oh, no, you won't. That pair of glamour boys might still be hanging around, and then what would you do?"

"At least I wouldn't start a fight," she said viciously, shoving her hands in her pockets and standing exactly where she was.

"So that's the trouble.... What did you expect me to do, tap him politely on the shoulder and ask him if he'd please stop kissing you?"

"You could have tried. But, oh, no, you had to wade in with both fists flying." Her voice shook with the intensity of her feelings. "I loathe violence!"

"Do you think I like it?" Ryan demanded furiously. "But sometimes there's no other way—particularly with a guy like Rusty. It's the only language he understands."

"You *enjoyed* hitting him."

"I had no other choice but to hit him. Surely you can see that?"

But Karen was past the stage where facts would have made any difference. "You men are all alike! If you're not mauling some woman, you're fighting—that's all you know how to do."

She saw Ryan pale, his eyes cold as ice. Very quietly he said, "So you're putting me on a par with Rusty—thanks a lot, Karen."

"You're just like him," she repeated stubbornly.

"In that case you can hang around with him, not with me. And the next time I see him mauling you, I'll let you get out of it yourself. Or perhaps you didn't want to get out of it—perhaps you were enjoying it."

"You know damn well I wasn't!" she cried. "Oh, I hate all of you—why can't you leave me alone?" She turned on her heel and began running across the gravel, her one desire to put as much distance between her and Ryan as quickly as possible, her own words echoing in her ears.

He didn't come after her. When she reached the first row of bungalows she risked a backward look over her shoulder. He was walking away from the terminal in the opposite direction. She slowed to a walk, breathing hard, for her boots were too heavy for running. She had not wanted him to come after her—had she?

As if it were a videotape, the ugly little scene replayed itself in front of her eyes and her own voice, shrill with rage, echoed in her ears. After all the angry words she had thrown at him, it was hardly surprising that he should keep his distance from her. Yet she was honest enough to recognize that she had, nevertheless, expected him to follow her, to try and convince her she was wrong, to direct the whole force of his personality toward her and her problems. But he had not. He had walked away from her.

For a moment she was afraid. She couldn't see him any longer, for he had descended the hill beyond the runway, and his physical disappearance suddenly seemed symbolic. What if he had accepted her words as the final truth? What if he *did* leave her alone? It wasn't until she considered the possible withdrawal of his support that she realized how much she had come to depend on it. Lodged somewhere at the back of her brain had been the idea that someday, somehow, she would be as other women—normal, capable of loving a man in all senses of the word. And it was Ryan who had fostered that idea, engendering in her both a pride in her own womanly beauty and a faint, fragile inkling of what desire could be like.

But now he was gone. He had come to her aid once again, and far from being grateful to him, she had screamed at him to go away, hurling at him accusations that were totally unjust yet that contained enough grains of truth to hurt. Worst of all, she had likened him to Rusty. How could she have done that? Now that her temper had cooled, she knew how wrong she had been. Rusty and Ryan were as different as . . . as night from day, she thought tritely.

She began walking toward the hotel again, staring down at the ground. There was no need to ask herself why she had done it, for she already knew the answer: physical violence had been an integral part of the eleven-day ordeal she had been subjected to as a teenager. Her overreaction today—for an overreaction it had been—was yet another expression of fears and emotions locked up for too long in the depths of her own psyche. And once again Ryan had taken the brunt of it.

By the time Karen reached the hotel she had managed to smooth over the worst of her fears. Ryan would understand why she had acted as she had; and since his patience and his strength were facets of his character she had come to depend on, he would continue to be her confidant and friend. She didn't need to worry. She would apologize to him as soon as she saw him and everything would be all right. . . .

In her tent she changed into a pair of tan bush pants, man-tailored yet subtly flattering to her female curves, adding a very expensive navy blue shirt, a silk scarf, and a narrow leather belt. She made up her face, something she had scarcely bothered to do since she had come up here, flung her jacket around her shoulders and went to the door of her father's Parcoll. Knocking on it lightly, she called, "Ready for dinner?"

"Come in, dear."

Warmed by his endearment, she opened the door. He had been working at the desk, which was in more than its usual state of disorder. As she came in, he pushed himself to his feet with that slight sideways stagger she had almost come to expect. It was on the tip of her tongue to ask him about it, but she didn't want to drive the welcoming smile from his face—it was too new, too pleasing. So she contented herself with saying generally, "How are you?"

His reply was just as meaningless. "Fine, fine. Let me get on a sweater and we'll go and eat."

"Is Ryan coming?" The question sounded overly casual, even to her.

"Haven't seen him all day. He'll turn up when he's ready, no doubt." Patting his pocket to see if he had his pipe, Laurence added, "Got a lot done today—all those tables revised." He indicated an untidy pile of papers balanced precariously on the left-hand edge of the desk.

Karen walked over and looked at them. Done on foolscap in her father's crabbed writing, they had been erased and scored out and rewritten, with tiny arrows indicating incomprehensible shifts in the numbers, asterisks added with abandon. She said diplomatically, "You've made a lot of changes."

"I have, haven't I?" he said with considerable satisfaction.

On inspiration she added, "Would you like me to recopy them? They seem a little confusing. Only because I don't understand them, of course."

"Hmm." He surveyed the top sheet critically, holding it close to his eyes. The one below it looked to Karen as if at some stage in its career it had had a lengthy sojourn in the wastepaper basket. "I suppose you're right," he said judiciously. "But you're on holiday, my dear."

"I'd love to do it," Karen said promptly, knowing she was speaking the simple truth, for involving herself in his work would give her the chance to get closer to her father.

"Then after dinner I'll show you how to go about it."

They ate together. The workmen were there, Joe as usual causing vast quantities of food to disappear, and a couple of new people had come in, but there was no sign of Ryan, or of Rusty and Steve. In sudden panic Karen remembered Rusty's softly spoken threat, wondering if the absence of all three of them was somehow related. When Lucas came in, she was emboldened to ask where Rusty and Steve were.

"Checked out for a couple of days. Fine with me. A bunch of government people arrived today so we're full up."

"You mean they've left?"

"Yeah. Had to go to Frobisher, they said."

She frowned, wondering why they had gone, then rousing herself to hear her father say, "Rather tough-looking men, I thought they were. No great loss.''

"You're right,'' she said with considerable feeling. Then she changed the subject, drawing her father out to talk about his work. It was always interesting to hear an expert speak on his topic, particularly if he had the gift of making it seem clear and logical. Laurence had that gift, and before long the two serviettes and the paper place mats were covered with maps, diagrams and sketches. Totally absorbed, Karen didn't notice until they got up to leave that Ryan had come in with another group of the government workers and was seated at a table with three other men and two very attractive young women. He was laughing at something one of them had said, and he didn't even seem to notice her and Laurence leave the room. It was definitely not the time to make her apology.

The next couple of days Karen was thankful she had her volunteer work with Laurence to occupy her attention, since it was becoming increasingly obvious that Ryan had taken her at her word. She had asked to be left alone; he was obeying her to the letter. That was bad enough, because it made her realize how significant a person he had become in her life. What was worse was that when he wasn't working he was rarely alone. One or the other, or both of the two young women, whose names were Elise and Marilyn, were nearly always with him—or so it seemed to Karen. The men were, too, but that wasn't what worried her. He was very much a part of their group in a way that she was not, and he, certainly, made no efforts to include her. A couple of the younger men did, but dictated by an urge to show she did not need any of them, including Ryan, she coolly declined their tentative overtures.

She enjoyed working with her father, and the hours she spent with him brought about a closeness between them. Although Karen studiously avoided references to the kidnapping, they could chat comfortably about the past now, about Nancy and Mandy and the house on the Tantramar Marshes. It was an intimacy Karen treasured, because it was becoming more and more obvious that something was wrong with Laurence. Spending as much time with him as she was, she could not remain oblivious to certain physical symptoms that recurred with alarming frequency: the tremors she had noticed before, and the loss of balance, a debilitating tiredness, a slurring of his speech. His impatience with his own weaknesses was such that she hesitated to say anything, feeling that the initiative should come from him. But on the third evening they spent together, she abandoned this pose of tactful silence.

Laurence had been sitting at his desk for a couple of hours while she had been attempting to understand the intricacies of his filing system so that she could clear away some of the confusion on the bookshelves. He went to stand up, but his whole leg must have gone numb, because he staggered and would have fallen to the floor had he not grabbed one of the metal supports of the tent. Dropping the papers in her hands, Karen ran to support him. Although he wasn't very heavy, she was still breathing hard by the time she managed to steer him over to the bed. He collapsed on the edge of it, leaning forward and rubbing his knee. "No feeling in it at all," he muttered, more to himself than to her.

"What's wrong, dad?" she asked. She was kneeling beside him, her gray eyes very direct.

"Nothing for you to worry about...."

She began rubbing the leg herself, for she could see that his hands were shaking badly. "That's not true," she said calmly. "I'm your daughter and I love you, you know that. So it does concern me."

It almost made her cry to see how his hand trembled as he tried to pat her shoulder. "I'm so used to being on my own that I keep my troubles to myself," he said apologetically.

She grinned at him with open affection, taking the sting from her next words. "What you mean is that you're an independent old cuss who doesn't want anyone else feeling sorry for him."

He couldn't help laughing. "Didn't take you long to figure me out, did it?" Speaking quickly, as if he wanted to get it over with, he said, "I've got multiple sclerosis, Karen."

Unconsciously, her fingers tightened on his leg. Shocked eyes fastened on his face, she stammered, "What... I don't know much about that. What does it mean?"

The facts came so smoothly off his tongue that she knew he must have gone over them in his mind many times. "It's a disease of the central nervous system. For some reason the insulation substance on the nerve fibers breaks down and is replaced by scar tissue, which in simple terms means that the messages don't get through to the brain correctly. It was first diagnosed when I was in my mid-thirties, before Nancy inherited all the money. But then it went into remission for years and I more or less forgot about it. In the past few months, though, I've had a number of attacks and the symptoms keep recurring." His voice roughened. "I go to pick up a book and I drop it. I try and get up from my chair and fall flat on my face."

"Is it fatal?" she asked in a small voice.

"No, although there are days I almost wish it were. It'll just keep on getting worse and worse, until eventually I'll end up in a wheelchair. Helpless. Dependent on other people all the time."

He would hate such dependence; she knew him well enough for that. She sought in her mind for words of comfort. "Could you not have another remission?"

"I could, certainly. One of the characteristics of the disease is that it comes and goes."

"Then you'd still be able to travel and do your work."

"Yes... but for how long?" He glanced down at her. "I'm sorry, Karen. I shouldn't be telling you all this."

She rested her cheek on his knee. "It's all right... I'm glad you did. Tell me—was it because of your illness that you didn't want me up here?"

He seemed relieved that she had opened up the subject. "That's right. Your arrival was so unexpected. When Ryan told me you were actually here, in the next Parcoll, I didn't know what to think. On the one hand I was desperately anxious to see you again, because after all it had been nine years, hadn't it? But on the other hand, I saw you as just another complication. Someone else to deceive and keep at a distance. I was having a hard enough time fobbing off Ryan, let alone my own daughter.''

"I see. I wish I'd known—I just thought you didn't want to see me again.''

"I'm sorry, Karen. One of the things Nancy used to criticize, and I think rightly so, was my tendency to keep everything to myself. Particularly unpleasant things. . . .''

"It's a natural enough tendency,'' Karen interposed gently.

It was doubtful if he even heard her, for he was following his own line of thought. "I feel as though my body—my own body—is letting me down. And there's nothing I can do about it.'' He banged his fist on his knee in a frustration she could understand all too well. "There are so many things I still want to do!''

"Do you have drugs to take?'' she asked, not knowing what else to say.

"Oh, yes. They help. I should go to Montreal myself for a checkup, but I keep putting it off.'' He patted her cheek. "At least the next time I go there, I'll be able to see you, Karen.''

"And Mandy, too.''

"I have the feeling she's more like her mother than you are.''

"Perhaps so. But I know she would want to see you.''

Rather to Karen's relief the talk wandered off in other directions, until Laurence yawned and stretched. "Do you mind if I pack it in now, Karen? It's been a long day."

She got to her feet and kissed him good-night. "Sleep well, and I'll be along in the morning. And, dad—thanks for telling me."

"You're a good daughter, Karen. Good night."

Although she was walking in the direction of her own tent, Karen knew she was not ready to go to sleep. She had not wanted her father to see how badly his disclosures had upset her; now that she was alone, she felt the full force of them. Doing up her jacket, she began walking down to the shore, wishing with all her heart that she could go the opposite way, toward Ryan's tent. But although the government crew had left earlier in the day, he had made no effort to see her, and was working alone rather than with her and her father. She couldn't blame him; she could only blame herself. Nor could she expect him to make the first move—that was up to her. But tonight, upset as she was, she lacked the courage.

Then she thought of Mary Ann. Mary Ann would cheer her up. Moreover, she would be able to give more details about her father's illness. But when Karen reached the nurse's bungalow, it was in darkness. Either Mary Ann was in bed, or she was at Don's; either way, Karen didn't want to disturb her.

She went down to the shore, sitting on the bank and watching the slow-moving chunks of ice float on their way to Baffin Bay. The sun, low in the sky over the mountains, cast a gold band across the still water, while the clouds were flushed a gentle pink, presage of the sunsets to come in the weeks ahead. It was very quiet.

The last time she had sat by the shore and looked out over the water, she had felt peaceful and at one with her environment. But tonight she felt isolated, attacked by loneliness and something akin to despair. She had found her father again after all these years, only to discover that he had a crippling illness, one that would destroy his spirit as well as his body. Yet as she gazed sightlessly over the inlet, she was unable to cry. It might have been better if she had; it might have eased the tightness in her throat and the tension between her shoulder blades. But she could not.

She might have been there one hour or even two. What finally brought her to her feet was the realization that she was cold, chilled to the bone. She had been too sunk in her own thoughts to have noticed the drop in temperature or the freshening of the wind. Huddling deeper in her jacket, she walked up the hill, knowing she was no nearer to being sleepy than she had been when she had left her father.

It was as if her thoughts had conjured him up, for as she approached the hotel, Laurence was coming down the steps. "I thought you'd gone to bed," she called.

"Couldn't sleep," he said economically. "Where were you?"

"Oh, I went for a walk," she said vaguely.

He gave her a searching look. "You look cold. Why don't you come inside and we'll make a pot of tea?"

Knowing that was exactly what she craved, warmth and people and the feel of solid walls around her, she said, "Sounds lovely."

They went inside. The lounge was wreathed in smoke, for Guillaume, Claude and Joe were watching the late movie, a brilliantly hued affair that appeared to be set on a tropical island, a setting more than usually incongruous in Pond Inlet. She couldn't help wondering what Lucas, Noah and Tuglik would make of it.

The dining room was deliciously warm. While her father put on the kettle, she rubbed her hands together to get the circulation going again, already feeling much better. Creature comforts were by no means to be despised. Somehow it seemed a natural progression that this should bring Mandy to mind. As Laurence carefully carried two cups and saucers over to the table—and it seemed important to Karen that she not offer to help him—she looked up at him and said, "Do you know what I'd like to do?"

He smiled at her. "I couldn't possibly guess."

"I'd like to phone Mandy and see if she'd come up here for a couple of days."

He sat down rather quickly. "Why?"

Although she had not had time to think it through, Karen found the answer coming readily enough off her tongue. "Because I think you should see each other again and get reacquainted. To be honest, I don't think she'd stay long. Roughing it isn't really her thing, and Pond Inlet would certainly be roughing it by her standards. But I might be able to persuade her to come for a short visit."

Laurence got up to make the tea, bringing it back with him. "I wouldn't want you to tell her what I told you earlier this evening," he said seriously. "If I decided to tell her when she got here, all well and good. But it's not something I'd want discussed on the telephone. Nor am I sure I want your mother to know about it yet."

"I can understand that. But it *is* a factor. I think you should see Mandy now, while...." She floundered for words.

"While I'm still on my own two feet," he finished for her with a touch of grim humor.

"Will you let me phone her?"

Moodily he stirred his tea. "Do you think she'll come?"

"I don't know," she answered honestly. "She gets pretty caught up in her social life. But I can try."

"Go ahead then. Now, let's talk about something else." Firmly he led the conversation back to the paper he hoped to publish on the Thule dig he and Ryan had worked on the past two summers, and obediently Karen followed his lead. When they had finished their tea, Laurence looked more relaxed. "I think I'll try again," he yawned. "Should be able to sleep, now. Good night, Karen."

She went to the bathroom, then on impulse went back to the dining room where the telephone was. It was late, but Mandy was an inveterate nighthawk. Getting the Ottawa operator, she placed a collect call. Mandy answered on the second ring. "Yes, I'll accept the charges. Karen! How are you? Are you still in the frozen north?"

"Very much so, and loving it. And I'm fine. What about you?"

"Oh, I'm so *cross* with Craig. Do you know what he did? Last Thursday when we were out with Sheila and Doug, he and Sheila...." Karen listened with half an ear, for it was a story, with other names, that she had heard many times before. In her more cynical moments she wondered if Mandy was any more likely to marry than she herself, for her sister seemed to be incapable of a deep, lasting commitment. The first sign of a problem in a relationship and Mandy vanished in a cloud of hyperbole.

At intervals Karen murmured the appropriate responses, knowing there was no sense in raising the purpose of her call until Mandy had let off steam. "So I told him there was no way I'd go to the Merritts' garden party with him, and if he wanted to go he could take Sheila. Maybe I'll go with Doug." Mandy giggled. "That would serve them both right. Do you think I should?"

"I'll tell you what I think you should do. Phone the airline and make your reservations and come up here for a couple of days." Cunningly she added, "That'll really give Craig a shock. He's too used to having you available."

"Really?" There was a pause while Mandy indulged in some concentrated thought. "You might be right. Is there a proper bathroom up there?"

"Running hot and cold water, lots of good food and comfortable beds. And the place is crawling with eligible men," Karen said flippantly, wondering what Joe would think were he to hear himself so described.

"Men! I'm off them," Mandy sniffed. "By the way, how are you and father getting along?"

"Very well," Karen said readily. "He'd be glad to see you, I know he would."

"Is that gorgeous hunk of a Ryan still there?"

Karen's hesitation was so brief that hopefully Mandy hadn't noticed it. "Oh, yes."

"Then I will come," Mandy said decisively. "I'll give you a call as soon as I make the arrangements. What's your number there?" A pause while she scribbled it down. "Great! You must be psychic, Karen. I was really feeling at loose ends. And mother's away for a few days, so I don't have to worry about her. I'll see you soon!"

They said goodbye and Karen put down the receiver. For her own sake as well as her father's, she was glad Mandy was coming, although she did rather wish her sister hadn't decided quite so promptly once she'd learned Ryan was still there. Not that it was anything to do with her, Karen thought miserably; Ryan plainly had no intention of picking up the threads of their friendship. She was beginning to understand that she had not properly valued what she had had. It was only now, when he had withdrawn from her, that she realized how important he had become to her since that first day when he had seen her running in the rain.

CHAPTER ELEVEN

MANDY DID NOT PHONE the following day. But as Karen was going to the hotel for dinner, she heard the growl of an approaching plane and recognized it immediately as the First Air flight. She found herself hoping Mike was on it; it never occurred to her that Mandy would be.

She and her father were halfway through their meal when there was a great commotion at the front door, the clump of boots, the sound of voices. Then the entrance to the dining room suddenly seemed to be full of new arrivals. The air crew. A couple of men who turned out to be working for Petro-Canada. Mike Riley. And a girl standing confidently in the circle of Mike's arm, very much the focus of attention. Mandy.

Mandy's only concession to the latitude was that she was wearing a pantsuit. It was of navy blue corduroy so soft as to look like velvet, and very fashionably cut. Her blouse was a froth of ruffles, and her shoes had to be handmade Italian with their tiny heels and pointed toes. She should have looked and felt totally out of place. Instead she looked delighted with herself and with everyone else.

Before Mandy saw them, by one of those coincidences that seemed to follow her around, Ryan came into the room behind her. She must have seen him out of the corner of her eye. She turned and flung her arms around him, shrieking, "Ryan! How lovely to see you again!"

Ryan lifted her clear off the ground as she kissed him—on the mouth, Karen saw with a nasty sinking feeling in the general vicinity of her heart.

"So that's Mandy," Laurence said dryly. "Does she take everywhere by storm?"

"Yes. . . you have to admit she's gorgeous," Karen replied, trying very hard to be fair and wishing she could find it in her to laugh at the look of chagrin on Mike's face.

"Indeed."

Ryan had put Mandy down. He must have said something to her, because she looked over her shoulder directly at Karen and Laurence. "There you are!" she exclaimed, running across the room to them, Ryan following more slowly. She hugged her sister, then with a touch of unusual shyness said, "Hello, father." Her cheeks were glowing with color, her auburn hair cascading to her shoulders, and her eyes were very bright. Beside her, Laurence looked. . . old, Karen thought with a painful twist of her heart.

"Mandy," he said gently, getting to his feet. "It's been a long time." He kissed her on the cheek. "How did you manage to get up here so quickly? Was there a cancellation?"

Mandy began chatting about her dealings with Nordair and First Air, from whom she appeared to have extracted reservations by sheer charm alone, and then about the flight up. Ryan sat down at the

table with them. It was the first time he had joined
them for a meal since the fight with Rusty, and
almost immediately Karen noticed the grazes on his
knuckles. He must have seen the direction of her
gaze, but he said nothing to her, preferring to question Mandy about the weather at Clyde and the state
of the sea ice along the coast. Karen sat quietly as the
talk ebbed and flowed around her, hearing Mandy's
delightful laugh and Ryan's deep, achingly familiar
voice as they bantered back and forth. Later, as they
lingered over their coffee, Laurence purposely drew
Karen into the conversation, making her part of the
group in spite of herself.

Then Ryan stood up, stretching to his full height.
"I've got an hour or so of work to do. Then why
don't we all go for a walk?" He grinned at Mandy.
"You'd better change your shoes."

She put out her slim and elegantly shod foot, pout-
ing prettily. "I did bring a pair of boots. . . like the
ones you brought, Karen. But they're not very
glamorous, are they?"

"Practical, though," Karen responded a touch
sardonically. "I don't think I'll go for a walk, thank
you. I've got fifty or sixty pages left of one of the
books you loaned me, Ryan, and I want to know who
did it. I'm never any good at guessing the murderer."

It was a flimsy excuse and she knew it, but he offered no demur. "You'll come, won't you, Mandy?"

"Sure I will. In the meantime I'd better check in."

Lucas put Mandy in the same tent with Karen.
Mandy looked around their quarters in wide-eyed
wonder. "It's not exactly the Ritz, is it? Where's all
this running water you talked about?"

"In the hotel. But it's trucked in, so you have to go easy on it."

"Good thing I washed my hair this morning then. I have this new shampoo, absolutely fabulous stuff, but you have to rinse three times." She started rummaging in her suitcase for the despised boots and pulled them out, scattering lacy underwear all over the carpet. "Damn—why am I so messy? And where are my socks? Surely I didn't forget them. I packed in such a hurry, I wouldn't be surprised. Oh, no, here they are." She slipped her feet out of the beautiful shoes, kicking them casually under the bed, and grinned at her sister. "You look kind of tired," she said frankly. "Is anything wrong?"

"No, everything's fine," Karen said untruthfully. "But I've been doing some work for father. His handwriting is atrocious, and it's enough to make anyone tired."

"Oh." Mandy flung her jacket on the bed, pulling a white cashmere sweater over her head. "I thought I picked up a few bad vibes between you and Ryan."

Whatever Mandy's faults, she was not stupid. "Did you?" Karen murmured. "Not really. . . but the trouble is with this place that you can't get away from people. You see them at every meal, you keep bumping into them around the village. Besides, you know me—I never was one for getting too close to anyone."

"I somehow thought Ryan would be different. He's nothing like Duke, you've got to admit that."

He certainly wasn't. But Karen didn't want to discuss Ryan. How could she tell anyone else about the strange intimacy that had grown between them, an intimacy she herself had destroyed in a few careless cruel words? "I'm just not interested," she said dismissively, bending to pick up the scattered clothes and consequently missing the shrewd glance Mandy sent her way.

"Well, if you're not, I am. If you wanted him for yourself, I certainly wouldn't interfere. But if you're really not interested, I'll try my luck. I'd forgotten how devastatingly attractive he is. Anyway, it'll serve Craig right," she added darkly.

"Craig won't know," Karen said reasonably.

"Oh, I'll tell him—you can be sure of that." She hauled a gorgeous fox jacket out of her other bag and threw it around her shoulders. "Let's go and see father for a while before I go for this walk."

The visit with Laurence could not have been called an unqualified success, for Mandy and Laurence were as different as it is possible for father and daughter to be, Mandy all on the surface, Laurence intensely private. Each thought the other's life-style a waste of time, although neither was impolite enough to say so. Uncomprehendingly Mandy looked at Laurence's collection of artifacts and documents; quizzically Laurence listened to a highly colored description of Mandy's activities over the past month. It was, no doubt, a relief to both when the visit ended.

Karen was going to stay and work for a while. As Mandy left to find Ryan, the younger girl winked at her sister and whispered, "Wish me luck!"

Wishing instead that she could blot out of her mind all thoughts of Mandy and Ryan together, Karen tried to bury herself in a more than usually convoluted piece of writing. But she found her ears were straining for sounds of their departure, and then, after an hour or so, for sounds of their return. Finally she pushed the chair back, knowing that normally she would accomplish more in fifteen minutes than she had in the past hour. It was time to quit.

She bade her father good-night, mistakenly under the impression that he had no idea what her problem was, and went to her tent, one swift glance having ascertained that Mandy and Ryan were nowhere in sight. She read for a while, then went to bed, there to toss and turn for what seemed like hours. It was past one o'clock when she finally heard Mandy's exaggeratedly quiet steps on the planks outside, and then the squeak of the opening door.

Face turned to the wall, Karen pretended to be asleep. But inwardly she was sick at heart. What had they been doing, the two of them? Walking all that time? It didn't seem likely. Mandy would walk from *a* to *b* if there was no other way of getting there, but fast cars were more along her line. Talking? Again she found it difficult to imagine that her sister would be interested in sustaining a conversation of any depth for very long. So what else could they have been doing? Her imagination, always rather too vivid for her own good, flashed a series of images across her tired mind. Ryan kissing Mandy, his big hands that could be so gentle cupping her face. Mandy holding him close, all the strength and solidity and warmth of him that she, Karen, could remember so well...and then what? Beyond that her mind refused to go, partly from ignorance, more from a fear of confronting something she didn't think she could bear. But the floodgates opened just a tiny chink, and the innocuous little question floated to the surface. What if they had made love?

The emotion that welled up in her could only be jealousy. She, who had never wanted a man enough to be jealous of him, was jealous of Mandy and Ryan. There could be no other name for the ugly mixture of pain, anger and fear that ripped through her at the thought of Ryan sharing that mysterious, terrifying intimacy with her own sister. Hating herself, hating her own thoughts, she buried her face in the pillow, not helped at all by the fact that Mandy's quiet movements had ceased and that her even, regular breathing indicated she was already asleep. It was a long time before Karen was able to follow suit.

THE NEXT TWO DAYS were repetitions of that first evening. Karen worked religiously for her father. Mandy and Ryan dominated the conversation at mealtimes and spent every evening together. Mandy was glowing with health and vitality, and Karen knew her well enough to be certain that Craig was long since forgotten, eclipsed by a man Mandy herself had called devastatingly attractive. Mandy in love had always been a source of amusement to Karen, but not this time. For it seemed to her that Ryan was equally attracted, that he laughed more than usual, looked younger and more carefree. And why not, she thought, trying to be fair. Mandy was lovely and vivacious and fun to be with. *She* wasn't burdened with all the hang-ups of her elder sister. *She* didn't jump if a man came within ten feet of her. Of course Ryan would be attracted to her—any normal man would be.

It was one thing to rationalize all this, to have fruitless inward discussions that went around and around in circles. It was another to be presented with proof. Knowing Ryan and Mandy had gone in the opposite direction, Karen went for her favorite walk to the shore on Mandy's third evening at Pond Inlet. When she'd almost reached the sea she settled on the rocks and gazed out over the water at the familiar prospect of mountains, glaciers and hovering sun. She had tucked herself into a crevice to be out of the wind, which also meant she was virtually out of sight, but she heard them coming, heard Mandy's lilting laughter and high-pitched voice with Ryan's deeper accompaniment. She contemplated getting up and confronting them, but her body refused to obey her. So she cowered deeper into the rocks, hugging her knees, then remaining motionless, her dark jacket and pants merging into the shadows. A pair of snow buntings, disturbed by the others' approach, flitted along the ground, one of them perching only three feet away from her.

Ryan was helping Mandy over the rocks, her hand resting trustingly in his, her hair and the lush fur jacket the same rich blend of colors. She was looking in Karen's direction. Although Karen was sure she couldn't be seen, she was nevertheless glad it was Mandy rather than Ryan who was facing her way. Then Mandy's foot slipped. She gave a tiny shriek of alarm, falling gracefully into Ryan's arms and grabbing hold of his jacket, murmuring something that made him laugh. Her hands slid from the jacket to encircle his neck. She raised her face, closing her eyes so that her long, curled lashes fluttered on her cheeks.

It was a kiss that seemed to Karen to last forever. Frozen into her hiding place, the image of the two merged bodies, silhouetted against the mountains, burned itself into her brain. Mandy was pressed into the protective curve of Ryan's big frame, her hands caressing his hair. When he raised his head, she ran her fingertip along the line of his mouth, reached up and kissed him again, then moved back from him, shaking her hair from her face, her whole body a provocative invitation. "Let's go back, shall we?" she said, and each word fell like a blow on the silent witness huddled in the rocks.

Karen missed Ryan's reply. Through a haze of pain she saw the two of them walk back up the hill toward the hotel, hand in hand, Mandy managing to stay very close to Ryan despite the roughness of the path.

Afterward, Karen had no idea how long she stayed there; it could have been fifteen minutes or it could have been an hour. When she got up at last, her movements were stiff and awkward and her face was pale and set. She didn't expect to find Mandy in the Parcoll, nor did she. Wincing away from the thought of what Mandy might be doing, she got into bed and, oddly enough, fell instantly asleep, a deep, unrefreshing sleep from which she woke the next morning feeling tired in body and soul.

Mandy was already dressed and gone. And if she

didn't hurry she'd miss breakfast herself, Karen realized, looking at her watch and wondering if it was worth the effort. In a spurt of defiance she decided it was. She couldn't hide from Mandy and Ryan forever, and after last night, surely nothing worse could happen? She put on her tightest jeans and a red silk shirt, making up her face with liberal quantities of blusher and a bright red lipstick. With a couple of gold clips she fastened her hair in a loose knot on the back of her head, letting stray tendrils fall around her ears. That should fix them. Be damned if she was going to crawl around with her tail between her legs.

But when she walked into the dining room, the first person she met was Ryan, standing by the counter pouring himself a cup of coffee. He was wearing navy blue cords and a T-shirt so close fitting that it was molded to the hard muscle and bone of his torso. She had never been so aware of his physique, of his essential maleness; to think of him with Mandy was sheer agony.

He gave her a single keen glance that took in the brave red shirt and the flushed cheeks, and went beyond them to the clouded gray eyes and the faint blue shadows under them. "What's wrong?" he said. "Didn't you sleep well?"

"I'm fine." She reached for a cup and saucer to pour her own coffee.

His hand clamped around her wrist. "I asked you a question. Don't fob me off, Karen."

It was too much. She had got used to being ignored by him, and almost used to seeing him always in company with Mandy. What she could not bear was his concern for her. Spurious concern, for what did he care? "Let go," she snapped, her eyes blazing. "I *was* fine until you came along."

He dropped her wrist so quickly that the cup and saucer rattled in her hand. "If this were anywhere but a public place, I'd make you take that back," he said with dangerous quietness. "You can't even let anyone close enough to you to express a little genuine solicitude, can you?"

"I don't want your solicitude—I thought I'd made that clear to you," she hissed.

His face closed. "So you did. Here, let me pour you some coffee."

She held out the cup, knowing he would not miss the slight unsteadiness in her hand, hating herself and him in equal measure. "Thank you," she said tightly, adding cream and sugar and stalking over to the table where Mandy and Laurence were sitting.

"I love your blouse," Mandy said. "Did you get it in Montreal?"

She might hate herself and Ryan, but it was impossible to hate Mandy; Mandy, after all, had checked out the situation first and had only set her cap for Ryan after being assured that Karen did not want him for herself. So they began to talk about clothes in a very sisterly way and before long there was a little genuine color in Karen's cheeks and some of the haunted look had left her face.

"I'll leave you my angora sweater if you like," Mandy was saying. "It would go beautifully with that blouse."

"Leave it for me... what do you mean?"

Mandy opened her eyes very wide. "I'm going home today. Surely I told you that?"

"You certainly did not! You only just got here."

"I'm invited to a party tomorrow night," Mandy said, obviously thinking no other explanation was necessary. "I've got reservations on the flight that comes in this afternoon and leaves after supper. I'll stay at Frobisher overnight and be home tomorrow by noon." Her brow furrowed. "I hope I've been away long enough for Craig to have missed me."

But what about Ryan, was on the tip of Karen's tongue. She risked a glance in his direction. He was looking at Mandy with a kind of tolerant amusement, apparently not at all upset by the news of her imminent departure. But perhaps he had already known about it. Perhaps, she thought with a cynicism that shocked her, that was the reason for his concern a little earlier. Now that Mandy was leaving, he wanted to be back on good terms with Mandy's sister.

He's not like that, a little voice screamed in her brain. She ignored it, drenching her pancakes with syrup and beginning to eat.

After a while Ryan left to type up some notes, and the three family members loitered over second cups of coffee. Despite an almost total absence of common ground, an undemanding affection seemed to have sprung up between Mandy and Laurence, and Karen found herself cherishing the sensation of family closeness as they sat around the table. She might regret Mandy's visit for other reasons, but not for this. Nor did Laurence regret it, she was certain.

When they finally got up, Laurence said gruffly,

"Karen, I want you to take the day off and spend some time with your sister. You've been working too hard. You look tired today."

So it was not only Ryan who had not been deceived by the bright red shirt. Mandy said cheerfully, "Great idea! Come with me up to the Hudson's Bay store, Karen. I want to get a few souvenirs."

They walked to the store, where Mandy purchased a T-shirt for Craig, which proclaimed Pond Inlet, N.W.T., under the stencil of a very large polar bear marooned on an unlikely looking ice floe in the midst of a bright pink sunset. "I'll insist that he wear it." Mandy chuckled.

"You sound almost serious about him," Karen said tentatively.

"I am rather." Mandy sounded faintly surprised. "I've been going out with him for nearly a month, haven't I? If I can last two more weeks, that'll be a new record for me."

The question that she had suppressed at the breakfast table burst from Karen's lips. "But what about Ryan?"

They had paid for the shirt and were outdoors again. Mandy said innocently, "What about him?"

"I. . .I thought perhaps you were falling in love with him," Karen said lamely.

"Goodness, no!"

"Well, it looked that way to me."

"So you were watching, were you? I rather thought you might be." This with a demure, sideways smile.

"What have you been up to, Mandy?" Karen demanded.

Mandy stopped in the middle of the road. "I don't think you're being very honest with yourself, Karen Smythe. I think you're more than half in love with the man yourself."

"I'm not!"

"No? You sure didn't like seeing me with him."

It was true. She hadn't. "Did you talk about me, the two of you?" For some reason she disliked the thought that they might have.

"We did not," Mandy said ruefully. "I tried a couple of times and got royally snubbed for my pains. Not a man you can twist around your finger."

"No, he's not, is he? But that doesn't mean I'm in love with him," Karen said helplessly, starting to walk again. "I...like him. He's been a good friend to me. But...."

"Have you ever told him that?"

"Quite a while ago I did. Not lately."

"Why not?"

"We had this fight, you see. I said some dreadful things to him. Things that weren't true at all. But he thought I really meant them."

"If anyone should be an expert on fights, it's me," Mandy said complacently and ungrammatically. "It's a great way to get rid of a man you don't want anymore. But if you do want him, then my advice is to kiss and make up.... I just hope it works with Craig," she added thoughtfully.

"That's easier said than done."

"Nonsense! If you want something in this world you go ahead and take it. That's my philosophy."

It was not coincidental that the image of Mandy

and Ryan kissing each other should flash across Karen's vision. "I noticed that," she said with a touch of acerbity.

"Good. I hoped you would."

"So you did it all on purpose."

"I might have."

"Is *he* in love with *you*?" Karen hadn't meant to ask that.

Again that innocent, wide-eyed stare. "You'd better ask him that yourself, hadn't you?" Then Mandy looked around her briskly. "Noah lives down this street. His wife makes those crocheted hats with the tassels that so many of the men wear, and sealskin slippers. He said she'd sell me some if I liked them. Let's go and ask."

"Subject of Ryan closed" was the message there, Karen thought with reluctant amusement. But their talk had lightened her spirits enough that she enjoyed the rest of the day, even down to helping Mandy pack. Her sister had ended up buying some sealskin boots and a hand-embroidered parka as well, as a result of which Karen fell heir to a number of Mandy's other garments that couldn't be squeezed into her bulging suitcases.

The four of them ate dinner together in the hotel. Afterward Mandy kissed Ryan goodbye in the full view of the whole dining room, oblivious to the fascinated hush that fell over the audience. "If you ever decide to live a normal life in Montreal, let me know," she said pertly. "I'm in the phone book."

"I'll do that," Ryan responded. "Bye, Mandy. Tell Craig he has my sympathy."

To Karen, who was watching, it didn't sound like the speech of a man whose heart was broken. Yet if he had just been amusing himself with Mandy, flirting with her much as she had been flirting with him, was it not possible he had also been doing the same with Karen? Instinctively she repudiated this. But how could she be sure?

She, Mandy, Laurence and the air crew piled into the van and drove to the airport, where Mike handed out tags for the luggage, then started loading it into the hatch at the nose of the plane, his copilot stowing it away. Again the scene was very casual, a far cry from the formalities of Air Canada. Mike climbed aboard and the propellers started to turn. Mandy kissed and hugged them both, her last words to Karen as she ran for the steps, "Don't forget my advice! If you want something—go after it." She vanished into the plane, which in a minute or two taxied down the runway and took off.

In silence Laurence and Karen watched it circle and head southeast until it was swallowed by the clouds. "I'm glad she came," Laurence said, the ghost of a smile on his face. "And I'm glad you're still here."

His simple words were enough for Karen, who knew him too well to expect flowery speeches or long-winded declarations of love. She said impulsively, "Did you tell her about your illness?"

"No. Would you have?"

"Probably not."

"I haven't told anyone but you, Karen."

Tucking her arm in his, she left the terminal with

him. Walking was difficult for him, for he tired easily and had to rest a couple of times on the short distance to the hotel. The tremor in his arm was far more pronounced by the time they reached the Parcolls, and when Karen suggested he lie down for a while, he made no demur, in itself a bad sign. She made sure he had everything he needed, then left him alone.

As always when she was troubled or upset, the sea beckoned to her. She wandered along the beach, scuffing at the sand, picking up the occasional oddly shaped rock, the mournful crying of the gulls wafting across the water. Her father's health was worse than when she had arrived. She could not deceive herself otherwise, much as she might have wanted to. Although Mandy's visit with all the accompanying complications had driven it to the back of her mind, she now found it weighing on her, a harsh fact of reality that she could not alter or ameliorate. If only she could share it with Ryan...that might help. But despite Mandy's departure he was as distant from her as he had been since the day of the fight with Rusty. According to Mandy, it was up to her to mend the breach, and originally she had had every intention of doing that. But how could she? And what if he rejected her? She shivered, thrusting her hands deeper in her pockets. She had forgotten to bring mittens.

After a while she turned back, for once oblivious to the beauty of the gold-tinted water and the majestic silence of the mountains. Staring at the ground, she clambered up the hill, the wind tugging at her hair and sending chills down her back. Because she was not really looking where she was going, she didn't see Ryan until she was almost up to him. He was standing by the door of her Parcoll, his own hands in his pockets, his blue eyes guarded. Trying to ignore the erratic pounding of her heart, Karen said feebly, "Hello."

"I saw you coming up the hill so I waited for you. You look cold."

Ordinary little phrases. She could throw them back in his face, as she had done this morning, or she could accept the concern behind them. She said, stumbling a little over the word, "I am. I was walking on the beach and didn't realize how cold the wind was." She hesitated, Mandy's advice uppermost in her mind. "Will you come inside for a minute? The stove's on, so it'll be warmer." Not exactly a scintillating invitation, but it was the best she could manage. She waited for his reply, with no idea whether he would accept or refuse, yet wanting him to accept with every fiber of her being.

"Sure."

Unconsciously she let out her breath in a tiny sigh. Preceding him through the door, she walked over to the stove and held out her hands to its warmth. He was here. The rest was up to her.

He joined her, kneeling to turn up the knob. Having no idea where to begin, she simply opened her mouth and let the words come out. "Ryan, are you in love with Mandy?"

"Good Lord, no!" He got to his feet, looking at her in blank amazement. "She's amusing and pretty, and fun to be with—but I'd never fall in love with her in a thousand years. What made you ask that?''

"I saw you kissing her. Down on the rocks." There, it was out.

"Did you now...? Did she see you?"

"I don't think so," she answered hesitantly.

"If she did, that would explain a number of things. I had the feeling the whole time she was here that some kind of a game was being played. And that kiss was part of it. Mind you, I fell in with the game, if that's what it was. You so obviously didn't want anything to do with me. You might as well have been a million miles away, so I suppose I was flattered when she set her cap for me, and glad enough to have her company. Whatever her faults, she's not dull."

He was not in love with Mandy; indeed, he had more or less seen through her tactics. Feeling immeasurably better already, Karen had the courage to ask her next question. "Ryan, do you remember the day of the fight?"

"Yes."

The watchful look was back on his face. "I'm sorry I spoke to you the way I did. Accusing you of being violent all the time and always mauling me. It's not true. I knew that at the time."

He moved closer to her. She had not switched on the light, and because the windows were covered it was almost dark inside. "I knew it, too," he said heavily. "At least intellectually I did. But I guess I was hurt just the same. I didn't like being bracketed with Rusty and Steve, as if I wasn't any different from them."

So she had hurt him. She had that power. It meant he must care for her even if only to a limited degree; the words of a casual acquaintance had nowhere near the power to wound as did those of a friend. "You *are* different from them," Karen said with passionate conviction. "You're honest and kind and true...." She came to a stop before the look in his eyes. "I-I've never even thanked you for getting rid of Rusty for me," she finished weakly.

"You haven't, have you? You could thank me now."

She knew what he wanted, and with a rush of sheer joy knew that they were back on their old footing again. And once again she understood how deeply she had missed him. More accustomed to the darkness now, she could see his steady blue eyes, the firmly held line of his mouth. Sensing that he was holding back, that perhaps the doubts caused by her accusations had not fully been banished, she knew the next move was up to her. He needed something from her—reassurance, the confidence that their relationship had not been permanently impaired by the ugly scene at the airport when physical and emotional violence had conspired to separate them.

He needed her...the words seemed to sing in her heart. She looked up at him, sliding her hands up his chest to cup his face. Pulling it down to her, she trustingly offered him her mouth and the sweetness of a kiss innocent of desire or complicity. Had she but known it, it was a kiss as different from Mandy's far more practiced one as a kiss could be.

It didn't last long. Still very close to him, her eyes

shining softly, she said, "Welcome back...I missed you," and knew her words would need no explanation.

Ryan stroked her hair back from her face. "I missed you, too—so much. The trouble is, this place is too small to avoid anyone, and it seemed that every time I turned around, there you were. Beautiful, desirable and totally out of reach."

"Ryan, I'm still not—"

"Hush." He silenced her with his mouth, his arms drawing her against him. She didn't want to argue with him; she didn't want to worry about the future or the demands he might make on her; she only wanted what was happening now...the warmth of his mouth, the pressure of his body, the sense of rightness, of belonging....

He couldn't have failed to sense her surrender. He teased her lips apart, and she felt the first touch of his tongue. It was an intimacy she had never imagined, nor could she possibly have imagined her response. A shaft of pure pleasure went through her. She clutched at his shoulders, sagging against him, as the kiss went on and on and with it the honey sweet exploration of her mouth. Her own response was shyer, less sure of itself, but it was undoubtedly a response. Ryan's arms tightened convulsively around her, his lips drawing the breath from her body until she thought she would die with the delight of it.

When he finally did release her, Karen could only cling to him, her eyes black pools of wonder. He was breathing hard. She rested her finger against the pulse at the base of his throat, feeling the blood pound beneath her touch, and it could have been her own blood.

He shrugged off his jacket, almost roughly pulling hers off as well, and letting it drop to the floor. Then she felt the imprint of his hands on her back, burning through the thin red shirt, and a kiss that didn't seem to have ended had started again. Although this time her response was bolder, it still had a touching innocence to it, for she had no idea of what forces she might release in him, nor what extremes of control he might have to exert to subdue them. Lips met, moved and deepened their joining; tongues touched, invaded, caressed; slim soft body curved into the hard arc of bone and muscle.

When Ryan thrust her away it was like the ripping in two of a lovingly woven tapestry, a desecration of a design that was as beautiful as it was inevitable. He was still holding her by the elbows, although there was a foot or more of space between them. He was panting for air, harsh lines engraved from cheek to chin.

Karen might have fallen had it not been for his support. Bewildered and bereft, not wanting their embrace to end, she said faintly, "Did I do something wrong, Ryan? Something I shouldn't have?"

"You did everything right," he said hoarsely. He drew two more deep, hard breaths, fighting for composure. "You don't even understand, do you?" He let go of her, putting more distance between them, his face in the shadows.

"Understand what?"

"Karen, I want you. Want you in the most primitive and direct way possible. And that doesn't just mean kissing. It means making love to you and all that that implies." He hit his fist into his palm, a small gesture with a world of frustration behind it. "I know I can't do that. Not yet, anyway—you're not ready for it. But when you kissed me a minute ago and responded to me so openly. . . I was in danger of forgetting."

It was the Karen of nine years ago who spoke through her lips. "You can't make love to me—not ever."

"I can't make love to you now. Never's a long time."

"You can't!" There was an edge of panic in her voice.

"Karen, a month ago I couldn't have kissed you as I did just now. You know that as well as I do. Who knows what will happen in another month? But I made you a promise, that I wouldn't do anything you didn't want, and I mean to keep that promise." There was the first sign of a smile on his face. "Even if it half kills me."

Now that he was no longer holding her or kissing her, now that he'd erected a barrier of words between them Karen couldn't imagine how she had been swept unresisting into that other, magical world. Not just unresisting, she thought with caustic honesty. Actively encouraging him. Abandoning herself to a wild excitement in her blood that had beckoned to an even greater possession, to that ultimate closeness between men and woman. But that was not for her. Nine years ago she had vowed she would never allow herself to be so frighteningly vulnerable to a man, and no one in those nine years had caused her to even contemplate changing her mind. No one until Ryan.

"Don't look so confused, Karen," he said, and the gentleness she cherished was back in his voice. "It'll all work out somehow. Things usually do."

Not this, she thought painfully. Shivering a little in reaction, she muttered, "You were different a minute ago, almost violent." It was an unfortunate choice of words, yet it best described that slam of fist into palm.

He said grimly, "Don't always expect sex to be a nice, pleasant little interlude, Karen. It's one of the most powerful forces in us."

"It doesn't have to be." She crossed her arms over her breasts in unconscious defensiveness.

Moving restlessly around the room, he said, "Let's drop it—we're not getting anywhere. Where's Laurence, do you know?"

"He's in bed." And it all came rushing back. Her father's illness, the weakness he despised in himself, the loss of independence he feared more than he feared death.

Something must have shown in her face. Ryan said sharply, "What's wrong?"

Earlier she had longed to share the burden with Ryan. Now she was not so sure. If Laurence had wanted Ryan to know, he would have told him himself, wouldn't he? Certainly he hadn't wanted Mandy to know. "Nothing," she said, intending to sound firm, but merely projecting irresolution.

"Is he ill?"

"Of course he's ill," she snapped. "You know that as well as I do."

With overdone patience Ryan said, "Is he worse, then?" He came closer, his eyes intent on her face. "He's told you what's wrong with him, hasn't he?"

It might only have been an inspired guess on his part; however, Karen was unable to disguise her flinch of acquiescence. "Yes, he has," she said dully.

"He feels very close to you, Karen. . .I'm not surprised he told you. Did he ask you to keep it confidential, or can you tell me?"

She was visited by a sudden strangé thought, something right out of the blue. She could fall in love with Ryan Koetsier, she thought blankly. Perhaps she already had. Perhaps that explained why she had so minded his withdrawal and his subsequent flirtation with Mandy. *I'm in love with Ryan Koetsier.* Tentatively she played the words over in her mind, scarcely knowing what she meant by them, yet at the same time recognizing their power. He was sensitive enough to understand Laurence's need for privacy, and if she were to say the matter was confidential, he would not persist. Other men might urge her to reveal it anyway, might rant and rave until she did; not Ryan. He would accept her word as the truth and leave her with her secret.

But love? She didn't love him—she couldn't! She was mistaking an appreciation of his integrity, a trust in his strength, as another emotion altogether. She did not love him; she liked him. Not at all the same thing.

It had taken only seconds for all this to flash through her brain. Her voice seemed to come from a long way away as she said calmly, "He didn't want

Mandy to know. But he didn't say anything about you.'' She knelt to unlace her boots, wanting something to do with her hands and, as unemotionally as she could, described the nature of Laurence's illness.

By the time she had finished she was back on her feet. Ryan looked as though she had hit him between the eyes. He muttered, more to himself than to her, ''I should have guessed, I suppose. It's the logical thing to explain all those symptoms—oh, hell, Karen, that's the worst possible disease for your father to get. He's so damned active and independent. It would kill him to be confined to a wheelchair.''

Her own thoughts exactly. ''I know,'' she said in a low voice. ''I think that's why he hasn't told anyone—he wants to pretend it doesn't exist. And that's why he gets so angry when he drops things, or stumbles, or starts to shake.''

''When did he tell you?''

''The day before Mandy came.''

''So you've been carrying the burden all by yourself since then. I wasn't much help to you, was I, avoiding you like the plague. I'm sorry, Karen.''

''You couldn't know.'' She had had enough of words, she thought wearily. Ryan's shock had been as great as her own, and he had given her no easy platitudes, for which she was grateful. But now what she wanted was the comfort of being held, the knowledge that she was no longer alone in the dark. ''Ryan,'' she said in a small voice, ''hold me.''

In an instant she was enfolded in his arms, and it was all the security she had craved for years. For the first time since she had learned of her father's illness she began to cry, softly and naturally, unafraid of sharing with Ryan her pain and anxiety.

When she had finished, he said, "Stay there a minute while I get a Kleenex. If I were the hero in a book, I'd have an immaculate handkerchief in my pocket, wouldn't I, for just these contretemps. Here." He pressed several tissues into her hand.

She blew her nose, feeling at once tired and strangely peaceful. "Thank you," she said, knowing she was thanking him for far more than the Kleenex.

"Anytime," he replied, and she knew he meant it very literally. "You look worn out. You'd better get to bed." He hesitated, then added with elaborate casualness, "Why don't I turn my back while you get undressed, and then I can kiss you good-night before I leave?"

Karen scarcely hesitated at all. She didn't know enough of love to know if she loved him; what she did know was that she trusted him and needed him. Boldly taking what was a giant step into the dark, she said equally casually, "All right."

He went to stand in the opposite corner of the room while she stepped out of her clothes, folded them neatly and put them on the chair, and then pulled her nightdress over her head. It was a full-length knit nightshirt in a soft shade of pink, with flowers embroidered around the neckline. It was not intended to be a seductive garment, and she had chosen it for warmth and practicality, yet it clung to the swell of her breasts and the curve of her hips. Had she known just how seductive it did look, she would have got into bed and pulled the sheets up to her chin before saying a word; as it was she said softly, "I'm ready, Ryan," and stood still, waiting for him.

He turned, staring at her pale, slender figure as though he could memorize it. Then he walked toward her, slowly closing the distance between them. Dropping his hands to her shoulders, he said huskily, "Good night, Karen."

She raised her face in mute invitation, her eyes closing so that the long dark lashes fanned her cheeks. His kiss began gently, wooing her into submission, until she forgot everything but the warmth of his lips and the heaviness of his hands. Wanting both to please him and to reassure him that all was well between them, the rift forgotten, she pressed her body against his. There was the dizzying touch of his tongue again, then a new sensation, the slow slide of his hands from her shoulders down the length of her back. They caressed the concavity of her waist, the swell of her hips, and the thin fabric of her nightgown seemed less and less of a barrier to the warmth and sureness of an exploration that left her trembling. And then his hands moved upward to cup the firmness of her breasts, and the shock ran through her whole body, a mingling of pleasure and pain, of fear and sheer delight. The seeking of his tongue at her mouth, the searching of his fingers at her breast... feelings so new, so overwhelming, that she was lost, helpless to resist.

Then his arms went hard around her, so tightly that she could scarcely breathe. His lips, no longer gentle or tender but fierce and hungry and unrelenting, demanded a response from her. She whimpered deep in her throat as fear mastered pleasure, banishing it as if it had never been. Bound to him by arms like steel, unable to move, Karen felt another sensation thrust itself on her consciousness—a remembered hardness between her legs, a savage male demand that knew nothing of words or gentle phrases, that would not heed her even if she screamed against its claims.

Nevertheless, the scream gathered in her throat, filling her mind. With all her strength she jerked her head free, drawing breath into her air-starved lungs, and the scream came out as a hoarse, desperate cry. "No, Ryan—please, no!"

His features were blurred with feeling, his blue eyes drowned in it. He was a stranger to her. "I'm sorry," she said more strongly, "but you scared me."

Her words must have reached him. He looked at her, appalled, as cold reality banished desire. His jaw tightened, deep lines scoring themselves in his cheeks so that he looked like a man being tortured. "I did it again, didn't I?" He said harshly. "I frightened you. God knows, I meant to be gentle. I was only going to kiss you." Suddenly becoming aware that he was still holding her, he pushed her away, dropping his clenched fists to his sides. "I don't know what happens to me when I get near you, Karen, but I can't keep my hands off you. I want to make love to you, to hold you until we're not two but one."

He was breathing as hard as if he had been running; she could see beads of sweat on his forehead, a corrosive self-contempt thinning his mouth. Forgetting her own fear, and almost incoherent with compassion, she reached out a hand, palm upward in supplication. "Ryan. Ryan, dear—"

He didn't even hear her. Retreating from her, he muttered, "I'm sorry, Karen, more sorry than I can say. I'm no good for you—I only want to help you and I end up hurting you every time. . . ." He looked around, as if not even certain where he was. "I've got to get out of here."

He lunged across the room and was through the door, slamming it shut behind him before Karen could say a word. Her hand fell slowly to her side. For a moment her eyes flickered around the Parcoll, as though she would still find him there. How could he be gone, he who had filled the room with his presence and ignited her body with his hands? Unconsciously she smoothed her nightdress over her hips, remembering how he had done the same as if they were his lips; she pressed her fingertips to her mouth. But he was gone; she was alone. The fears that had haunted her for years had won again, defeating her fragile awakening to passion, driving away the one man who could bring that passion to its fruition.

She stood very still, staring wide-eyed into the empty, shadowed corners as she realized just exactly what message her brain had given her. By some strange alchemy she now believed that in Ryan lay the key to her cure, that he could make of her a whole woman. She didn't know how, for the fears were still black-winged and powerful, trying to beat down her new confidence; but she knew it was so. She needed him. Needed him desperately. Because she knew something else—she no longer wanted to be the old

Karen, standing on the sidelines of life, believing that she was forever exiled from love and intimacy and all the normal human needs. She wanted to express all of her female nature, to liberate the passion and generosity that she now knew she was capable of. And she wanted to do it with Ryan.

She stared down at her hands, remembering how they had buried themselves in the silkiness of his hair and smoothed the hard lines of his shoulders; remembering, too, the agony on his face as he realized how he had frightened her. So he had left her, not trusting himself to be with her.

For a moment she contemplated going to his tent and confronting him with her discoveries. But then, from some secret source of wisdom, she knew that would be wrong. It was too new, too raw in his mind. But tomorrow was another day, and the tomorrow after that. The time would come when it would be right to tell him.... She smiled secretly to herself, feeling happier and more sure of herself than she had for days.

CHAPTER TWELVE

THE OPPORTUNITY KAREN SOUGHT was to come sooner than she'd expected, although perhaps not quite under any circumstances she might have imagined. She got up the next morning feeling rested and content. She dressed in slim-fitting wool slacks and Mandy's angora sweater and brushed her hair until it crackled and shone. Boots and her jacket and she was ready.

She stepped outside into a fresh, shining morning of sun and blue sky, the mountains etched sharply against the horizon. A beautiful day, she thought, knowing it echoed her own optimistic mood. Then her attention was caught by the sound of an engine high in the sky. It was a plane, a white plane that for a moment she thought was Rusty's. Realizing it was smaller than the Twin Otter, she gazed up at it, frowning slightly. Rusty and Steve hadn't come back to Pond Inlet. So were her suspicions about the gyr-falcons quite unfounded? Was Rusty simply an itinerant ornithologist as he claimed?

The door of the farthest Parcoll opened with the rub of hinges she had come to expect. She turned, watching Ryan come outside, the sun gilding his fair hair. When he saw her he stopped dead, and she knew this was not the time. Not yet. Instead she called casually, as if the devastating scene between them last night had never happened, "Whose plane is that, do you know?" and began walking toward him.

He glanced up at it. "Petro-Canada, I think. Why?"

"I've just realized Rusty never came back. I didn't tell you what happened on that flight I took with them, did I?" Greatly daring, she tucked her arm in his, smiling up at him. "Are you going to breakfast?"

She felt the stiffness in his arm and saw the wariness in his blue eyes, as blue as the sky behind them. Blithely ignoring both, she chattered on, "The day of the fight, I'd been up in the plane with Rusty. We went up to Utuk Lake, over Oliver Sound and Frechette Island to Bylot." Firmly steering Ryan toward the hotel, she described the ostensible purpose of the trip, to locate snow geese, and told how they had seen what she was sure was a gyrfalcon even though Rusty had said it was a goose. "The fight and everything that happened afterward put it right out of my mind," she confessed as they helped themselves to coffee before going to sit down. "But I was sure he knew it was a gyrfalcon, and I figured he'd try and catch it. Instead, he and Steve took off and they haven't been back."

Thoughtfully Ryan stirred his coffee. He was treating her more naturally now, she was glad to see, talking to her not as the woman he wanted to seduce but as a friend. "Do you know where they went?"

"Lucas said they'd gone to Frobisher, but that they'd be back."

"If what you say is true and they are trying to capture the falcons—and I wouldn't be a bit surprised, Rusty looks like the type who'd be after a fast buck—then they could have gone to get the equipment they'd need. Or to make arrangements for overseas transportation." He began to peel an orange, and Karen found herself watching the movements of his long, sensitive fingers, recalling with a tiny shiver of excitement how those same fingers had caressed her breasts. "Tell you what, Karen," he went on. "Are you game to hike up to Utuk? It's a good fourteen miles. We'd have to leave as soon as possible and camp overnight." His mouth hardened. "Maybe that's not such a good idea."

She had to say it. She encircled his wrist with her hand, speaking quietly so they wouldn't be overheard, yet with absolute sincerity. "Please don't blame yourself for what happened last night, Ryan. I instigated it just as much as you did."

Briefly he rested his own hand on hers, and her fingers were swallowed in his much larger grip. "Thanks, Karen, that's sweet of you. But I'm the one who let it get out of hand. Don't worry, it won't happen again." He smiled crookedly. "Although, as I recall, I said that once before, didn't I?"

The waitress arrived with bacon and scrambled eggs and a mound of hot buttered toast. Waiting until she had left, Karen said calmly, "What would we do at Utuk? Look for the falcons?"

"Yes. See if there really is a nesting pair there. Even if we're mistaken about Rusty, it would be a useful sighting because there's so little information about them.''

''I think it's a great idea. What should I bring?''

Trying to make a joke of it and not quite succeeding, Ryan said, ''You wouldn't be afraid to go way back there, just the two of us?''

''No.'' Her face was very serious.

He appeared to make a decision. ''Okay. I'm due for a couple of days off—after I left you last night I couldn't sleep, so I worked on those bloody reports until four o'clock this morning. Finished them, thank goodness.''

She could have asked him why he hadn't been able to sleep. Instead she said, ''What will I bring?''

''I'll rustle up some food from the kitchen. Your father's got a tent we can borrow. And I'll take a gun, just in case. Pack a change of clothing, a towel and a sleeping bag, and we'll take two pairs of binoculars.''

After breakfast while he was organizing the gear, Karen had a quick bath and packed her clothes. A day and a night with Ryan. . . the prospect filled her with happiness, and she was humming as she folded the down sleeping bag, shoved it into a waterproof bag and tied it under the flap of her backpack. Checking to see that she had everything she needed, she propped the pack beside her bed and went to see her father. ''Can I come in?'' she called, tapping on the door.

''Sure. Morning, Karen.''

He was already hard at work, his desk the usual untidy clutter of papers, his pen scratching away on the paper. ''Can you do without me today?'' she asked. ''Ryan and I thought we'd hike to Utuk and camp there overnight." Briefly she described her sighting of the falcon and their suspicions of Rusty and Steve.

Laurence listened intently, capping his pen and pushing his notes aside. "There's a lot of money to be made in the smuggling of those birds—you could well be right. If Rusty and Steve turn up here again, I'll get Lucas to keep an eye on them. Or better still, the constable."

"We've got no proof—it's pure conjecture."

"A minor detail," he said grandly. "I never did think Rusty was much of an ornithologist."

She smiled. "We'll be back tomorrow. By the look of things you'll have plenty for me to do."

"I'm starting to analyze the new data from the summer's dig. Very interesting, indeed." His eyes gleamed with enthusiasm.

She rested her hand on his shoulder. "Well, take care of yourself, won't you?"

"I will." Briefly he covered her hand with his. "I know I don't have to worry about you with Ryan along. A very capable fellow."

There was no reason for her to blush. Knowing her father had noticed, she blushed even more. "Yes, he is," she mumbled. "He's probably waiting. I'd better go."

Laurence heaved himself upright and kissed her on the cheek. "See you tomorrow, dear."

"Bye." Without the slightest touch of premonition, Karen blew him a kiss over her shoulder and went outside.

Ryan was waiting for her. He gave her some of the food to carry and a set of metal cooking utensils and swung his own pack up on his back, adjusting its straps. Then he helped her with her own pack. By nine-thirty they were on their way.

They stopped for lunch near the lake where Karen had camped and then pressed on. It was astonishingly warm, warm enough for both of them to travel in their shirt-sleeves. It was also very hard work, for the terrain was never flat. Either they were clambering over rocks and gravel, or striding from tussock to tussock trying to keep their balance and avoid the clinging black mud in between. But the beauty of their surroundings was, for Karen at least, compensation enough. Behind them was the satin-smooth ribbon of the inlet edged with the jagged mountains; ahead of them the towering cliffs of the canyon, its plateau dusted with snow. And all around them was the silence of the tundra, broken only by the shrill call of the plovers and the murmur of the river.

Midafternoon they stopped for another break, munching on apples and raisins. By mutual consent they had kept the conversation away from the vicissitudes of their relationship. Instead they had a lengthy and very satisfying discussion on religion, during which they discovered that they believed—and disbelieved—more or less the same things. It would never have occurred to Karen to discuss religion, or the meaning of life, or her own personal philosophy, with Duke or Mandy; neither one of them would have appreciated it. Yet with Ryan she felt free to express concepts she believed in yet had never disclosed to anyone else. She was delighted with his penetrating questions and with his own ideas, more thoroughly worked out than her own and more concisely defined, yet very much along the same lines. It was a new kind of sharing, and one she very much enjoyed. Besides which, on an altogether more mundane plane, it helped to take her mind off her aching feet and the pull between her shoulder blades from the backpack.

They finally reached the base of the bluff, where the waters from the lake tumbled over the rocks in a hundred streams that joined and rejoined to form the river. The cliffs were awe inspiring, bare rock devoid of life, gouged and worn, mute sentinels of a deep, ice-cold lake that guarded its own secrets. There was no sign of the gyrfalcons and even the plovers were silent.

Ryan picked out a campsite on a slight rise that overlooked the river, where a heap of rocks carelessly dumped by a long-ago glacier would shelter them should the wind come up. Together they smoothed out the ground and put up the tent, a two-person tent that left barely six inches of space between their spread-out sleeping bags. Neither of them chose to comment on the fact.

Ryan set up the stove, and by combining the contents of several packages he produced a mouthwatering stew that was thick with meat and vegetables. He also baked a bannock so hot that the butter melted on it. With tea and tiny cans of sweetened fruit, the meal was a feast. Karen sat back on her perch, a rather lumpy chunk of granite for which she was not adequately padded, and licked her fingers quite unselfconsciously. "That was marvelous," she sighed. "I don't know when a meal has tasted so good. Maybe you should give up being an archaeologist and become a chef instead.''

''Remember I dragged you up hill and down dale for eight hours first to make sure you had an appetite.''

She wrinkled her nose at him. ''True—perhaps you'd better stick with archaeology.''

He grinned. ''Just for that I'll finish off the last piece of bannock. Then I'll heat some water so you can wash the dishes.''

''So *we* can, you mean.'' As she laughed at him, that elusive emotion called happiness enveloped her again, and she knew she would never forget this moment, with Ryan crouched on the ground beside the stove, his tanned arms bare, his hair stirred by the breeze. She said impulsively, ''You like me, don't you, Ryan?''

''Yes, Karen, I like you very much.''

''I like you, too. Liking is important.''

''Very.''

''That's good, then,'' she said, with an air of naive satisfaction that made her companion smile. ''Why don't I go down to the river and get some water?''

''Okay.'' Not at all impulsively, he added, ''In the long run I wouldn't be surprised if liking isn't more important than loving.''

''Oh.'' Unaccountably she blushed, hot color staining her cheeks until he couldn't possibly have missed it. Grabbing an aluminum pot she fled down the bank, and as she did so she wasn't thinking of the little scene that had just passed, but of the touch of his hands on her breasts and the sweetness of his kisses. That was surely not as simple as liking—was it? But perhaps it had nothing to do with love, either.

She dallied by the river's edge until her cheeks had cooled, then scrambled up the bank, spilling out a quarter of the water as she went. As they washed the dishes, Ryan suggested, "Why don't we hike up to the foot of the lake? If you can face the thought of putting one foot in front of the other, that is." Unsympathetically ignoring her groan of protest, he went on, "The odds are better that we'll see the falcons in the morning, but it wouldn't hurt to try tonight."

It was, after all, why they had come, Karen knew. But tired feet didn't make for an overweening interest in ornithology. "As long as we don't go too far."

"You could stay here if you like."

"By myself? No, thanks! I did that once before." She stifled a yawn, for the food had made her sleepy. "Let's go and get it over with. Don't you ever get tired?"

"I'm a man, remember? One of the stronger of the species."

She threw a clump of lichen at him, then ran down the slope, giggling helplessly as he followed her in mock pursuit. She was soon out of breath, for they had to climb steadily to reach the foot of the lake. Tossing pride to the wind she said eventually, "I'm going to stop and have a rest, Ryan—you go ahead."

"Can't take it, eh?" he teased. "Tell you what—do you see that ravine over to the right? Why don't I go and investigate that? It looks like a probable nesting spot. Then when I come back we'll go on to the lake together. It's no distance now."

"A fine idea," Karen said, seating herself firmly on a rock and loosening her boots. "Be careful."

For quite a while she was able to keep him in sight, then the contours of the land hid him. She sat quietly, feeling the profound silence of the tundra press down on her, a silence that the tumble of the river only served to emphasize. Idly her eyes roamed the cliffs, her thoughts on anything but the purpose of the trip. When a flicker of white crossed her vision, therefore, it took her a moment to realize its import. There it was again, disappearing into a deep fissure high on the face of the bluff. Suddenly excited, she got to her feet, doing up her boots again and reaching for the binoculars. She'd get a better view if she crossed the little creek ahead of her and rounded that clump of rocks.... There was no sign of Ryan, but surely he'd figure out where she'd gone.

Her neck craning upward in the hope of catching that illusory flash of white again, she clambered over the rough ground. The creek was more difficult to cross than she had anticipated. Some of the rocks wobbled when she put her weight on them, and the water that had looked harmlessly shallow from a distance was deep and shockingly cold. Using every handhold that she could, she inched her way across. Then she was on dry ground again, hurrying across a bed of sand and around the boulders until her angle of view altered enough that she could see into the fissure. For a moment she stood still, conscious only of disappointment. There was nothing, only bare, furrowed rock reaching to the sky, its foot in the opaque green waters of Utuk Lake.

Then her head swung around. From farther up the lake she heard a shrill, piercing cry. Unmusical, totally wild, it echoed between the walls of the canyon. She saw the bird in the same instant. With its pointed wings beating the air, it came swooping toward the cliff. Karen fumbled for the binoculars and more by good luck than skill focused directly on the falcon. Her heart skipped a beat. Its plumage was as dazzling as snow, the wing feathers tipped with gray, the breast and tail pure white. She could see the predatory hooked beak, the great dark eyes, and all the grace of its flight, so economical, so swift, so beautiful that it brought a lump to her throat.

The gyrfalcon circled, falling lower and lower in the sky. For a moment it hovered, then it plunged toward the cliff. With a gasp of wonder Karen saw its aerie, an undistinguished collection of sticks and moss, soiled with droppings. The female and a couple of dun-colored chicks were crowded in the nest; the male had perched on a rock close at hand.

Her heart was racing, her muscles aching from holding the binoculars. Slowly she lowered her arms and found that without aid of the glasses it was so difficult to locate the nest that she could have passed over it a dozen times and not seen it. Memorizing its location, which was surprisingly near the water, she turned on her heel and began to hurry back the way she had come. She must tell Ryan. He would want to see it for himself.

Still bemused by the bird's wild beauty, her mind full of what she had seen, Karen forgot to be cautious. She came to the creek and began hurrying across, automatically searching for footholds. She was a third of the way over when, with her boot perched hazardously on a rough-edged boulder, she tried to jump across a cascade of rushing water to a cluster of rocks. At the critical moment, however, the boulder shifted. Thrown off balance, she wavered in the air, flinging herself forward in a frantic effort to steady herself. The boulder gave way altogether, crashing downstream from the force of the current, and her foot followed it. She had time to scream once. Then she fell sideways into the roiling water.

The cold jolted her like an electric shock, emptying the breath from her lungs, paralyzing her. Water rushed over her face, her nose. She was flung against a rock, her shoulder striking it with bruising force. Disoriented, terror-stricken, she scrabbled for a toe-hold, and by a superhuman effort managed to get her head above the water.

She didn't see Ryan running toward her. She only knew she couldn't move, that she was immobilized by a cold unlike anything she had ever experienced, that she was going to drown in a foot of water.... When he grabbed her under the armpits, she was a deadweight, her head flopping forward on her chest, her arms dragging. By sheer brute strength he pulled her out of the water, the muscles standing out in his neck. Half kneeling, he flung her over his shoulder and lurched toward the bank, his breath rasping in his throat for she was weighed down by her wet clothing and sodden boots.

His own feet were wet, but he ignored them. In a shuffling run he carried her to the tent, where he put her down on the ground as gently as he could. She lay there in a crumpled heap, water dripping from her jacket and her soaked hair.

Ryan knew the dangers of shock, knew time was short. Shucking off his clothes, he left them lying in an untidy heap and knelt beside her, almost ripping the garments from her body. He could feel the wind on his own bare skin and knew it for yet another enemy. When she was naked, he pulled her into the tent, drying her icy flesh with a towel, then thrusting her limp body into one of the down bags. It took only a minute to fasten the two bags together. Sliding in himself, he gathered her into his arms, pressing her as close to him as he could, covering her without resting all his weight on her.

Perhaps anticipating that they would wash in the creek, he had brought an extra towel. Reaching for it, he wrapped it around her head and clumsily tried to dry her hair. It was the tugging at her scalp that brought Karen back from the hazy underworld of blue white glaciers and frigid rushing waters to some semblance of normality. She was cold—shivering and quaking with a cold that pierced her very bones. Something was pulling at her hair, and there was a weight on her chest, smothering her. She couldn't move.

Her eyes flew open. The noise she had been dimly aware of was the chattering of her own teeth. She tried to stop them, but couldn't; they would not obey her. Nor could she speak. But she could hear, and that was the next thing to register in her brain. The voice was Ryan's. The face hovering over her, taut with anxiety, was Ryan's, but the message in his face was at variance with the soothing murmur of his voice. "You'll be all right, sweetheart. Just lie still, you'll be all right." Over and over again he spoke, as if a record had stuck and could only repeat itself.

Why was she so cold? She couldn't remember.... But Ryan wasn't cold. From his naked skin came warmth, and like an animal she burrowed into it, thrusting her head into his shoulder, curling her legs between his thighs. He guided her hands into his armpits, letting a little more of his weight rest on her and pulling the soft folds of the sleeping bag closely around them both, trapping every bit of precious heat.

Time passed. Karen had drifted into a kind of daze, in which she only gradually became aware that she was growing warmer, that her shivering was only intermittent now and that her teeth were no longer clattering together like castanets. Ryan had been rubbing her hair again with the towel, his fingers firm on her scalp. She gave herself up to him completely, cocooned in the warmth of his body, utterly safe.

She must have slept. When next she opened her eyes, it was to full consciousness. She remembered her foolish dash across the creek, her tumble into the water, the terror she'd felt when her limbs wouldn't obey her and take her to safety. And then everything was hazy. Obviously Ryan had rescued her. He couldn't build a fire, for there was no wood. He had no heater for the tent. So he had done the only thing possible and used his own body heat to bring her back to life.

He was sleeping, his breathing deep and regular,

his face only inches from hers. His lashes were a shade darker than his hair and, she thought with a faint quiver of amusement, thicker and longer than her own... it wasn't fair. In sleep he looked younger, less in control. His chin was as formidable, his nose as strong, but his mouth was relaxed, gentled, in a way that could only move her.

Karen lay very still, becoming aware of something else: they were both naked. Obviously he wouldn't have left her in her wet clothes, for modesty at such a time had no place. Equally obviously he would want every bit of his own warmth to reach her. For a fleeting moment, a capsule of her past, she wanted to move away from him and put a safe distance between them; she had never envisaged that she could lie with a naked man as intimately as she was doing with Ryan.

But she didn't move away. Conscious of her heartbeat, which sounded loud enough to wake him, she allowed her eyes to wander where they would. His shoulders were very broad, his arms powerfully muscled, yet the shadowed hollow above his collarbone had a touching vulnerability. Under his skin the pulse at the base of his neck marked his own heartbeat. Greatly daring, she pressed her lips to it, feeling it throb with a strong, elemental rhythm. She slid her cheek down his hair-roughened chest.

Unconsciously his arm tightened around her. Hardly breathing, she waited until she was sure he still slept. Then her eyes continued their leisurely exploration.

The heat crept into her face. She was curled up to

him so closely that her breasts were lying against his chest. Her skin was very white compared to his own tanned flesh, very smooth against the mat of his hair. Excitement kindled within her. Trying to analyze it rather than be swept up in it, she realized it was sexual excitement, an emotion that was as storng as it was selective. An emotion, moreover, that she had never thought she would feel—yet she was feeling it now. Her nipples hardened, tight as buds in springtime.

"Karen...."

Her lashes flew upward, then dropped in confusion. Ryan had awakened and was watching her. He couldn't be unaware of what she was feeling—nor of the softness of her breasts or the giveaway hardness of their tips. When he spoke again, she knew he was fighting to keep the conversation on an ordinary plane. "Are you warm enough?"

"Yes." Bravely she looked into his eyes. "You seem to be making a habit of saving my life."

He grinned crookedly. "Or your virtue—remember Rusty?"

"How could I forget?"

He stirred restlessly, not meeting her eyes. "Talking about your virtue, I'd better get up and get some clothes on."

The moment of choice. She said gravely, "I like it the way we are."

"So do I...too damn much," he agreed feelingly, reaching for the zipper on the sleeping bag.

Boldly she stayed his hand. "Couldn't we stay like this? If you leave, I'll get cold again."

"But if I don't leave—oh, Karen, I want you so

much.'' With a muffled groan he buried his face in her neck.

She held him there, noticing abstractedly that her hair was still damp. Against her thigh she felt his manhood stir to life, felt him move hastily away from her. He pulled his head free of her hands, the relaxation gone from his face and with it the youth; in it instead willpower battled with instinct. She said urgently, "Ryan, listen to me a minute—please, don't look like that. I. . . .'' She couldn't find the words. Instead she deliberately moved closer to him, putting her arms around him and feeling under her fingertips the scarred flesh of his back. "Put your leg over mine,'' she whispered. "I don't want to get cold again.''

There was a kind of agonized amusement in his face. "Karen, I can't. I want you—and I can't hide that. One of the penalties of being a man.''

She smiled, her gray eyes soft with tenderness. "I'm not asking you to hide anything. I just want you to hold me.''

With his eyes trained on her face, he brought his thigh over hers, where it lay heavily, pinioning her. Deep within her surged an ache of longing too strong to be denied. She gazed straight at him, glorying in it, wanting to share it with him, a tiny smile of wonder tilting the corners of her mouth. And suddenly the words were all there, just waiting to be said.

"A month ago, when we met, if you or anyone else had told me I could be here with you like. . .like this, I'd have told them they were crazy. I would never have thought it possible—never. You've turned my life upside down, Ryan, and I'm beginning to realize

I'm not at all the kind of woman I thought I was. I don't know how much more I can change. I still get terrified when I think of actually. . .of actually. . . ."

"Making love," he finished for her.

She stared at his breastbone as if it was the most interesting thing in the world. "Yes."

"Why, Karen? Can you tell me?"

A month ago she would have said no, adamantly and unhesitatingly. But now she knew differently. The silence of nine years needed to be broken, and Ryan was her friend, the man she trusted. It was time that she tell him.

Her eyes darkened as she steeled herself to go backward in time to the eleven days and nights that had changed her life. "I was fourteen," she said. "You know that. My mother had inherited all that money and it made a big splash in the papers. Not that she did anything to curb the publicity—she thrived on it, and even went on a television quiz show. You know the sort of thing, 'How It Feels to Inherit a Million Dollars. . . .'

"Oh dear, I sound bitter, don't I? But it affected us all. We left the home that I loved and moved to the city. The rift between my father and mother deepened, and the house was always full of people—sycophants who adored my mother because of her money. Not that she knew that. She was too excited by it all to understand or care." She shivered, as if the ice-cold water had again touched her skin. Ryan put his arms around her, not tightly or passionately but as though she were a child in need of comfort.

When Karen picked up the thread of her narrative,

her voice was toneless. "I was on the way home from school one day when a car stopped and a man leaned out to ask directions. It was raining, just like the day you stopped the car. I went closer to talk to him and another man got out, grabbed me and threw me in the back seat. They put a cloth over my face—it was chloroform, I found out afterward—and I passed out. When I came to I was in a small room that had no windows, lying on a hard, lumpy mattress. I had a terrible headache and I was scared to death...." Her face was blank as she relived those first minutes of consciousness in all their sickness and fear.

"There were three of them," she went on unemotionally. "A very big man, as big as you although older and overweight. He was always dirty, and he bit his nails. They called him Paul. The other man was smaller, and rather like a rat. He was scared of Paul, but he didn't want anyone else to know that. And there was a woman called Rosie, who had black hair and wore a red skirt. Looking back, I suppose she was slatternly and foulmouthed, but she was kind enough to me, and at least she was a woman. She was Paul's mistress.... I hated him. He's the one who told me I was being held for ransom, and that if my mother didn't pay up, they'd kill me. He liked telling me that sort of thing because he liked to see people squirm. I once watched him twist Rosie's arm until she screamed—he liked doing that kind of thing, as well."

"Did he ever do anything to you?"

Karen blinked, coming back to the present, hearing the repressed anger in Ryan's voice with faint surprise. "He hit me a few times," she said slowly. "I wasn't always in that little room, you see. They let me out into the other rooms sometimes, usually when they were all there. The day he twisted Rosie's arm I kicked him and yelled at him to stop, and he hit me so hard I went clear across the room." She smiled faintly. "But he stopped twisting her arm."

"You're tougher than you look, Karen," Ryan said quietly. "That was a brave thing to do."

"Was it? I'm not so sure. There were other things he did, you see, and I didn't fight back." She swallowed hard. "One night I needed to go to the bathroom, and for some reason they'd forgotten to lock me in. As soon as I opened the door I heard the noise—panting and thumping and Rosie sobbing. Without understanding what was happening—I was a very young and naive fourteen—I crept down the hallway. It was dark. The house was old and dirty, and it smelled of grease and sour food and sweat. I still don't know where it was. Buried in the woods somewhere south of Montreal, I guess. But if I were to walk into it today, I'd know it. . . . Well, you know what I saw, of course. Paul and Rosie were making love, though there are cruder words for what they were doing. It was more like rape really, because I don't think Rosie wanted to. She was scratching and kicking, and he was hitting her, and all the time she kept on sobbing. He was like a beast, a big, ugly, cruel beast." For a moment she closed her eyes. "I didn't interfere that time. I couldn't—I was too scared. I ran back to my room and closed the door and tried to shut out the noises. Eventually they stopped, although it seemed like forever before they did.''

"So that's why you're afraid of sex, and afraid of being a woman.... Paul was bigger than you, stronger and behaved like a brute—or worse than a brute. So you thought all men were like him...and that sex was painful and violent, to be fought against with all your might.''

"I had nothing to compare it with, you see. It was so...ugly. And then, he used to—" She broke off, her lip trembling.

Up until then Ryan had scrupulously kept his anger under control. But Karen could feel the steel strength in his arms as he pulled her closer and heard the roughness in his voice. "Tell me, Karen.''

"It was nothing, really," she muttered. "But I was so frightened of him. I tried not to show it, but he knew. Maybe his kind always does.'' She was clutching Ryan's shoulder, her nails digging into his skin. "I think he...wanted me. He used to come into my room sometimes to bring my meals, and he'd just stand there looking me up and down as if he was mentally undressing me. Other times he'd...touch me. I'd be paralyzed with fright, but I couldn't have screamed to have saved my soul. I suppose that's why Rosie never realized what was going on.'' The words came tumbling out now that she had started, as if she couldn't wait to get it over with. "He kissed me only once. It was in the room in the dark. I—I fainted.''

"Just as you did with me that first time.''

She squeezed his shoulder in mute acknowledgment of an anger she knew was directed at himself.

"You couldn't have known. Another time the others were outside and he caught me in the hallway. He was telling me the things he'd like to do to me—horrible things. And then the other two came back in and he stopped. I don't know why I was so frightened of him, Ryan, but I was. He only had to look at me and I'd freeze."

"By the sound of it you had damn good reason to be frightened of him. A bully and a sadist...."

"He'd pick fights with poor Roy, too—that was the other man. The whole house reeked of violence. I'm sure that's why I reacted so strongly when you hit Rusty."

"How did you get out of there in the end?"

"My family paid the money. It was my father, actually, although I never found that out until the other night, remember? Paul chloroformed me again, making sure first that I thought I was going to be killed, and when I came to, my father was there and I was taken home."

"And you've never told anyone what you've just told me."

"No. I couldn't. For ages I was afraid they might get me again—they never were caught, you see. So I buried it all as deeply as I could and tried to pretend it had never happened."

"I'm glad you told me, Karen. It helps me to understand."

She rested her cheek on his own, the grip of her fingers slowly relaxing. She felt very tired yet at the same time very peaceful, Paul, whom she had loathed and feared in equal measure, began to recede into the distance again. On the basis of him alone she had decided all men were cruel and brutal. But Ryan was not like that, she thought wearily. Ryan was different....

He heard the rhythm of her breathing and knew she was sleeping again. He held her gently, seeing a leggy, coltish fourteen-year-old who had been exposed to cruelty and lust beyond her imagining. He could picture her fighting gallantly in Rosie's defense; he could also picture Paul's fat, dirty fingers on her breasts. Ryan gritted his teeth, wishing he could smash his fist into Paul's face, beat him until he screamed for mercy. As Rosie had screamed. As Karen hadn't been able to....

He must have moved convulsively, for Karen's eyes blinked open. "What's wrong? Ryan, don't look like that—"

"Sorry," he muttered. "I could kill that bastard."

"It's over now—better forgotten."

"Is it over, Karen? Will it ever be?"

"I want it to be," she whispered, her gray eyes anguished. "But—"

"Will I ever be able to make love to you? Fully and completely?"

"I—I don't know. The trouble is that I saw them, Rosie and Paul. I saw them actually.... It was so horrible. When I think of someone doing that to me, I get so frightened."

"It doesn't have to be that way."

"I think I'm beginning to understand that, Ryan, and you're the one who's done it for me. But I'm still afraid. I wish I weren't, but I am."

"Do you really mean it, Karen? Do you really want to be free of the past?"

She let her eyes wander over every detail of his face, a face she knew almost as well as her own. As she did so another image dropped into her mind, that of the great white bird flying so freely among the cliffs and rocks that were its home. She did want to be free. Free to respond to him, free to be his woman as naturally and as easily as the bird cleaved the sky. "Yes," she said softly. "Yes."

"Then will you trust me, Karen?"

"I already do," she said simply.

"Let me make you a promise. A promise that will hold until we—both of us—decide it should be changed. I promise nothing will be consummated between us. That I won't do to you what Paul did to Rosie. But what I will do is make love to you in the sense of touching you and caressing you. Helping you to explore the different responses of your body, and encouraging you to touch me in the same way. But I promise not to—" He smiled suddenly. "There's really no delicate way of putting it, is there? But you know what I mean. You see, I think that might free you, Karen. You'll know that in one very real sense nothing is going to happen. So you won't have to worry or be frightened, and hopefully you'll enjoy the pleasure two people can give each other."

That he could talk to her so intimately was in itself a revelation. Not even giving herself time to think, she said breathlessly, "I agree."

For a moment Ryan looked taken aback, and she guessed he had expected her to argue or procrastinate her decision. Then he laughed, gathering her into a bear hug that was more brotherly than loverlike. "Good girl!" Sobering, he added, "You were right to be frightened of Paul. Don't ever think that means you lack courage—you don't, believe me."

Glowing from his words of praise, she said with a pertness that deceived neither of them, "So where do we begin?"

"Well, we could begin by you kissing me," he drawled. "Or touching me here." He pressed her hand to his chest. "Or here." He drew her fingers across the flatness of his belly.

A smooth V of hair narrowed to his navel, where the muscles were ridged and taut. Karen felt her heartbeat quicken and a certain elation seize her. She was safe. Ryan had said so. So she could do, or say, whatever she liked.

Very slowly she ran both hands from his waist to his shoulders, letting her fingers learn every contour of bone and sinew. Then with deliberate sensuality she pulled his head down and kissed his mouth, teasing his lips with her tongue. Against her breast she felt the thudding of his heart; he must like what she was doing. Darting her tongue in and out, she stroked his hair and the nape of his neck, exulting in her newly discovered freedom.

He had let her take the lead. Now he brought his own hands up, smoothing the long curve of her back, then drawing her hips close to him. He was fully aroused, and for a moment all the old fears surfaced, the shock running through her body.

He said gently, "It's all right . . . I promised."

She relaxed, saying shyly, "I like what we're doing."

"So do I—as you can tell."

She blushed, in a rush of womanly pride knowing how desirable he found her. Boldly she traced the arc of his rib cage and the hard ridge of his pelvic bones, reading passion as naked in his face as his body was naked. Then she brought his hand to her breast, saying in a low voice, "Touch me there, Ryan."

His answer was to cup her breast in his hand, then to lower his head, his lips traveling along the pale silky skin in a trail of fire to her nipple, which hardened in an instinctive response she could not have prevented had she wanted to. Deep within her, where it had lain chained for years, passion burst from its bonds and leaped to engulf her. Her body arched in unconscious provocation; her face was rapt.

"Oh, Ryan," she said helplessly. "Oh, Ryan...."

His mouth still held her breast captive, but his hands were free. They slid from her breast to her waist, almost spanning its slenderness. Lifting her on top of him, he began kissing her mouth again, fierce, hungry kisses, while his fingers stroked the curve of her spine and the swell of her hips in a soothing, hypnotic rhythm.

In a miraculous wave of passion Karen lost all sense of time and place. Paul, the room, the black-winged fears—all vanished. There was only Ryan, the hardness and strength of his body, the low murmur of his voice as he called her endearments she had never heard him say before, the sure, sweet movements of his hands on her willing flesh. And overlaying it all was her own wondrous sense of freedom to give and to enjoy.

There was also a host of tiny details that later she would be able to recall with utter clarity: the sight of Ryan's lean fingers caressing the white curve of her breast; the slow, lazy way his lips traced the line of her throat; the pounding of his heart as he rolled over on top of her, and the blue of his eyes, now blurred with tenderness, now blazing with desire. His hands were feather light, then strong as steel, binding her to his will until she was lost to everything but the bittersweet wonder that was desire unassuaged.

That their mutual pleasure was gathering to an inevitable conclusion Karen did not fully understand. All she knew was that her hips were moving under his in a rhythm she did not need to be taught, and when his fingers drifted down to her thighs and touched her where no man had ever touched her before, she shuddered in violent response, her nails clawing his back.

Had he broken his promise then, she might scarcely have realized it. Instead he flung himself off her, his chest heaving, his head resting on clenched fists.

The spell he had woven around her shattered in a thousand pieces. Shocked back to reality, she tried to speak. "Ryan?"

"I'll be all right in a minute."

She touched his shoulder and saw him flinch. Suddenly terrified, she cried, "What's wrong?"

"It's all *right*," he snapped, everything in his bearing suggesting the contrary.

She felt suddenly cold and pulled the thick folds of the sleeping bag around her. "I shouldn't have—"

"Karen, for heaven's sake!" He looked over at her, his mouth still a tormented line. "Remember that promise I made you? I'm keeping it, that's all."

"I'd forgotten about it," she said blankly.

"Well, I hadn't."

The tumult in her body was gradually subsiding. But the transition from intimacy to distance had been too fast. A few moments ago she had been caught up in a hunger that was as old as time, rejoicing in the touch of flesh on flesh, wanting Ryan as she had never wanted anyone before. And now she was alone again. It was impossible not to remember some of the things he had done to her and she to him. Although at the time it had seemed natural and right, now she was not so sure. She had never thought to call herself wanton or shameless, yet those were the words that came to mind. She had forgotten the promise he had made; she had wanted him to take her. Her body would have welcomed him; it would have been not an invasion but a coming home. If only he had consummated their lovemaking then, when she was so caught up in the emotions he had evoked that caution and fear had vanished, and all inhibitions had fled. If only he had. . . .

But how could she tell him that now? She couldn't, she knew she couldn't.

She watched him warily, and when he looked over at her, her face was unsmiling. "Sorry, Karen," he said somberly. "I thought I could handle this whole situation with rather more panache. I'd never have forgiven myself if I'd broken my promise. Not when you trust me as you do.''

But I wanted you to, she screamed inwardly.

"I'm going to get dressed and stay outside for a while. I won't go far, don't worry." He brushed her cheek with his fingers. "Try and get some sleep."

She couldn't think of anything to say. Burying her face in the sleeping bag, she heard him leave the tent and move around outside. Her limbs suddenly leaden with exhaustion, she pulled the folds of the bag around her and closed her eyes, her only desire to block everything out in the oblivion of sleep.

KAREN WOKE SOMETIME IN THE NIGHT to see in the gray light a man's checked shirt only inches from her nose. Her lashes flickered. It was Ryan, of course, but a Ryan now fully clothed and with his back to her. She was still naked, and in sleep she had curled her body up to his, one arm tucked around his waist, her cheek against his shoulder blade.

She could feel the slow rise and fall of his chest and knew he was sleeping. Suddenly she was filled with happiness to be so close to him, and the thin yellow walls of the tent became home to her in a way the gracious Tudor-style mansion in Montreal had never been. Snuggling up to him, she closed her eyes again....

CHAPTER THIRTEEN

THE NEXT TIME KAREN AWOKE it was to the hissing of the stove and the mingled aromas of frying bacon and hot coffee. She lay still for a moment, remembering all that had happened during the night—and, she thought with a wry twist of her lips, all that had not happened. Shy of even seeing Ryan again, she called out weakly, "Can you pass in my backpack, please? I've got some dry clothes in it."

The tent flap opened and Ryan pushed her pack in. She was sitting with the sleeping bag pulled up to her chin. Not looking at him directly, she murmured, "Thank you."

"Did you sleep well?"

Busy with the straps, she said politely, "Yes, thanks."

"I've had your boots by the stove for quite a while, trying to dry them out."

"Oh, that's good." She pulled out a clean pair of wool socks.

"There's four feet of snow on the ground." Her eyes flew over to him and he grinned at her. "Thought that would get your attention. Good morning, Karen."

"It didn't snow," she said accusingly.

"Quite right, it didn't. Why are you clutching the sleeping bag so modestly?"

"Will you please go away and let me get dressed," she seethed.

He had levered himself into the tent so that he was almost alongside of her, his big body relaxed, his eyes watchful. The smile fading from his lips, he said, "Are you regretting what happened last night?"

Her eyes dropped, her fingers restlessly pulling at the edge of the bag. "No," she said, but so uncertainly it was almost no answer at all.

He reached over and very gently stilled her fingers. "You'll tear it and all the feathers will come out."

His hand was close to her chin. She could see the blond hair on the back of it, the tanned skin stretched over the knuckles, the well-kept nails. Ryan's hand. . . . In a tiny gesture of surrender she rested her cheek against it, her eyes closing.

"Sweetheart. . . ." He was kissing her hair, her forehead, her cheek. Blindly she offered him her mouth, her lips soft and warm from sleep. There was no need for words; their bodies spoke for themselves. The sleeping bag fell to her waist, and once again she felt the magic of his hands on her breasts, stroking them until her head whirled with the unimaginable delight. Unaware of doing so, she was making tiny sounds of pleasure deep in her throat. When he half fell across her, she gloried in his weight, holding him with all her strength to prolong kisses that banished the old, frightened Karen and created in her place a warm-blooded and passionate woman. A woman who felt as free as the falcon. . . .

The ending was pure farce. From outside came a sudden hissing and spitting. Ryan tensed. Against her mouth he muttered, ''Oh, hell—the coffee.''

Weakly Karen began to laugh, even though her eyes were still slumberous with desire. ''You'd better go and rescue it. Don't think I'm going to walk fourteen miles without my cup of coffee.''

He pushed himself upright and made an undignified scramble for the coffeepot. Her cheeks flushed, her heart racing in her breast, Karen grabbed a sweater and pulled it over her head. She felt like singing at the top of her lungs or doing a mad dance on the tundra, and all because of one man. She loved him, she thought lightheartedly. She must love him. How else could he make her so happy?

She had wriggled into her jeans and was pulling on wool socks when Ryan poked his head in the flap of the tent. Her hair was tumbling about her face; she looked young and carefree, the gray eyes clear and unshadowed. She gave him a wide, generous smile and said saucily, ''I hope my breakfast's ready.''

''Bacon and two eggs, coffee, and some rather burned toast. And I saw the gyrfalcons.''

''You did?'' As she crawled out of the tent, he helped her to her feet. ''Where?''

''Flying near the foot of the lake.''

Although her eyes swept the sky, it was empty of any life. ''That's where their nest is. And, Ryan, they have two babies! I'm so glad we've seen them,'' she murmured. ''You know, we may be quite wrong about Rusty and Steve. I know they saw at least one of the falcons that day, but they're obviously not doing anything about it. Maybe we were being too suspicious.''

''I hope you're right,'' Ryan said, not sounding particularly optimistic. ''If they do come back, we'll have to keep an eye on them.''

Karen sat on a rock and began to eat. The food was delicious, even the blackened toast, and coffee had never tasted so good. The talk turned to other matters; there was an easy companionship between them as they broke camp and loaded their packs for the long hike home. Neither of them referred directly to their lovemaking. But it was there when their hands brushed as they washed the dishes, or when they accidentally bumped into each other reaching for the same thing. A spark of awareness, a shared memory of intimacy and of secret, unspoken caresses. When they were ready to leave, Karen gave one last look around, knowing she would always remember this wild and beautiful place, where Ryan had taken her body by storm and made it his own. Technically he had done nothing, for she was still a virgin; yet in her heart she knew she belonged to him, that with hands and mouth he had set his seal on her.

By maintaining a steady pace all day, they reached the hotel in time for dinner, although they were the last ones to arrive. There was no sign of Laurence in the dining room, so Karen concluded he must already have eaten. Because she was ravenous, the beef stew and lemon-meringue pie disappeared in short order. They were drinking their coffee, Karen gradually becoming aware that every muscle in her body was aching with tiredness, when Lucas came in. He saw them immediately and his face brightened with relief. "There you are! Have you seen Laurence?"

"No," Karen replied. "But we only just got here. Isn't he in his tent?"

"No. He took the boat and he hasn't come back."

"Took what boat?" Ryan demanded.

"My boat," Lucas explained patiently. "Yesterday at noon he said he had to go to the dig to check some measurements. Said he'd be back this morning at the latest. I was busy most of the day and only just noticed my boat's not on the beach."

"You mean he's not back?" Karen asked, her mouth dry.

"The boat's not back. He's not in his tent. There's a note on his desk, but I'm not so good at reading his writing. Maybe you better go and look."

Ryan was already pushing his chair back. "Come on," he said tersely to Karen.

She hurried after him, not bothering to lace up her boots at the door. She saw the note as soon as they entered Laurence's Parcoll, for he had propped it against a pile of books. Its brevity was so characteristic of him that she could almost hear him speaking.

Ryan,
Need more data on the measurements of the winter house and the caches—maybe I lost the sheet. I'm sure I'll be back before you. Tell Karen the papers in the left pile need typing.

                                    L.

Speaking more to himself than to Karen, Ryan said, "There's probably no reason to be worried. He's gone to the dig and he's no doubt got involved in something and completely lost track of the time. I wish he hadn't gone by himself, though."

There was a hollow feeling in the pit of Karen's stomach. "He...he must know how to handle a boat?"

"Lord, yes. But he's so damned shaky these days, and all he'd need to do is lose his balance...." He came to a decision. "Karen, I'm going to borrow a boat—Lucas's cousin has one—and go up there."

"I'm coming with you."

He nodded as if not at all surprised. "All right. You realize he'll be as mad as hell when we both arrive there?"

"I don't care. I just want to know he's safe."

"Bring an extra sweater and let's go."

It took five hours to reach the dig, for the boat was only an aluminum canoe with an outboard motor clamped to its transom. During that five hours Karen had plenty of time to think, remembering with a pang of anxiety how greatly her father's strength and sense of balance had deteriorated even in the short time she had been there. He should never have set off alone. However, knowing him as she did, she understood only too well how his independence and impatience would not have allowed him to wait until she and Ryan returned from Utuk Lake. He would interpret that as a sign of the weakness and dependency he feared.

Her hands clenched in her lap, and she hoped with all her heart that her apprehensions were exaggerated, that Laurence had simply become absorbed in his precious data and lost all track of time. That when they arrived at the dig they would be greeted by a testy, "What the devil are you doing here?"

The boat chugged along. The scenery was spectacular, the midnight sun spilling its gold and pink hues on the water in a profligate display, the cliffs and headlands rising dark and snow-covered from the sea. They saw dovekies and fulmars; loons and oldsquaws flew at their approach; the black heads of seals watched them pass. They crossed the deep, still waters of Oliver Sound and rounded the sheer headland called Qerbignaluk, where the islands heaved out of the water like killer whales. For the first time in over an hour, Ryan spoke. "The dig's in that little bay. Take the binoculars and see if you can see anything."

The tundra leaped into focus. Karen saw heaps of rocks, bones scattered around them, and a yellow tent. But although she searched the approaching shoreline as it came into view, she saw no signs of a boat or of her father.

There was a little beach of pale sand. Ryan drove the canoe up on it, and Karen jumped out. Ryan went over to one of the excavated winter houses, where the boulders were neatly shaped into walls and platforms surrounding a flagstone floor, and then hurried over to the tent. But Karen did not bother looking. She knew Laurence was not there, for the place breathed of emptiness and desolation. Only ghosts lived here, she thought painfully, the ghosts of a people long gone. Toonoonik-Sahoonik, the land of many bones. . . . She shivered, for the silence was oppressive, the very stillness of the sea a menace. The waves of their passing had vanished as if they had never been.

Ryan came up to her. "He's been here, I can tell."

"But he's not here now."

"No. And we didn't pass him on the way." He dropped a hand on her shoulder, making no attempt to mask the anxiety in his eyes. "Something's gone wrong, Karen. I think he's had an accident in the boat."

Ryan was saying nothing she did not already know. She bit her lip, her eyes searching the horizon before coming back to his face. "What do we do now?"

"There are strong currents between all the islands," he answered carefully. "I think we should look for the boat there. I don't see how it could have sunk with the sea this calm."

"You think he went overboard."

"We don't know that yet, Karen. He may have run out of gas and been stranded."

She knew Ryan didn't believe what he was saying; nevertheless, she seized on his words as a last crumb of hope. Not even looking back at the bleak little settlement set against the hillside, she sat in the prow of the boat, sweeping the sea with the binoculars as the canoe chugged away from the shore. They passed a huge chunk of drift ice, surrealistically tinted in rose and yellow from the sun, but Karen was oblivious to its beauty, just as she was oblivious to the gaunt, elegant geometry of the rocky islands. They cruised slowly among them. A half-dozen ringed seals flopped into the sea with a great splash, and her head swung around. The crackle of a loon ricocheted off the water, making her start nervously. When Ryan finally did say, ''Over to your right, Karen—there's the boat,'' she had to search for it. She might easily have passed it by without seeing it, for it was also aluminum, gray like the rocks. It was drifting with the current. It looked empty.

Ryan eased up on the throttle and they approached it slowly. Grabbing it by the gunwales, Ryan turned off his own outboard. The silence echoed in Karen's ears, as alive as the crying of the loon had been. The boat was empty.

She sat very still as Ryan carefully reached over and picked up the red gasoline container, hearing the liquid slosh around inside it. Then he checked the other outboard. ''It's out of gas,'' he said evenly. ''His gear and papers are in that haversack. He must have started out for home and fallen overboard. The boat kept going until it ran out of gas, and then it just drifted with the current.'' He hesitated. ''We'll search around the rest of the islands just to make sure he didn't manage to crawl up on one of them. But I don't think it's likely. He wouldn't have come way out here to start with, and the water's so cold he wouldn't have been able to swim.''

Karen was almost glad for Ryan's brutal honesty. ''You mean he's dead.''

''I think he must be, Karen. You couldn't last any time in these waters.''

''Dead. . . .''

''Let's check the other islands. There's still a chance he might have made it to safety.''

Numbed and cold, she sat in the bow while Ryan routinely circled the rest of the islands. She didn't think they would find her father's body, nor did they. She suspected they would never find it, for she knew enough to realize it would probably be swept out to sea and lost for eternity.

When she heard Ryan speak, she tried to concentrate on his words. "I'm sorry, Karen. More sorry than I can say.... I don't suppose we'll ever know exactly what happened, but I would think he must have reached for the gas can and overbalanced. You know how shaky he could be sometimes."

Twisting to face him, she said with difficulty, "So the disease he feared killed him anyway."

"Maybe in the long run it was a merciful ending," Ryan said quietly. His blue eyes were trained on her face as if by their very intensity he would force her to at least consider what he was saying. "It killed him quickly in the land that he loved—and respected. Laurence of all people was never blind to the dangers of the north and the penalties it exacted of those not physically able to cope with it. Maybe he would have preferred this kind of death to a protracted illness in a city hospital or some kind of institution."

Karen could hear every word, and in an abstract way she recognized their truth. But in front of her eyes, superimposed over anything Ryan could say or do, burned the image of the empty boat lying in wait for them, floating like a dead whale among the ancient rocks. Empty of her father, who had vanished as if he had never been, his moment of weakness paid for in the most costly coin there was.

She heard Ryan speak again, and even discerned the pain behind his halting words. "Laurence loved the north, sweetheart—he felt at home here as he never did in the city, you know that. In time I hope you'll be able to accept how fitting it was that he should die here. His spirit will join those of a long-ago people who also loved this land. . . ."

Despite herself, her eyes were dragged back to the deserted settlement at the base of the cliffs, where the hunters of whales had lived out their lives. She hugged her knees against her breast, feeling very cold. "What do we do now?"

"Let's go back to the campsite for a minute. I want to put my arms around you and hold you, Karen."

She would fall apart if he did. Shatter into a thousand pieces that would never fit together again. "No. I don't want to go back there."

There was a long pause. "I can't even see your face. Sweetheart, I'm so sorry. . . ."

Dazed with shock, she looked around at the steel-gray waters of the fiord and the distant, snow-covered peaks. "Take me back to the hotel." She shivered. "I'm cold."

"All right," Ryan said heavily. "We should report this as soon as possible so the police can conduct a search for the body. I'll tow the other boat back with us."

The journey back was like a long drawn-out nightmare, but like all nightmares, it had to end. Lucas met them at the wharf, for he must have heard them coming. He went to notify the police while Ryan guided Karen back to the hotel. She was on the verge of collapse, so tired that she scarcely knew where she was. When they reached her Parcoll she was dimly aware of him helping her undress and then carrying her over to the bed. She felt him kiss her and then pull the covers over her. She huddled under them, letting sleep wash over her, obliterating everything that had happened in a black tide of forgetfulness.

KAREN SLEPT FOR NEARLY FIFTEEN HOURS. When she woke up, there was a moment when she wondered why she dreaded this awakening, before memory rushed back and with it the knowledge of her father's death. Their reconciliation had been so brief, she thought sadly. She had found him only to lose him again. She stared up at the ceiling, remembering herself and Mandy and Laurence sitting around the table in the dining room, remembering how she had struggled to decipher some of her father's handwriting and how they had joked about it. Her throat felt tight and all her emotions frozen; although she wanted to cry, for it would have eased the pain, the tears wouldn't come, and eventually she got out of bed and got dressed, her movements awkward and stiff.

She was brushing her hair when she heard footsteps outside and a tap at the door. Ryan came in. She was standing by the bed, and something in her set, white face made him stop several paces away from her. "Did you sleep well?" he asked.

"Yes, thank you." Her words were polite, as if he were a stranger.

"Karen, there's to be a brief inquest in an hour. They'd like you to be there, if possible. It's not much notice, I know, but I didn't want to wake you earlier."

"What's the time?" she asked, confused.

"It's nine in the evening. You slept the whole day."

She tried to gather her wits. "I see. Yes, I'll go."

"Someone will have to contact your mother and Mandy. Maybe you'd like me to do that for you?"

Another hurdle. "No. No, I'll do it." Belatedly she added, "Thank you anyway."

"And the Anglican priest wanted to know if you'd like a memorial service—tomorrow, perhaps."

She did not need to hesitate over that decision. "Yes. Do I need to see him?"

"No, he'll make all the arrangements. You'd better come and have something to eat now."

"I'm not hungry."

"You must eat. Come on."

There was a note in his voice that was meant to be obeyed. He took a step closer to her and instinctively she moved back. "I—I have to get my jacket," she stammered, going over to one of the beds, where the jacket was lying on top of her backpack. She didn't know why she was avoiding him; perhaps she was still afraid that if he touched her she would fall apart. Start crying and never be able to stop.

He didn't press her. In silence they walked to the dining room, where she ate homemade bread and drank tea and afterward couldn't have told anyone what she had eaten. But the food at least gave her the strength to place the call to Montreal. As she heard Mandy's perky hello, she felt a surge of relief that Nancy had not answered the phone.

"Mandy, it's Karen. I've got bad news," she said

bluntly. She couldn't have borne it for Mandy to embark on her usual lighthearted chatter about Craig's misdoings.

Mandy's voice altered. "What's wrong?"

"Father's dead." Her voice tight with strain, Karen described the events of the day before. She was careful not to mention Laurence's illness, however; that would remain his secret. "There's an inquest this evening and a memorial service tomorrow," she finished. "Is mother home?"

"She's out at the moment, but I'll tell her when she gets back.... I don't think she'll want to come to the memorial service, Karen."

"No, I don't imagine she will." How could Nancy react to the death of a husband whose existence she had ignored for years?

"So I won't come, either. I'd better stay here with her. It isn't because I don't want to come—you understand that, don't you?"

Oddly enough, Karen did. "It would be better not to leave mother alone."

Across the hundreds of miles between them, Mandy sounded uncharacteristically unsure of herself, and Karen guessed she was crying. "I can hardly believe it. I came back from Pond Inlet so pleased to have seen father again. And now he's gone...."

Karen's throat tightened. "I feel the same way."

"Is Ryan looking after you?"

"Yes."

Mandy blew her nose. "Did you follow my advice?"

Trust Mandy not to forget that, even under these circumstances. "Yes, I did. How's Craig?"

"He's here now."

"Good—I'm glad you're not alone."

Unmistakably a sob came over the line. "Oh, dear... it's useless to say I wish it hadn't happened, that he was still alive, isn't it? But I do wish that." Unexpectedly her voice gained strength. "I'll tell you one thing, though—I'm so glad I did see him again. I'll never regret that. And you're the one who brought it about. Thanks, Karen."

A uniformed policeman had just walked into the dining room and was talking to Ryan. "I'd better go, Mandy, I think it's time for the inquest. Give my love to mother, and tell her I'll phone again tomorrow. My love to you, too."

"Likewise. Take care of yourself, Karen—I'll be thinking about you."

Karen put down the receiver, staring blankly at the cheaply paneled wall, the artificial wood grain blurring in front of her eyes. Her sister could be flip and casual to the point of aggravation, but when the chips were down, Mandy had shown both love and sensitivity.

The inquest passed in a kind of haze. Karen automatically answered the questions that were put to her and listened as Ryan described their journey to the dig. The police officer reported that so far there was no sign of Laurence's body, and a verdict of death by misadventure—a peculiar word, Karen thought abstractedly—was handed down.

When it was over, Ryan escorted her back to her room. But when he bent his head to kiss her, she turned her face so that his lips brushed her cheek rather than her mouth. "Good night," she said stiffly, wanting only to be alone. Even though she hadn't been up long, she felt exhausted again. All she wanted to do was fall asleep again and forget it all. It took an effort to add, "Thank you for all your help."

His blue eyes were hooded. "You'll come and get me if you need me, won't you, Karen? Don't be alone if you don't want to be."

Go away, her mind screamed. She smiled falsely, already starting to close the door. "No, I won't."

It was sheer relief to shut the door and get into bed. A dreamless and deep sleep claimed her immediately, and it was noon the next day before she left the Parcoll and went into the hotel. Ryan was in the lobby with Josh Crooks, the local police officer, a burly young man from northern Cape Breton with level brown eyes and tightly curled dark hair. They stopped talking as soon as they saw Karen, and when Ryan spoke again, she knew the subject had been changed. "I was just about to go and get you," he said.

Her brief smile did not reach her eyes. Turning to Josh she said, "Have you found anything?"

"No, ma'am. But we've got until this evening before the search is called off. I'm on my way up to the airstrip now to relieve the other guy."

As he left them, Ryan said quietly, "Rusty and Steve are back. They flew in last night. If they're up to no good, they're not likely to try anything as long as the RCMP plane is around. I may scout around their plane later on, see if I can see anything."

It was the first thing that had been said to her in

two days to touch her with reality. "Be careful. I couldn't bear it if anything happened to you, now."

"I will." Gently he smoothed the hair back from her face. The fluorescent lighting was merciless to the dark shadows under her eyes and the pallor of her cheeks. "I wish there were more I could do to help you, Karen."

She stiffened. "I'm all right," she said with patent untruth. "What time's the memorial service?"

"Three o'clock. I'll walk up with you."

No point in arguing. And when the time came Karen was glad enough for his company. Afterward she was to retain only a few scattered impressions of the service, for everything seemed to happen at a distance. There was the tolling of the bell punctuating the distant grumbling of the search plane at the mouth of the inlet. Sealskin was stretched on the altar, emblazoned in *inuktitut*, and the choir stalls were shaped like *komatiks*. The service itself mingled the two languages, something her father would have liked, Karen was sure. There was Guillaume stumbling over his condolences, Lucas's firm handclasp and Tuglik's wide-eyed stare. And last but not least there was the steady, undemanding presence of Ryan at her side.

They walked back to the hotel together, Ryan with his hands thrust in his pockets, his face set. Finally he said, "Karen, I'm worried about you. You haven't shed a tear since your father died, have you? You need to do that—it's a part of mourning."

"I'll do it when I'm ready," she said tersely, hunching her shoulders and staring down at the ground.

"I don't think you're facing what's really happened. You're hiding from it." Only silence from his companion. "Don't shut out the living because of the dead, Karen."

She whirled to face him, stamping her foot, her eyes blazing with the first signs of life in two days. "Leave me *alone*! Do you hear me?"

"I hear you. But I won't do it."

They had reached the row of Parcolls. Without another word, Karen stalked into her own and slammed the door. Why couldn't he leave her alone? She didn't want to feel the pain, to weep, to lose control...she wanted to keep the deadness that enveloped her and preserve its peace. She didn't want a storm of emotion to overcome her. She didn't want to cry....

She undressed and got into bed. Her eyes were aching and her whole body was tense, her nerve ends twitching and jumping. It was a long time before she fell asleep, and when she did she was haunted by nightmares: long, silver boats overturned in the water; polars bears roaming the winter houses amid a clutter of dry, white bones; sheet after sheet of crabbed, spiky handwriting flung over a coffin shaped like a whale, petrified into gaunt, gray rock.... And then the dream changed. Flowers were growing on the rock, and she was lying on the grass, stretched out in the sun. Its warmth was soothing and healing her, stroking her taut muscles until they relaxed, touching her with fingers of fire that made her moan with pleasure.

Karen wasn't sure when she crossed the boundary

between sleep and wakefulness and realized that the warmth in which she was enfolded came from Ryan's body, that it was his hands that were bringing her such exquisite pleasure. She had been lying on her stomach; now she twisted to face him, slipping her arms around him with unselfconscious grace and lifting her face for his kiss. Her lips moved languorously, her body as pliant as the fragile yellow poppies in the wind. And like the poppies, she opened to the sun, glorying in its life-giving heat.

Neither of them said a word. As slowly and delicately as if they had been doing it for months, they explored each other's bodies, fashioned so differently yet pulsing with the same needs. They kissed, tasting each other's flesh. They touched, giving each other with equal generosity equal delight. His hands moved lower, to where her pale, slender thighs parted, and she lost the last vestige of control. As the insistent, primitive rhythms gathered strength, she clutched Ryan's shoulders, her face distorted with pleasure.

It was only afterward, after the waves of release had subsided, that she began to weep as she had never wept in her life. The sobs seemed to tear her apart. The tears streamed down her cheeks, dropping onto his chest. Ryan held her quietly, knowing this outburst had been inevitable, glad that it had finally come.

She cried for a long time. For her father, lost when she had scarcely found him. For the slaughtered narwhale, and the dead bear with the red blood on its white fur, and the falcons carried to captivity in an alien land. But also for herself, for the frightened young girl she had had to bury deep within, for the sexuality she had for so long denied.

Eventually she grew quiet in Ryan's arms. As he held her, she could feel the strong, steady beat of his heart against her breast, all the comfort she needed. She said shakily, "You did that on purpose, didn't you?"

"Yes. I felt you needed to cry. I was afraid you'd bottle up your grief in the same way you'd buried all your fears after the kidnapping, and I didn't want that to happen. But it wasn't just that. I wanted to be close to you, as well. You seemed to be a long way away the past couple of days."

"I was," she said honestly. "I was scared to let you near me in case I fell apart." She bit her lip, adding in a low voice, "I wish I hadn't lost him so soon."

"I wish you hadn't, too. In time, though, perhaps you'll be glad that he didn't have to suffer through a long illness."

"I think I will be." She hesitated. "I've been very selfish the past couple of days, Ryan. Wrapped up in my own feelings. If I lost a father you lost a friend, and you must have been grieving for him, too."

"Yes," he said in a low voice. "A friend whom I loved, and a co-worker whose knowledge and insight I deeply respected. His name will live on through his work, Karen, that much I can promise you."

"Would it be possible to publish his latest work? From the last two summers?" she suggested tentatively.

"Certainly it would be—you could help me."

"I'd like to do that." It would be a fitting memorial for her father, one he would have appreciated.

"There's one other thing I've been wanting to say, Karen." He brushed her hair back from her face. "Laurence will live on in you. We've talked a lot about your mother's inheritance, of the money that changed your life. But your father has given you an inheritance as well. Courage and independence. Intelligence. A free spirit. You have all of them."

She felt a lump in her throat and said hoarsely, "If I'm free, it's because of you."

"It's because of your own courage and your will to fight."

"Thank you," she whispered, not knowing what else to say. Her head was tucked under his chin, her cheek resting at the base of his throat. Although she felt calm now, she was also very tired. She gave a tiny sigh as her eyes drooped shut, and within minutes she had fallen asleep again, her body curled trustingly into his.

Ryan stayed where he was for a long time before he carefully eased himself out of bed, dressed and left her alone.

CHAPTER FOURTEEN

WHEN KAREN GOT UP the next morning, the first thing she did was to root in her backpack for the little ivory ptarmigan her father had given her. She had shoved it out of sight two days ago, for she had not been able to bear looking at it. Now she held it in the palm of her hand, seeing the light glint on its smooth surface and feeling its coolness. She must speak to Ryan about her father's papers. It would be wonderful if between the two of them they could ensure that his latest findings were published; Laurence would want that, she was sure. Today she could face going to his tent and finding the inevitable muddle on the shelves and the desk. Yesterday she couldn't have done it.

Running her fingers over the flowing curves of the tiny sculpture, she thought of Ryan. If he had been around nine years ago, her phobias would never have developed. He wouldn't have allowed it, just as last night he had not allowed her grief to remain frozen, banked up inside where it might have festered and poisoned her.

But he had said something else last night. He had said he wanted to be close to her. Blushing slightly, she remembered just how close he had been, and remembered, too, how she had kept him at arm's length since Laurence's death. No longer, she vowed silently. Twice now he had brought her to such a pitch of longing and desire that he could have taken her and she wouldn't have protested. Nor would she have feared him. More than that, she would have welcomed him, for their physical joining would be an integral part of a lovemaking that had become both natural and right, something to be longed for, not feared.

She must find the courage to tell him this, she thought resolutely. He must be released from his promise, for it was no longer necessary.

She got dressed, putting Mandy's fluffy angora sweater over the red silk shirt and carefully making up her face to hide the traces of her weeping. Because her watch had stopped, she had no idea of the hour, but her stomach was unquestionably telling her it was time for food; hopefully she hadn't missed breakfast.

It was five past nine when Karen went into the dining room, which was deserted except for herself. She was served the last of the oatmeal along with eggs and bacon, then went in search of Ryan. His room was empty, the bed neatly made and the clothes folded on the chair. Nor was he in her father's tent, where the characteristic mess and confusion gave her a poignant sense of loss. She checked the hotel again, wishing she could ask the smiling waitress if she had seen Ryan, but knowing the language barrier made it impossible. Still no sign of him.

She went outside again and stood irresolutely on the steps. For some reason she felt uneasy, far more uneasy than the circumstances warranted; Ryan could be in any one of a dozen places and he was quite capable of looking after himself. Nevertheless, she checked the co-op and the Hudson's Bay store, and on her way saw the RCMP van and the water truck, neither of which had Ryan as a passenger. Back to the Parcolls. No Ryan.

By now her unease had changed to fear. She would have given anything to see Ryan walk along the plank boardwalk toward her, the breeze ruffling his thick, fair hair and his blue eyes alight with the pleasure of seeing her. But the boardwalk remained stubbornly empty, and her fear intensified. Where else could she look?

Chattering and peeping, a flock of snow buntings fluttered to the ground a few feet away from her, their wings flashing white. They reminded her of another bird whose white wings had carried it high above the cliffs and the green waters of Utuk Lake, and as clearly as if he stood beside her she heard Ryan say, "Rusty and Steve are back... I may scout around their plane later on, see if I can see anything."

Karen clasped her hands in front of her. That was where he was—she knew it in her bones. *Oh God, let him be all right,* she prayed desperately, beginning to hurry up the hill toward the airport. *Don't let anything have happened to him.*

It took her perhaps ten minutes to come up behind the terminal building, and in that ten minutes Karen learned more about love than a hundred romantic interludes could have taught her. She knew now that she loved Ryan and was bound to him body and soul for the rest of her life. Terror-stricken as she was for his safety, she wondered how she could ever have repulsed him. Nor was this the kind of love that Mandy knew, that depended on extravagant dinner dates, fast cars, and gifts of roses and perfume. It was instead an elemental human need: Ryan was her complement, the other half of a whole. Without him she would, she supposed, survive. But she would never be complete.

She halted behind the building, steadying her breathing. The Twin Otter was parked partway up the runway, its door open, but there was no sign of Rusty, Steve or Ryan. No sign of anyone, for that matter. But at least if the plane was there, they had not all disappeared; she now acknowledged to herself that she had been afraid of that happening.

Stepping as quietly as she could, she rounded the corner of the building. Through the open door she could hear static from the radio and hoped it was muffling her approach. Creeping up the stairs, she saw the posters warning against polar bears and the empty benches in the waiting room. A man was in the office, bent over some charts on the desk, his back to her. It was Rusty.

Karen shrank back into the doorway, her heart hammering. Then she scuttled down the steps again and back into the shadow of the building. Ryan was not in the terminal. So he must be in the plane.

Had Karen stopped to think, she would probably have run for help from the police or from Lucas. But she was pervaded by the intuition that time was running out, that five minutes from now would be too late, and that Ryan would be lost from her forever.

Dodging low, she ran along the edge of the runway, trying to approach the plane from behind in case Steve was in the cockpit. Ducking under the tail, she crept alongside the fuselage, took a deep breath for courage, and peered inside.

Lustrous white plumage was the first thing she saw; it seemed to have a life of its own in the dingy cabin of the plane. Then she saw details. Seats had been removed to make room for wooden-framed cages that were covered with thick wire netting, each cage with a stout wooden perch to which the gyr-falcons had been tethered with leather thongs. Two adults and a young bird, the latter a dull, speckled brown. All three were hooded. She saw the hooked beaks and the cruel talons, heard the rustle of their restless movements, and forgot even Ryan for an instant in a rush of pure rage that obliterated caution and good sense. Falcons were meant to be free! Rusty wasn't going to get away with this.

As carefully as she could she climbed aboard. Swiftly her eyes searched every inch of the cabin; still no Ryan. She began to edge her way forward past the cages, but found only a briefcase flung on one of the seats and a jacket she recognized as Rusty's hanging over the back of another.

"That you, Rusty? Let's get the hell outta here."

Karen froze into place, her hand clamped on the collar of the jacket. But worse was to come. From outside she heard footsteps approaching, confident, noisy steps that could not possibly be Ryan's. Rusty was coming back.

Almost simultaneously two things happened. Steve

levered himself out of the pilot's seat and poked his head around the corner, and Rusty climbed up into the cabin.

"What the hell..." Steve began.

"It's okay," Rusty said lightly, his pale eyes glinting. "I saw her from the terminal. Figured she was going to poke her nose where it didn't belong."

Two men closing in on her. It was the old nightmare back again. As Karen shrank into the seat, something hard in one of the jacket pockets brushed against her hip, but it didn't even register. Rusty said silkily, "You shouldn't have come here, Karen. You've seen the falcons now, so we can't let you go. You'll have to come with us."

Steve ran his eyes over the slender lines of her figure and said coarsely, "I'd rather have her along than the other—"

"Shut up," Rusty said with lethal speed.

It was the last clue Karen needed, for she had seen something else as she crouched there. Dark bruises and torn skin on Rusty's knuckles, a puffiness to his mouth and a raw patch on his cheekbone. He had been fighting.... Once more she felt anger race through her blood and with it strength came back to her limbs. She couldn't afford to be afraid or to faint, because someone else was involved. Ryan needed her. Straightening up, again feeling a hard object bang against her hip, she said loudly, "Where's Ryan?"

"Somewhere where he won't cause any trouble for quite a while," Rusty said smoothly.

Steve guffawed. "Right on."

Cold fingers closed around her heart, squeezing it until she could hardly breathe. "What have you done to him?"

"Just roughed him up a bit." Steve grinned.

"I owed him one, after all," Rusty added.

She stared at Rusty, her eyes huge in a paper-white face. "You've killed him," she whispered.

Something flickered over Rusty's features so that for a moment he looked as predatory and as merciless as the falcons. "I don't want a murder rap slapped on me. He'll recover."

She had been clutching the jacket for support, and slowly the shape under her fingers reached her numbed brain. She said slowly, "Where is he, then? He's not on the plane."

Rusty was plainly losing interest. "You don't need to worry your head over him. Steve, I'll get the door and check the bolts on the cages. You start her up. There's good visibility all the way to Frobisher."

"What about me?" Karen gasped, letting her lips start to tremble and her eyes widen pathetically.

"You're coming with us, sweetheart."

"But I don't want to!"

Rusty didn't bother veiling his contempt. "You should have thought of that sooner." He turned and began squeezing past the cages on his way to the door, while Steve headed for the cabin.

Karen's fingers fumbled in the pocket and closed on the cold, metallic barrel of a gun. Just to hold the weapon gave her courage. Pulling it free, she felt for the trigger and breathed a quick prayer that it was loaded. For Ryan's sake she had to use it. She had not been deceived by Rusty's claim that Ryan was safe... he was in danger and she was the only person who could save him.

Again she cowered in the seat, hearing the heavy thud as Rusty slammed the door, the rattle of the bolts lost in the engine's roar. Knowing she had to wait until he headed for the cabin, she sat down, pretending to do up her seat belt. He passed her without a glance.

Through the window she saw the propellers start to whirl. It was now or never, for once they were airborne she would not dare to use the gun. Clutching it in her hand, she got to her feet. The plane started to move, and she stumbled a little as she went up the aisle. But Rusty was sitting down, and now was her chance. Above the noise of the engines she yelled, "Turn back to the terminal!"

Two heads swiveled around, and from the expression in Rusty's eyes Karen knew with a reckless surge of triumph that the gun was loaded. Steve reached for his seat belt, and she raised the barrel until it was pointing directly at him. "Don't move."

Out of the corner of her eye she saw Rusty lunge for her. She swung the barrel around and pulled the trigger. There was a sharp crack and, horrified, she saw him stagger back, clutching his shoulder. Rooted to his chair, Steve croaked, "You shot him!"

Karen smothered a hysterical urge to giggle, for apart from her overwhelming anxiety about Ryan, the scene had all the elements of a grade B movie: "Steve, take the plane back to the terminal or I'll shoot again.... *Which makes it time for the death-*

less line, "and this time I'll shoot to kill," she thought wildly, wondering what she would do if Steve didn't obey her.

But like all bullies, Steve had little courage when the tables were turned on him. The nose of the plane came around. Karen had had time to see that she had only inflicted a flesh wound on Rusty; painful it no doubt was, but it would be nowhere near fatal. The sight of the blood oozing between his fingers sickened her, and she thought of Ryan to give herself strength.

Steve said sulkily, "Now what?"

Ducking down, she saw they had reached the terminal. What now, indeed? There was no one around and she didn't know how long she could continue to hold the two men at bay. On sudden inspiration she shouted, "Keep going! You can take it down the street between the houses."

Again Rusty reared up in his seat and again she turned the gun on him, something in the desperate set of her mouth warning him to subside. He called her an unprintable name and she spat back. "Where's Ryan? What have you done to him?"

"I'll never tell you where he is. By the time you've finished searching for him, he'll be dead." Rusty uttered another epithet that made her flinch.

The plane rocked unsteadily as they left the level surface of the runway. Karen waited until they were well along the street, where, fortunately, the two rows of houses were spaced widely apart, before she yelled, "Shut down the engines."

The silence was deafening. Through the Plexiglas

window of the cockpit she saw the Inuit start to gather, giggling and gesticulating. Not moving from her stance by the doorway, she braced herself to wait, knowing that sooner or later Josh Crooks would be notified that a plane was parked in the middle of the street.

It took fifteen minutes, and it seemed like an age. Karen had to force herself not to think of Ryan, or she would have ended up in a screaming heap on the floor. As it was she had to wait another ten minutes while the door was pried open from outside, for she didn't dare move away from the two men to help Josh. But finally he was there with her and she could lower the aching arm that had been holding the gun and blurt out a confused explanation. "They won't tell me where Ryan is," she finished despairingly. "We've got to find him!"

Josh made no comment. He had her leave the plane before he herded Rusty and Steve out, then he searched them and handcuffed them to opposite sides of his truck. When he'd had a low-voiced conversation with Steve, he rejoined Karen. "Ryan's in the old warehouse down by the beach. Steve says Rusty left a note in the office at the airport saying where they'd put him. What Rusty didn't know—or maybe he did—was that the likelihood of anyone finding it before the next First Air flight was pretty slim. And that's two days from now. We'll take Lucas's van. Let's go."

She faltered, "Rusty will be all right, won't he?"

"Lord, yes. It's only a flesh wound. Another half inch and you'd have missed him altogether. Come on."

Leaving Lucas to stand watch at the plane, Josh drove at a breakneck speed down the hill, stopping at the medical building to pick up Mary Ann and throw a stretcher and some blankets in the back of the van. It was Josh who had to explain to Mary Ann what had happened, for now that Karen was almost at the point of finding Ryan she was unable to talk or even to pray. She sat bolt upright in her seat, her eyes staring straight ahead. But instead of seeing the untidy buildings that straggled along the shoreline, she was picturing the ugly marks on Rusty's face, and his bruised knuckles.

They bumped along a narrow, rutted side road and pulled up by an old metal shed, its doors hanging crooked on the hinges, its windows shuttered, graffiti scrawled on the walls in white paint. It looked deserted; moreover it looked as though it had been deserted for years. In sudden panic Karen realized that Ryan might not be there. That both Rusty and Steve might be lying, and that Ryan was somewhere else where they might never find him. Drowned, like her father. Or buried under a heap of rocks on the tundra.

She discovered she was trembling and clenched her hands together in an effort to stop. Josh said calmly, "Why don't you stay here until we find him?"

She shook her head, for any kind of activity was better than doing nothing. Mary Ann opened the van door and Karen slid to the ground, misjudging the distance so that she jarred her knees. The first thing she noticed was the cold. The wind was blowing on-shore, carrying with it the icy chill of the glaciers. Wherever he was, hurt or unhurt—and she was sure he was hurt—Ryan had been exposed to that cold for hours.

She stumbled after Mary Ann and Josh as they circled the building, Josh checking all the doors. Finally at the rear of the shed he found what he was looking for. "They forced this door," he said with a grunt of satisfaction. "See the marks on the wood? They're new."

He was carrying a wrecking bar, and it took him only a couple of minutes to pry the door open, the screech of metal on wood sounding very loud. Grasping the flashlight that swung on his hip, he went through the door, directing the beam around the dirty, litter-strewn floor. Wooden crates were piled against the walls. Two broken-down snowmobiles stood nose to nose, the metal dented and the seats torn. The sound of Josh's footsteps reverberated hollowly under the high ceiling.

Then he steadied the beam of light downward and they all saw what he had seen: fresh footsteps crisscrossing in the dust, and three dark spots that had to be blood. Karen pressed her hand against her mouth, fighting back the scream that was rising in her throat.

Josh began to follow the tracks, stepping to one side of them and motioning the women to do the same. They were almost at the far end of the shed before he halted. "There he is."

They had left Ryan on the bare floor behind a pile of oil drums. A casual observer would never have seen him. He was lying on his back, one arm flung wide at an awkward angle, his cheek resting on the dirt. His eyes were closed, his hair matted with blood. He looked dead.

Mary Ann and Josh dropped to their knees beside him, but Karen stayed standing, her eyes glued to Ryan's face. She was deaf to the low murmur of conversation between the two people on the floor. *He's dead,* she thought numbly. *Dead. And I never told him I loved him.*

Josh had got to his feet. "We're going to fetch the stretcher and the blankets," he said to Karen. "You stay here." He was stripping off his jacket as he spoke, and he bent to spread it over Ryan's still body.

"Why are you doing that?" Karen asked blankly. Her voice seemed to come from a long way away.

"To keep him warm, of course," Josh said with a touch of impatience. He looked at her more closely. "He's alive, Karen. In bad shape, but alive."

Karen sat down suddenly on the nearest oil barrel, burying her head in her hands. "I thought he was dead," she muttered. She grabbed Josh by the sleeve. "You sure he's alive? You're not just telling me—"

Mary Ann said matter-of-factly, "Of course we're not. Put your jacket over him, too, Karen. We'll be right back."

Obscurely grateful that Mary Ann had given her something concrete to do, Karen sank down on her knees beside Ryan's sprawled body. As she very gently tucked her jacket around him, she saw other things. His shirt was torn and filthy, while the side of his face was bruised and scraped. She rested her hand on his cheek, feeling how cold his skin was, noticing the stubble of beard on his chin. As the door of the warehouse creaked open again, she dropped a kiss on his lips. When Josh and Mary Ann came back she was kneeling beside him, holding one of his hands between her own.

With swift competence the other two slid Ryan onto the stretcher and covered him with blankets, then carried him out to the van. Josh barred the shed door again while Karen climbed in the back with Ryan. There was nothing she could do but stay by his side; although he was deeply unconscious, she cherished the irrational hope that he would know she was there.

Josh left them at the medical building, saying cryptically to Mary Ann, "I'll be back as soon as possible."

"Where's he going?" Karen asked, puzzled.

"To lock up Steve and Rusty and to get the plane back on the runway. Ryan will have to be taken to Frobisher right away, Karen. I can't look after him here." Mary Ann hesitated. "Maybe you should go in the other room while I clean him up a bit."

"No."

"Okay. Then you can fill the hot-water bottles for me and put them alongside his chest."

By the time this was done, Mary Ann had conducted a swift but thorough examination and had cleaned the ugly wound on Ryan's scalp.

They both heard the van pull up outside. Lucas came in. "The plane's nearly ready to take off. Can he go now?"

"All set," Mary Ann said calmly.

The two of them had obviously worked together

before. Swiftly Ryan was transferred to the van, where the heater was pouring out a blast of hot air, and as carefully as he could Lucas drove up the hill toward the airport. He drew up near the Twin Otter, which was parked on the runway, its double doors open and the wire cages resting on the ground. Josh had been photographing them. As Lucas let Karen out, telling her in a low voice to stay near the van, Josh undid the hasp on the first cage and pulled on a pair of big leather gauntlets. Lucas went to help him. Awkwardly Josh transferred the first adult bird to his wrist, bracing himself for its weight. As he unbuckled the leather thong, Lucas removed the hood that had been covering the falcon's eyes.

At first the bird seemed confused, blinking in the light. Then it suddenly spread its wings, so that Josh had to duck. With a clumsy lurch it took to the air. A harsh scream burst from its throat, and then it was winging its way skyward, the wind whickering in its feathers. Twenty feet, forty feet, a hundred feet, higher and higher it flew, veering south toward the distant canyon that was its home.

Karen watched until it was only a speck against the clouds, her vision blurred with tears. For a moment the deadweight of anxiety for Ryan was lifted, for the bird's regained freedom touched a chord in her heart. Moving as quickly as they could, Josh and Lucas freed the young bird and the other adult, and they, too, soared upward, released from confinement to the wide expanse of the Arctic skies, the element for which they had been fashioned, the environment that was their own.

Ryan had been carried to the plane, the stretcher resting on a mattress on the floor. Karen had time to say a quick goodbye to Lucas before the doors slammed shut and the plane was taxiing down the runway. "Josh is the pilot," Mary Ann said comfortably. "Paulasee Atak is the copilot—he works for Petro-Canada. So we're in good hands. And Josh radioed ahead for an ambulance to be waiting for us at Frobisher. Mind you, they may decide to send him right on to Montreal."

Karen looked over at the other woman; they were sitting across from each other, fastening their seat belts for the takeoff. She said with a careful lack of emotion, "What do you mean?"

Equally carefully Mary Ann replied, "I'm sure he's going to be all right, Karen. But he's very badly hurt, there's no getting around that. There's a strong possibility of pneumonia setting in, and he may have internal injuries as well. He might be better off in Montreal."

"His parents live on the Gaspé coast. We'll have to let them know."

"Josh will notify them from Frobisher."

As if she couldn't bear to think of what Mary Ann had said, Karen added at random, "I didn't pay my bill at the hotel."

"We'll look after that, too—don't you worry about it."

The plane had left the ground and was rapidly gaining altitude. Karen looked back over her shoulder for a last glimpse of Pond Inlet, seeing the rows of bungalows already dwarfed to doll-house proportions, and across the inlet the line of mountain peaks looking as pretty and benign as a postcard scene. It was impossible not to wonder if she and Ryan would ever come back here together; it was also impossible to know the answer.

They were over the tundra now. Karen could see the winding course of Salmon River, the lake where she had camped and the canyon at Utuk Lake. So many memories, and all them centered around the man who lay so still on the stretcher behind her. . . .

Once they had reached their cruising altitude and were on course for Frobisher Bay, Mary Ann crouched on the floor beside her patient. Karen joined her, leaning back against one of the seats. A musky odor lingered in the cabin from the caged birds, and she remembered how they had overcome the bewilderment and fear of their captivity to fling themselves into the sky. Suddenly she felt a fierce joy. She was glad they were free. Glad. And she knew that Ryan would have felt the same way. She could only pray that the price of their freedom would not be too high.

Mary Ann must have been watching the play of expressions on Karen's face. As if she felt it was better for Karen to be talking rather than gazing so fixedly at the unconscious man on the floor, she began asking about the capture of the gyrfalcons. Had Karen and Ryan known of Rusty's plans. How had Karen ended up in the plane? And how had the plane ended up trundling down the middle of the street?

Karen had to speak fairly loudly to be heard over the droning of the engines, and the actual physical effort of finding the words and saying them out loud helped relieve some of the tension she was feeling. She finished by describing how she had held the two men at gunpoint, fired at Rusty and coerced Steve into driving the plane off the runway. "I didn't know what else to do," she confessed. "I figured at least I'd get someone's attention that way."

Mary Ann chuckled. "You sure did! Half the village was there according to Lucas. All joking aside, you did a very brave thing, Karen."

"I don't think it was particularly brave—I was desperate, that's all. I knew they'd done something to Ryan, and I knew if we took off he might never be found. So I had to stop them. Finding the gun was pure luck."

"*I* think you were brave." Mary Ann leaned over to take Ryan's pulse and blood pressure, noting the results in a black-covered book.

Up until now Karen had not had the time to assess her own actions, for everything had happened too fast and she had been too sick with worry about Ryan to even think about what she had done. But now, with faint wonderment, she realized that she had outwitted two criminals. Men who would do anything for money and—she looked at Ryan, her eyes clouding—who wouldn't hesitate to hurt anyone who got in their way. Yet she had stopped them—she who had been terrified of physical violence ever since the kidnapping. For the first time she saw what she'd done in the light of a personal victory, as an overcoming of deeply ingrained fears. Inexorably her brain carried it one step further. The reason she had been able to do it had been her concern for Ryan. If she had not been half-crazy with fear for him, she would never have had the strength to threaten two dangerous, unscrupulous men with a gun, and even shoot one of them. But because she loved Ryan, she had found the courage to do just that.

Love, she'd discovered, was all-consuming, demanding everything you had to give, and because you loved, you were able to give far more than you had ever dreamed possible. It had produced in her a kind of audacity she had not thought she possessed. Not only the gyrfalcons had been freed, she thought humbly. She herself had been liberated from yet another burden from the past. And all because of Ryan....

He had to recover. He *had* to. She had to tell him all that he had done for her and show him that she was free now to express her love for him. Physically and emotionally free, a whole woman...he *had* to recover.

THE NEXT FEW HOURS were a nightmare for Karen. At the airport in Frobisher Bay they were met by an ambulance and all four whisked off to the hospital. There, Ryan was wheeled away by a white-coated attendant, Mary Ann disappeared to report to the doctor and Josh went to report to his superiors. Karen sat in the waiting room, committing to memory the pattern of tiles on the floor and the tiles of the dog-eared magazines on the table, most of which seemed to date from at least a year ago.

Eventually Mary Ann came back in, sitting down beside Karen and chafing her cold hands. "They're going to operate,'' she said straightforwardly. ''They're a little concerned about internal bleeding because his blood pressure's been falling. Assuming all goes well, they want to fly him to Montreal tomorrow on the Nordair flight. The equipment and facilities here are limited, of course.''

Karen had scarcely heard all this. Her mind had stopped at the word ''operate.'' ''When will I be able to see him?''

''Within the next couple of hours, I'm sure. I just saw Josh and told him what was up, and he's getting in touch with Ryan's parents. I think he's going to advise them to meet you in Montreal rather than come up here.''

Josh confirmed this when he came back twenty minutes later. ''Here's the Koetsiers' phone number, Karen. They asked you to call once the operation's over. I explained who you were.'' He looked over at Mary Ann and added apologetically, ''I'm afraid we're going to have to leave—I've got a constable going back with us to take Rusty and Steve into custody. We can phone the hospital once we get to Pond Inlet.''

Karen went through the routine of saying goodbye, somewhat comforted by Josh's bear hug and by Mary Ann's whispered, ''I know he's going to be all right.'' She promised to see them again at some unspecified time in the future, then she was left alone in the waiting room.

Time passed. She sat stiffly in the uncomfortable, vinyl-covered chair, trying to occupy herself by methodically recalling every interchange she had ever had with Ryan, good, bad and indifferent. Meanwhile her ears were strained for the sound of someone's approach.

The nurse who finally arrived was a very efficient bleached blonde, who in a clipped voice informed Karen that Mr. Koetsier was as well as could be expected and would no doubt be flown to Montreal the next day. She looked askance when Karen demanded to see him. "He's still under the anesthetic, you know," she reproved.

"I don't care. I just have to see him."

The nurse clicked her tongue disapprovingly. "There's really no—"

"I shall see him if I have to go from room to room myself until I find him," Karen said levelly, aware that she wasn't conforming to the way a visitor should behave and that she didn't care. "It would be far simpler if you were to take me to him."

"Very well. This way, please." With a starched rustle of skirts and a reproachful sniff the nurse led her away.

Ryan's room was immaculately clean, the exact duplicate of thousands of other hospital rooms across the land. The sign on the door said Do Not Disturb. "You may stay exactly ten minutes," the blonde said. "I'll come back then."

Karen ignored her. Dismayed by the bottles and tubes, by the bandages on Ryan's head and arm, by the flatness of his figure under the white coverlet, she stood silently at the foot of the bed. His breathing sounded very loud, but apart from that he could have been dead, so still was he lying.

When the nurse came back in precisely ten minutes, Karen was still standing there. She allowed herself to be steered out into the corridor, and waited until Ryan's door had been pulled shut before she said clearly, "There's a chair in the corner of Mr. Koetsier's room. I shall stay there until he's ready to go to Montreal." As the nurse began to sputter something about rules and regulations, Karen added with a touch of rueful humor, "There's really no choice. You see, I have no money, no charge cards, nothing. I left it behind in Pond Inlet."

There was no answering smile in the nurse's face, which was as starched and prim as the uniform. "I shall have to check with the doctor."

"Thank you," Karen said smoothly. "I promise you I'll be no trouble. After all, we both want Mr. Koetsier's recovery, don't we? Which reminds me, I promised I'd phone his parents. You don't have to bother coming with me, I can find my own way back." Quickly she went back toward the waiting room before the nurse could come up with a reply.

There was a telephone at the entrance to the waiting room. Karen dialed the operator, giving her the Koetsier's number. As she waited for the connection to be made she wondered what she was going to say.

The phone was picked up on the first ring, and the operator checked that the charges would be accepted. "Go ahead, ma'am," she said nasally.

"Mrs. Koetsier? This is Karen Smythe."

"How is Ryan?"

Karen passed on what little news the nurse had

given her. "The Nordair flight arrives in the evening, I believe," she finished.

"Yes. There'll be an ambulance there to meet you. My husband and I will go straight to the hospital."

The voice was pleasantly pitched, with a trace of an Irish accent, but there was no real warmth in it. Awkwardly Karen said, "I'm sorry I had to call collect. I have no money, because—"

"That's quite all right. Just a moment, please." There was a silence, presumably while Mrs. Koetsier talked to someone in the background. Then, "My husband wishes to speak to you."

"Karen?" The voice was so like Ryan's that Karen clutched the phone, her knees weak. "Karen, are you there? Gerard Koetsier speaking. Ryan's father."

"Yes, I'm here," she said weakly, then heard herself blurt, "You sounded so much like Ryan, you startled me."

He chuckled. "We've been told that before. Karen, we're looking forward to meeting you."

You might, she thought silently. *Your wife's not.*

"I'll go to the hospital in the ambulance with Ryan."

"Fine. Let us know if there's any change in plans, or any change in Ryan's condition. Phone anytime, day or night. We'll see you tomorrow evening."

Slowly Karen replaced the receiver. She wished she'd been able to explain to Mrs. Koetsier why she had no money. She had the feeling Ryan's mother was blaming her for the whole situation. Slowly she began to walk back to Ryan's room, knowing she should try to get some sleep. She would need her wits about her tomorrow.

Ryan was lying just as she had left him. She curled herself up in the chair, which fortunately was more accommodating than the one in the waiting room, and leaned her head back. Oddly, she felt almost content now that she was back in the same room with him. Although everything rational within her told her he could not know she was there, somehow she found herself hoping he did know.

As the night hours went by, one by one, Karen dozed fitfully, waking each time stiff and cramped. Nurses came in and out, the blond one first, then a much friendlier redhead. Once or twice Ryan stirred, muttering something under his breath, and each time Karen sat bolt upright, praying that his eyes would open and he would see her there. But each time he subsided into unconsciousness again and she had to settle back in the chair, trying vainly to get comfortable.

The red-haired nurse brought her some breakfast in the morning, but the disapproving blonde was on the day shift again, so she was given no lunch. She intended to eat on the flight to Montreal, but the plane was very crowded, and except for takeoff and landing she spent most of the trip beside Ryan's stretcher. He still hadn't fully recovered consciousness. The doctor in Frobisher had explained that this was partly due to concussion and partly to the onset of pneumonia, for which Ryan had been given massive doses of antibiotics. Karen had hoped that the journey would rouse him and that, if only fleetingly, he would recognize her, but this was not to be; as the ambulance screamed its way through the streets of Montreal toward Mont-Royal he remained sunk in a torpor.

She herself was dizzy with fatigue. Part of it stemmed from a simple lack of food and sleep; part from culture shock, for the ceaseless flow of traffic, the crowded buildings, and the incredibly tall trees and luxuriant gardens seemed as alien as another planet after the stark, bare beauty of the tundra. In addition, there was the burden of anxiety about Ryan, which Karen had been carrying for twenty-four hours now. Coupled with this was a perfectly normal anxiety about meeting his parents. What if they didn't like her? What if they blamed her in some way for his condition?

By the time the ambulance drew up to the emergency department, Karen was in a pitiable state of nerves. She jumped to the ground, clutching the door handle for support, and followed the stretcher as it was wheeled through glass doors into the hospital proper. She saw them immediately—a big blue-eyed man with fading blond hair, and a petite, pretty, red-headed woman at his side. Ryan's parents.

She heard Mrs. Koetsier cry, "There he is!" and saw her run forward to clasp Ryan's inert hand. Gerard Koetsier followed more slowly, gazing in silence at the unconscious body of his eldest son. Karen hung back, not wanting to intrude.

"Are you Mr. Koetsier's parents?" It was one of the attendants speaking.

"Yes, we are." Karen would have recognized that deep voice anywhere.

"Perhaps you could follow me, please? I need some information for the admitting clerk."

The three of them went with the stretcher into one of the side rooms. Karen stayed where she was, leaning back against the wall as a wave of depression overwhelmed her. She had become redundant. Ryan didn't need her anymore; he had his parents at his side. Wondering vaguely what she should do, for she didn't even have money for a telephone call to her mother, she took the line of least resistance and stood still, closing her eyes for a moment. Around her the staff of the emergency department went about their business, busy and involved. She might just as well not have been there.

"You must be Karen."

For a crazy moment she thought it was Ryan speaking—that she would open her eyes and see him standing there under the white glare of the overhead lights, that familiar quizzical expression on his face.

It was not Ryan, of course. It was his father. Karen swallowed hard, terrified that she was going to disgrace herself by bursting into tears. "Y-yes," she stammered. "I'm Karen Smythe."

Her hand was enveloped in his much bigger one. "Gerard Koetsier, Karen. I'm sorry we didn't speak to you a minute ago. I think we were both so concerned for Ryan. Shelagh is nearly finished filling out the forms. Come and join us."

She managed a smile, for there was genuine friendliness in his manner. However, as she started for the room, the attendant began wheeling the stretcher out again. "Mr. Koetsier will be admitted to room 1428, sir," he said. "If you were to come back in an hour or so, the doctors will have seen him by then and you should be able to get more up-to-date information."

Gerard nodded. "Thank you."

Unwilling Shelagh Koetsier detached her fingers from her son's. She had beautiful hands, Karen thought irrelevantly, slim and tapered, with diamonds and emeralds blazing against the white skin. The stretcher disappeared onto the elevator, the double doors slid shut, and the three of them were left in the hall. Very quietly Ryan's mother said, "Gerard, he will be all right, won't he?"

Gerard put a hand on her shoulder. "Dear heart, of course he will be. And he'll be getting the best of care here."

Briefly his wife rested her cheek on his hand before looking up. She was beautifully dressed in a beige shantung suit with a figured silk blouse, her makeup and softly waved hair in perfect taste. Her eyes, which were as green as the emeralds on her fingers, rested dispassionately on Karen, neither friendly nor unfriendly, and Karen suddenly realized how she must look to the two of them. She was wearing jeans and hiking boots, and Mandy's white angora sweater was not nearly as clean as it had been when she had put it on. Her hair was uncombed. She wore no makeup and her fingernails were dirty.

Shelagh smiled perfunctorily. "I'm Ryan's mother, as you've no doubt realized. Gerard, can we go somewhere for a coffee?" She looked around distastefully. "I don't want to stay here."

"*Ja.* Come along, Karen."

Too tired to argue, Karen followed them outdoors and across the tarmac to the parking lot. Their car was a Jaguar; she wasn't surprised. Climbing into the back seat she murmured, "I'm not dressed for a restaurant...."

"No matter," Gerard said dismissively. Shelagh said nothing.

He took them to a *patisserie* on a quiet little side street, where the clientele was dressed in everything from suits like Shelagh's to jeans like Karen's. Their table was very private, tucked against the wall. Karen stared at the menu that the peasant-skirted waitress had given her, the French words jumping in front of her eyes.

"What's wrong?" Shelagh Koetsier asked sharply.

Karen raised her head. "Since yesterday morning I—I think I've only had one meal." She attempted a smile. "And that was a hospital breakfast."

With a massive calm that was somehow very comforting, Gerard said, "They have very good open-faced sandwiches here. A glass of milk and perhaps a fruit dessert. How would that be?"

"It sounds heavenly." She took a deep breath, knowing she might as well get it over with. "Mr. Koetsier, I'm going to have to ask you for money to use the phone. My mother lives in Montreal. I must call her and tell her I'm here."

"You have no money?" Shelagh Koetsier sounded faintly scandalized. But more than that—wary.

She thinks I'm after Ryan's money, Karen thought wildly, not sure whether to laugh or cry, for nothing could be further from the truth. Perhaps fortunately, she didn't laugh. Instead she felt a healthy lick of anger warm her veins. Confronting the emerald eyes

squarely she said, "That's right. Everything happened so quickly I didn't have time to run back to the
hotel and get my handbag." Already half-ashamed
of her anger, she ruefully touched her hair. "No
money, no comb, no lipstick, and only the clothes
I'm wearing."

"Which is why you haven't eaten," Gerard Koetsier interposed.

"That's one reason. I was very worried about
Ryan, too."

"You care for him a great deal."

Karen raised her chin proudly, the soft lamplight
darkening her eyes. "Yes, I do."

Gerard nodded, as if he had settled something to
his satisfaction. "Here comes your sandwich. Eat
first, then tell us what happened up there. We spoke
to the policeman, but the connection was poor and it
only confused us."

The food was delicious. Trying not to wolf it down,
Karen began to feel better, and a little color crept back
into her cheeks. Slowly at first, but then with more
assurance, she began to tell them about the events that
had led up to Ryan's injuries. It took a long time. She
had to tell them of her father's death, and discovered
they had both met Laurence in Pond Inlet the summer
before and had liked him; she had to describe her
flight with Rusty and Steve, and the fight afterward;
the trip to Utuk Lake where they had sighted the gyrfalcons. She had to relate Ryan's disappearance and
her takeover of the plane. She ended by telling them
how she had forced the two men at gunpoint to drive
the plane down the street. "I had to get someone's

attention and that seemed the only way to do it.''

Gerard slapped the table with the palm of his hand and began to laugh. ''Good for you! I'd love to have seen it.''

Even Shelagh managed a smile before saying directly, ''How did you find Ryan? Where was he?''

''Rusty had left a note in the terminal building saying Ryan was in the old warehouse by the beach.''

''So that's what the police officer was talking about. He mentioned something about a note, but I didn't really understand him.'' Her brow furrowed in recollection. ''He also said something to the effect that the note might not have been found in time—what did he mean?''

''There wouldn't have been another scheduled flight from Frobisher until today,'' Karen said reluctantly. ''So I suppose it could have been possible that no one would have seen the note until today.''

''And Ryan was left in an unheated warehouse?'' Gerard interjected. ''Where—on the floor?''

''Yes.'' For a moment Karen's fingers clenched on the tablecloth. ''When I first saw him, I thought he was dead,'' she said, her voice trembling a little. ''It was horrible.''

Gerard was not to be put off. ''So if you hadn't stopped the plane, Ryan might not have been found until it was too late.''

''I—I suppose so.''

It was Shelagh who spoke next, a sheen of tears over her brilliant green eyes as she placed her hand on Karen's. ''Then we are forever indebted to you,'' she said simply.

"When Ryan gets out of hospital and we're able to take him home, you must come and stay with us," her husband added.

When, not if. Gerard, at least, believed Ryan was going to recover. "Thank you," Karen said. "I'd like that."

Gerard made a great play of consulting his watch in an attempt to dispel the emotionally charged atmosphere around the table. "We'd better get back to the hospital. Karen, I booked an extra room in our hotel, not realizing you lived in Montreal. Do you have far to go?"

"To the Lakeshore." She thought of her mother, of all the inevitable questions and upheaval, not the least of which would be questions about Laurence. Suddenly her heart quailed.

"I think you should stay with us tonight," Shelagh said decisively. "You look very tired."

"I would prefer that." For the first time since they had met, Karen smiled at Ryan's mother, a generous, full-lipped smile that lifted the shadows from her eyes and gave her face its haunting beauty. "Thank you, Mrs. Koetsier."

The older woman smiled back. "Please call me Shelagh," was all she said, but Karen sensed it was the proffering of friendship. Feeling much readier to face whatever they might find at the hospital, she left the restaurant with Ryan's parents, and the city did not seem quite so alien to her as it had when she arrived.

CHAPTER FIFTEEN

THE EARLY SEPTEMBER SUN was warm on Karen's face. She lay back in the chair, her eyes closed. The waters of the pond lapped pleasantly against the shore, and in the willow trees that hung so gracefully over the pond, the tips of their branches almost touching the surface, the birds chirped back and forth. Wafted on the breeze was the sweetness of honeysuckle and the fragrance of velvet-red roses growing on the trellis behind the house. Without opening her eyes she knew that Ryan was stretched out beside her, only two or three feet between their chairs, near enough that she could reach out and touch him. She should have been perfectly content, but she was not.

She had been staying at Valkenburg, the Koetsiers' country estate on the Gaspé coast, for nearly a week now. She had fallen in love with the place at first sight, with the lush green fields dotted with cattle, with the forest of tall trees that carpeted the gently rolling hills, with the sparkling view of Baie de Chaleur from her bedroom window. The house, although relatively new, was modeled after an old French farmhouse, with a stone facade, shuttered, leaded windows and a huge oak door. The slate roof had several brick chimneys, and old-fashioned scented roses rambled up the walls. In its comfort and quiet air of welcome the house reflected Gerard's easygoing personality, whereas the understated beauty of its furnishings, paintings and floral arrangements had to be credited to Shelagh.

Karen had arrived there a week after Ryan had been released from hospital, three weeks after the long journey from Pond Inlet. It was perhaps as well that that first night at the restaurant she hadn't realized what lay ahead. Ryan's recovery had been slow and difficult, for his injuries had been far more extensive than she had expected. He had succumbed to pneumonia, and for forty-eight hours, until the crisis was past, the three of them had almost lived at the hospital. Three ribs were broken and bones around his wrist had been crushed, while an infection had developed in his incision—one thing after another, it had seemed to Karen. But when he finally did begin to mend, her concern over his physical condition was superseded by another, more private concern, one she couldn't verbalize to anyone, least of all Ryan. He had changed. He was no longer the open, vigorous, strong-willed man she had known him to be.

At first she had attributed this to physical weakness. Because of his ribs, it hurt Ryan to talk, while the long battle with pneumonia had left him thinner than she had ever known him, and drained of energy. It was natural enough that he should lie silently in the hospital bed for hours at a time, and at first she was happy just to be in the same room with him and know that he was alive.

But matters didn't seem to improve. Oh, he would smile at her and ask how she was and inquire after her mother and Mandy, but nothing more. She knew Gerard had described to him the events of that last day in Pond Inlet, and she had expected him to question her, even if just to ask about the gyrfalcons. However, he never did, and something in his pallor and frightening weakness prevented her from bringing the subject up. So when they were together in the hospital they talked commonplaces, and more and more often Karen began to time her visits to coincide with those of Gerard and Shelagh; that way she was no longer alone with him, sustaining artificial conversations about the weather and Mandy's blossoming romance with Craig.

It was all wrong; she knew that. What she didn't know was how to alter the situation so that they could return to their old footing.

Partly to placate her mother, but partly for her own reasons she delayed her visit to Valkenburg, so that Ryan had been home a week before she arrived. He looked much better, his skin tanned from lying in the sun and the bruises finally fading. But it soon became clear to Karen that she was there at Gerard and Shelagh's insistence rather than Ryan's, for he kept her at a distance both physically and emotionally. Back in Pond Inlet she had never doubted that he wanted her, welcome or unwelcome though his attentions might have been. Here at Valkenburg it was becoming horribly clear he did not want her at all, not in any real sense. His manners were beautiful, his courtesy unfailing. She would have preferred anger and discord. At least then she would have known she existed for him.

The only times there was even the pretense of closeness between them was when they worked on the archaeological research. Karen had written to Mary Ann, who had bundled up all of Laurence's and Ryan's papers and mailed them to Valkenburg. For a couple of hours a day Ryan and Karen sorted them and annotated results, with Karen typing to Ryan's dictation. Gradually a kind of order was emerging. But here, too, Ryan stuck strictly to business. None of their conversation could even remotely be considered personal, and certainly he never touched her; it was as if he was intent on maintaining a distance that was as much physical as emotional.

Yesterday evening, after he had gone up to bed, Karen had steeled herself to speak to Gerard and Shelagh about it. She had grown to like them both a great deal over the past weeks. Gerard she had warmed to from the start, probably because of his likeness to Ryan; it had taken her longer to understand Shelagh, whose intense, passionate nature could in a crisis focus on only one thing at a time. Wrapped up in Ryan's recovery, Shelagh had been polite, even friendly, but it was not until she had assured herself her son was on the mend that her natural warmth and gaiety had spilled over onto Karen. Now, as the three of them sat in the library around the first fire of the autumn, an applewood fire with dancing flames and an intense heat, Karen said hesitantly, "Shelagh, I think I'd better go back to Montreal tomorrow."

"Back home, you mean?"

The elegant Tudor-style house had never been home. "Yes, that's what I mean," she answered hastily.

"Why, Karen?"

The firelight flickered over the young woman's delicate features and shone in her hair. She was sitting on the floor hugging her knees. "For one thing classes start in a couple of weeks and I suppose I should get ready for that. But the real reason is that Ryan doesn't want me here."

Shelagh didn't deny it. She said thoughtfully, "He's not himself. I don't know what the matter is. When I asked him, he told me more or less politely to mind my own business." She tossed her head with its tousled red curls, remembered indignation in her voice.

Gerard laughed indulgently. "Fools rush in, my dear."

"He's my son—I thought he'd tell me." Her eyes narrowed speculatively. "But he didn't. Which means it must be something to do with you, Karen."

"With me?" Karen repeated weakly.

"Yes. Is he in love with you?"

"Shelagh—" Gerard expostulated.

"Now, Gerard, we might as well get this out in the open. Something's wrong, you know that as well as I do. You didn't answer my question, Karen."

Karen had had time to think. "Had you asked me that a month ago in Pond Inlet, I would have said that perhaps he was. He never said so in so many words, not really. But—" She blushed and fell silent.

"But he was behaving like a man in love," Shelagh said briskly.

"I—yes."

"Whereas now he's behaving as if you're some kind of distant cousin in whom he's not particularly interested. Hmm...have you asked him what the matter is?"

"No. You mean what he's been like—would you ask him if you were me?"

"She probably would," Gerard said dryly. "Karen, why don't you give it at least another week? We like having you here, and apart from the new college term I don't get the impresasion you're in any particular hurry to go back to Montreal."

Her eyes dropped. Gerard, like Ryan, saw too much. "I'd like to stay. You're being very kind to me and I love the farm, it's so beautiful.... Maybe I'll try and speak to Ryan."

"An excellent idea," Shelagh said promptly, wrinkling her charmingly upturned nose at Gerard's reproving frown. "Don't be so stuffy, darling."

"You're a bossy, opinionated woman," Gerard murmured. "Why then do I love you so much?"

As Shelagh impulsively kissed him, the gentle firelight made them look like the young lovers they must have been thirty years ago. Karen quickly looked away, not wishing to intrude. She wanted the same thing for herself and Ryan, she thought wistfully. Love, trust and laughter, burnished by the years into a bond flexible yet strong. Once she had thought it might be possible. Now she was not so sure.

As she lay beside Ryan by the pond the next day,

Karen was thinking back over that conversation. If she were Shelagh, she would ask Ryan outright what the trouble was. He and she had always been honest with one another, hadn't they? Why should it be any different now?

She opened her eyes, turning her head to look at him. Because they were sheltered from the wind, he had taken off his shirt. The tape across his ribs was very white against his skin as his chest rose and fell steadily with the rhythm of his breathing. He looked relaxed and peaceful. . .and remote. She bit her lip indecisively, searching in her mind for the right way to introduce the subject. Or was there a right way?

Then the problem was solved for her. Through the drooping branches of the willow a tiny yellow bird darted, coming to rest on a branch only feet away from her. Its feathers were the color of dandelions, its breast streaked in cinnamon, while its dark eyes seemed to look at her inquiringly. She said very softly, "Ryan, are you awake? There's a little yellow bird in the willow tree—what is it?"

He opened his eyes. "Yellow warbler. Male," he answered economically.

"I suppose the female's a dirty brown color," Karen said in disgust.

As he chuckled, the bird gave an affronted twitch of its tail and vanished into the shadowy depths of the tree. "As a matter of fact, the female is nearly as bright a yellow as the male."

"The exception that proves the rule."

"Do I detect a touch of Freudian envy?" he said lazily.

She smiled back, saying provocatively, "Maybe so...wasn't it Freud who said that sex was the strongest drive in us?"

"He said a lot of things."

She sat up, swinging her legs to the ground. She was wearing brief blue shorts and an open-necked shirt that she had knotted beneath her breasts; as she leaned forward, the shadowed valley between them was just visible. She said bravely, "Ryan, back in Pond Inlet you told me over and over again that you wanted me." She bit her lip. "Sexually, I mean. But right now I might just as well be a stick of wood as far as you're concerned. Is it something I've done?"

She must have taken him by surprise, for, briefly, she saw his fingers tighten around the arm of the chair before he consciously relaxed them. Taking his time, he sat up, turning to face her. "That was in Pond Inlet, Karen. But we're home now. Back to reality."

"You mean it was only because of the place?" she said, taken aback. "I can't believe that."

"We all behave differently when we're in faraway places. There's not the same sense of responsibility. The rules change."

"That's true enough, I suppose. But I don't think it relates to us."

"It was a summer affair."

"It wasn't an affair at all," she retorted.

"Then perhaps that's why it hasn't continued. Because it was unsatisfactory for both of us."

She had the feeling he was fencing with her, using words as a means of keeping her at a distance. "You mean you don't want me anymore," she persisted, knowing she had to discover the truth no matter how much it hurt.

Something in her voice must have touched him. "It's not you who's changed," he said. "You're as lovely and as desirable as ever. It's me. I let myself get carried away in Pond Inlet—and forgot certain things." As she stared at him in perplexity, he added forcefully, "You must believe me. It's nothing you've done."

Strangely, in the peaceful, sunlit garden Karen felt as though she was fighting for her life. The adrenaline began to pump through her veins. She sank down on her knees beside him and took his hand between hers. It was flaccid, neither accepting nor rejecting her advance, and she tried to ignore a stab of fear. "How have you changed?"

"Up there I tried to play God," Ryan said bitterly. "Never a wise thing to do." He glanced down and must have seen the bewilderment in her eyes. Roughly he added, "Let's go up to the house and get something to drink."

"Please—not yet, Ryan. I still don't understand what you're saying."

"It's very simple," he said impatiently. "I thought I could change you. You were so inhibited and frightened, and in my arrogance I thought I could bring you to life. Make you forget your fears. And I suppose to a certain extent I succeeded. But I should never have done it."

"You *did* succeed," she said urgently. "I'm not the same woman I was."

"I didn't succeed, Karen. You're as much locked in that dark little room as you ever were."

"I'm *not*!" Unconsciously she was gripping his fingers so tightly that her nails were marking his flesh. "Don't you remember what happened in the tent at Utuk Lake? And in my room after my father died? The times you made love to me? You can't have forgotten—"

"No. I haven't forgotten." He stared down at the grass, his brows meeting in a frown.

"I—I wanted you then, Ryan. Truly, I did," she blurted.

"You only wanted me because you knew you were safe, because I'd promised nothing would happen."

"That was true to start with—"

"That's the way it was." He moved restlessly, pulling his hand free. "I'm thirsty. Let's go and get that drink."

"Not yet. We still need to talk," she pleaded.

"There's nothing to say, Karen."

"There's everything to say!" He was sitting on the edge of the lawn chair, his elbows on his knees, his head bent. She rested her palms on his shoulders, achingly aware of the sun-warmed skin, and looked straight into his eyes, her own wide with appeal. "I want you, Ryan. Please don't leave me."

"You don't even know what you're saying!"

"Yes, I do. I want you to kiss me and touch me the way you did in the tent."

Maybe he was right...it was no longer time for words. Taking her courage in her hands, Karen reached up and kissed him full on the mouth, her lips

soft and warm, yet with an endearing touch of
shyness. For a moment she thought she had won,
for she felt his instinctive response as if it were
her own. He grasped her bare arms, drinking from
her mouth as if he was indeed thirsty, a man given
water after days in the desert. Boldly she let
her hands slide down his chest and around his
rib cage, holding him gently because of his injuries, her heart alive with joy, for in the circle of
her arms was the one man she needed for life to be
complete.

Ryan wrenched his head free, striking her hands
away. She fell back, giving a single shocked gasp, the
color draining from her face.

He stood up, flinching with pain because he had
moved too fast, and said harshly, "Are you coming
up to the house or not?"

She had never before offered herself so blatantly to
a man—and he had rejected her. Thrust her away as
though she was anathema to him. Moving very slowly, she stood up, too. "Why did you do that?" she
whispered.

His voice was raw with an emotion she couldn't de-
fine. "Because it's no good, Karen." He must have
seen the blank incomprehension on her face. "You
don't understand at all, do you?" he grated. "Look,
let's leave you and all your fears out of it for now.
There's another reason I can't let you get close to me.
Because it's happening all over again. I told you about
my sister—because of me, she's dead. And the same
thing nearly happened with you and Rusty and Steve.
If you hadn't found that gun, they'd have taken you

with them as a hostage, and sooner or later they'd have killed you. They couldn't have afforded not to. And that would have been the second death—"

"Ryan, it had nothing to do with you! *I* was the one who went poking around the plane—"

"You were looking for me, weren't you?"

"Yes. But—"

"I wasn't there, of course." There was no mistaking his self-contempt. "When you needed me, I was flat on my back in that bloody warehouse."

"You could hardly help that. There were two of them, after all, to your one."

"Oh, for God's sake!" he said savagely. "Stop finding excuses. I should never have let them get the better of me. But I did—with the result that you were left alone with them."

Her temper was rising. "So now you're blaming yourself because two men, both of them armed when you were unarmed, managed to knock you out. You're only human, Ryan."

"I wasn't there when you needed me—that's what I'm blaming myself for."

"Do you know what? It's your pride that's hurt, Ryan Koetsier," she said roundly. "A hell of a lot more than your ribs."

For a fleeting moment a glint of humor crossed his face, and she saw the old, familiar Ryan. More quietly, he said, "There's doubtless more than a grain of truth in that, Karen. But it's not that simple. You were lucky and brave, so you escaped from Rusty and Steve. But if you hadn't, if something had happened to you, I would never have forgiven myself.

I've never really been able to forgive myself for Sally—you know that.''

"But I did escape and I'm here," she said, spreading her hands in desperation.

"Not for me, you're not. I can't risk letting you get close to me again. I'm beginning to believe I must carry some kind of jinx around with me—I jeopardize the women I care for.''

"Ryan, that's crazy!''

The blue eyes were bleak. "No, it's not. Look what else happened to you in Pond Inlet, Karen. You nearly got mauled by a polar bear, and then you fell in the creek and might have drowned. And it was because of me you went there in the first place. It's no use... I'm not risking it again.''

Karen shivered, as if the black wings from the past had brushed her again. She had never heard such cold certainty in anyone's voice. It was an effort to keep on fighting, for deep within her she was growing afraid that she had lost, that logic and reason could not alter his decision. "You can't take responsibility for other people,'' she argued. "It was the truck that killed your sister—her death wasn't your fault!''

"Oh, Karen, those are just words,'' he said wearily, bending to pick up his shirt and awkwardly putting it on. "Let's go.''

She *had* lost. Blackness roared in her head, so that Ryan's body wavered in her vision, as insubstantial as a shadow. As though another woman was speaking, she said, "You don't really want me here at Valkenburg, do you?''

"It would be easier if you were gone.'' He had buttoned his shirt and was waiting for her. In the merci-less sunlight she could see the lines of pain around his mouth and felt her heart clench with despair. He was wrong. She was sure he was wrong. But how could she convince him?

In sudden terror she cried, "Ryan, you said you were my friend and I believed you. I trusted you. But now you've changed—you're not the same." She closed her eyes, swaying on her feet. "Was any of it true? Or was it just what you said—a summer affair? Something to be forgotten as soon as possible?"

No answer. She opened her eyes, saw him standing irresolutely, his face a mask of indecision, and had her answer. Blinded with pain, she lashed out at him wildly. "I hate you! I never want to see you again—never!"

Pivoting, she ran away from him, around the pond and into the concealment of the trees, knowing he couldn't run after her even if he wanted to. Leaves slapped her face and arms, and branches scratched her legs. Not until she tripped over a protruding root and nearly fell did she slow her steps, panting like a terrified animal in the quiet of the forest.

There were wild flowers around her feet, the soft murmur of birdsong in her ears. The trees were tall and green, the sun dancing between their boughs. Karen sank down on her knees on the grass as tears crowded her eyes and spilled over. It was very beauti-ful and very tranquil, and she would have given her soul to be back on the bleak, chill slopes of the tun-dra with Ryan. . . .

She cried for a long time until there were no more

tears to come. Without having considered it at all, she knew she had decided to leave Valkenburg that day. She would go back to the house, pack and ask Gerard to drive her to the station. And somehow, over the autumn, she must learn to do as Ryan had already done. . . forget her summer loving. Forget the man who had brought her to life only to fling her aside. Sending up an incoherent prayer that she would not have to see him again, she stumbled to her feet, wiping her eyes on her sleeve, and began threading her way through the trees back to the house.

CHAPTER SIXTEEN

"PASS ME THE CARROTS, will you, dear? You should have some yourself. You're not eating enough."

If her mother had said that once in the past week, she had said it a dozen times. When Karen had first returned from Pond Inlet, Nancy had been on her best behavior, for her daughter had taxed her with the matter of the unmailed letters so many years ago. But contrition was not Nancy's best suit, and now things were back to normal with a vengeance.

Biting back the retort that came to her lips, Karen said evenly, "I'm not very hungry."

Nancy, having started, would not let well enough alone. "It's a pity you ever went away in the first place. All that gallivanting around the North Pole and then the Gaspé coast didn't do you a speck of good. You'd have been better off staying home where you belong."

"It wasn't the North Pole, mother. It was Baffin Island."

With an airy gesture Nancy dismissed her words. "You look like a ghost since you came back. Just because your father died—"

"Mother, please!"

"Leave her alone, mother," Mandy said with uncharacteristic sharpness. ''Hadn't we better hurry? You're going out with the Rawlinsons tonight, aren't you? And I'm expecting Craig very shortly. Did I tell you what he bought yesterday?'' And Mandy was off on one of the rambling anecdotes, always amusing, that she had used successfully ever since she was a child to divert Nancy's attention.

Breathing a sigh of thanks for her sister's intervention, Karen took another mouthful of potatoes and methodically chewed. Evening was always the worst time, particularly when Nancy and Mandy were out, as they so often were. She would walk from room to room or go down to the shore and stare at the waves. Sometimes she put on her sneakers and ran until she was too tired to think. But nothing she did could remove the pain of Ryan's rejection. At times it was a dull ache, dominating everything she did. At other times it flared to agonizing life, terrifying her in its intensity.

She knew now without the shadow of a doubt that she loved him—now, when it was too late. For as the slow days and the devastatingly lonely nights passed one by one and Ryan made no effort to contact her, she was forced against all evidence to conclude that what he had said was true. For him it had been an interlude, an unsatisfactory one at that, that he had no compunction about bringing to a close. It was a view she fought against, raged against even, for it refuted the tenderness and passion and simple friendship that she remembered so well. But he neither telephoned nor wrote to her. Certainly he didn't try to see her. He was allowing her to drop out of his life as if she had never been.

The dinner plates had been removed and coffee had been poured. Both Nancy and Mandy were dieting, so no dessert was offered, not that Karen cared. She was stirring cream into her coffee, watching the two liquids swirl together and mix, when the telephone rang. Mandy leaped up from the table. "It'll be for me," she said breathlessly.

Nancy smiled fondly. "I do believe she and Craig are going to make a match of it. Most suitable. He comes from a fine family."

"Plus there's all that money," Karen said cynically.

Mandy poked her head around the door. "It's for you, Karen."

Her heart stopped. "Who is it?"

"He didn't say...although it sounds a bit like Ryan now that I think of it."

Karen's spoon dropped from her fingers and clattered on the saucer. *Let it be Ryan, please let it be Ryan,* she found herself repeating over and over again as she walked from the table out into the hall; it seemed a very long way. She picked up the receiver, held it to her ear and said faintly, "Hello."

"Karen? Gerard Koetsier."

Her heart plummeted. "Hello," she repeated foolishly. "How are you?"

"Shelagh and I are here in Montreal. We are visiting friends for a few days. Karen, we are wondering if you will do us a favor."

His Dutch accent seemed thicker on the telephone. "Yes, of course," she stammered. "How's Ryan?" The question burst out in spite of all her intentions to say nothing.

"That is why we are telephoning. Before you left last week you explained to us why you were leaving, that you didn't feel Ryan wanted you there. We had to take your word for that, although we were sorry to see you leave. We think you should go back, Karen."

"No!"

There was a pause. "We cannot force you, obviously," Gerard acknowledged. "We can only appeal to you as Ryan's parents. He needs you, we are both convinced of it."

"That isn't what he told me. In fact, the exact opposite was true. He wanted me gone."

"He may have said that—"

"He did say it." Karen grasped the receiver, her voice threaded with pain. "Gerard, let me be frank with you. I love Ryan. I wish I didn't, but I do. But he doesn't love me. I was just a summer romance to him, he told me so. I can't face going back to Valkenburg and seeing him again. It hurts too much. So please don't ask me."

"I see." Another heavy silence. Then Karen heard the sound of another, lighter voice and Gerard's murmured reply. She was not surprised when Shelagh came on the line. "Karen, I'm on the extension, so I've been listening in. I promised Gerard I wouldn't interfere, but I'm going to anyway. *I* think Ryan is in love with you, whatever he says to the contrary. He hasn't been fit to live with since you left—"

"Then if he's in love with me, Shelagh, let him tell me that himself," Karen interrupted furiously. "He's a grown man, and surely capable of it."

"But he won't!" Shelagh wailed. "Because of

what happened to Sally, he won't. You...you know about Sally, don't you? Our daughter?''

"Yes," Karen said more gently. "Ryan told me. He still blames himself for her death.''

"He told you that, too, did he? I've never known him to share that with anyone else. Oh, Karen, I'm sure he's in love with you, and that only you can help him...I don't know how, but if you love him, you can find a way. He's lost without you. I'm so worried about him. Please, please—won't you try?''

Karen leaned against the wall, feeling battered and torn. "Why are you so worried?" she procrastinated.

Gerard overrode Shelagh's impetuous reply. "He is not himself," he said simply. "Not the son we know and love.''

Shelagh broke in again. "Somehow I'm sure it's related to Sally. After she was killed, and long after Ryan had gotten out of hospital, he was...depressed doesn't seem a strong enough word. Withdrawn. Unreachable. Given to working himself into the ground, driving himself unmercifully, and then sleeping for hours at a time.... He's like that now.''

"That's nothing to do with me," Karen replied, knowing she was being less than truthful. Hadn't Ryan himself said he couldn't risk her becoming another Sally?

"Oh, yes, it is...we heard him one night when he was asleep," Shelagh said. "He must have been dreaming about you, because he kept calling out your name....''

Karen closed her eyes, swaying on her feet. She was defeated, as Shelagh had surely known she would be. She heard herself say, "All right, I'll go."

"If you take the train, you could be there tomorrow evening," Shelagh said eagerly. "We left a key under the flowerpot by the front door."

"I'll probably take my car. That way I can leave if and when I want to," Karen responded, already regretting her decision.

As if he had read her thoughts, Gerard said formally, "We are most grateful, Karen. I am sure you are doing the right thing."

"I wish I was as sure," she answered. "Perhaps you should give me your phone number, in case I need to get in touch with you." She jotted down the number on the pad beside the telephone.

"We'll be thinking about you," Shelagh said tremulously. "He's very like his father, Karen, so I know he's worth fighting for...good luck."

There didn't seem to be anything else to say. Goodbyes were exchanged and Karen replaced the receiver on the hook

It was too late to start out tonight, she thought numbly. She'd leave first thing the next morning and be there by evening. But what on earth was she going to say to him when she saw him? "I was just passing by and thought I'd drop in for a chat.... Oh, God, why had she let herself in for this?

"Who was that, darling?"

Her mother. Lifting her chin, Karen walked back into the dining room. "It was Ryan's parents. They want me to go back for another visit before classes start, and I think I will," she said lightly. "I won't leave until tomorrow, though."

"You've only just came back from there."

"It's a beautiful place, mother. Particularly at this time of year." Oddly, verbalizing the thought made Karen realize she had been missing Valkenburg as well as Ryan. She had spent only a few days there, but even in that short time it had become home in a way Nancy's house had never been.

"Good for you," Mandy said briskly. "You can give that gorgeous Ryan a kiss for me. Come along, mother, or we're both going to be late. Anyway, I want you to show me what you're going to wear."

"I'd much rather you stayed home, Karen."

"Of course she's not going to do that," Mandy exclaimed. "He's worth lots of money and he has devastating blue eyes. I'd be off like a shot myself— you wouldn't catch me waiting until tomorrow." She gave Karen a quick, meaningful glance. "Now come along. I think you should wear the blue suit with your sapphires."

As Nancy suffered herself to be led away, Karen heaved a sigh of relief, grateful to Mandy for coming to her rescue. Maybe her sister was right; maybe she should leave tonight, even if she only went as far as the outskirts of the city. That way Nancy couldn't have one of her last-minute weak spells.

In the end that was what Karen did. She stayed in a motel only thirty miles from home, where she slept so soundly that it was midmorning before she woke. She had needed the rest. Now that it was daylight and she knew she would be seeing Ryan again that very day, she was aware of both anticipation and, against all the facts, optimism. He couldn't send her away again—he couldn't.

She showered, dressed in jeans and the red shirt for

good luck, breakfasted and was on her way. It was a four-hundred-mile drive, and several times she stopped for a stretch, for a light meal or a coffee. The sun had set by the time she reached Matapédia, and it was well past ten o'clock when she pulled in to the driveway of Valkenburg.

The house was in darkness. For a horrible moment she thought Ryan might not be there. Then she saw his sports car parked outside the garage and knew he must have gone to bed. His room was at the back of the house; he probably wouldn't have heard her arrival.

Taking only her handbag, she went up the steps and found the key to the house under a pot of geraniums. The lock turned silently and she stepped inside, closing the door behind her and standing quite still until her eyes adjusted to the gloom. She had no clear idea of what she was going to do. She only knew she had to find Ryan....

Slipping off her shoes and leaving them by the door with her purse, Karen crept along the hallway and up the thickly carpeted stairs. In the time she had stayed there the house had become very familiar to her, so it was with a comforting sense of coming home that she saw the bronze bowl of chrysanthemums in the alcove at the head of the stairs, and the magnificent seascape on the wall across from Gerard and Shelagh's room. She knew Ryan's bedroom was at the end of the hallway even though she had never been in it. Tonight she would be seeing it for the first time.

Her footsteps were soundless on the carpet. Unconsciously she was holding her breath, for now that she was here, she had no idea what she was going to

say. For a moment she halted, wondering if she
should take the coward's way out and go to her own
room, waiting to see him until tomorrow. She was
tired from the long drive, and suddenly panic-
stricken at the thought of confronting him. What if
Shelagh and Gerard were quite wrong? What if he
didn't want her here at all? Where would she go?
What would she do?

The door to his room was ajar. It occurred to her
that the pounding of her heart alone might be enough
to waken him, and somehow this gave her courage to
approach his doorway and slip through. It was a very
large room, with tall, uncurtained windows open to
the night and bookshelves and a desk along the opposite wall across an expanse of pale carpet. But it
was to the bed that her eyes were drawn, the bed and
its single occupant.

Ryan was lying on his back, his arms flung wide,
the sheets a tangle about his hips; he was naked. The
hand lying on the mattress was clenched into a fist,
and even as she watched he stirred restlessly, muttering something under his breath before his cheek fell
back on the pillow. Remembering how relaxed he
had looked when he was sleeping in the tent at Utuk
Lake, Karen knew this was not the same man. Something *was* wrong. And it was up to her to supply the
cure.

Earlier she had wondered what she would do when
she saw Ryan again. Now she knew exactly what to
do. With exquisite care so as not to disturb him, she
began undressing, sliding her jeans down over her
hips, unbuttoning her shirt and letting it fall to the

floor. Finally she removed her lacy underwear, so that it dropped on top of her shirt. Her body a pale shadow in the dark room, she walked across to the bed and very carefully eased her weight onto it. He stirred again and she froze into position. But then he became quiet, his breathing deepening, and inch by inch she edged across the mattress, lifting her knees and sliding them under the sheet until she lay beside him. Then she deliberately closed the gap between them, savoring the delicious shock as her flesh touched his.

With her hands she began to stroke him, relearning the contours of his throat and shoulders. Dropping her head, she rested her lips in the hollow under his collarbone, where the skin was smooth and warm. She could feel the abrasive roughness of his hair tantalize the softness of her breasts.

As she rubbed against him, she felt his first shudder of response. Then his arms went around her, crushing her with a strength she gloried in. Raising her head, her dark hair tumbling over his shoulder to the pillow, she welcomed his fierce, possessive kiss and the thrust of his tongue, opening to him with all the generosity of her nature. It was he who finally pulled his mouth away, the pulse pounding at the base of his throat. "Karen—am I dreaming again? God, you feel so real!"

"I *am* real." She didn't want him to talk; they had talked beside the pond and it had done nothing but harm. So she closed his lips with another kiss, taking one of his hands in hers and moving it to her breast, where her heartbeat hammered under her soft, silky skin.

Ryan groaned deep in his throat, his free hand entangling itself in her hair as he ravished the sweetness of her mouth. In a contrast that was almost painful, so pleasurable was it, his fingers were stroking her breast with a gentle, infinitely sensual repetitiveness, cupping its softness, brushing the taut nipple with his palm. When his lips left her mouth to slide down her throat and join the tender assault of his fingers, the touch of his tongue was the blaze of sunlight and the heat of flames. She arched against him, unconscious of everything but that sunburst of unimaginable pleasure.

She had come to his bed to seduce him and was herself being seduced. Or was it that simple? For as he buried his head between her breasts, she was dropping kisses on his hair and throat, her hands massaging the muscled planes of his back, her nails tracing the long line of his spine where the scars pulled the skin. But more than that, against her thigh she could feel the throb and pulse of his need for her, and her whole body arched in response. She wanted him. She wanted to be taken in the most primitive way possible. Invaded, ravished, filled with him, man to her woman. Her hips began to move in a slow, seductive rhythm, seeking to gather him in.

His tongue was still tormenting her breast, until she cried out his name in sweet agony. For a moment he raised his head, looking straight into the wild beauty of her face. "I want you so much," he said huskily. "I—"

Very gently Karen rested a fingertip on his mouth. "Then take me," she said softly. "We don't need your promise anymore, Ryan." It was true, she realized in wonderment. His happiness was far more important than the ghosts of the past. Holding his head between her hands, she smiled at him, a pagan, glittering smile of triumph and desire; when she spoke her voice was a paean of sheer joy. "Make me yours, Ryan—show me that you want me, how much you want me."

"Yes."

A single word, but the only one she wanted to hear. His hand slid from her breast to her waist and from there to her hips. She felt him lift her so she was lying on her back, and for a moment he raised himself on his hands, his eyes moving from her flushed, rapt face, over her swollen breasts to the narrowing of her waist and the very center of her womanhood. And then he touched her there, where only he had ever touched her before, and a shaft of longing lanced through her so that her face convulsed and again she cried out his name.

It was all he needed. He lowered his body, his mouth seeking hers, like hands stroking her thighs until they parted for him as easily and naturally as the clouds part for the sun. The drive of his desire became the gathering of her own, indistinguishable, until he was lost in her and she in him, a single frantic rhythm claiming them both. It spiraled them through the dazzling white sky to the sun's very heart, then dropped them on a gently shimmering shore where the tide had receded and there was only tranquillity and a vast silence.

Only very slowly did Karen become aware of reality again. The silence was infiltrated by the mingled beating of their hearts, gradually slowing to normal. Ryan's face was resting against her neck; she felt his breath wafting her skin and brought her hands up to stroke his hair. He was very heavy, lying on top of her as he was, and she was content that it be so. She had never in her life felt as she felt now—suffused with peace and calm and the sure knowledge that her union with Ryan had been essential, inevitable and right.

He said, his lips tickling her ear, not looking at her, "Karen, are you all right?"

She couldn't help the bubble of laughter that escaped her. "All right? I've never felt better! Whole, and at peace, and..." she hesitated, adding in a lower voice, "And as if I belong here. With you."

He did look at her then, his blue eyes very direct. "Truly?"

She could only smile at him, all her love shining in her eyes. "Truly. Thank you, Ryan. That's all I can say—thank you."

"The room where you were locked up—it's gone now, isn't it?"

"Gone forever." Tears blurred her vision. "And all because of you."

"No...because you had the courage to come back here."

"Courage or desperation. I'm not sure which."

"Courage, I think. Because I sent you away, didn't I? I thought I was doing the right thing for both of us. But once you'd gone, I knew how wrong I'd been.

I was lost without you. I thought about you night and day. Wondered what you were doing. Tormented myself with the possibility of your being with another man. Dreamed about you...and then tonight when I woke up, the dream had become reality." He smoothed her hair back from her face. "It's my turn to thank you, Karen."

She nuzzled her face into his chest, giving him a series of tiny kisses. "You're welcome."

Laughter reverberated in his throat. "You'd better stop that, or you'll be in trouble."

She chuckled. "Is that a promise?"

He silenced her with a kiss, a long, slow exploration of lip and tongue and mouth that left her breathless. "Are you daring me?" he murmured.

"I'm not sure I need to."

He rolled off her, resting on one elbow, letting his eyes wander over her possessively. "You don't."

A delicious languor was stealing over her. There were still things that needed to be said, but they would keep, for the whole night was theirs. "Show me," she said provocatively. "Show me that you still want me, Ryan Koetsier."

"I'll show you more than that," he said huskily. "I'll show you how much I love you."

Her breath caught in her throat. Impetuously she sat up, a lock of dark hair falling forward over her breast. "*What* did you say?"

He too sat up, leaving a foot of space between them. "I said I love you, Karen. I've loved you, I think, from the first moment I saw you, running along the sidewalk in the rain. Do you remember that?"

She nodded soberly. "Yes, I remember it. I was frightened of you that day, and for many days afterward. Because I knew you meant change, and I thought I was fine as I was. You did mean change, and thank heavens for it." With a sudden delightful smile she looked down at her naked body and, more shyly, over at his. "I never thought I'd be able to do this. Never."

With sudden intentness, he said, "Why did you come back here, Karen?"

"Your parents phoned me. Last night," she added with a faint note of surprise, for it seemed much longer ago. "They were worried about you. They said that you were in love with me, even though you had virtually sent me away. At first I didn't believe them. I was scared to, I guess. But they're very persuasive—your mother in particular! So I risked it and came. Because, you see, I love you, too." She smiled at him gravely. "I have for a long time, I think, although I was scared to admit it. Love wasn't for me, or so I thought. Until bit by bit you made me see that I was as capable of loving a man as any woman—and as passionate and as hungry for sexual love as any woman, too. You did that for me, Ryan. I'll never be able to thank you enough."

He said carefully, "You're not confusing gratitude with love?"

"When I say I love you? Heavens, no!" The laughter died from her eyes. Fiercely she added, "You're my man, Ryan. The one I need to be whole. I want your body. I want to bear your children. And I want our souls to be one. That's what I mean when I say I love you."

For a moment she thought he was near tears, and it touched her in a way that even their lovemaking had not. She said, although she scarcely needed to, "You understand what I mean, don't you?"

"Of course I do. Because it's the way I feel, too." He reached out and touched her, as if he was setting his seal on her. "I want to learn every inch of your body, and I'll never cease desiring it. I want to see our child nursing at your breast... who knows, maybe we've started one already."

"Perhaps we have." She felt her blood quicken at the thought.

He grinned suddenly, a boyish grin that made him look much younger. "Just in case we have, I think you'd better marry me. For the sake of our parents, of course."

She loved it when he teased her. "Of course," she agreed primly. "But imagine the terrible time I'm going to have once I'm married spelling your last name on the telephone. Smythe, even with a *y* and an *e*, is much simpler."

"Complaining already." He smiled. Then he grew serious. "You will marry me, Karen?"

"With all my heart."

He drew her down on the pillow beside him, his arms around her. "I wish your father could know. I think it would have made him very happy."

Karen nodded, blinking back tears. "It would, yes... although heaven knows what mother will think of it."

"Don't you worry about that—I'll bring her around."

And he would, she knew. She gave a sudden start. "Oh! I'd forgotten—classes start next week."

"We'll work that out somehow," he murmured comfortably. "I want you to have a career, Karen—it's important for both of us. It'll no doubt complicate life at times, but the rewards will make it worthwhile."

"I'm glad you think that way." There was only one more thing she needed to say, something of desperate importance. "You'll never send me away again, will you, Ryan? I don't think I could bear that."

"Never." He threw his thigh over her to pull her closer. "I should never have done it then. But I was overwhelmed by feelings of failure and depression and fear. It seemed as though disaster followed in my wake. And you were right, my pride was hurt because I'd left you alone to face those two thugs. You, of all people."

"It all worked out for the best, though, Ryan." Her voice rang with conviction. "Yes, I did have to face those two men alone and it was very frightening, no question of it. But I did it, and I won. In more ways than one. Because of the gun, I managed to prevent them from taking the falcons, certainly. But I also conquered my own fear of violence, the fear that Paul and Roy had left me with. I needed that experience on the plane, just as I needed us to make love. The past will never disappear, I know that—but it will take its rightful place now and will allow me the freedom to love you."

"I hadn't thought of it that way," he said slowly.

"You were too busy blaming yourself." She took the plunge. "Sally's death was terrible and wasteful, of course it was. But surely you've absolved yourself, Ryan. I was only half alive when you met me. You've given me the gift of love and laughter, the promise of children, the happiness of being at your side...it's almost as though you've brought me to life."

He kissed her. "I'll need time to think about that, Karen, but maybe you're right. There's risk in everything we do, isn't there? Loving you is a risk, because if I lost you a part of me would die—but I can't stop loving you because of that."

"Nor I, you."

He held her in silence for a few minutes in an intimacy that needed no further words. Then all he said was, "I love you," as he began kissing her again— long, deep, kisses without haste. Together they began to explore, learning what pleased each other, giving pleasure for pleasure in a slowly gathering crescendo of passion. "I like that," she said. "Oh, yes...."

"Touch me here," he said. "Again...now here."

And then control was lost. Words became incoherent as her body welcomed its passionate invader and his found both shelter and release. Together, like the great white falcons, they broke free of the earth and soared into the infinite skies, carried on wings of love to the place that was truly home.

ABOUT THE AUTHOR

Jocelyn Haley flew to Baffin Island last summer for a week—and fell in love with the Arctic. She loves being outdoors anyway, and the high north, far above the tree line, held a special magic for her. She couldn't wait to write about it in a book and has carefully and lovingly woven several elements of the north—wild flowers, mountains, animals and the Inuit people—into *Cry of the Falcon*.

Jocelyn lives in a farmhouse surrounded by orchards and meadows in the Annapolis Valley of Nova Scotia. Fortunately there's a university town four miles away, so she has the best of both worlds—nature *and* cultural stimulation.

Gardening and listening to classical music are two of Jocelyn's favorite pastimes. And since she's become such a successful writer she's been able to indulge another passion: traveling. Her next trip will be to England to visit relatives. She hopes eventually to visit Fiji, China, Japan and India—as well as another area of the Arctic.